THE DEVIL'S BONES

THE DEVIL'S BONES

LARRY D. SWEAZY

FIVE STAR

A part of Gale, Cengage Learning

GALE
CENGAGE Learning·

Detroit • New York • San Francisco • New Haven, Conn • Waterville, Maine • London

GALE
CENGAGE Learning®

LIBRARY OF CONGRESS CATALOGING-IN-PUBLICATION DATA

Sweazy, Larry D.
   The devil's bones / Larry D. Sweazy. — 1st ed.
    p. cm.
   ISBN-13: 978-1-4328-2571-3 (hardcover)
   ISBN-10: 1-4328-2571-2 (hardcover)
   I. Title.
PS3619.W438D48 2012
813'.6—dc23   2011038666

First Edition. First Printing: February 2012.
Published in 2012 in conjunction with Tekno Books and Ed Gorman.

Even in our sleep, pain which cannot forget falls drop by drop upon the heart . . .

—*Aeschylus*

To Sherry, for your love and encouragement

Chapter 1

November 10, 1985, 3:15 P.M.

Tito Cordova sat on the porch steps, staring at the barren tomato field and empty migrant shacks across the road. Everyone had left for Florida, or Mexico, to spend the winter. He hugged his knees to his chest, trying to keep warm. It had snowed for the first time the night before. The snow didn't cover the ground, just spit from the gray sky, teasing his imagination with a chance to go sledding, make snow angels, and stay home from school.

He hated school. Hated the boys who taunted him on the playground and called him names. They called him a little wetback or a spic. The words stung worse than a fist to the face, made him feel dirty, and confused him. He wasn't a real wetback, a *mojado,* but the boys were too stupid to know the sense of pride the men in the fields carried with them when that word was used in their native tongue. They had swam across the big river, made their way through the desert, following a coyote like little *pollos,* little chickens determined to find work and a better life for their families, for their *madrecitas.*

His mother had made the trip when she was twelve, a few years older than he was now. She was just a little girl, following her father and mother through the night. She had said the stars were so bright she could see her shadow dance on the spiny cactuses, and hear the snakes slithering past her feet. She was not allowed to talk for fear the *migra,* the Border Patrol, would find them and send them back home. A coyote had left them just inside Texas with a promise he would return with a ride, took what money they had, and was never seen again. They waited for a day, parched and alone, huddling in the shadow of a big rock. His grandfather was enraged that he had allowed himself to be tricked, but they moved on, finding work picking cucumbers, cauliflower, strawberries, and finally, tomatoes in Indiana. His mother and his grandparents, they were *mojados,* but not him.

Tito knew he was different, saw it in the mirror every morning when he combed his hair. Sometimes, when he was in the bathtub he tried to scrub his skin off so it would be white like all the other kids. But it never worked, his skin just turned pink and purple. His mother would yell at him, tell him he should be proud of his blood. Even in summer, when the others came up to harvest, he felt like he did in school. His skin was not as dark as theirs, no matter how much time he spent in the sun. He didn't know the language like they did, only bits and pieces, words his mother used when she was angry, sad, or told stories of her childhood home in the mountains. He was part white, part Mexican. A *gringo* and a Mexican. He didn't fit in either world, no matter how much his mother insisted that he did. She could not change the color of his eyes from blue to brown, or the lightness of his hair to coal black, or the deafness of his ears when she would speak Spanish with the others.

Sometimes Tito was so lonely he thought of running away, of stowing away in the back of a pickup truck and picking grapefruits in the bright Florida sunshine with the rest of the families. But there was nowhere to go. He knew nothing of the work, of the world beyond the little town they lived in. There was no family of aunts and uncles, no grandparents, they had died long ago. It was just him and Momma once winter came on. And José Rivero, the field boss at the tomato plant, that his momma hated. She said he had traded his beautiful skin for a white heart.

Other times, he dreamed of going back to the village of his mother's birth, where winter did not exist and the volcano, Juanconi, slept among the peaks of the mountains. Where the thick forests were filled with creatures he could not imagine, and birds every color of the rainbow flew effortlessly, with joy, as they sang from morning until night. Vendors sold tamales on the street corner, and in the spring the whole town gathered to celebrate the Passion with a big pageant, a *representación*. It did not sound like such a sad place, and many times, Tito had asked his mother why she left if it was so beautiful there. A question she answered just like everyone else did when he asked: "To come to the other side. To come to paradise."

He pulled himself up from the porch, and walked to the front door. He knew it was locked. All of the doors were pulled tight; he'd tried to open them three times already.

His mother was not home and he didn't know where she was.

The lady came yesterday, just like she came every month. She brought them medicines, and always on the day after the lady visited they went into town and bought groceries. His mother had sent him to his room, but he heard their voices grow loud.

The lady always looked at him with sad eyes, but he never felt like a poison apple around her. His mother said the lady was a *bruja*, a witch, a healer, but she could not heal the wounds in their house. He knew they were arguing about him. They always argued about him. This time seemed different though, and he was afraid. After the lady left, his mother went to her bedroom and closed the door. He could hear her crying, saying the rosary over and over again. A pot of *menudo* simmered on the stove until he went to sleep. He could still smell the spicy stew in the morning.

When he awoke and prepared to leave for school, his mother looked sick, like she hadn't slept all night. Candles flickered on the small altar in the front room, a tall votive with the face of the Virgin of Guadalupe the brightest of all. A statue of Christ stood over a picture of his dead grandparents, arms stretched out, a forlorn look on His face. Other statues of saints dotted the shelf, Saint Joseph with a long white beard, standing next to a pale Saint Martin. These were the only men in the house, ceramic and plastic, molded in eternal sadness and the promise of forgiveness.

Tito had never known his *papá*. From the time he was able to ask, his mother told him that his father was dead. "Was he Mexican or a white?" he would persist.

She would answer only that he was dead.

"Is he buried in Mexico?" Tito asked when he was old enough to understand what dead meant.

Silence was his answer, a cold turn to the kitchen where she would create a task of some kind to avoid him, or go to her room and say the rosary.

"Dead. He is dead." It was all Momma would ever tell him about his father. His questions fell flat, changed the air between him and his mother for hours. Tito was left with nothing of his father to see in his mind—no pictures, no name, just a ghost with blue eyes that stared back at him from the mirror. A man without a face, a voice, or a shadow. He searched for eyes like his own in every crowd, in every stranger's face, wondering, hoping, wishing that he could find someone to call Papá.

His mother hadn't said anything about leaving, about not being home after school. She just hugged him and cried as the bus honked its horn. Before he turned to run up the road, she had stopped him, took off her St. Christopher's medal, and shoved it into his hand.

"You will need this, Tito," she had said. "My papá gave it to me when I was a *chica*, and it is rightfully yours."

The medal was cold to his touch. Her name was etched on the back of it. *Esperanza*. It meant hope, and that had always made Tito smile. When he placed the medal around his neck, he felt sad even though he didn't understand why.

He had eased into the back of the school bus, ignoring the glares of the white boys, avoiding their feet as they slid them out to try and trip him. His mother walked to the middle of the road and waved until he could not see her any longer. She had never done that before. Tito waved back as hard as he could so she would see him. He wanted to make the bus driver stop and let him off once she had disappeared, but he knew he couldn't, so he sat down in the last seat and pulled his jacket over his head so the other boys could not see the tears welling up in his eyes.

Now, the sun was starting to fall from the sky and it would be dark soon.

He was hungry.

The thin blue jean jacket he wore wasn't keeping him very warm, so he started to pace back and forth across the porch, jumping over his school books, turning back and jumping again. There was nothing else for him to do. The nearest neighbor was half a mile up the road and Mr. Jacobson didn't like him or his mother too well. He figured if it got dark and she wasn't home yet, he'd walk down the road anyway and ask Mr. Jacobson if he knew where his mother was.

Unconsciously, Tito touched the medal around his neck. He rubbed the face of the saint softly and shivered. "Momma, where are you?" he said out loud.

He heard a car coming up the road and a flicker of hope warmed his face. The road was gravel, and sometimes in the summer you could see a dust plume long before you saw the car, but not today. The car had appeared out of nowhere. He stopped jumping and eyed the road.

The car was moving very slow. He knew immediately it was not his mother's car. For a moment he was relieved, almost happy at the prospect of being rescued.

As the car pulled up in front of the house, the driver flipped on its high beams. Tito was caught in the light, standing twenty feet in the car's path.

He strained to see inside the car, but he was blinded, stunned like a raccoon in the road.

The door opened and he saw a man stand up, while another person stayed in the passenger seat. All of his relief and hope faded.

He backed up against the house, wishing he were like one of those moths that blended into the bark of maple trees. The same scary feeling he'd had last night after the lady stormed out of the house flooded his whole body. His mind screamed at him to run instead of just standing there, but when he tried to move, his stomach clenched so tight he thought he was going to vomit the ham sandwich he'd had for lunch. Sweat beaded on his forehead and he was afraid.

He couldn't scream for help. His voice was stuck in the base of his throat.

The man moved closer, saying his name over and over again, calling him a little wetback bastard.

Tito started to run. He ran so fast that he thought he was going to be able to jump up into the sky and fly away. But he was not fast enough. He could feel hot breath on the back of his neck and hear the hate in the man's voice as he was wrestled to the ground and dragged to the car.

"Please Momma, come home!" he screamed. "Please come home!"

CHAPTER 2

August 21, 2004, 4:34 A.M.

A dog barked outside the bedroom window, distant, but close enough to force Jordan McManus to open his eyes. He hesitated to move—his arms and legs were tangled in the sheets with Ginny Kirsch's body. She had her back to him, their bodies molded to a perfect fit, their fingers still entwined, though the pressure and force of hanging on to each other was gone. Her breathing had returned to normal and they both had been silent as they drifted in and out of a dream world, in and out of the past, fifteen years before, when their love was new. The dog's sudden alarm put a final end to making love, and to the start of a gnawing feeling in the pit of Jordan's stomach that he'd just made a big mistake.

The past slipped away quickly for Jordan as he began to pull away from Ginny. The familiar touch they once had for each other no longer existed. It had vanished over the years when they'd see each other on the street, both married to someone else, their lives separate, but bound by the closeness of the small town they lived in, by the connections they still shared. Jordan's marriage had ended a year before, and Ginny's was, and always had been, more than a little rocky. This was the first time in nine years they'd let themselves cross the line, touch in any way beyond a knowing, longing glance.

"I've got to go," Jordan said. Ginny opened her eyes halfway, as if she didn't believe him. His police radio sat on the night-stand, silent except for a steady low-level buzz. The window was open and a pair of sheer white curtains had been pulled aside and fastened to the wall with a thumbtack. A fan sat on the floor, aimed at the bed, blowing warm muggy air over the sweat-soaked sheets. The small bedroom at the back of the fourteen-by-seventy-foot trailer was as hot as a jungle at noon.

Dim light from the bathroom softened the cracked wood paneling that covered the walls, a jumble of half-empty perfume bottles on the dresser at the foot of the bed, and the pile of dirty laundry that lay in front of the open closet. There was nothing Jordan could see through the window that made him think anything was wrong beyond the walls. It was just a feeling. The kind you learn to trust when you wear a gun and a badge. A dog doesn't start barking at four-thirty in the morning for nothing.

"Can't you stay a little longer?" Ginny whispered. Her deep blue eyes were wide open, masked with a hardness he did not know.

"No, I'm still on shift."

He reached to the floor and grabbed his boxers and uniform pants. His shirt was by the door, next to the dresser. Somehow, he'd managed to lay his utility belt and 9mm Glock on top of the dresser without knocking over any pictures or perfume bottles. His socks and shoes were lost in a pile of clothes that had not found their way to the laundry pile, tossed in an anxious, heated moment without any regard to where they'd landed. He was really in no mood to go on a scavenger hunt for his uniform through the mess on the floor. The fog was lifting from the drunkenness of his desire for Ginny's body, and he was surprised to find it had left a sour taste in his mouth.

"Like anything's gonna happen," Ginny said, sitting up. "It's been a long time, Jordan." Her voice was scratchy and weak, like she'd smoked a pack of cigarettes in the last ten minutes.

"No, I've really gotta go." As quickly as the dog started barking, it stopped. Silence returned beyond the window, almost oppressively—even the crickets stopped chirping. All Jordan could hear was the fan whirling a million miles an hour and his heartbeat racing at the same rhythm as the blades of the fan. This was more than a trip back to his teenage fantasy world—the land of no consequences, the pleasure palace of new experiences. It was a fall. A headlong dive into home base when it was obvious the game was over a long time ago. He took a deep breath and headed for the bathroom.

Ginny reached out to touch him, to stop him, but it was a half-hearted attempt. Her hand fell back to the bed, and she closed her eyes and exhaled. Contempt was already spreading between them. Love for them had never been easy outside of the bedroom.

Jordan wanted a cigarette, but they were in the police cruiser parked a block away, hidden behind the Sunoco station that had been closed since they were kids. He relieved himself, washed his face and hands, and avoided looking in the mirror or at Ed Kirsch's razor and shaving cream that sat on the side of the iron-stained sink. There was barely enough room in the bathroom for him to bend over and pull on his boxers and pants. He immediately felt closed in, trapped, suffocated by the smell of another man's after-shave. He washed his hands and face again to try and regain his senses. It didn't help.

This time, though, he caught a glimpse of his reflection in the mirror when he looked up. Like his mother, Jordan had sandy blonde hair, and wore it cut close to his skull, exposing a thin line on each side of his head, a pattern of baldness already genetically predetermined. A faded three-inch scar zigzagged under his right eye, nothing more than a blemish now that his skin had tanned from the hot summer sun. The scar was too difficult to think about, and for the most part, he rarely noticed it. He kept the memory of the scar hidden away in a dark and unreachable place in his heart, in a dungeon of anger he'd fought most of his life to keep bolted and locked.

He had his father's blue eyes—a misty blue that always held a hint of sadness, like dusk settling onto the horizon after a perfect summer day. If he could change anything about his appearance it would be his eyes. He saw nothing but betrayal in his father's eyes, and now, in his own. Jordan always swore he'd never be anything like his father. But he'd failed to live up to that vow when he slipped into bed with another man's wife. The door to the dungeon was cracked open, and the old rage made his head throb—he looked quickly in the medicine cabinet for a bottle of aspirin. He closed the mirrored door as soon as he saw a needle and a small wad of aluminum foil stuffed behind a half tube of toothpaste, and hurried out of the bathroom.

Ginny was standing at the bedroom window, still naked, her arms crossed over her breasts. She had unfastened the sheer curtains and they fluttered in the breeze from the fan. The light from the bathroom mingled with the break of dawn, and Ginny's shoulder-length blonde hair glowed against her sun-bronzed body.

A small blue and pink dragonfly tattoo, wings spread in flight, shimmered in the moisture on the small of her back. She was thirty-three, three years older than Jordan was, and her body showed little sign of bearing a child nine years earlier—she was thin, thinner than he ever remembered. She still looked ethereal, though, otherworldly, and forever young. For a moment, Jordan forgot about the needle, forgot again that he was a cop. But the pure image of Ginny at nineteen he'd held onto for so long faded quickly when the police radio buzzed again with static.

"I don't know how much more I can take," she whispered.

"The heat?" he asked, searching for his socks. It had only

rained a quarter inch in the last twenty-three days, and the temperature had hovered in the nineties for just as long, dropping into the mid-seventies at night. It was the hottest, muggiest August anybody in central Indiana could remember. The night air was so humid he could barely breathe, but seeing her standing there, he couldn't resist touching her velvet skin again, couldn't resist asking the question that was screaming in his head. He slid his hands around her waist and pulled her as close as possible.

"Are you using?" Jordan couldn't see the expression on her face, but he felt her stiffen and then relax as she arched into him. Her neck smelled of jasmine.

"No. Why would you ask me that?"

"The needle in the medicine cabinet. I thought maybe there was some aspirin . . . I wasn't snooping."

Ginny pulled away and turned her back to the window, facing him. She was a good six inches shorter than he was, five-foot six to his six-foot one, and she had to reach up to touch his face. "It's Ed's, he's diabetic. Why? What were you thinking, that I'm shooting up?"

"I thought Ed might be." He was relieved that he was wrong, but he wasn't sure that she was telling him the truth. The answer came too quick—but he wasn't going to pursue it, for all he knew Ed Kirsch really was diabetic. Even though diabetes didn't explain the aluminum-foil rock. They both knew Ed Kirsch's history, knew he had used and sold pot and speed in the past, when they were teenagers. But as far as he knew Ed had given up that life a long time ago—at least the dealing part. Jordan wasn't sure Ed had ever quit using.

There was no way he could make a bust for possession if the foil was a rock of cocaine, or crystal meth. How would he explain being in the bathroom?

Ginny's fingers were like short shocks of electricity on his face as she touched the scar under his eye. Jordan recoiled, and she looked at him oddly, forced a smile—she knew she was out of bounds and she didn't care. She never had.

"No, Ed knows better than that. Daddy doesn't like him the way it is. He's not going to give him a reason to arrest him," Ginny said, shaking her head. "I just don't want to live the rest of my life like this. It has to be better than this, Jordan, it just has to be. I never dreamed marrying Ed would turn out like this. Let's run away. Go to Arizona or Florida, anywhere but here. Let's start over. Change our names. You could work on a fishing boat or be a guide in the mountains for tourists. I'll get a job at a grocery store, be a waitress. I don't care, as long as I don't have to be what I am now."

"We had our chance for that a long time ago. It didn't work out too well, if I remember right. You weren't ready, remember?"

"I was young and stupid. I was scared. I didn't know what I wanted."

Jordan hesitated. He wanted nothing more than to rescue Ginny, take her out of the life she'd gotten herself into. He knew how bad things turned out—he had watched her fade a little more every day. But he'd stayed out of her life for so long . . . and he wasn't up to getting his heart broken again. At least not so quickly. If they got back together, it would have to be the right way. Not like this.

He could watch Ed, arrest him if he was using or selling, but taking him out of the picture for Ginny wouldn't be a great start to any kind of relationship. They had enough baggage the way it was. "So now we'd just be stupid?" he asked. "I don't want to live anywhere else, Ginny. I can't just walk in here one day out of the blue and pick up and leave. Why would I want to do that? Why would you even think I would do that? Is that why you called me? You thought I'd sweep you up and take you away from all of your problems? Take you away from Ed? Come on,

Ginny, tell me that wasn't your reason? We're not kids anymore. It's just not that easy—we'd have to give it some time. You'll have to leave Ed on your own."

Ginny sat down on the edge of the bed and grabbed up the sheet to cover herself, her eyes moist, on the verge of tears. "No. He won't let that happen," she said, turning her head away.

"I'm not scared of Ed Kirsch."

"You should be," Ginny whispered. She took a deep breath. "I'm sorry, I just wanted to touch you. Feel alive again."

"You know something? I don't believe you."

Her lip sagged into a frown like it always did when she didn't get what she wanted. "You're nothing but a goddamned third-shift security guard, Jordan," Ginny yelled. "Whether you want to admit it or not, and a gopher for my father. You've been under his spell since you were twelve. Look at you now. You're a grown man and it's no different. You're just a deputy in a stinking small town in Indiana. A big fish in a little pond with a gun on your hip to make you feel powerful. How could you like your life? Nothing's changed. Not even you, climbing in and out of my bed when the mood strikes you."

Jordan couldn't argue with her, she was right about most of the things she said. Being a cop in Dukaine, Indiana, with a total of two stoplights, was not like being a cop in New York City. It had its challenges, especially in late summer when the migrants came to town, but mostly he wrote speeding tickets and checked on locked doors at night—he really was a security guard on a basic level. But crystal meth had become a problem in the last couple of years, a rural scourge that had worked its way from the South and into the big cities—Indianapolis and Chicago—that Dukaine sat squarely between. Keeping an eye on the ammonia tanks, a key ingredient that could be found in the homemade drug, at the co-op was high priority. But even that only required sitting and watching. Users that made their own meth were a big concern and a drain on time—but the bigger problem was the mega-labs out west, rumored to be operated by Mexican drug lords.

It was the Mexican connection and the transportation of the drug, considering the influx of migrants during harvest season, that concerned most of the law enforcement officials in Carlyle County. Jordan hadn't seen any sign of big-time operators in Dukaine, but that didn't mean they weren't there. He had seen, though, the devastating effect meth had on its users; he'd been involved in three busts in the last six months, and each time there were children in the house where the meth was being cooked. The users lost everything, and it was almost impossible to break the addiction. Security guards didn't have to deal with seeing that.

"I didn't say everything in my life was perfect," Jordan said. "Would I be here if it was?" He put his uniform shirt on—it stuck to his sweaty skin, making him even more uncomfortable. "I knew I shouldn't have come here."

"Don't go."

He kissed her on the forehead.

She drew back and looked at him harshly. "You still love me. That's why you came."

The dog barked again. Jordan tried to ignore the remark, and took a step over to the window and looked outside. She was right about that, too. He'd never stopped loving her. How could he?

There were seventeen trailers in the Royal Lane trailer park, all lined up ten feet from one another, facing a single unpaved road that led in and out to Main Street. Beyond the road was a set of railroad tracks that skirted an eighty-acre tomato field. Over the field, he could see the bright lights of the SunRipe plant glowing against the early morning sky, a warehouse the size of two football fields, all lit up like it was the last Friday night football game of the season.

The plant was operating at full capacity, pumping out ketchup, spaghetti sauce, and various other products made from tomatoes, twenty-four hours a day. Tomatoes were the lifeblood of Dukaine, and the plant was the single largest employer in the southern half of Carlyle County. While the rest of Indiana was mostly covered with corn and soybean fields, there were over fifteen thousand acres of tomatoes in a hundred-mile radius of the SunRipe plant. During the picking season, an army of migrants descended on the town, more than doubling Dukaine's population from three thousand to seven thousand, straining the demand on every service in town, especially the police department. In all, thirty to forty migrant camps sprang up across the county every summer.

The police department consisted of Jordan; Ginny's father; the marshal, Holister Coggins; and Johnny Ray Johnson, the other full-time deputy. In the summer, off-duty deputies from the county sheriff's department filled in on a part-time basis. Even with the help, the days were long for the three of them, working a minimum of six days a week, twelve hours a day. Jordan always worked the night shift. He liked the quiet. Johnny Ray liked the noise of the day, the joy of being a cop, the sun glaring on his badge, so the schedule worked out for the both of them. Holister, for the most part, was always on duty.

Jordan didn't see anything out of the ordinary beyond the window, just the neighbor's cat crawling up onto a stained yellow brocade sofa that sat on the patio. He was jumpy because he knew he was somewhere he wasn't supposed to be. Breaking rules for the pure pleasure of it was something he thought he'd given up a long time ago. He was overreacting and he knew it.

"Ed and me have been in trouble for a long time, Jordan," Ginny said. The anger faded from her face as she dropped the volume of her voice and lowered her head. "You know that. Ed's been sleeping with that little redheaded tramp down at the truck stop for months. He says he's on the road, but we never have any goddamned money. I know where he is. I always know where he is, and he's not on a run to Texas like he's supposed to be. Damn it, Jordan, *you're* my safe place. My rock. The one I could always turn to . . . the only person who's ever been there for me. And I need you now, more than ever."

"Is this just a way to get back at Ed?" he asked, eyeing the door. "Call it even? Pretty easy to do if you ask me. Just call Jordan, he'll come running?"

"It's been nine years, Jordan. If that was my reason, I would've done it before now."

Jordan knew about Ed and the redhead at the truck stop. He'd seen them together more than once, and he'd used that information to rationalize his own behavior a few hours earlier when he'd slid from the shadows and into Ginny's open arms. There were a million times he wanted to tell Ginny what was going on, but he'd vowed to stay out of their relationship, just like she'd vowed to stay out of his. And he'd vowed not to break the code of silence that came with his job. He knew a lot of secrets—knew more about most of the people in Dukaine than he wanted to. Every vow he'd ever promised himself seemed to be empty now, all in a matter of a few hours. What the hell had he been thinking?

"It'd be different this time, I promise," Ginny said. "You're the only man I ever truly loved."

"Sometimes, love's not enough." Jordan drew in a deep breath of muggy air from the fan. For a second, he thought he saw fear flash across Ginny's face, like she wanted to tell him something, but the look disappeared as quickly as it had appeared.

"I don't believe that," Ginny said.

"If it's time to leave Ed, then leave. I'll make sure he can't hurt you."

"You can't promise me that."

"Yes, I can. I can make sure he can't hurt you or Dylan—and I'm sure Dylan's old enough to understand what's going on. He probably knows you two can't stand the sight of each other. Trust me, you'd be doing him a favor. But I won't play second fiddle to Ed Kirsch ever again."

Ginny stood up, her eyes twisted as if Jordan had just slapped her. "You're a son of a bitch. A self-righteous asshole just like you've always been. You take what you want when you want it, and then you run. You always run, Jordan, when things get a little close, a little too complicated. You're hot on the outside, but cold as ice on the inside," she said. "Get out. Get out of my house. Get out of my life, and stay out. I mean it."

"You're going to wake Dylan up."

"Are you afraid he'll tell Ed you were here?"

"I'm sorry. This won't happen again." He grabbed his utility belt and 9mm Glock off the dresser, snapped it on quickly, and walked out of the bedroom.

"Don't go," Ginny said, following him to the door of the bedroom. "Please don't go. I need you . . ."

Her sobs followed him down the trailer's hallway and he heard a door open. He turned and saw Dylan, blonde hair tussled and sleepy blue eyes on the edge of tears, peering out of his bedroom door.

Damn it, he thought, *this is the last thing I wanted to happen.* He put his index finger to his lips and whispered, "Go back to bed, everything's all right."

When the nine-year-old boy responded with a half-smile and disappeared back into the bedroom, Jordan eased out of the front door just as the birds were starting to sing and the street-lights were going off.

CHAPTER 3

August 21, 2004, 5:48 A.M.

The sun was already a white disk in the pale blue sky when Jordan pulled into the police department parking lot. He'd driven the streets of Dukaine three times looking for something out of place, a reason for the dog to be barking, but he didn't see anything, not even a loose dog. He reasoned that his uneasy feeling was nothing more than his overactive imagination all mixed up with a heavy dose of guilt. It would have been easier to blame the heat for his nervousness. Everybody else was blaming the drought for everything. Like the call he got a couple of shifts ago. "I'm sorry, Jordan, I punched my wife because the A/C quit working, and I just lost my temper. It won't happen again, I promise." In the winter, domestic disturbance calls came in because the furnace went out. He decided the weather really was responsible for stupidity. It was something to keep in mind, but it didn't make him feel any better.

Like most small Midwestern towns, the road that ran through the center of Dukaine was named Main Street. All of the other side streets were named after dead presidents: Jefferson, Adams, Tyler, Kennedy, and Harrison. The police station sat at the corner of Jefferson and Main in the back of a two-story brick building that had once served as a hardware store until it went bankrupt and was bought by the town. The Town Hall occupied the front half of the building, windows replaced by plywood and painted dark brown to match the color of the brick, and the second story was used for storing Christmas decorations and old office equipment.

The gravel parking lot was empty, with the exception of Louella Canberry's ancient Buick. A single water tower rose from a barren brown grass field between the police department and the volunteer fire department, freshly painted white with a ripe tomato on each side. The fire department was housed in a blue metal building with four-oversized garage doors. A basketball hoop stood alongside the driveway, the net torn and dangling on one hook, and a tornado siren sat atop the building, four rusted horns, one for each direction, to alert the entire town.

Louella Canberry was the sole dispatcher for the police department. She was a retired second-grade teacher and had talked Holister into letting her try her hand at dispatching the day after she quit teaching. It turned out she was pretty good at giving orders over the radio, but Jordan wasn't surprised—she was the teacher everybody'd feared the most in elementary school. He didn't like her any more now than he did when she was his teacher. Somehow, they managed to tolerate each other, but it still pissed her off when he called her Louella instead of Mrs. Canberry.

He grabbed up his gear to go inside the police station and put an end to the shift. There was nothing more he wanted than to go home and take a nice long shower, sit in front of the air-conditioner, have a few beers before he went to sleep, and pretend last night with Ginny never happened. But a rumbling engine at the stoplight at Jefferson and Main made him hesitate.

He looked over his shoulder and saw a SunRipe semi, a red Kenworth cab pulling a long white trailer dotted with tomatoes wearing smiling faces bouncing into a bottle of ketchup. The driver was hard to distinguish, but Jordan was pretty sure it was

Ed Kirsch heading for home. The semi lurched forward and drove out of sight.

A bead of sweat formed on his upper lip as he watched the diesel exhaust dissipate, heard the vibration of the big engine shift as the driver picked up speed. If it was Ed, there was no recognition on his part to wave, but that was normal. Ed and Jordan were good at avoiding each other, if they could. If they couldn't, the tone was as cordial as two prison inmates bumping shoulders.

He knew he wouldn't be able to help himself—he'd watch Ed a little closer, find out if he was dealing again. But he wasn't sure what he'd do about it other than talk to Holister, see if he had the same concerns.

When he went inside, Louella was sitting at the dispatch console, a battleship gray metal desk with an odd collection of twenty-year-old radio equipment piled on top of it, filing her nails.

Jordan was glad to be out of the sun. One of the perks of working the night shift, six in the evening to six in the morning, was that he pretty much got to keep vampire hours, which lately, especially since the drought took hold, was worth all of the Friday and Saturday night fights he'd had to deal with.

The police department consisted of the main entry, the dispatch desk, and two small offices. There was an odd musty smell that accosted Jordan's nose every time he walked in the door of the police station. The white ceiling tiles were stained, little splotches of brown that looked like Rorschach tests, and mold on the window sills all contributed to the smell, but he wasn't sure that was all there was to the odor. He was almost certain there was a dead mouse or two decaying somewhere, probably in the ductwork. Or the smell was Louella's perfume. Either way, it wasn't pleasant.

"Holister just called, he wants you to meet him out at

Longer's Pond," Louella said, spinning in her chair to face him.

Holister Coggins had been the marshal in Dukaine for thirty-one years, and his daily routine was as rote as the change of seasons—always on time, always predictable, always in the same place at the same time every day. He reminded Jordan of a turtle basking in the sun, not moving off his log unless he absolutely had to.

Jordan was becoming just like Holister. He liked his routine, liked things in their place, where they belonged. But his last shift had been anything but normal, and instead of his world being black and white, like it normally was, his life was suddenly as gray as a funnel cloud just before it touched the ground and became a tornado. He knew, deep in his heart, that things hadn't ended with Ginny when he walked out of her trailer. It had only been a start, and finishing it was not going to be easy, no matter how it turned out.

"What's he doing out at the pond? He's usually at the café having breakfast about now," Jordan said. He was really in no mood to see Holister, all things considered, but he was mildly curious why the old man was at Longer's Pond so early in the morning.

"I don't know. He doesn't tell me anything until he comes in the office. He tried to call you earlier, but you didn't answer," Louella said. She had the face of a bird, and she changed expressions constantly, always pursing her lips or squinting her eyes through the thick plastic herringbone glasses she'd worn forever. Her hair was tied up in a tight bun with spindly silver hairs poking out haphazardly, and she constantly pulled the miniature knitting needle that held the bun together in and out, never satisfied with its position. Louella Canberry couldn't sit still if her life depended on it. If she wasn't typing a report, she was on the phone talking to her brother, Albert, who owned the local funeral home, or some other family member, keeping up with all the latest gossip around town. She not only annoyed Jordan, she drove Holister nuts too. Johnny Ray treated her like she was Gladys Presley.

"Nobody called me," he said, unsnapping his gunbelt.

"I'm just telling you what he told me."

He looked at the clock over the console. "I'm off shift in ten minutes."

"Holister said he wanted you out there, now," Louella said, imposing a reserve of authority she'd once used ruthlessly on disobedient second-grade students. "I'm pretty sure he knows what time it is."

"Call back and see what he wants. It's time for me to go home and go to bed. This heat's drained me," Jordan said. It was not necessarily a lie, but he wasn't about to tell Louella why he was in such a hurry to get out of there.

The air-conditioning was on full-blast, but it was still warm inside the room. The two offices were directly behind the dispatcher's station, Holister's and the one he shared with Johnny Ray Johnson. There was no jail in Dukaine. Any apprehensions required a trip to the Carlyle County jail in Morland, twenty miles away. The temperature of the police station bounded in extremes. In the summer it was always too hot, and in the winter it was always too cold. Radiant heat and window air-conditioners did little to steady the comfort in the aged building, and the Town Board's budget was so tight that the thought of upgrading any equipment that wasn't vitally necessary was never put on the table for serious discussion. They wouldn't hire another deputy for the same reason. Sweat ran down Jordan's back, but Louella showed no sign of being overheated. She looked like she'd just walked out of an icebox.

Louella muttered something under her breath, spun back around to the console, and did as she was told.

Jordan walked into his office, a ten-by-ten room painted light gray with a small nicotine-stained window next to the gun locker, a desk similar to Louella's, a file cabinet, and a corkboard full of wanted notices and memos from INS.

The Immigration and Naturalization Service used the office when they were in town checking green cards and work permits. He didn't look forward to those times, which came predictably three times a year: at the start of harvest, followed by a "surprise" visit every August, and then again at the end of the harvest. The INS agents treated the entire department as if they were nothing more than low-life rent-a-cops, po-dunk Barney Fifes who knew nothing about law enforcement. It was easier to let the agents think what they would, because there was nothing that would change their minds. But as far as Jordan was concerned, there were very few small-town police departments that had to deal with the situations the Dukaine Police Department was forced to deal with every migrant season. The crime rate in Dukaine doubled in the summer, and they received very little help beyond what the county sheriff's department provided. And now that meth had burst onto the scene, it was starting to seem like the crazy season was going to last all year long.

The INS visits were geared more toward finding drug smugglers and coyotes than they were for deporting illegals. Once the agents filled their quotas, they were gone. The only real use Jordan had for the INS was when they weren't around. All he had to do to get the attention of a migrant was utter "INS" under his breath. No matter how drunk or vigilant a Mexican was, when a cop said INS, they understood English perfectly. His Spanish was adequate, and he knew just enough to get what he wanted, at least most of the time, like asking for license and registration when he pulled a migrant over for speeding. *"¿Su licencia y registro por favor?"* But he used the INS ploy with restraint. Unlike Johnny Ray.

He sat down at the desk to fill out his shift report and prepare the lone speeding ticket from the night before, when Holister's voice boomed over the radio. "Tell him to get out here, now. I need him."

Jordan dropped the pen, raced out of the office, and said, "Radio him back. Tell him I'm out the door and on my way." Holister's tone finally got his attention. There was no mistaking panic, even over the radio. Louella pursed her lips into a hard smile. He knew her "See, I told you so" expression better than he wanted to, and refused to acknowledge it as he ran by her desk.

Whether it was from the heat, fatigue, anxiety, or all three, he felt numb. Every step felt like it was in slow motion, every breath consciously taken. He pushed his way out the door of the station, slid into the hot leather seat of the cruiser, and hit the lights and siren.

He spun out of the parking lot and squealed the tires on Main Street. The cruiser's engine rumbled as he lit a cigarette and focused his eyes on the road.

The town blurred by quickly. Big Joe's Tavern sat on the opposite corner of Jefferson and Main. The Farmer's Bank & Loan with its gold Queen Anne dome towered over the other buildings across the street. Marlee's Beauty Shop sat in a converted white bungalow next to the Dukaine Café, and a row of Victorian-style houses that sat on each side of the street in various degrees of repair rounded out downtown as he headed east toward Longer's Pond.

The last house on Main Street belonged to Buddy Mozel, the third-generation owner of the SunRipe plant. It was a huge Victorian with twin turrets that sat back off the road, pretty much hidden by sculpted shrubbery and a six-foot black iron gate that surrounded the five-acre property.

Jordan flicked ash out of the window and noticed the front

gate was standing wide open. Which was unusual, as the mansion was always locked up tighter than a military fortress.

He had no time to stop and ask questions—and figured if something was wrong he'd know about it anyway. Buddy Mozel had been a recluse since Jordan was a kid, and a person was more likely to see Elvis eating a tenderloin at the local café than to see Buddy Mozel out and about.

It only took Jordan five minutes to reach the outskirts of town where the Little Blue River widened into a floodplain. Tomato fields bordered both sides of the road. At least a hundred migrants were at work in the fields, bent over filling bushel baskets with quick deliberate movements to protect the tender tomatoes, and to save as much of the crop as they could from the unrelenting sun and lack of rain. It was too early to use the mechanical pickers, so the cost of losing even one tomato was too high.

The sight of migrants working in the fields was a timeless event that had occurred each and every summer of Jordan's life. The Mexicans were nameless bronze-skinned ghosts who disappeared after the sun went down, and vanished completely when the first cold wind blew them out of town in October.

The road was lined with pickup trucks and beat-up cars with license plates from Florida, Texas, and Arizona. A big red GMC pickup that belonged to José Rivero, the field boss and Buddy Mozel's right-hand man, sat separately from the other cars.

José was standing in front of the truck with one black cowboy boot propped up on the shiny chrome bumper, talking on a cell phone. He waved casually as Jordan zipped by.

He barely had time to wave back. Jordan had known José since he was a kid. One of the few Mexicans he'd ever spent any time around. And then, it wasn't openly.

Whites and Mexicans didn't mix under any circumstances beyond the fields. Most of the townspeople held the migrants in low regard; they were wetbacks, spics, dirty people who didn't know how or didn't even care to learn to speak English. The line of prejudice was a sad fact of life in Dukaine, and was clearly drawn on both sides. The Mexicans avoided whites as much as possible, coming into town only when they had to, always traveling in crews of fours and fives.

A sign on the front door of Miller's Grocery said it all: NO MORE THAN 2 MEXICANS INSIDE AT 1 TIME. There was no sign on the front door of Big Joe's Tavern though, it was just common knowledge that the migrants weren't allowed there—if a Mexican wanted a good ass kickin', that was the place to go. For alcohol, the migrants had to go to Peg's Keg & Spirits just on the other side of the railroad tracks. On Friday nights the liquor store parking lot was filled with cars blaring Mariachi music. Jordan was normally parked across the street, watching for the first sign of violence. The cruiser's presence was usually enough to keep the peace. But there were times when the tequila and Tecate took hold and things got ugly, especially lately, with the yields down from the drought. Money was tight and tensions were high.

José had worked for the Mozel family for over thirty years, and was a friend of Jordan's grandmother, Kitty. It was not uncommon for José to knock on her back door, in need of some herbal cure for one of the migrants who had fallen ill. They were not welcome by any of the white doctors, and Kitty had made it her life's work to treat the Mexicans the best she could once she'd retired as a nurse—standing outside the lines drawn by religion, the town, and even Holister, who was her next-door neighbor. But since Jordan had become a cop, seven years ago, José rarely spoke to him, and avoided him just as the rest of the migrants did. José never asked for favors, but Jordan had turned his head more than once when an illegal made a misstep.

Ginny was wrong about his hunger for power. Her rules for

right and wrong changed on a daily basis. But consistency was key to Jordan, even if it meant *not* following every letter of the law, even if it meant allowing an illegal to continue to make a living. He was more apathetic than righteous, but the rationale for his thinking was simple: Arrest and deport one illegal only to have them replaced by another. In his mind, it was better to keep a known face under a watchful eye than continually have to deal with new faces, a new unknown.

The migrants faded in the rearview mirror as he slowed the cruiser and turned onto the gravel road that led to Longer's Pond. He immediately noticed that it was lined with devil's plague, three-foot-tall white flowered weeds that were brittle and dry.

It had been months since he had been to the pond. Oak and hickory trees showed little sign of bearing nuts, and their leaves were tainted with fragile brown edges. The woods surrounding the pond looked more like mid-October than mid-August. For the first time in weeks Jordan was chilled to the bone, and he didn't know why.

He scanned the parking area and saw Holister's police cruiser, a three-year-old unmarked white Impala, sitting under a seventy-foot cottonwood tree. The windows were down, the doors unlocked. Holister was nowhere to be seen, and there were no other cars in the lot. He took a deep breath, ground out his cigarette in the ashtray, and radioed his location to Louella.

As he got out of the cruiser, a mockingbird sat in an elm tree singing a song that was a three-part chorus of chickadee, kill-deer, and police siren. The song ultimately sounded like a jumbled Hank Williams song turned up on high speed. Otherwise, the pond was silent. He whistled at the mockingbird. When the bird didn't whistle back he unsnapped the strap on his Glock, slid his nightstick into his belt, and reached for the handheld radio.

A well-worn path led down to the pond from the parking lot, which wasn't anything more than a small field covered with dead grass and sparse gravel. Holister appeared on the path just as Jordan called him on the radio. In a hurry, limping badly, the marshal looked like he was a Saturday night drunk, except it was Tuesday morning.

"You all right?" Jordan asked.

"There's somebody out there," Holister answered. A wild, unfamiliar look danced across the marshal's eyes. His solid white hair was a mess. His uniform shirt was splotched with sweat and untucked, hanging from his protruding belly like a flag. "I heard 'em running," he continued, gaining his breath. "Laughin' like it's funny. Like it's all a big goddamned joke. My legs gave out, or I'da showed them how fucking funny it is." He had his .38, a service revolver from the Korean War, drawn with his finger heavy on the trigger.

Jordan couldn't do anything but stare at Holister warily. He'd never seen his boss in a state like this before.

"I heard a mockingbird when I got out of the car. You sure it wasn't just a bird you heard?"

"It wasn't a goddamned bird, Jordan."

"Back up. Tell me what the hell's going on. You sure we don't need to get you to the doctor?"

"Damn it, I don't need another mother hen, Ginny and Celeste do a good enough job at that." Holister paused, looked up at the sky, and then back to Jordan, holding his gaze with steel blue eyes. "You won't believe me."

"I'd believe just about anything right now."

"I found Tito Cordova, Jordan. I finally found him."

CHAPTER 4

August 21, 2004, 6:32 A.M.

Holister might as well have said he'd come face to face with The Bogeyman and invited him to speak at the Founder's Day breakfast.

"I sure wasn't expecting that," Jordan said.

"You think I was?" Holister answered.

Tito Cordova's name bounced around in Jordan's head like a wraith released from its chains. Of all of the secrets Jordan knew about the people in Dukaine, Tito's story was the one that hit closest to home. He'd done his best—just like most everyone else in town, to forget about the little light-skinned Mexican boy—to act like Tito never existed, that nothing out of the ordinary happened on that November day so long ago.

It took a few days, but the search for Tito Cordova became an event. Holister had told Jordan more than once, when he recounted the story of Tito's disappearance, that he could not bear to see Esperanza Cordova camped outside the police station waiting for news about her son, but he had hesitated to do anything because she was a Mexican. After receiving a stern request from Buddy Mozel that was more like an order, Holister organized a formal search that eventually consumed everyone in town.

It was Holister's failure to act swiftly, and his suspicion that there was more to the disappearance than it being just a random act, that drove him to look for the little boy long after the search ended. Long after the trail had gone cold, until the memory of Tito Cordova slowly became a whisper.

They searched everywhere in Dukaine, yelling, "Tito, Tito," over and over again. Jordan remembered the hopelessness and frustration in Holister's eyes, who seemed old even then, as he looked inside every garage, every empty house, for a sign that Tito had been there. It was like the boy had just vanished, gone for the winter like the rest of the Mexicans.

And Jordan could never forget Tito's mother, hysterical, standing alone on her porch day after day as Holister told her there was no news. Esperanza Cordova screamed at Holister in broken English, and then in Spanish, "I will never forgive you! I will never forgive you if you do not find my son!" Afterward, she would collapse in a bundle of sobs and moans that made his own heart quiver and shake.

Jordan knew better than anyone that Holister was still obsessed with the Tito Cordova case. Holister brought up the search, and his guilt, every year after the harvest ended and cold weather became a promise fulfilled, recounting each and every step he'd taken looking for Tito.

The file was hidden and locked away, but pulled out and dusted off annually, like a memory book of a long-lost relative who'd died tragically and did not deserve to be forgotten. For Jordan, the recounting of the past, of the time after Tito had disappeared, was just as painful to him as it was to Holister. But regret and professional failure had nothing to do with Jordan's pain.

He was twelve when Tito Cordova had disappeared, and his own sense of loss had more to do with the knowledge of what his own life was like in 1985. That was the summer when he learned the word *divorce*, followed by the reality and certainty of death and the scars it left behind.

Now, as an adult, when Holister pulled out the file to celebrate their own Day of the Dead, their own *Día de Los Muertos,* he would pretend to listen. Holister never showed him all of the file—he guarded the contents fiercely, even from Jordan, and then put it away for another year.

Afterward, Jordan would go directly across the street to Big Joe's Tavern and drink until he was numb, glad that the annual review of Tito's case was over, glad the Mexicans were gone for another year.

"Where'd you find him?" Jordan finally asked Holister. His mouth was dry. It was as if the sun had burnt his tongue from top to bottom. But he knew the heat wasn't the cause. It was the past rising up in the back of his throat.

"Down at the pond. Half-buried. There ain't much left. Just bones. Probably been there all along." Holister drew in a deep breath and looked to the sky. "We looked here, goddamn it. We covered every inch of these woods. A few of the deputies from Carlyle County even got their scuba gear and searched the pond, remember?"

"I remember. You've told me about this a million times. The sheriff's department divers said it was just too damn deep and muddy down there to find anything," Jordan answered, staring down the path that led to the pond.

He always wondered if it had been a white kid instead of Tito Cordova who disappeared, if the divers would've looked a little longer or dived a little deeper.

"It started snowing, and then the pond froze over, that's why we stopped looking for him," Holister said.

That's not the only reason why the search stopped, Jordan thought, but could not bring himself to say aloud. Holister always left that part out of the story, left out what happened to Esperanza Cordova. That pained Holister as much as never finding Tito did.

"Somebody's out there, Jordan," Holister repeated. "Somebody thinks this is awful goddamned funny."

"Are you sure you're all right? I can call an ambulance out here . . ."

"Would you *just* listen to me?"

"All right. Just who in the heck do you think is out there?"

"I don't know. I just heard a laugh. Heard somebody runnin' through the woods screamin' like a wounded banshee."

"Louella said she got a call about a meth lab out here last week. County didn't find anything. I was out here a month ago for the same reason. You know what goes on in these woods. Why didn't you call the sheriff's department for backup when you heard the laugh?"

Holister fidgeted and glanced away. "I didn't need them."

Jordan knew Holister well enough to know he wasn't telling him everything. But the fact remained that Holister *had* discovered some bones. Whether the bones belonged to Tito Cordova was yet to be seen.

He needed to get his bearings. The heat made it almost impossible to think straight, and he was tired and guilt-ridden. He not only had betrayed his own vows by sleeping with Ginny, he had betrayed Holister and created another secret to keep from him. It almost felt as if the world had stopped moving— the drought had changed everything, exposing events of the past rapidly.

Jordan could not help but wonder if he could keep his break in character, his secrets, hidden away so they wouldn't hurt the ones he loved the most—or would they be exposed to the whole world like the skeleton?

Now was not the time to bring up his suspicions about Ed Kirsch to Holister.

The air was still, like the moment before a storm hits. Even the insects were silent. Any cicadas that had survived their seventeen-year birth cycle were not celebrating, and the shadows underneath the canopy of leaves stood motionless, in prayer for the next breeze.

Jordan shivered again, stared at Holister, and then looked toward the pond. He had an unnerving feeling that he was being watched. "You're not making any sense. Why'd you come out here in the first place? It had to be more than a lark. You're usually having breakfast at the café right now. This isn't normal."

"It don't matter," Holister snapped. He started to walk away. "Come on, you need to see this."

Jordan reached out and grabbed Holister's shoulder. "It does too matter. Why in the hell were you out here?"

Holister was still stout for his age, heavy but not overly laden with fat from his years of sitting behind the wheel of the cruiser and living on a diet made up mostly of biscuits and gravy and cheeseburgers. There was nothing about his appearance that suggested old age had weakened him. Until now. Holister looked like he'd aged ten years since Jordan had seen him the day before.

"I didn't want to tell you until I knew what was goin' on," Holister said.

"Tell me what?"

Holister reached into his back pocket and handed an envelope to Jordan. "Go ahead, open it."

Jordan reluctantly pulled a letter out of the envelope. A gold medal fell to the ground. He ignored the medal for a second, unfolded the paper, and read it:

> *Be at Longer's Pond on Tuesday at five o'clock. Don't bring no one with you. Go to the spring and wait.*

The writing looked like chicken scratchings. It wasn't signed, and the paper looked like normal typing paper.

"Somebody wanted you to find the bones," Jordan said.

Holister nodded.

Jordan flipped over the envelope to look at the postmark. The letter had been mailed two days prior from the post office in Dukaine. "You've been out here since five o'clock this morning?"

Holister nodded. "I got a little scared when I couldn't chase after him when he started laughin'. That's why I called you."

"Him? Was it a male?" Jordan asked.

"I don't know. I didn't see anybody, goddamn it. I'm just assumin' it's a man."

"But it was one person?"

"I think so. I don't know for sure. I ain't got X-ray vision, Jordan. If I did, I'd be eatin' breakfast like usual, and you'd be home asleep."

Jordan nodded. "All right, all right. You got this letter yesterday?"

"I didn't know if it meant evenin' or mornin'. I figured if nothin' happened then I'd have Johnny Ray come out with me this evenin'."

"But something did happen?"

"I guess so. He's out there, but when I called for him to show himself everything got quiet," Holister said.

Jordan reached down and picked up the gold piece that had fallen out of the envelope.

It was a St. Christopher's medal. There was an inscription on the back. Etched in thin, tiny letters was the name *Esperanza*. Even in the dim light, Jordan could see tarnish and the dullness across the face of the protector saint. He grazed the full length of the cloaked figure with his thumb and felt the pain of failure, not only for Holister, but for Esperanza and Tito.

"It looks like you might be right," Jordan said. "You might have finally found Tito. But I'm calling the sheriff's department to get a few more sets of eyes out here. Somebody's up to no good, playing games with the past or with you. Either way, I don't like it. Gives me the creeps is what it does."

"I don't like it neither. Not after seeing them bones."

Jordan folded up the letter, dropped the medal back in the envelope, and handed it back to Holister.

"You hang on to it for now," Holister said.

"All right." Jordan stuffed the letter into his back pocket. "Can you make it back down to the pond and show me?"

Holister nodded and headed slowly toward the path.

"Hold on." He radioed Louella and had her request a sheriff's deputy come out to the pond, unholstered his Glock, and chambered a round. "All right. Let's go have a look."

The path opened up to the pond and the bright morning sun danced across the surface like a flashlight shining on a cracked mirror. Cattails, russet brown and cottony, shot up out of dried, crusty banks. The water had receded ten feet from its normal bank, exposing a desert dotted with fallen trees and trash. Red and white fishing bobbers and tangles of stray fishing line hung from bare tree limbs. A lawn chair, the webbing rotted away, lay on its side next to an old tractor tire.

Longer's Pond had changed, just like everything else in Dukaine had changed, after Tito Cordova disappeared. What had once been a getaway for fishing and swimming was now a nearly stagnant puddle, the water tainted by years of fertilizer runoff and neglect. There was an overgrown sandy beach on the north bank of the pond. A small cement block building that had housed a concession stand sat vacant, marred by graffiti, its windows broken, the inside a haven for raccoons, meth cookers, and other vermin.

Twenty feet out into the water an aluminum slide rose up out of the muck, rusted and leaning heavily to the right side. At the height of summer a water hose would be extended from the concession stand to the slide, creating a makeshift water-slide. A huge cement foundation that was once a diving board platform, cracked and crumbling, jutted up a little farther out into the water. The depth of the pond back then was at least twenty-five feet. The bottom was comprised of a thin layer of sand, on top of a limestone base that had holes and caves that went to depths unknown. Jordan had spent a lot of time at Longer's Pond in the old days, during summer vacation. It saddened him to see it as it was now.

A huge NO TRESPASSING sign was posted in English and Spanish, *NO PASSÉ,* at the entrance to the wetlands beyond the pond. Unlike the days when he was a kid, the migrants were not legally allowed to camp anywhere but on SunRipe land. After Buddy Mozel bought the land surrounding Longer's Pond a year or so after Tito disappeared, he convinced the Town Board to prohibit the migrants from squatting in the wetlands, which was public land. And if they didn't have the money to pay him rent for one of the forty or so ramshackle houses and trailers he owned, he'd either deduct the rent out of their pay or make sure they didn't work at the plant.

Holister pointed to the pond. "The bones are over there by that big sycamore. I heard 'em run just up over the bank and into the woods toward Huckle Road," he said as he pushed through the thick stand of cattails and disappeared.

Jordan followed and stopped when he got to the edge of the pond.

A small, four-foot skeleton lay half-submerged in the dirt. A frail, bony hand reached out to the right. The other arm and hand were still buried. The rib cage was partially exposed and Jordan could see about half of the pelvis and most of the right leg. Both feet were still lodged in the hard ground. One visible eye socket, dark and empty, pointed upward to the sky, and the mouth was locked open, like it was crying out, screaming silently.

Holister turned to Jordan and started to say something, but

the only sound he made was a quick wheeze and gasp.

Jordan heard a loud noise behind him. At first, the noise didn't register in his mind, it sounded like distant thunder, but the echo was close enough and he quickly realized what he'd just heard was a gunshot.

He spun toward the woods where Holister said he'd heard laughter, and raised the Glock into firing position. Another shot went off, striking the ground a few feet from his boots. Jordan jumped to the ground, tackled Holister, and rolled up onto his knees firing blindly into the trees. After unloading his magazine, his body went into full reactionary mode. His training kicked in so forcefully it was like an out-of-body experience. He grabbed another magazine, reloaded, and searched the woods for movement before firing again.

Holister's shirt was covered in blood, starting just above his pocket, and the old man rolled over and began to struggle to his feet, pulling himself up on all fours. His eyes were wild with pain. When he tried to say something his voice was a garble of bloody spit and grunts. "Son of a bitch," he muttered, grabbing his chest. Another shot came out of the woods and the bullet exploded squarely in Holister's back, sending him sprawling facedown into the dirt.

CHAPTER 5

January 17, 1986, 3:15 A.M.

There was blood everywhere. Hard pebble-sized sleet bounced off the cracked windshield, but all Jordan could hear was the reverberation of the crash. Metal against metal ringing in his ears, as the family Pontiac station wagon slid sideways and came to a sudden stop against an oak tree. He could not quit screaming.

He tried to move, but was trapped in the backseat between the driver's seat and the twisted door that rested against a tree. Tears streamed down his twelve-year-old face and he could barely see. Blood mixed with the tears from a cut that was caused by biting his bottom lip during the crash, and from the glass shards embedded in his face, under his right eye. His left hand was free, and he inched it up to his face to wipe away the blood to clear his eyes. Each time he moved glass stabbed through his pants.

The smell of gasoline and antifreeze burned deep in his throat, making it difficult to breathe as he gasped in between screams.

A single siren seemed to grow closer. But it was distant, and Jordan could not be sure that it was actually a siren he was hearing. It could be his ears still ringing from the crash. He was dazed, and could only hope that it *was* a siren, that someone, somewhere, was on the way to help.

His father, Big Joe McManus, was sitting upright, his skillet-sized hands still gripping the steering wheel, eyes wide open, staring straight ahead. Only his right finger twitched. His mother, Katherine, was slumped over, her head against the window, blood dripping out of her ear onto Jordan's brand-new white Chuck Taylors he'd gotten as a Christmas present from Kitty. Her eyes were closed and she was moaning softly.

Every second seemed like an hour as Jordan replayed the crash over and over in his mind a million times. He tried to think of something else while he screamed, hyperventilated. His voice was catching. His vocal chords were starting to freeze up.

What he really wanted was to still be at Kitty's, asleep in the spare room behind the kitchen, so he could have pancakes for breakfast when he woke up. But his parents had shown up, waking him at three o'clock in the morning. Kitty was not happy, but she was accustomed to the uncertainty of Saturday nights, the uncertainty of the life her only daughter had chosen when she'd married a man who owned a tavern.

The radio had been on low when Jordan got into the car half-awake, tuned to a crackling AM country station out of Indianapolis. It was still on, but now the music was nothing but static. His father loved Porter Wagoner and Dolly Parton. His mother liked quieter music, Johnny Mathis, John Gary, and Perry Como, but she never got to pick the radio station in the car, only in the mornings on the Philco radio in the kitchen before his father got out of bed or after he left for work. She referred to his father's choice of music as "hillbilly music," as if it were somehow beneath them all.

His parents had always seemed like an odd couple, a mismatched pair of socks, even to Jordan. One was neat and quiet, and the other was loud and a slob. And lately, they had been like magnets opposing each other, with him and Spider caught in the middle. He heard them talk about divorcing over the summer, and Big Joe had spent a few nights away from home. But after Tito Cordova disappeared, he came home for good. Nothing had changed between his parents. They argued even more intensely, and it was worse than it was before Big Joe left.

One minute Jordan was on way his way home, safe and secure in the backseat, but uncomfortable with the wall of silence that was cemented between his mother and father. The next minute his parents were screaming at each other. The interior of the car smelled of beer and whiskey, but that was not unusual. His father always smelled like a tavern, a mix of yeast and cigarette smoke, harsh yet comforting.

Jordan's father owned Big Joe's Tavern at the corner of Jefferson and Main. Joe McManus was a hulking man, well over six feet tall and solid as a two-hundred-and-ten-pound Indiana University linebacker, which he was for one season until he lost his scholarship for poor grades and too much partying.

Jordan's sixteen-year-old brother, George, who everybody called Spider, was the spitting image of his father. All the way down to the unmanageable cowlick in his thick black wavy hair.

Jordan, on the other hand, favored his mother. His features were softer, his chin less chiseled, his hair sandy blonde instead of black, his eyes blue though, just like Big Joe's. And it was already obvious, at the age of twelve, that he lacked the coordination and natural athletic ability that had allowed his father a brief stint in college, and Spider a reputation that was almost legendary in the high school gym, which is where he'd got his nickname from. When George ran across the basketball court, his long, black, hairy legs made him look like a giant spider scurrying down its web, intent on killing the unfortunate moth that had flown into his trap.

Big Joe always blamed Jordan's clumsiness on his mother's side of the family, and was quick to show his disappointment at every football or basketball game Jordan sat the bench. The distinction between Jordan and Spider did little to build a brotherly bond. They navigated the four-year difference the best they could as their father pitted them against each other. Jordan's refuge was Kitty's house, while Spider's refuge was wherever Jordan wasn't.

His mother did not work outside the house, but sometimes she worked at the bar on Saturday nights when there was a live band playing. She'd wait tables if needed, but she'd rather dance if the band played music she liked.

Saturday night was the only night his father drank at the bar. At least that was the way it was for a long time. Lately, he'd been drinking a lot more than normal. Staying at the tavern long after it closed, while his mother slept in their bedroom alone. He'd seen his mother's eyes fill with tears, standing over the sink scrubbing burnt macaroni and cheese out of a casserole dish, and while she had been folding laundry the day before the accident.

Big Joe had an obvious dislike for the Mexicans that came into town in the summertime, and he made no bones about how he felt about Buddy Mozel and the SunRipe plant in general; he thought the plant had ruined the town, growing into a dominating force that allowed foreigners to soil the town with brown skin. Buddy was the enemy, the gatekeeper, and lately, he'd been buying every piece of land in Dukaine that became available for sale. And some that wasn't. Buddy had even tried to buy the tavern, but Big Joe swore that would never happen. Not as long as he was alive. People had to have some place to go where they didn't have to smell Mexican dirt, is what Jordan heard his father say one day when he was talking about Buddy trying to buy the tavern.

Jordan's mother was more tolerant of the migrants, of Buddy Mozel. She was, at times, enamored by Buddy's class, his knowledge of fine things, and his ability to put on a pair of boots and walk in the mud like an everyday person. Buddy called his mother Katherine, a formal nod that made her smile, while Big Joe called her Katie like everybody else in town.

She always encouraged Jordan to be nice to the Mexican kids that showed up in school for the first six-week period. Tito was neither, and that's what confused Jordan. His father helped with the search, his mother did not, and then after the search was called off, the constant drinking and arguing began.

Jordan just tried to stay quiet, back in the shadows. He had learned a long time ago to stay out of the line of fire when his father was drinking. You could never tell if Big Joe was going to be mean or nice. Mostly it was mean. He didn't trust the nice times—knew it was like a break in the clouds, a ray of sunshine on a stormy day.

The argument his mother and father were having in the car was about another man, Buddy himself asking his mother to dance, and she obviously had obliged, ignoring Big Joe's famous jealous streak. Jordan thought it was strange that Buddy was in the tavern at all on a Saturday night, but the tavern was a grown-up world. One that he had very little understanding of. He rarely went there, unless he absolutely had to.

Since Tito disappeared, his mother seemed to ignore most of his father's rules, and Jordan had withdrawn even further from both of them, just waiting for the next argument to explode out of nowhere, the next lightning bolt to land directly on his head. He didn't walk on eggshells, he tiptoed. Spider disappeared as much as possible, hanging out with his best friend, Charlie Overdorf, as far away from the house and tavern as possible. It was dumb luck that Spider had gone to Kitty's that night— Charlie was out of town at his grandfather's funeral—and Spider couldn't stand the thought of missing homemade sloppy joes.

The car had started to slide sideways as his father pressed the accelerator to the floor, promising to get them home as soon as possible.

"I'll take you home and leave. I'll sleep at the tavern," Big Joe had said. It was not the first time Jordan had heard him say that, knew it was a veiled threat, a promise of things to come.

"Fine," his mother said.

"Damn it, Katie, what in the hell were you thinking?"

"I was in the mood to dance."

"I don't know what that son of a bitch was in the bar for anyway."

"I asked him," his mother answered, her voice rising to meet the level of Big Joe's. "It's my turn, Joseph. It's my goddamned turn."

Jordan knew there had been other women in his father's life, but until that moment he had chosen to ignore it—even though it seemed like a divorce was really going to happen. More than once he had seen his father and a woman leaving the back of the tavern, in a more than friendly way. When he'd said something to Spider about what he saw, his brother had threatened him within an inch of his life if he said anything to their mother.

He had been staring out the window and into the darkness wondering if Tito Cordova was warm, and was more than shocked to hear his mother swear. It was her belief in God, or at least that's what she'd said during a recent argument, that kept her from leaving Big Joe.

He wondered if Tito was buried underneath the banks of snow, hidden away by some monster to feast on when it got really hungry. Jordan had never looked for monsters in the dark until Tito Cordova had disappeared. Now he seemed to be doing it all the time, trying to remember what the little Mexican boy looked like, and wondering if the monster was going to come for him, too.

Tito, Tito, where are you?

Big Joe reached over and slapped Katherine, the crack so sudden it was like glass shattering. The echo lasted forever, overcoming Dolly Parton wailing at Jolene. Tears immediately streamed down his mother's face, but the rage in her eyes grew. Jordan thought she was going to hit Big Joe back.

There was a car coming toward them in the other lane. Headlights glaring off the snow bank alongside the road, blinding Big Joe momentarily. They sideswiped the car as the rear end of the Pontiac swung out from behind them. Sparks shot up into the air as the two cars raked alongside each other in opposite directions. And then their bumpers caught, sending both cars into a high-speed spin.

Even when Jordan closed his eyes, he could still see the crash, still feel his stomach turn upside down as they spun and spun and spun, and still hear his own screams as he saw the tree come closer and closer in slow motion. The impact deafened him, the immediate pain strange and frightening, but distant, like it was happening to someone else, and the explosion seemed as if it was going to last forever.

His mother screamed and then became silent as her head slammed against the window multiple times. Cold air whisked inside the car, and the music faded, disappeared, and everything, including the dashboard, grew dark.

Once he got his breath, Jordan began screaming, began trying to free himself. Neither did any good. He was stuck, alone in the dark, more afraid than he had ever been in his entire life. He thought the sleet was glass, still showering over him, even ten minutes after the station wagon had come to a stop.

A bright light shined in Jordan's eyes, and he began to scream again.

"It's all right, Jordan, I'm here to help."

He blinked and saw Holister Coggins standing in the open

door at the other end of the backseat, behind the driver's seat. Red and blue strobe lights pulsed across the icy road, casting dancing spires of light onto the trees and the ground, covering the world with sharp diamonds that at any other time would have looked beautiful and festive. A large chorus of sirens throbbed in the distance, suddenly transforming the black night into a rousing carnival.

"Can you move, son?" Holister asked.

Jordan shook his head.

"Does it hurt anywhere?"

Jordan nodded.

"OK, you just hold tight while I check on your mom and dad."

A question began to form on Jordan's lips. A question filled with terror and dread that had been building since Jordan had opened his eyes after the car came to a stop. After he realized the door Holister was standing in had flown open and the seat next to him was empty.

"Where's Spider?" he whispered. He could see Holister exhale heavily.

"Just hold on, I'll be right back." Holister stood up out of the door and shined the light on Jordan's father. Big Joe moaned— blood dripped out of his mouth as he tried to speak.

The flashing strobe lights multiplied as the ambulance and fire trucks arrived. There was yelling. Orders flying back and forth, voices carrying on the cold wind like trumpets blaring at a Christmas concert.

"You're going to be all right, Joe. Just hang on. Hang on for God's sake," Holister said.

"Katie," Joe mumbled.

Holister's flashlight disappeared. "I got three over here," he hollered out, and then said, "She's gonna be all right, Joe, don't you worry," in a lower voice as he shined the light on Katie's face.

Images and shadows danced around the Pontiac. Holister's face appeared and then disappeared. Big Joe moved his head and groaned. The smell of gasoline was even stronger now—it made Jordan's nose and throat burn, and he tried not to breathe. Darkness came and went, lasting only a moment, but always returning, and the cold kept getting colder.

"I'm gettin' him out there before the car blows." A pair of hands reached in and grabbed Jordan's shoulders. "This might hurt," Holister said. Jordan opened his eyes wide as he felt a shock of pain like he was rolling in a rose bush. He heard the crunch of glass, and then felt his legs pull free as Holister wrapped him in his arms and lifted him out of the backseat.

The wind hit his face, and a blanket appeared out of nowhere and tightened around him like a cocoon. More faces. More blood. In and out of reality. Big Joe being laid on a stretcher. Steam rising from the front of the Pontiac.

Where was his mother? He wanted her . . . and he struggled in Holister's arms, reaching out for her, calling her. Holister's huge, strong arms held him tight, and he whispered that it all would be OK, for Jordan to calm down. But even in the rush of movement, in the flashes of light, Jordan could see tears in Holister's eyes, and he knew the man was lying.

The other car was in the middle of the road, a mass of black twisted metal. The driver's door was open, the front of the car pushed back like a closed accordion facing the opposite direction from his father's station wagon. Jordan recognized the car; it was Buddy Mozel's big black Lincoln Continental, but there was no one behind the steering wheel.

Darkness ate at the blue and red streaks of light, and the voices dimmed, vibrated—it was like nothing Jordan had ever experienced before. He was falling into a hole. He wanted his mother. Big Joe. Spider. Kitty. He wanted to wake up from the nightmare . . . have pancakes. Smell Kitty's violet perfume, and hear his mother sing.

Halfway to the ambulance, Holister put Jordan on a stretcher. "Is my mother going to be all right?" he managed to ask.

"She'll be fine, son, just fine," Holister said. His voice was distant, cracking like the static on the radio. As Holister lay another blanket over him, Jordan turned his head, looked back at the Pontiac.

He finally saw Spider, finally got the answer to his question. But he wasn't sure what he was seeing was real. It was so far away. Spider was lying in the middle of the road in a pool of blood, his legs twisted under him.

January 17, 1986, 6:12 A.M., Patzcuaro, Mexico

The air coming under the door to the infirmary was cool. Footsteps approached, but the boy kept his eyes closed. The pain was finally gone from his head, but the fingers on his left hand were still splinted, and both legs were still in casts, still broken. He could not move, and he did not speak. The nuns thought he was a mute. But it was only because he did not understand their language well enough to speak back. They spoke softly to him in Spanish, stroked his hair, fed him, prayed over him as he silently wished for his mother to appear. But she never did.

The days were all the same. Warm sunshine pouring in the windows. Children's voices echoed in the distance. Laughing and playing knew no language barriers. The nights were quiet. Sometimes he heard singing. He was the only one in the infirmary. Six other beds were empty. But he was always afraid, even though the nuns had shown him nothing but affection and concern. He opened his eyes when the door creaked open, and when he a saw a man dressed in black follow the nuns inside. Tito Cordova could do nothing but scream.

CHAPTER 6

August 21, 2004, 6:33 A.M.

Without a thought, Jordan ducked, rolled Holister over, and dragged him into the middle of the stand of cattails. He fired off three rounds as they made it safely into the thick cover.

And then came the quiet, like the long wait after a lightning strike for a loud clap of thunder. No one laughed, no one ran. Jordan could hear his heart pounding. Mosquitoes buzzed near his ear. He felt like a rabbit that had outran a pack of dogs, waiting for the next sound, the next gunshot, to send him running again.

Holister's body was lifeless. His eyes were blank, staring upward. Jordan listened for a breath, felt for a pulse, and could feel nothing. He knew he was taking a chance, but he began to pump furiously on Holister's chest.

He stopped CPR after a minute or so, flipped his radio on, and called Louella for help. She didn't answer.

Jordan went back to Holister, felt for a pulse again before resuming CPR. He found one this time, a faint beat, enough to give him a little bit of hope.

He hit the radio again, opening the frequency to the county sheriff's department and state police. "10-53! Man down, man down," he said as quietly as he could, and gave his location.

The Carlyle County Sheriff's department immediately responded that they were on their way, so was the volunteer ambulance from Dukaine. Louella finally answered, panicked. She had probably fallen asleep. The volume squawked loudly. Jordan couldn't understand her, so he squelched the radio.

Thunder erupted and bullets peppered the cattails, high, low, at his feet, and over his head. He jumped on top of Holister's body to protect him as hot metal grazed his right arm.

He screamed unconsciously, rolled over and fired the fresh magazine in the direction of the shooter, and reached for another as pain exploded through his entire body. Jordan could barely grasp his utility belt. It only took him a second to realize he'd used both of his spare mags. Holister had dropped his weapon when he was hit the first time. The service revolver was lying next to the skeleton, and the bullets from the old .38 in Holister's belt wouldn't do Jordan any good anyway.

The firing stopped, and he heard a laugh just like Holister had. A deep, guttural laugh that sounded like a hawk screaming as it dove from the sky to finish off its prey. There was nothing human about the laugh. It was neither male nor female. To him, it was pure evil.

Fear paralyzed Jordan. He knew he was a sitting duck, a dead man if the shooter continued to take blind pot shots into the stand of cattails. There was no flash of the past, no churning of regret in the pit of his stomach. He ignored the pain in his arm and the blood soaking his sleeve as he reached for his nightstick and tucked it under his arm. He wasn't going out of this world without a fight, but he had no choice but to wait and see if the shooter was going to come and claim his prize. No choice but to wait and try to crack the motherfucker upside the head, even if it was the last thing he did.

A siren throbbed in the distance. The radio buzzed distantly with voices. Louella called Jordan, but he didn't answer, he didn't move. He held his breath and clutched the stick tighter.

A pool of blood began seeping out from under Holister's

body. The marshal wheezed again and took a deep gasp of air. His eyes were open, blinking. He tried to speak, but failed. A frustrated tear eased out of the corner of the old man's right eye. Jordan put his cheek up to Holister's face so he could hear him when he tried to speak again.

"Tell Celeste I tried to make things right . . . ," Holister said. "Tell Ginny this was all my fault . . ." His voice was distant and weak, but he struggled to move, struggled to say something else.

The sirens grew closer.

Beyond the cattails Jordan heard the weeds rustle with movement, coming toward them. He motioned for Holister to be silent, eased himself up on his knees and squatted, ready to leap at the first thing that moved.

A chattering of starlings swooped down from the clear blue sky and lit atop the sycamore tree that marked the skeleton's grave. In a matter of seconds the birds evacuated in a burst of fear and squawked all the way across the pond.

Jordan teetered on the balls of his feet, startled by the sudden outburst. Sweat poured down his face, stinging his eyes. The stick was in his left hand, and he knew the swing would be weak and uncoordinated since he was right-handed, but he was only going to have one chance to save Holister and himself. He jumped up as soon he saw a human figure emerge into view.

An EMT stopped. "Whoa, Jordan, it's me!"

He didn't immediately recognize Sam Peterson. They both played on the same softball team and went all through school a year apart. They weren't enemies, but they weren't beer-drinking buddies either.

Sam was just a blur to Jordan, a creature from a horror movie rushing toward him.

The stick was six inches from Sam's head on the downward swing, and Jordan was too weak to stop it. Sam threw a blue vinyl bag at Jordan and jumped out of the way, cowering. The bag deflected the swing, and Jordan staggered back into the weeds. He was disoriented, enraged. He ran at Sam, tackling him to the ground.

Sam Peterson was not a lightweight. He matched Jordan pound for pound and was in better shape from lifting weights at the fire station five days a week. Sam pushed Jordan off him and delivered a swift punch to Jordan's right eye. Jordan fell backward, dazed.

"You move another inch, McManus, and I'm going to kick the shit out of you," Sam Peterson said.

Charlie Overdorf, the other EMT, arrived pulling a gurney. He stopped dead in his tracks. "Damn it, Sam, what the hell is going on?" Charlie asked as he rushed to Jordan.

"He fuckin' attacked me, what the hell was I supposed to do?" Sam said.

Jordan's heart was still racing. He exhaled deeply and tried to pull himself up. "Shit, Sam, I'm sorry. I thought you were the shooter," he said. He shook his head to clear his vision.

Sam Peterson stepped back, his right hand still clenched in a fist.

Holister's eyes were glazed and fixed, his eyes focused on the skeleton.

"It's all right, Jordan, we're here to help," Charlie Overdorf said.

Charlie Overdorf kneeled down, strapped an oxygen mask on Holister, and after a minute or two, said, "Jesus, Jordan. What's that out there?" He pointed twenty yards away at the skeleton.

Jordan was breathing heavily. His face was throbbing from the punch and his arm felt like it was on fire. The bullet had only grazed him, but it felt much worse now that the adrenaline had left his system. He ignored Charlie's question and alerted the Carlyle County Sheriff's department of the shooter's last 10-20, which was the northwest corner of Longer's Pond, where

Huckle Road intersected with County Road 300 South. He was glad Holister was getting the attention he needed, glad that he'd taken a chance and performed CPR, but the marshal was still weak, still in bad shape. Jordan had only been this scared of losing someone he loved one other time in his life.

Sam forced Jordan to sit on the ground with a blanket over his shoulders to prevent him from going into shock, and began to wrap the wound on his arm.

"Those bones are the last fucking thing you need to worry about right now, Charlie," Jordan said.

"Just asking, man. You really need to get a grip on yourself," Charlie answered.

Charlie was as inch taller than Jordan and skinny as a cornstalk. He was thirty-six, had three kids, all girls, a year apart in age, the oldest being ten. He was an imperturbable man, calm and reserved even in the most stressful situations, not a crisis junkie like most of the EMTs Jordan knew. Charlie was an ever-present figure in Jordan's life, though not as much in the last ten years, and Spider's best friend, and just his presence helped calm him down.

"You got a sheet, Sam. I want to make sure Holister's all right before I deal with this. And if you don't mind, I'd rather neither of you said anything to anybody about the skeleton until I get things sorted out," Jordan said.

Word would get out that there was a skeleton at the pond soon enough. It would spread like wildfire through town. He knew there'd be speculation that the skeleton was Tito Cordova as soon as everybody heard what had happened. But there was no way of knowing that the skeleton *was* Tito. The letter was mailed from Dukaine, so the shooting sure did seemed linked. As far as Jordan was concerned it was not a random act—just like Holister's theory about Tito, which did not escape his attention. Somebody in Dukaine was behind the shooting. But why? Why now? After all these years?

"You're not in any shape to deal with anything, Jordan, except for a ride to the hospital," Charlie said evenly.

Jordan tried to relax, but couldn't push the regret he was feeling away. Maybe if he'd ignored Ginny's call, none of this would be happening. Maybe if he'd trusted his gut a little more, he wouldn't have felt the need to climb into Ginny's bed again. Or if he would've paid more attention to his ex-wife, Monica, maybe she wouldn't have slept with her boss. . . . There were too many maybes to think about, and Jordan knew none of them mattered at the moment. The shooting had nothing to do with his personal life. Whoever was behind the shooting had lured Holister to the pond—for whatever reason, the marshal was the target, not him.

Two Carlyle County Sheriff's deputies appeared, weapons drawn. They stood guard fifteen feet from the EMTs, silent, eyeing the tree line in opposite directions.

The deputies' appearance relieved Jordan, but he was not calmed entirely. The shooter had remained phantom-like, and for the first time since the shooting had ended, he began to question whether or not there was more than one of them.

A familiar feeling began to rise in the back of his mind; a certain knowledge of events, a knowledge that life can change in an instant, a storm can rise from nowhere and catch you unaware in its path, through no fault of your own. And then nothing would ever be the same. He was in the midst of another storm, and no matter how hard he tried, he would not be able to get the life back he had a few hours ago. He was angered by the crack in his perception of himself, his own desire to be a person that could end the storm for others. For as long as he could remember he wanted to be the one to extend his hand and say, "I'm here to help."

He'd found a way of escaping his own darkness, his own

uncertainty, by becoming a calm force in a moment of chaos, by righting wrongs and putting everything back where it belonged. Regardless of Ginny's, or anyone else's, opinion, Jordan knew there was more to his life, to his badge, than being a lowly gopher for Holister.

But he had failed to save the marshal from harm, a man that he loved like a father, and he knew he would replay the shooting over and over, questioning what he could have done differently.

"Charlie's right," Sam said. "Look, I'm sorry about punchin' you, I wasn't expecting it."

"Not a problem, don't worry about it, man. I was . . ." Jordan said. He couldn't finish the sentence, bring himself to admit aloud to Sam Peterson that he was scared.

Instead, he wanted to argue with Charlie and Sam about going to the hospital. He started to say he was fine, that he was going to catch whoever shot Holister and beat them till they begged for mercy, but he knew Charlie was right. He was in no shape to deal with anything. He was lucky to be alive.

A chill swept over him again and he began to shiver. His skin felt like it was swelling, and he itched all over. He was drenched with sweat and covered in muck. The rancid pond water smelled even worse now that he was sitting downwind. A north breeze drifted over the pond, churning the mugginess of the air but doing nothing to cool it. The pond smelled dead. Not the rotting stink of a roadkill raccoon but more like a vacant slaughterhouse where death attached itself to the cobwebs and dust piles. It was an old smell, almost like the blood meal Kitty used in her garden to keep the rabbits out of her petunias.

The sky was dotted with small puffball clouds that held little promise of rain. Jordan felt sick to his stomach and immediately leaned over and threw up a mass of nervous bile. "I hate fucking hospitals," he said, catching a breath of air.

"See, I told you you needed lookin' after," Sam said.

"I'm all right," Jordan said. "Take care of Holister, I'm gonna need him."

Sam nodded, flipped his radio off his belt, and called to check on backup.

"Get down here, Sam," Charlie ordered. "I'm losing him. We need to bag him now."

"Shit, Charlie, you know I'm no good at that," Sam said, staring nervously at Holister. "I've just done it on that mannequin in training class."

"I'll do it," Charlie answered. "But I'll need your help."

Sam scurried to Charlie's side, following Charlie's orders at every move.

Jordan's radio was buzzing with voices. The Carlyle County Sheriff's department had blocked off Huckle Road and three cars were patrolling the roads surrounding Longer's Pond. Bill Hogue, the sheriff, was arriving at the parking lot, and Johnny Ray Johnson was on his way.

Louella was calling every other minute, checking on Holister's condition. Sheriff Hogue finally had to tell her to stay off the frequency.

Two more EMTs pushed by the deputies. Sheriff Hogue was two steps behind them.

"Damn," Hogue whistled. "You all right, McManus?"

"I won't be singing at the Christmas party anytime soon."

"Why did I know I wasn't going to get a straight answer?"

"I'm a predictable person, Hogue, haven't you figured that out by now? It's not me we need to worry about," Jordan said, shedding the blanket from his shoulders. He tried to stand, but immediately sat back down.

The world started to spin in opposite directions. Bill Hogue looked like a man standing in front of a circus mirror, the kind that shrank the head and inflated the belly. The blurred image wasn't much of a stretch. On a normal day, Bill Hogue looked like a bowling pin dressed in a brown sheriff's uniform. Take the Smokey the Bear hat off his head to expose his smooth bald head and he was a dead ringer for a tenpin.

"I can see that," Hogue said. He turned his attention to Charlie Overdorf. "Is Holister going to be all right?"

"Doesn't look good," Charlie said as he inflated the bag in Holister's mouth.

"What about him?"

"From the looks of it, it's a flesh wound," Charlie answered. "A few stitches, and he should be as good as new."

"You up to telling me what happened, McManus?"

"He's going to the hospital," Sam Peterson said.

"I can tell you," Jordan answered, ignoring Sam.

CHAPTER 7

August 21, 2004, 7:22 A.M.

Jordan took a deep breath and tried to regain his senses. He needed to stop and think, make sure he knew what he was dealing with. Having a conversation with Bill Hogue was like playing one-on-one basketball on a hot summer day; you never had time to catch your breath, and the man was smart, always two steps ahead of you. Jordan was never any good at one-on-one, and he was even worse when it came to talking to Bill Hogue.

He could give a shit about Hogue's position. Any authority over him belonged to Holister and the Town Board, not the sheriff's department. Maybe it was Hogue's disregard for all of the small-town deputies in the county, much like the INS agents, or maybe it was something more—like the fact that Bill Hogue was Ed Kirsch's uncle. Either way, Jordan didn't like the unsettling feeling Hogue's presence always seemed to evoke, especially now.

Bill Hogue was first and foremost a politician. He was in his first year of a four-year term, but it was Hogue's third term as sheriff. He was deeply entrenched in the structure of the county law-enforcement community. Hogue had been elected eight-and-a-half years ago as an alternative to a corrupt one-term sheriff who was presently on the waning end of a tax evasion and attempted murder sentence. The Carlyle County Sheriff's department had been clean of scandal ever since the then fifty-year-old Hogue took office, and no one questioned the iron-fist policies that kept it that way, or Hogue's political abilities to make sure he attained whatever goal he set for himself.

Jordan was well aware of the rumors that Hogue was considering a run for the Morland mayoral seat when that election came up in two years. So, there was no question that he was intent on taking charge of the investigation to bolster his image. He didn't fault Hogue for that, and Jordan also knew there was no way that he or the Dukaine Police Department could handle an investigation of this magnitude. But he intended to be involved as much as possible, to be in the loop, to be in the hunt for the shooter.

"I'm going to need a full report on this, McManus," Sheriff Hogue said.

Jordan ignored the demand. He wanted to ask the sheriff if he thought he was a fucking idiot, but he already knew the answer. He watched as Sam Peterson and Charlie Overdorf tried to lift Holister onto the gurney. Hogue turned away, surveying the landscape, pushing the toe of his boot into the dry dirt.

Holister was limp, as heavy as a dead horse, and the other EMTs from Carlyle County joined in to help. They had to tilt him sideways to completely lift him up onto the gurney.

"You need to come with us, Jordan. That arm needs to be looked at," Sam said.

"I'm fine, really. The sheriff and I need to talk first."

"After I get Holister on his way, I'll be back down for you," Sam said. "What about that?" he asked, pointing at the skeleton.

"Don't worry about it. There's nothing you can do."

When Jordan turned back to Bill Hogue, the sheriff was staring at the skeleton.

"That's part of what happened," Jordan said.

"I noticed. You better start from the beginning, and don't

leave anything out. You've never been in a situation like this before. Probably don't know your ass from a hole in the ground when it comes to investigating a shooting."

Jordan took a deep breath, ignored Hogue's supercop attitude the best he could, and told the sheriff everything that had happened from the moment he'd got the call from Holister.

Everything except the letter Holister gave him. He wasn't sure why he felt the need to filter information, especially information concerning the shooting. It was a gut feeling, a reaction to Hogue's arrogance—and the fact that Hogue had family in Dukaine, too. The sheriff's sister was Ed Kirsch's mother. Ed's father, Lee, was the real rounder of the bunch, a small-time crook who'd served two years in prison in the early seventies for burglary. After fathering nine children, Lee ran off with another woman, leaving Ed's mother to fend for herself. Jordan didn't know how tight Hogue was with Ed or any of the Kirsch kids—he'd seemed to distance himself from Dukaine and his family once he started to climb the ranks in the department. But Jordan still didn't trust the connection.

"Ginny and Celeste are going to take this hard," Hogue said, casting Jordan a glance that penetrated his heart.

The comment left Jordan speechless, even more on guard.

"Let's go have a look," Hogue continued without missing a beat. "If you can." It was not a question of concern; it was an order. Hogue didn't wait for an answer. He headed straight toward the skeleton. Jordan nodded yes and made his way through the cattails close behind Hogue.

They edged along the bank of the pond and stopped about ten yards from the skeleton.

"The first shots came from over there," Jordan said as he pointed to the big sycamore tree. Horse nettle and ragweed surrounded it, rising about six feet tall against the trunk of the tree. There were scrub trees in front of the tall trees, and even with the sun bright overhead there was a shadowy world of withering vegetation beyond the pond banks. A few game paths wound through the weeds about twenty feet from the sycamore, apparent only to a hunter or someone who knew the ways of deer and raccoons. Jordan guessed that the shooter had used the trails, at least initially, to navigate and hide among the weeds.

"We need to check those trails," Jordan said, making sure Hogue was aware of them.

"You don't need to worry about that. I got boys all over the place, checking every trail, every path in and out of here. Just like I got to do."

Jordan's arm throbbed and he felt light-headed. The blaring sun hurt his eyes and he had a pounding headache, but he tried to ignore the pain, tried not to show Hogue any weakness.

Holister's .38 lay on the ground a few feet from the skeleton. Hogue pulled a handkerchief out of his back pocket and picked the weapon up to examine it. "This Holister's?"

Jordan nodded.

"The damned old fool never would change, would he? If he'd been carrying a Glock things might've turned out different," Hogue said.

"He didn't trust plastic."

"I don't know that I'd trust a fifty-year-old weapon."

"It shoots just fine."

Hogue looked at Jordan oddly and smirked.

Jordan walked away from Hogue, restraining himself from striking out, and took his first close-up look at the skeleton. The butterscotch brown bones were covered with dried mud, but everything looked intact; the rib cage poked out of the ground perfectly, even the fingers were still attached. Flies had lost the opportunity to lay their eggs in the flesh long ago; there were no signs of insects anywhere, except the ever-present cloud of mosquitoes that swarmed over the pond. It looked like the bones had been there for a long, long time, hidden under the water and muck. At its normal level, Longer's Pond would have been about five feet deep where he stood, and Jordan wondered how the divers could have missed the skeleton when they searched the pond.

The skull bothered Jordan the most. He hesitated, and then reached down and touched the top of the head. It was warm from the sun, and he recoiled quickly. The skeleton was real. Just like the blood on his shirt.

He had never seen anything like it. The only skeleton he could recall ever seeing was in his eighth-grade biology class, and it was made out of plastic. It felt strange standing in an open grave, exposed by the lack of water and the erosion of time. All sorts of images flashed through Jordan's mind: Halloween decorations dancing in the wind; a faceless little boy struggling to breathe, sinking deep into the water, stuck in the mud; and finally, fish and snapping turtles picking flesh off the bone as if it were bait, an unexpected feast.

A siren blared in the distance. The ambulance with Holister was pulling away, heading toward St. Joseph's Hospital in Morland. Jordan glanced up, then returned his gaze to the skeleton. "Are you really Tito Cordova?" he asked silently.

Hogue gently returned the .38 to the spot where he found it. "Doesn't look like he had time to get a round off," he said.

"No, he didn't."

The sheriff didn't immediately respond—it looked like he was thinking, plotting out his next question. "Hard telling how long it's been here," Hogue finally said, easing up next to Jordan, looking down at the skeleton.

"Holister seemed to have a good idea. Pretty close to twenty years, if he's right."

The sheriff looked at Jordan curiously.

"Holister thought the skeleton belonged to Tito Cordova."

"Why in the hell would he think that?"

Jordan started to tell Hogue about the letter, again, but remained quiet. He would put the information in his report, turn in the medal and letter as evidence, once he was certain Hogue was going to allow him to be involved in the investigation, once he saw where things were going from here. "Holister was obsessed with the Cordova disappearance. We reviewed it every year. I think he really wanted to solve that case before he retired."

"These bones could belong to anybody."

"That's what I thought," Jordan paused. "Do you remember when Tito Cordova vanished?"

"I'd just started with the department when that happened. Nothing but a greenhorn looking for a way to show myself off to old Ben Gunther, the sheriff back then," Hogue said with a nod. "I sure as hell remember it. Things like that just didn't happen around here. Kids disappearing with no trace. I was over here every day walking through fields, checking every nook and cranny in the SunRipe plant. If it would've happened during harvest, I would've thought one of the Mexicans was responsible, but they were gone."

"All of them except José Rivero and Tito's mother, Esperanza," Jordan said, watching Hogue closely. "But Holister talked to José and ruled him out from being involved because he'd been away when the kid disappeared. If I remember right he left a few days before, and returned a few days after the search ended. Everyone Holister questioned led to a dead end. I don't think he ever accepted the idea that Tito was abducted by a stranger, but that was the final word."

"Well," Hogue said. "That's the way it looked to me, too. If something like that happened now, I might look at it the same way Holister did. I'm going to want to see Holister's original report. I'm sure our department's report is still on file, too. I

71

need to refresh myself on the details."

"I know where the report is. I think," Jordan said. Holister's office looked like a rat's nest. Piles of unread papers covered his desk and his filing cabinets were ancient, burgeoning with faded manila folders and old newspapers. Holister hated doing paperwork, and no matter how much Louella goaded him and tried to keep him organized, he resisted, almost like a teenager staking his ground, not cleaning his room. But the Cordova file was special to Holister. So special, he kept it hidden in the false bottom of a briefcase he kept secured in the gun locker. Jordan never understood why, and never asked. He wished he would have now.

"The way it looks now, the boy might've just wandered in here and drowned. It might not have been a crime at all," Hogue said.

"The Cordova place was on the other side of town. That would've been a five-mile walk. Somebody would've surely seen him before he got here."

"Could be. But they checked the pond."

"That's what I was thinking. Holister and I talked about that. The water wouldn't have been that deep here. How'd they miss him?"

"Hard to say. The report should name the divers. If they're still around, I'll talk to them and find out. Then again, maybe the skeleton isn't Tito Cordova. Maybe it wasn't here when the divers went in," Hogue said. "Looks like I'm going to need a forensics team out here to find out for sure." He turned away from the bones and walked back over to the .38. "How about you, McManus? Did you get a shot off?"

Jordan stood up. "I told you, I unloaded three magazines."

Hogue nodded. "Let me see your weapon."

Jordan hesitated, then placed the Glock in Hogue's puffy right hand.

"If you don't mind, I think I'll hold onto this," the sheriff said.

"Excuse me?"

"I'm going to hold onto it until we get the ballistics back. It looked liked Holister was shot more than once."

Jordan could barely breathe; he felt trapped. "Are you accusing me of shooting Holister?"

"No offense, McManus, but it was just you and him out here. I don't see any sign of your shooter. I got boys crawling all over this place. Maybe we'll find something, maybe we won't. Ballistics will tell the story about your weapon. Hard to say whether I'm accusing you of anything or not. So, let's just call it procedure."

"Why in the hell would I shoot him?"

Jordan wasn't sure if Hogue was trying to intimidate him or humiliate him. There was no better way to degrade a cop than take his gun from him. And to make things worse, make him a person of interest or a suspect in the shooting of another cop.

"I don't know, McManus, why don't you tell me? I'm just considering all the possibilities, just doing my job. This whole situation seems a little fishy to me."

"And I *was* just doing mine," Jordan said, his voice rising. "This is the craziest fucking thing I've heard all day. Damn it, like I'd have a reason to shoot Holister Coggins?"

"Are you sure you've told me everything?"

Jordan hesitated. He was about to lie, about to break another rule, and he didn't like it, but felt like he had no choice now. If Hogue was going to make him a suspect the letter *could* help clear him—but something told Jordan the sheriff wasn't going to budge, letter or no letter. The letter might not have cleared him of any suspicion with the angle Hogue was taking. He could easily say Jordan had written it as much as anyone else—there was no proof otherwise. Along with ballistics, there'd be a handwriting expert involved. Besides . . . Holister had given him the letter. Hogue was an outsider. An outsider that Jordan didn't trust, at the moment.

"Yes," Jordan said.

"Well I'm sorry, McManus, that's the way it's going to be. The gun's going in for ballistics testing. I'll inform the proper people in Dukaine about my decision, and it'll be up to them what to do with you from there. From the looks of that arm you're going to have a few days off anyway. Maybe by then, this will be all cleared up."

"What the hell did I do? Shoot myself to make it look good? That's stretching it a little bit, don't you think?"

"I thought about that. But it's a flesh wound. Could have happened a million different ways other than the story you gave me. I have to look at all of the possibilities, McManus. I'm sorry if you don't agree with my methods, but I quit believing in stories a long time ago. I need evidence. Cold, hard evidence. Can you prove to me that the blood on your arm is a bullet wound?"

"No. You just have my word."

"Well, that's not good enough today."

Sam Peterson appeared at the foot of the path that led up to the parking lot. "Jordan, come on. We need to get you looked at."

Jordan stared at Hogue. "I didn't shoot Holister, goddamn it."

"Well, you don't have anything to worry about then, do you? Just make sure you stay close to town. I'll want to talk to you once the report comes back."

Sam walked up next to Jordan. "Come on," he said as he grabbed Jordan's good arm. Jordan pulled away and started to say something; he wanted to make his case against the shooting no matter what. But the world began to spin again, his head throbbed like a marching band was using it for drum practice, his fingers tingled, and everything went black.

CHAPTER 8

August 21, 2004, 11:55 P.M.

Luckily, the bullet had only torn flesh. A jagged cut just below Jordan's shoulder looked more like he'd been in a knife fight instead of being shot. The wound required eight stitches. Another inch or two and it would have entered and exited his arm, shredded his muscle or changed course, and done far more damage. It would have been easier to prove to Hogue that he wasn't responsible for the shooting if that had happened.

After a couple of hours in the ER, a pert little blonde nurse who didn't look old enough to be out of high school wheeled Jordan to a hospital room. He objected to being admitted, but the ER doctor insisted that he be held for observation because they couldn't stabilize his blood pressure, and every time he tried to stand up he almost passed out.

He hated hospitals, especially this hospital. It looked the same as it did the first time he remembered being taken there, when he was seven and broke his ankle when he fell out of the oak tree in Kitty's front yard. And again, after the car wreck, when he learned firsthand what it was like to lose someone he loved.

He kept arguing with the nurse, insisting he was fine, but all she did was smile, take his temperature, and give him a shot of Demerol. Five minutes after he disrobed and climbed into bed, he was fast asleep.

He woke up hungry and sore. His sleep was deep and without dreams or nightmares. But as he struggled to wake, the events of the day seemed foggy, and he had to question whether the shooting had actually happened or not. A touch to his arm told him all he needed to know. The world had done a flip-flop. Nightmares happened in broad daylight instead of in the lonely dark of night.

The hospital room was silent, lit only by the light that reached in under the closed door. He could hear distant muffled voices, someone padding by the door, a large air-conditioning unit humming on the roof. Jordan had no idea what time it was. He eased out of bed, grappling with the Houdini-inspired hospital gown.

The room's sole window overlooked the emergency room entrance. The parking lot was lit with towering incandescent lights that funneled a green diffused spectrum of light onto the asphalt. The bright white heat of the day had faded into a cover of solid blackness. A thin veil of vapor snaked up from the parking lot as the night air cooled and the humidity escaped into the air, casting long flittering shadows from the swarms of insects that attacked the lights.

"I can't stay here," Jordan said.

He found his clothes in a closet next to the bathroom. His watch and wallet were in a plastic bag, his utility belt and police gear were lying on top of the pile.

It was almost midnight. The entire day had been lost, and he did not feel rested at all.

His thoughts turned to Holister as he noticed the blood on his shirt, wondered if he had survived, if the marshal was dead or alive. There were two things he knew he needed to do. The first was to check on Holister's condition, and the second was to get the hell out of the hospital as fast as he could.

He washed his face in the sterile bathroom, trying to get rid of the Demerol hangover. His arm was completely wrapped in bandages, and he was supposed to wear a sling, but the confinement was worse than the distant pain he felt when he moved the wrong way. As he got dressed, he tried to ignore the blood on his shirt, but couldn't. The itchy feel of his uniform brought the entire day back to him, almost taking him off his feet. He sat on the toilet, catching his breath, fighting away the tears as he relived the moment when Holister was shot. Anger welled up from deep inside him, surpassing his sadness so strongly that he just wanted to start yelling at the top of his lungs.

"Get a grip, man. Just get a grip," he said to himself, using his good arm to hoist himself up.

He tapped the pocket of his shirt, an unconscious reflex, feeling for a pack of cigarettes that wasn't there. Steadying himself along the wall as he went, he made his way to the phone to call the front desk.

A female operator answered the phone.

"I need to check on the condition of a patient," Jordan said.

"Name?"

"Holister Coggins."

"Are you a member of the family?"

The question took Jordan by surprise. "I work with him, he's my neighbor."

"And your name?" the operator asked, cutting him off.

"I just want to check on his condition."

"Your name, sir?"

"Jordan McManus."

"Your name's not on the list, sir. I'm sorry, I can't give you that information."

"Is he all right?"

"I'm sorry, sir, I can't give you that information."

"Jesus Christ, is he dead or alive?"

The operator hesitated. "You'll need to call the family for

that information, sir."

"You can't even tell me if he's in the hospital or not?"

"No, sir, I can't."

Jordan slammed down the phone.

He immediately picked the phone back up and dialed Holister's house, hoping Celeste would answer. It rang three times before he realized how late at night it was, and he hung up.

"Damn it, I gotta get out of here," he said, sitting down on the edge of the bed. His first instinct was to call Monica, his ex-wife, but they hadn't spoken since the day their divorce was final. That life, that love, seemed like a bad memory hanging in the distance, a smoky haze of anger reignited by the spark of his own betrayal. Their marriage had started on rocky ground, Jordan rebounding from a broken heart after Ginny married Ed, and Monica anxious for love to fight her own demons. Looking back, Jordan was surprised the marriage had lasted as long as it had, seven years. But his stubborn streak and finish-what-you-start attitude kept him tied to the vows, even though it was obvious years before that neither of them could make each other happy. So he drank more, and she worked more. In the end, they had both simply married the wrong person.

The ghost of Ginny's love haunted Jordan every time he touched Monica. And Monica had physical and material needs that Jordan could never fulfill. She had ambitions that Jordan could never comprehend, and she was willing to do whatever it took to climb the ladders she'd put before herself. And there were no children in that plan.

Then he thought about calling Charlie Overdorf's younger sister, Lainie, who lately had been making a point to speak to him at softball games, wave whenever he slowed the police cruiser to a crawl in front of Miller's Grocery where she worked. Jordan was certain there was an attraction between them. Lainie was a tall brunette with perfect carved legs and a happy smile that made her hard not to notice. She had two young kids of her own, six- and seven-year-old boys, and had gone through a rough divorce herself. But he wasn't sure if he was ready to step into the shoes he would obviously be required to fill. Not yet, not this soon after his own divorce. Not with his feelings for Ginny alive and well, no matter how hopeless that might be. He wasn't going to use Lainie as a rebound—he thought too much of Charlie, of Lainie, to allow that to happen, so there was no way he was going to call her now.

After another second or two of thought, he called the only other person he could this late at night, and asked for a ride home.

He exhaled as he set the phone in its cradle. The drive from Dukaine to Morland, to the hospital, took about twenty minutes, but Jordan knew it would take his ride a little longer.

His mood was sour, made even more so by the fact that he couldn't find out about Holister. And it got worse when he went to gather up his utility belt and realized that his gun wasn't there. Jordan still could not believe Hogue thought he was a suspect, that he could be involved in the shooting.

He had no choice but to wait until the ballistics test came back. Surely the report would clear him, prove the bullets that took down Holister didn't come from his gun. *And then*, Jordan thought, *I'll be on Hogue's doorstep demanding my weapon back with an apology wrapped around it for good measure.*

Then what? he wondered. He had no idea where the investigation stood, where it was heading. There was a skeleton buried in Longer's Pond, and a shooter on the loose. It made sense to him that the two were related, they had to be. The letter Holister received was nothing but bait. If Holister was right, and the skeleton was truly Tito Cordova, then that was a place to start asking questions. But of who? Most people had either forgotten or buried the memory of Tito deep in the mud of their own past. Nobody would be comfortable answering questions about Tito. Jordan wasn't sure that he was.

He shook his head, made his way back to the window. Morland was only fifteen miles from Dukaine, but it seemed like a different world. There were three major factories, all serving the automobile industry. His grandfather, George, worked at the plant that made alternators for forty-four years, so Jordan had witnessed strikes, union walkouts, layoffs, as well as the good times when the factories could not produce enough alternators to fill the demand. Grandpa George always smelled like metal and oil.

Morland had changed since the days of Jordan's childhood. The Woolworth's store downtown had closed, along with most of the businesses. Now there were strip malls and fast-food restaurants at the north end of the city, close to the only interstate exit that served the town. The pace of life was more hectic, not like the comfortable rhythm of life in Dukaine.

Jordan could only think of one thing as he looked out the window: the person who had shot Holister and him was walking free. Would he strike again? Or had he accomplished what he set out to do?

A pair of headlights swept into the parking lot. Jordan recognized the van and drew a sigh of relief. It came to a stop at the ER just like he had instructed. He headed for the door, peeked out to make sure he wouldn't get caught leaving by the night-shift nurses, and then headed for the elevator. He pushed the button and the door opened immediately. The little blonde nurse who had wheeled him to his room yelled at him to stop, but Jordan jumped inside the elevator and hit the door-close button quickly.

The ride down was quick and Jordan breathed a little easier, sure that his escape was uneventful. The nurse had no idea where he was going; he'd be in good shape if she didn't follow him.

The elevator door opened into a dimly lit lobby. A bronze statue of Jesus greeted him, arms stretched out, two lambs at His feet. Jordan looked past the statue without regard to the implied invitation or promise of salvation, trained his vision on the exit, and hurried toward it.

"Jordan."

The voice stopped him in his tracks. He turned and saw Ginny stand up from a chair in the shadows of the waiting area. A TV flickered in the corner. Another person sat in the chair next to Ginny, but Jordan couldn't make out who it was for sure, but he was certain he knew, and the last person he wanted to come face to face with at the moment was Ed Kirsch.

He looked over his shoulder at the lights on the elevator, making sure the nurse hadn't followed him. The elevator was stopped, the numbers were not moving.

Ginny hurried across the room to meet him. Jordan did not open his arms to greet her. He stood motionless, eyeing the exit like an escaped convict that just got caught ten feet from the main gate. Ginny buried herself in his chest. Tears soaked through his shirt as she sobbed. He stood with his arms at his side.

"I'm so glad to see you. Are you all right?" Ginny asked, staring up at him. Her hair was disheveled, her face void of makeup, and she was dressed in blue jogging pants and a plain white T-shirt without a bra.

"I'm okay," Jordan answered, pulling away from Ginny as Ed Kirsch walked up to them.

Ed was five years older than Jordan was and his hair was already graying, his face was heavily lined, especially under his pale blue eyes. He was a slender man, almost fragile, and wore tight black jeans, a big silver belt buckle the shape of Texas, scuffed yellow snakeskin cowboy boots, and a long-sleeved black western shirt with pearl buttons. Ed shared little resemblance to Bill Hogue. Other than his eyes and nose, Ed favored his father, Lee, in stature, gait, and attitude. The apple had not fallen far from the tree.

Jordan reached out and shook Ed's hand.

"Good to see you up and walking, Jordan. We was going to come up and see you, but visiting hours were over by the time everything settled down. They let you out of here this late?" Ed asked.

"Yes," he lied.

"That's a hell of a shiner."

"It's not so bad," Jordan said, breaking eye contact. "Could've been worse, I imagine."

"I imagine so," Ed said.

Ginny eased away from Jordan and took her place next to Ed. "I'm sorry," she said. "Charlie said you were shot, and I couldn't even begin to think, what with Daddy in surgery and everything that was going on. All I could hear was sirens and my mother screaming into the phone that Daddy and you were hurt. I just can't believe this is happening."

"I called down to check on your dad, but they wouldn't tell me anything," Jordan said.

He could still feel her tears on his chest, smell her perfume, a light scent of familiar jasmine. Her touch revived him and he wanted nothing more than to hold her, push her hair aside and hug her as tight as he could. But he restrained himself, tried to shield his emotions, his desire to touch her, to comfort her and have her comfort him. Just seeing her with Ed twisted his stomach into pretzel-sized knots.

Jordan wanted to ask Ginny a question: *"Would this be happening if we would have run away like you wanted to?"* But instead, he asked, "How's Holister doing?"

"He's been in surgery a long time," Ed said. "I guess that's a good sign. You know Holister, he's strong as an ox."

"And stubborn as a mule," Jordan said, relieved that Holister was still alive.

"You two always were a good pair," Ginny said, forcing a smile.

"How's Dylan taking this?" Jordan asked.

"He's pretty upset. We left him with Louella," Ed said. "But he wanted to be here. I'll probably let him come in the morning if everything works out all right."

"He loves his Grandpa," Ginny said.

Ed nodded in agreement. "Family is real important to that boy."

Jordan looked out the front window, saw the van sitting in front of the door.

"Mother won't leave his room," Ginny said after casting a glance at Ed that was cold and loaded with quiet anger. "But she asked about you."

"Tell her I'll be back in the morning. If anything happens, you give me a call," Jordan said to Ginny. "I'm going home."

Ginny started to say something, then stopped mid-sentence. She reached up and touched his cheek, his scar, then whispered, "I'm really glad you're OK."

Ed cleared his throat and Ginny turned around and walked back into the shadows, toward the TV.

"Jordan," Ed called out as he followed Ginny. "Me and you need to have a talk once this thing with Holister is over with."

"You know where to find me," Jordan answered.

"Yes . . . I do."

He stepped outside the lobby and took a deep breath, gulping air that did not smell of death and sickness. Even more, he was glad to be free of Ginny and Ed, though he did have the urge to stay, to sit with her, to wait for word on Holister's condition. But there was no way he could bring himself to stay one more minute in the hospital, especially in the same room as Ed Kirsch.

Does Ed know about last night with Ginny? Jordan wondered. *Or is it something else?* In the end, did it really matter? He was going to have to face up to what he did, and it looked like that was going to happen sooner rather than later. He wasn't really all that surprised.

The guilt he felt for leaving both Ginny and Holister pushed his concerns about Ed to the back of his mind. He felt even worse about not seeing Celeste. He cared as much for her as he did Holister, sometimes even more, and promised himself that he would come back to comfort Celeste in the morning when he was rested.

The van, a ten-year-old Chevrolet with rusted wheel-wells and faded blue paint, revved its engine. Jordan shook his head, jerked open the door, and climbed inside.

"Damn, you look like you just had the shit beat out of you," Spider said.

"I did," Jordan answered.

CHAPTER 9

January 21, 1986, 1:00 P.M.

A light snow began to fall as the hearse pulled through the black iron gates of Haven Hills cemetery. Kitty took Jordan's hand in hers and patted it gently. All Jordan could do was stare at his lace-up dress shoes. The limousine from the funeral home smelled like the inside of an old woman's purse, a mix of after-dinner mints and lavender perfume. It was the first time Jordan had ridden in a Cadillac. The soft brocade seats felt like he was riding on air, but he could not find it in himself to be excited or thrilled; he just wanted to cry.

His tears had dried up and he just felt empty. The past three days were a blur of whispering voices, slamming doors, visits to the hospital to see Spider, and people coming to the door dropping off cakes, pies, and fried chicken. Jordan knew what dead meant. When Grandpa George had died seven years before, Spider dared him to touch the dead man's hand in the casket, and he did. But he didn't know how it felt when you lost someone close to you. Someone who lived in your own house, someone you loved and thought would live forever.

The hearse stopped and the door opened. Albert Patton, the mortician and Louella Canberry's brother, stood back and extended a black umbrella with his bony hands. Snow fell straight down from the gray sky as Kitty exited the car. Cold air blew into the limousine and Jordan shivered, pulled his navy blue wool winter coat tight around himself, and sunk back into the seat.

Kitty held out her black-gloved hand for Jordan to join her.

He shook his head. His left hand was free and his right arm was in a sling. If he moved wrong, pain shot through his entire body, adding to the soreness that seemed like it would never go away. He had scratches from the broken glass across his face, and a large bandage under his right eye. His face looked and felt very much like when he had chicken pox when he was in second grade; the stitches itched constantly.

"You have to, honey. I'm sorry," Kitty said firmly.

"I want to go home."

"I know. We will soon. Now come on."

At first glance, Kitty's angular face made her look angry all the time, but there was a softness in her eyes, in the way she walked, and in the way she spoke that immediately put any fear of her to rest. Kitty Coltraine would not hurt a fly. Jordan had seen her shoo flies out the window rather than kill them with a flyswatter, carry spiders to the door and watch them scurry away with a satisfied smile on her face. Each night just before dusk, Kitty put a bowl of milk on the back porch. It was not a lure for the stray cats in the neighborhood, but rather a reward for the black snakes that lived under her porch for eating the mice and rats that thrived in the grain elevator just beyond the backyard fence.

Her softness emitted from her gentle heart like a beacon to Jordan. The lessons he learned from her gave him as much comfort as they gave him guilt when he let his own rage and anger overcome his will, and he squished a bug or tore the legs off a spider for the pure pleasure of it. "No one has the right to judge the value of another life," Kitty would say when she saw him act out. "Not you. Not me. Not another man on this earth. Not if he truly believes in any kind of God and has any decent view of himself at all."

At the moment, Jordan wanted to pull off God's arms and legs for taking his mother away, but he decided to obey Kitty's demand to get out of the limousine, responding to the stern but soft look in his grandmother's eyes.

He crawled out of the backseat slowly, looked over his shoulder, and saw his father get out of the car on the other side. Big Joe McManus moved stiffly as well, tenuously, as if every step caused him a great deal of pain. He used a cane to steady himself and a bandage covered a row of stitches on his forehead.

Jordan's feet moved without command and he closed his eyes so he wouldn't see his mother's casket being unloaded from the hearse. Kitty led the way to the gravesite through a path of freshly shoveled snow, clutching Jordan's hand so tight he had to open his eyes. Kitty was dressed in a simple black coat, a black hat that flopped over her eyes and ears, and she wore a pink rose corsage over her heart. Pink roses were Jordan's mother's favorite flowers.

A blue tent stood over the open grave, the mound of dirt covered with a green blanket that was supposed to look like grass. The blanket looked stark and out of place against the snow-covered ground that surrounded the gravesite. A brass frame had been erected over the hole in the ground. Jordan resisted the temptation to look over the side to see how deep the grave was, to see if it was frozen and filled with snow. Four aluminum folding chairs faced the grave and Albert Patton hurried to place funeral bouquets in front of each tent pole, fresh springtime flowers the color of a dozen rainbows sitting on a pile of snow.

Kitty sat in the first chair and Jordan sat next to her. Big Joe walked behind them and sat at the other end, leaving the chair between him and Jordan vacant, a place for Spider, at least in spirit.

Car doors slammed and a parade of mourners followed the simple oak casket to the grave. Peter Hunt, Holister, Corney Lefay, Junior Johnson, Lem Jacobson, and Wally Peterson served as pallbearers.

Jordan squirmed in his seat.

"Be still," Kitty said.

"It's cold," Jordan answered.

"We won't be here long."

Jordan leaned over and whispered, "But I have to go to the bathroom, and I'm cold."

Kitty patted his knee and put her index finger to her lips to quiet him as the pallbearers slid the casket onto the brass frame.

Pastor Gleen from the Methodist Church on Lincoln Street stepped up to the casket. The snow began to fall harder and a slight wind whipped the grass blanket, raising it off the ground and setting it down gently.

"We are gathered here to commit the body of Katherine Joanne McManus to the grave," Pastor Gleen said.

More words followed, but Jordan didn't hear them. He heard his father sniffle, and he turned his head to see Big Joe shed the first tear he had ever seen fall down his face. Jordan looked away quickly. He stared across the casket at the crowd that gathered on the other side, a sea of faces mostly dressed in black. Snow covered a sea of tombstones. Tree branches looked like the arms and hands of a skeleton. Charlie Overdorf towered over his parents, his head down, staring at the ground. Corney and Edith Lefay held hands. Louella Canberry stood at the corner, unconsciously stroking a tall white lily. Lee and Marita Kirsch stood surrounded by all nine of their kids, almost lost in a gaggle of ratty hand-me-down winter coats. It seemed as if the whole town had come to his mother's funeral. Everybody was there except Buddy Mozel and Esperanza Cordova.

Jordan stopped searching the crowd as soon as he saw fifteen-year-old Ginny Coggins.

She was standing next to her mother, Celeste, wearing a thin yellow coat with a white dress underneath. Her blonde hair flowed gently over her shoulders. She did not wear a hat or gloves. She looked warm, like a ray of sunshine, out of place, almost like she was attending an Easter service instead of a funeral.

"Ashes to ashes," Pastor Gleen said, continuing the service.

They made eye contact and Ginny smiled at Jordan. And for the first time since his mother had died, Jordan smiled back.

"Dust to dust."

The pastor ended the service. A breeze whipped through the tent, and the mourners slowly returned to their cars.

Kitty stood up and took a rose from the top of the casket and gave it to Jordan. She leaned down, kissed him on the forehead, turned back to the casket and kissed it.

"Goodbye, baby," Kitty said, her voice breaking. "I love you." A tear dripped on the casket. She quickly wiped it away, stood up straight, and glared at Big Joe.

Jordan was still sitting in his chair, too cold to move, wanting to be warm, but not wanting to leave. "Can I see her one more time?" he asked Kitty.

"No, Jordan, you can't," Kitty said.

Kitty reached for Jordan's hand but hesitated. "Stay here a minute." She left the tent, skirted the grave, and made her way to a man standing apart from the crowd of mourners, twenty feet away.

The man was José Rivero. He was dressed in all black, the usual white straw Stetson replaced with a felt cowboy hat, and he wore a long leather overcoat that fluttered loosely in the wind. He nodded as Kitty approached him, took his hat off and put it back on quickly. Kitty was taller than José, but she did not seem to tower over him. José always seemed like a big man, even though he was shorter than most of the men Jordan knew.

Jordan could not hear what they were saying, but when José took Kitty's hand into his and tears welled up in his eyes, there was no question what was being said. He didn't need to understand a foreign language to know sorrow, he had seen plenty of it in the last few days to ever forget what it sounded like, looked like, and felt like.

"I told her I didn't want that wetback here," Big Joe said, easing up with the cane.

Jordan looked up at his father. Big Joe was dressed in the only set of dress clothes he owned; gray wool slacks, blazer, and a white shirt. Only his black tie was new.

"José didn't do anything," Jordan said, looking up at his father.

"You've been around her too long. That one is nothing but a liar and a thief, just like the rest of them."

Beyond the gravesite another light wind kicked up, buffeting the tent. Jordan's stomach growled, and then started to twist into knots. He'd heard his father rant about the Mexicans all his life, and had learned the hard way to keep his mouth shut. But for some reason, it didn't matter today if he got a swat across the face. He probably wouldn't have felt it anyway. "He's her friend, and mine, too."

"That's not saying much," Big Joe said, taking a step toward Kitty and José. "He needs to get the hell out of here."

Instinct mixed with fear and Jordan grabbed a hold of his father's coat sleeve. It surprised Jordan as much as it did Big Joe.

"He didn't do anything. José's just being nice," Jordan said, his voice rising from a quiver to a shout as tears streamed down his face. "You're the one that killed my mother! You killed her! Not him! Leave him alone!"

Big Joe wrapped his hand around Jordan's wrist, spun him,

took hold of his clip-on tie, and pulled him within an inch of his face. "Don't you fucking say that. Don't you ever fucking say that to me again, do you understand?" He let go with a push, propelling Jordan backward.

Jordan stumbled, bumped into the casket, and slid down to the cold ground. He had never felt rage before. His face felt hot and he could hear his heart beating a million miles a minute. He clenched his fists, and wanted more than anything to hurt something, hit his father in the face. But he couldn't see clearly, everything was blurry. His tears tasted salty, and he was surprised at how much they tasted like blood.

Holister appeared behind Big Joe and grabbed him by the shoulder. "Calm down, Joe, calm down. He's your son for Christ's sake."

"Shut the fuck up, Holister. This is none of your goddamned business," Big Joe said. He tore loose from Holister's grip and stepped back toward Jordan. "I didn't kill your mother, you little bastard."

Jordan could smell whiskey on his father's breath. The bitter smell made his stomach churn even more, and he lost control of the bile that was rising up in his throat. Vomit splattered on Big Joe's dull black shoes.

Holister wrapped Big Joe in a full Nelson, grinding him to a sudden stop. Lem Jacobson and Wally Peterson joined Holister, jumping into the struggle, and pulled Big Joe from under the tent toward the line of cars.

Jordan was panting, trying to regain his breath. He saw his father vanish in a swarm of black suits and shouts, like ants carrying a meal back to the nest. He wiped the vomit from his mouth with his sleeve and pulled himself up from the ground by leveraging his weight against the casket. When he blinked and regained clear vision, he saw Kitty standing before him with a panicked look on her face. She bent down, produced a handkerchief out of nowhere like a magician, and cleaned his face.

José and Pastor Gleen stood over her shoulder, staring down at him.

"Are you all right, honey?" Kitty asked.

He shook his head no. Without thought or explanation, he took off running. The bottoms of his shoes were slick and the snow was deep beyond the grave. Tombstones were a maze that had no end. They went on as far as the eye could see, and Jordan had no idea where he was going. His skin was pinprick cold, his face was throbbing, and his shirt was wet. But he didn't care about getting warm. He just wanted to get as far away from the casket and his father as he could. Kitty called after him, her voice distant. Her commands for him to stop only made him run faster, harder.

A line of twenty-foot white pines towered in front of him. Four crows lit from the tops of the trees and flew away in alarm. More tombstones lined the edge of the trees and beyond them, a mausoleum stood as a sanctuary, a limestone building as big as the Sunoco station, with an open airway that cut through the middle of it.

Jordan made his way inside and stopped. A few inches of snowdrifts covered the floor, and the walls were close enough to touch with his arms extended, lined with eight brass markers on each side. The walls blocked the wind, but it was still very cold. He took some deep breaths, settled into a rhythm of steady breathing, and leaned against a carved pillar of stone cherubs.

Voices called after him, fading in the wind.

Tito, Tito, where are you?

He had no intention of hiding, of staying there. He just wanted to get away from his father, from everything that was happening. All of the markers on the walls had the name Mozel on them. Beloved father. Dearest sister. Our baby boy. He recognized a few of the names. Hamilton Mozel III was Buddy's father. Buddy was Hamilton IV. But most of the names meant nothing to him. They were just names marked on a wall. But now he knew there were real people inside the walls. Real people, alone and cold, just like his mother.

"There you are."

Ginny Coggins was standing in the doorway. Jordan resisted running.

"Are you all right?" she asked, walking to him.

"I don't know," Jordan said.

Ginny smiled. "Kitty's pretty upset."

"I know."

"You want to go home?"

"No."

Ginny ran her fingers through Jordan's hair. "I heard Kitty talking to my mom. You're going to live with her for a while, at least until Spider gets better."

"Spider's not going to be better," Jordan said. "He can't walk. He can't run. He'll never play basketball with me ever again."

"It's sad," Ginny said. "But Spider's still alive. That's a good thing, right?"

"I'm scared."

Ginny nodded. Her yellow coat glowed in the murky gray light that filtered into the mausoleum. She ran her hand down the side of Jordan's cheek, pulled his face up, leaned down, and kissed him briefly on the lips.

"It'll be all right," Ginny said. "I promise."

January 21, 1986, 1:07 P.M., *Patzcuaro, Mexico*

The boy's legs were thin, and dead skin flaked to the floor as the last of the cast was cut away. Sunlight beamed through the eight-foot glass windows and illuminated all of the metal in the room. Even the doctor's face seemed to shine as he stood up and put the saw on a tray. A glint of light reflected off the stethoscope around the man's neck, and the boy clutched the medallion around his neck.

"Ah," the doctor said. "St. Christopher has done his job well."

The boy looked up at the doctor oddly, hearing words he understood for the first time since he had been awake. The man was obviously Mexican, but so far had only spoken in Spanish. "My mother gave it to me," he said.

Outside, children were laughing. Always in the distance. He still didn't know where he was. How he'd got there, how long he'd been wherever he was.

"You speak English," the doctor said, obviously surprised. He was a tall and slender man with thick hair the color of snow. His brown eyes softened as he stood staring at the boy. "Why would I think not to ask such a thing?"

"Where am I?"

"Casa de Elisabeth, *El Refugio*. An orphanage."

"In Mexico?"

"Of course, in Mexico, where else would you be?"

The boy took a deep breath and eased himself off the table. His legs were weak, but could hold his weight. He stood, gaining his balance by anchoring himself on the bed.

"Tener cuidado."

"I don't understand."

"I'm sorry. Be careful. *Tener cuidado*. Be careful."

The boy nodded and walked slowly to the window and peered out. He saw four girls and five boys kicking a ball. A town, all white buildings with red roofs, stood a mile in the distance. Beyond the town was a lake, bluer than anything he'd ever seen, with mountains behind it that reached into the sky, poking at the clouds. "But I am not an orphan," the boy said.

"*Sí*," the doctor nodded. "Yes, I'm afraid you are."

The boy didn't believe the old man. He pretended he did not hear what he just said. "The town, what is its name? Where am I?" His stomach growled with hunger.

"Patzcuaro."

"My mother's name means hope."

The doctor eyed the boy curiously. "Do you know your name?"

"Yes," the boy nodded. "My name is Tito. Is this a bad dream?"

"I should get the sisters. They will be happy you are awake, Tito."

"Patzcuaro. What does it mean?" the boy insisted, watching the children play.

The doctor hesitated and then answered, "The place where darkness begins."

CHAPTER 10

August 22, 2004, 12:43 A.M.

Spider shifted the van into gear and accelerated with the hand-control on the steering wheel. His wheelchair creaked as they exited the parking lot. The van had a hole in the muffler and the engine rumbled, leaving a trail of blue smoke in its wake. The air-conditioner was on high, but it was only blowing slightly cool air on Jordan's face, so he rolled down the window. The floor of the van was littered with empty water bottles, fast-food bags, and old newspapers. The ashtray was open and a half a joint sat on the corner, just within Spider's reach, and the familiar sweet smell of recently extinguished pot permeated the van.

"Bring any cigarettes?" Jordan asked. He ignored the joint, knew it would be there next to the ever-present plastic bottle of water. Spider's pot use put him in an uncomfortable spot, and he'd decided a long time ago to ignore his brother's habit as much as he could. The conclusion was simple: Spider wasn't going to quit smoking pot and Jordan wasn't going to arrest him for being a casual user. Maybe that didn't make him a good cop, the kind where duty to the law never ends. Jordan knew cops like that, hard-liners who stood behind a polished badge but struggled with their own private demons: alcohol, sex, drugs, or money. They would surely condemn him for turning his head when it came to Spider's drug use, and that was fine, but Spider was the only family he had left, even though their relationship was often tenuous and distant. He didn't see how he was any different than the cop who had an affair or drank away their problems on or off duty—and there were his own demons to consider, too.

Spider motioned to the console. A pack of Marlboros sat next to the ashtray, lying on a pile of cassette tapes that had been there ever since Jordan could remember. Howlin' Wolf, B.B. King, and Eric Clapton were the staples of Spider's musical diet. Jordan preferred more traditional country, George Jones, Johnny Cash, and some bluegrass, like Del McCoury and the Stanley Brothers.

Jordan grabbed the pack and flipped out a cigarette.

"How'd you get the black eye?" Spider asked.

"Sam Peterson punched me."

"No shit?"

"No shit," Jordan said.

"So he finally got his chance to clock you. Man, I bet that made him happy."

Jordan shrugged. "I attacked him, he really didn't have much of a choice."

"You attacked him?" Spider chuckled. "You guys used to fight like dogs when you were kids. At least you beat his ass then. I guess revenge really is sweet."

"He was a pest."

"So were you."

"It wasn't revenge. I was a little freaked out."

"Why?

"I don't want to talk about it right now."

Spider nodded and drove silently for about a half mile then said, "This is bullshit, you know." They turned a corner and his wheelchair shifted in its brace. The wheelchair had long ago become part of Spider's body. The front seat of the van had been removed and there was a lift on the side to allow him entry and exit, which he'd learned to navigate seamlessly.

His legs had been damaged beyond repair in the accident, crushed by the car they hit when Spider was thrown from the backseat. It had taken a while, but Spider applied his athletic prowess to his life after the accident, from the waist up, to allow as normal and mobile a life as possible.

Spider lived alone in an apartment behind Big Joe's Tavern, which he'd managed for their father since the day he turned twenty-one. That was the day Big Joe up and left Dukaine for Florida. Jordan had not seen or spoken to his father since. The years after the accident were difficult for all of them, as Spider adjusted to life without legs under Big Joe's roof, and Jordan adjusted to life without the familiarity of his family, of his mother's love, under Kitty's roof.

Jordan was seventeen when his father left town, at the height of his rebellion, at the height of his rage, and Big Joe was the target, the source of his anger. He was glad to see his father go, but oddly, it was like suffering another death once he figured out Big Joe was gone for good.

Spider was dressed in blue jeans and a white tank top, exposing two tattoos on his right arm. One was a skull with fiery red eyes and a gaping smile, and the other, a little larger than the skull, was a simple black spider dangling from a web. His thick black hair was tied in a ponytail and reached halfway down his back. Two small gold hoop earrings dangled from his right ear and his face was covered with an ever-present two-day beard.

"What's bullshit?" Jordan asked.

"That you didn't call me."

"I called," Jordan said.

"Yeah, when you needed a ride home," Spider said. He grabbed the water off the console and took a swig. He drove the normal route back to Dukaine, a well-worn path past the alternator factory and out to Highway 42 for the fifteen-minute ride home.

Jordan tapped the cigarette on the palm of his hand. "There was a lot going on."

"You know how I found out?" Spider said.

"Somebody came into the bar and told you, just like you find out everything."

"No, the fuckin' old man called me."

Jordan reached for the cigarette lighter next to the radio, but there was only an empty hole. He let Spider's words settle in his mind. *The old man called.* It was like getting smacked upside the head, which was probably the intention. So he tried to ignore it like he always did when Spider brought their father into a conversation. But that was like ignoring an itchy rash that wouldn't go away.

"Where's the lighter?"

"I don't know."

"Shit," Jordan muttered, sticking the unlit cigarette in his mouth.

"You shoulda called me," Spider said. "This is a big fuckin' deal. There's cops all over town. It's weird. Helicopters flying over like a fuckin' war movie. Then the phone rings and I hear you got shot. Real nice, fuckhead, real fuckin' nice." He dug into his pocket and tossed Jordan a disposable lighter.

"I wasn't hurt bad, so it didn't make sense for you to come and sit around and wait for me." He lit the cigarette, took a long drag, and exhaled out the window.

"You got shot, asshole. I talked to Charlie. He told me you were all right, so I said 'Fuck it, I'll just wait if that's the way it's going to be.' " Spider stopped at a red stoplight. The engine clicked, low on oil, and the smell of exhaust grew stronger.

"The bullet grazed me. I got some stitches. Besides, I know you don't like the hospital any more than I do."

"Sometimes you really piss me off, making decisions for other people, you know that? I sit wherever I go, or haven't you noticed? So, I was sitting at the bar wondering what the hell was going on. You just shoulda called. I woulda come to the hospital."

Jordan stared out the window, watching the streetlights go by. "He still in Florida?"

" 'Course he's still in Florida. It'd take an act of God to get him to come back to Indiana," Spider said.

"How'd he find out?"

"How the hell would I fuckin' know? He's still got his connections here."

"Obviously," Jordan said.

Spider shot Jordan a sideways glance, shook his head, and reached for the joint on the console, but retreated when he saw Jordan's face tighten. "If I could stand up, you'd have *two* black eyes right now. I oughta make you walk home."

"Like I never heard that before," Jordan said and then exhaled deeply. He drew on the cigarette, and wished the bottle of water on the console was a beer. "Somebody lured Holister to the pond, sent him a letter in the mail with a St. Christopher's medal."

"That's kinda weird, isn't it?"

"No. It belonged to Tito Cordova's mother. There's a skeleton exposed in the pond. Somebody wanted Holister to find it, then they shot him. And me."

"That's fucked up. You think the skeleton is *that* kid?"

"I don't know. The bones were all intact, they were small, child-like. How can anybody really know? But I think it might be. I just don't know why anybody would want to shoot Holister. He never gave up on that case. If anybody kept the memory of Tito Cordova alive, it was him. He didn't do anything but try to do his job."

"How'd you know he didn't have anything to do with it?"

"I know Holister."

"Charlie said the shit was about to hit the fan."

"What else did he say?"

"That's all."

"All right." Jordan took his last drag of the cigarette and tossed it out the window. "I have the letter and the medal. Holister wanted me to hold onto it. I don't know why, but I'm glad he did now. You can't tell anybody about this."

The stoplight turned green and Spider eased the van south, toward home.

"Isn't that evidence?" Spider asked.

Jordan nodded. "Hogue took my gun," he finally said.

"Whaddya mean Hogue took your gun?"

"He thinks I shot Holister."

"That's the stupidest thing I ever fuckin' heard. Why would you shoot Holister?" The question hung in the air for a second before Spider asked, "You didn't, did you?"

"Jesus Christ, hell no. Why would you even say that?"

"Ginny."

"There's more to that story," Jordan said, with no intention of telling Spider anything further.

"Always is. That's why I asked."

"There was no sign of the shooter when I left. It looked like it was just me and Holister at the pond. Ginny doesn't have anything to do with this."

"Well the note and that necklace thing ought to clear things up then. Why the hell didn't you just give it to Hogue?"

"I will, once I get my gun back. You don't understand. It's like a man who calls in and says he just found his wife murdered in their bed. The husband's always the primary suspect until he can clear himself, comes up with an alibi, you know? Hogue got it in his head that I was the only one at the pond, that there was no sign of the shooter, and I didn't have an alibi. That makes me an instant suspect, and he scores right away. It's a win-win for him."

"Other than you're a fuckin' cop, too."

"Cops commit murder. That doesn't matter. If I would've given him this piece of evidence the first thing he'd do is try to tie it back to me, check it for prints, check my handwriting to see if it matches. And then he'd start digging up shit between me and Holister. You know what he's gonna find there—the confrontation about Ginny before she ran off with Ed. It won't matter how long ago that happened, he needs a suspect fast to keep this from turning into a nightmare, and I'm it. But while he's wasting time checking me out, the real shooter is still out there."

"I wouldn't fuck with Hogue, man. He's a dick. He's been tryin' to bust me for years. I think you better tell him about this stuff. Besides, he's Ed Kirsch's uncle for Christ-sake. Not that I think they get along, knowing Ed the way I do, so I'm sure there's no love lost there. But he is family."

"I know—that's one of the reasons why I didn't give Hogue the letter in the first place. At the very least, I think Ed's using meth . . . maybe for his long runs to stay awake, who knows? But my gut tells me he's in deeper than that, maybe transporting. There's been a lot more activity this summer than usual—it's usually pot the migrants bring up with them."

Spider shot Jordan a sideways glance, but didn't say anything.

"I don't think Hogue knows what Ed's into, or that he's protecting him, he's got too much aspiration for that. But blood *is* thicker than water."

"How do you know Ed's using meth? Could just be speed," Spider said.

"Just a hunch," Jordan said, uncomfortably. "The shooting has nothing to do with Ed or Ginny." He sat up straight in the seat, caught Spider's eye in the passing light of a street lamp as they drove past the barber shop. "I want to catch the mother-fucker who did this. Gun or no gun. Hogue's not going to stand in my way. If there was a sign of the shooter, or they caught him, I'd know by now. This was a set-up, and that makes things even more personal. We were both sitting ducks. It was no ac-cident that Holister was there, and maybe me either. This wasn't a random shooting. Maybe they even waited for me to get there. It was thought-out. Planned. Premeditated. Maybe it has to do with Holister and me, but that doesn't make a whole lot of sense, at the moment. I didn't have anything to do with Tito Cordova when he was alive, or dead. Besides, Hogue knows an opportunity when he sees one. If those bones do belong to Tito Cordova, this thing goes back a long way. Hogue won't begin to know where to start asking questions. I do. For some reason, Holister made sure I wouldn't forget about all of this."

"Yeah? And where you going to start asking questions?" Spider asked.

"On Buddy Mozel's doorstep."

"Good fuckin' luck."

"Tell me about it—but you know as well as I do that Buddy was in the thick of things back then. Esperanza worked at the house, stayed here all year round instead of heading south like the rest of the Mexicans. And then there was rumor that he was Tito's real father. Nobody knew for sure. Holister always thought Buddy knew more than he was telling—and Holister's hands were tied to a certain point. If he pushed too hard Buddy would have had him fired, plain and simple. You know what happened from there."

"Yeah, I do," Spider said. "The son of a bitch still thinks he can buy his way out of trouble."

"I really need to get the file Holister had on Tito's disappear-ance. Hopefully, Louella will let me get a look at it. Holister was never convinced that a stranger took Tito, just like I'm not convinced a stranger showed up at the pond and started shooting. Whoever's behind this knew the history, knew when they found the bones how Holister would react if he saw them. That in itself shrinks the pool of suspects, don't you think?"

"Yeah, down to about three thousand people." Spider gripped the steering wheel and shook his head. "I hate it when you get all twisted up inside your head, and then go on a mission. I always get dragged into the wake of your shit somehow. I don't know if I'm in the mood to play big brother and cover your ass while this town gets turned upside down. I'm tellin' you, it reminded me of something you'd see in LA, fuckin' helicopters hovering, sirens going off everywhere. It was a little too weird for me. Hogue's gonna watch you like a hawk, and I don't want to be anywhere near that shit. If I get popped, you won't be able to help me."

"You said that more than once. I heard you. Just take me home," Jordan said.

"All right." Spider hesitated for a moment. "You sure you don't want me to stop at the tavern? I can loan you my .38 or the sawed-off under the bar."

Jordan let a half-smile cock across his face. Spider always had had a funny way of saying he'd help. "No, I think I can get through one night without a gun on my nightstand," he said.

"You sure?"

"Yeah, I'm sure."

Spider turned the van onto Harrison Street. They both saw the flashing lights at the same time.

"What the hell's going on?" Spider said.

Smoke wafted across the street in front of the van. An orange glow erupted two blocks away and hot embers jumped into the night sky like fireflies fleeing a nest. A fleet of fire trucks had the road blocked, along with a county cruiser and a Dukaine police car. Johnny Ray Johnson was motioning at them emphatically to turn down Lincoln Street away from the scene, but Spider stopped the van in the middle of the road.

"The house is on fire," Jordan said. "Jesus fucking Christ, the house is on fire."

CHAPTER 11

August 22, 2004, 1:23 A.M.

On the weekends, Johnny Ray Johnson worked as an Elvis impersonator in the lounge at the Super Six Motel. The motel was ten miles south of Dukaine, next to the interstate on the only on-ramp and exit in Morland. The lounge itself was dingy; a scattering of mismatched chairs and fake wood tables angled around a small stage made out of two-by-fours, cheap plywood, and painted flat black. Jordan had seen Johnny Ray perform once on the makeshift stage, an unrecognizable rendition of "Can't Help Falling in Love," and it was enough to know Johnny Ray's Elvis career wasn't going to take him to Las Vegas anytime soon.

As the deputy walked toward the van, Jordan saw a hint of the ever-present Elvis swagger that Johnny Ray practiced relentlessly. Even though it was late at night, Johnny Ray had on a pair of chrome sunglasses, and his dyed black pork chop sideburns gleamed in the presence of the flashing strobe lights. Johnny Ray was the old Elvis—the unfamiliar Elvis who took his last breath on a toilet—stuffed uncomfortably inside a blue Dacron police uniform. But he wasn't always that way—Johnny Ray had seen the last Elvis concert at Market Square Arena in Indianapolis as a teenager, and from then on he'd been devoted to all things Presley. He turned his graduation gown from high school into a blue and maroon beaded cape, and progressed from the young King to the old one with enthusiasm, all the way down to his car of choice, a white Cadillac Coupe Deville.

And it was, of course, the spirit of Elvis that led Johnny Ray into the realm of law enforcement. He studied Kenpo karate with a passion, took up target shooting with handguns, volunteered as a reserve deputy for the sheriff's department, and took criminal justice classes at the university extension in Morland. So when he applied to become a deputy, Holister could not deny his qualifications, and had no choice but to hire him fifteen years earlier. It was still a decision Holister was prone to complain about.

Johnny Ray shined his flashlight on Spider's face as he approached the driver's-side door.

Jordan was just about to jump out of the van and run toward the fire when the light swept over the console.

"Damn, it, Spider," Jordan said, motioning to the joint in the ashtray.

"Shit, I spaced it."

The light grew so bright Jordan could barely see. He snatched the joint, popped it into his mouth, and swallowed it whole.

"I thought that might be you, Spider," Johnny Ray said as he stepped up to the window. He shined the flashlight on Jordan's face. "There you are, Mac, Sheriff Hogue's been lookin' all over for you. He thought you took off from the hospital. Just about to put a call out on you, last I heard. I think you're in deep shit, Mac."

Jordan had gotten over being called Mac a long time ago, but there was something about how Johnny Ray said it that always pissed him off. Maybe it was the deep bass note he let dangle, that extended Elvis reverberation he added on the end of every sentence. Or maybe it was the countless times he'd asked Johnny Ray to just call him Jordan instead of Mac, all adding up to one giant wedge of dislike for the sloppy imitator.

Jordan reached over and grabbed Spider's bottle of water and chased the joint with a huge gulp. He shot Spider a disgusted glance. "Tell me that's not Holister's house on fire," Jordan said to Johnny Ray.

"It's not," Johnny Ray answered. "It's your house."

The air left Jordan's lungs. He could hardly breathe. He was stunned. Before he could reach for the door Spider was already unlocking the wheelchair.

"Go," Spider said. "Just go, I'm right fuckin' behind you."

"You're gonna have to move your van, Spider," Johnny Ray said, shining his light into the back of van, rising up on his tiptoes to get a look behind Spider's head.

"Shut up, Johnny Ray," Spider said. He spun the wheelchair around, preparing to release the lift. "You can move it yourself, or are you too much of a dumbass to figure out the controls?"

The last thing Jordan heard before he broke into a full-out run was Johnny Ray yelling at Spider, "Hey man, you can't talk to me like that, I'm The King—I mean, I'm a cop, damn it!"

Running two blocks was usually not a problem for Jordan. Even though he smoked, he ran three miles every other day. He had decided long ago not to become a turtle like Holister. But the day's events had left him completely depleted. He struggled for every breath, and pain shot through his arm every time his feet hit the pavement. His eye ached as the Demerol began to wear off, but the pain didn't seem to belong to him. His body was only reacting out of need. The fire pulled him closer, forced him to run toward it, much like a junebug banging against a streetlight, unaware of the consequences of its actions.

He ran through the intersection at Harrison and Lincoln, ignoring the sheriff's deputy who was demanding that he stop, and zigzagged up onto the sidewalk.

Each house on Harrison Avenue was structurally identical and looked almost like his. Most were built just after World War

II and faced the street with porches the width of the house. Some of the houses had been remodeled with enclosed porches and aluminum siding, but Jordan had chose to keep his house just as Kitty had left it: a swing on the open front porch, wood slat siding painted white, and original single-pane windows. There was no carpet inside, just forty-year-old rugs covering paths between the furniture that had been in the house long before Jordan had been born, leaving the original hardwood floors exposed. The rooms were small, three bedrooms, a kitchen, a bathroom, and a living room, but it was more than enough for him. Just as the simple house had been enough for George and Kitty Coltraine to raise their only daughter in.

From a block away he could see flames jumping out of the roof. The smell of smoke burned his nostrils, and he ran faster, trying not to pay any attention to the stories each house held for him as he passed by them. Tears began to run down his face and the pain from the gunshot wound traveled from his arm to his chest.

The fire mocked his rage, dancing uncontrollably against the starless night sky, and Jordan could feel the heat grow more intense the closer he got. There was noise all around him; engines rumbling from the stationary fire trucks, wood crackling and popping, people yelling, and overhead, two helicopters circling, shining bright white lights on the house.

He wanted it all to stop. His feet felt like cement, and his heart was beating against his chest with such tremendous force he thought it was going to explode. There was no way he could have believed how the day would turn out. Yesterday, his life was normal, on an even keel. He went to work on third shift, slept through the hottest part of the day, played on a softball league three nights a week, and didn't care to look too much into the future. He was satisfied. His love life, if you could call it that, was pretty much nonexistent since his divorce was final six months ago, except for the wink and a wave from Charlie Overdorf's sister, Lainie.

Then out of the blue, Ginny had called him. And all hell broke loose from there. Jordan knew there could be no relation to her call with everything that had happened, but it sure seemed like that mistake had set off a series of events that went from one nightmare to the next.

Two houses before his, just on the other side of Holister's house, a crowd had gathered behind a barrier of yellow tape.

Jordan felt like he was staring through glasses smeared with Vaseline, nothing was clear, and no one looked at all familiar. He eased his pace and stumbled to a stop behind the crowd on a small piece of grass and steadied himself on a cement lawn ornament, a gnome with green paint flaking off its face. Spittle ran out the corner of his mouth and he wiped his face with the tail of his shirt, paying little attention to the blood on his shirt.

Unconsciously, he sank to his knees. Ashes rained down from the sky, pelting the back of his neck like a swarm of bees had risen in the darkness and decided to attack for no apparent reason. He screamed using the last ounce of energy he had, and then fell face forward onto the grass.

The crowd slowly turned their attention to him. He heard alarmed voices. After a long moment of trying to catch his breath, someone touched him on the wrist.

He blinked to clear his vision and looked up to see Sheriff Hogue towering over him.

"There you are, McManus. You all right?" Hogue asked, leaning down, staring into his face. "Or do I need to call you an ambulance so you can take another swing at Sam Peterson?"

Jordan took a deep breath, and with every ounce of strength he had, forced himself back up onto his knees using the gnome for leverage. "I'm all right," he said, ignoring the reference to Sam. "Where's Spider?"

"Who?"

"My brother."

"Haven't seen him. Can you stand up?"

"You think you could give me a minute?"

"Why sure, I got all the time in the world. I might even go roast me a couple of wieners while you gather yourself together."

"What the fuck is your problem, Hogue? That's *my house* you're talking about."

Hogue stood up. "You're a smartass, McManus. You always have been. Your mouth's going to get you into trouble one of these days, if it already hasn't. Must have been the way you were raised."

Jordan bolted off the ground, his fist clenched as he steadied himself inches from Hogue.

"Jordan," Spider shouted from behind him. "Stop. You're just going to give him what he wants."

He heard Spider's command and his head immediately cleared. Hogue was standing squarely in front of him, his right hand inches from the 9mm he wore on his side, looking like a rock-solid wall, firmly planted, waiting for Jordan's next move.

"Look's like the sheriff here is trying to provoke you, Jordan. Now why would that be, Sheriff? You think my brother belongs in jail for some reason? And you haven't got shit on him? Sounds familiar."

Hogue stepped back a foot. The crowd had circled around them. The heat from the fire was intense, and the smoke was leaving a coating of ash on everyone's skin. But no one moved.

Three volunteer firemen ran hoses to the back of the house, while another one sprayed down Holister's house, trying to keep it as wet as possible so the fire wouldn't spread. There were flames coming from every window of Jordan's house. No matter how much water was put on the house, it was certain to be a total loss.

"How you doin', Spider? I haven't seen you for a while."

"George," Spider said.

Jordan stepped back and anchored himself against Spider's wheelchair.

"Pardon me?" Hogue said.

"George is my name. Only my friends call me Spider."

"I see," Hogue said. "Well you're right about one thing, George. I haven't got shit on your brother. Yet."

"What's that supposed to mean?" Jordan asked.

"The firemen said there was a heavy smell of toxic gas when they arrived. Looks like this fire might've been a meth lab gone bad. I got the hazardous material fellas on their way. They'll know with one good sniff."

"And now you're accusing me of setting fire to my own house? Of being a meth cooker?" Jordan yelled.

"Jordan, calm down," Spider said.

"You fucking calm down! I get accused of shooting Holister and now I'm a drug dealer? How in the hell can I calm down? Someone set my house on fire. Our house. Kitty's house. Everything I own is in that house, goddamn it!"

"He's looking in all the wrong places, and you know it," Spider said with an even tone in his voice, not taking his eyes off Hogue. "So, let him make a fool out of himself. Seems to me that's the one thing he's good at."

"You better watch yourself, George," Sheriff Hogue said.

"I will," Spider said. "Come on, Jordan, let's go."

"I'm not going anywhere. The house is on fire, if you haven't noticed."

"I noticed, and there's nothing you can do about it. You're comin' home with me. Now let's go."

"That's the smartest thing I've ever heard come from your brother's mouth, McManus. You better listen to him," Hogue said. "At least I know where you'll be. We're gonna need to have

113

a talk once we get things sorted out. That looks like it'll be a while, though."

A portion of the roof that surrounded the fireplace caved in, sending sparks straight into the air, a swarm of lightning bugs released into the black sky in a sudden burst.

"I'm not leaving, Spider," Jordan said, ignoring the sheriff.

"Yes, you are. Now come on." Spider spun his wheelchair and started to roll away.

"I'll be talking to you real soon, too, George. Real soon."

Spider pulled his hand off the wheels and hit the brake. The chair came to a sudden stop. "You threatening a cripple, Sheriff? I don't figure that looks too good for a man with high aspirations," he said as loud as he could without yelling.

Hogue's face turned red as he looked over his shoulder at the crowd that had gathered behind him.

Spider smiled. "Come on, Jordan. It's time to leave."

Jordan took a deep breath, stared at the house for a moment, watched the flames dance out of the front door, and wiped a tear from the corner of his eye. "Everything's gone," Jordan said.

"Not everything," Spider answered as he began to roll the wheelchair down the sidewalk.

Smoke hung so low to the ground it looked like they were walking through fog. There was a crowd of people all around them, but they parted, allowing them to exit without saying much of anything. A few of the neighbors—Corney Lefay, the local barber; his wife, Edith; and Wally Peterson, Sam's seventy-year-old father who had worked as a foreman at the SunRipe plant for forty years—stood back as he passed. Edith reached out and touched Jordan's arm as he passed. He smiled as best he could, and stayed close to Spider.

Other faces were less than recognizable. Jordan hadn't seen any sign of Ginny or Celeste and figured they were still at the hospital, unaware of what was going on at home. He knew it wouldn't stay that way long, since it looked like there was going to be some water and heat damage to Holister's house. But that was surely a secondary concern at this point, all things considered.

Just as they were about to cross Lincoln Street, Jordan stopped.

"Spider," he said, grabbing the handles of the wheelchair, bringing it to a stop.

"What? Ouch," he said, raising his right hand to his mouth. "Damn, it, I hate it when people do that. You ever have your fuckin' fingers pinched?" Spider said, sucking on his index finger.

"By the tree, across the street," Jordan said.

José Rivero stood in the shadow of the streetlight, next to a big elm that had buckled the sidewalk with its roots. Even in the shadows, Jordan could see José's shock of thick white hair against his dark, leathery skin. José was a little over five-and-a-half-feet tall, and always wore blue jeans, a denim shirt, a white Stetson straw cowboy hat, and angled-toed boots, black shit-kickers, permanently covered with dust. It was very unusual to see José by himself, off Mozel land, or out of his brand new red GMC pickup truck. Jordan moved from behind Spider's wheelchair to cross the street.

"What the fuck you doing now?" Spider asked.

He turned back to Spider and tapped his pocket. "If anybody knows what happened to Tito, it might be José. I don't know why I didn't think of that sooner."

"Might be because you feel the same way about Buddy Mozel as I do."

"Not entirely," Jordan said. Spider still blamed Buddy for the accident. Jordan still blamed their father. It was a quiet argument that neither of them would give up on.

"You think José set fire to the house?"

"I don't know, but don't you think it's strange for him to be here?"

When Jordan turned his attention back to the tree, preparing to cross the street, José was gone, nowhere to be seen. He'd vanished in the smoke and flashing lights, like he had never been there at all.

CHAPTER 12

August 22, 2004, 6:09 A.M.

As far as Jordan was concerned, there was no place lonelier than Big Joe's tavern at six o'clock in the morning.

The morning sun was already rising high in the cloudless sky, and bright, intense light invaded the tavern through the front window. Dust particles sparkled in the air, looking like an endless army of fireflies flittering about against the dark mahogany paneling that covered the walls. Memories of the fire were still close to the skin. The lighting beyond the reach of the sun was otherwise dull, soft from the blinking multicolored lights on the shuffleboard table's scoreboard and the dusty sconces that lined the walls. Ten tables and six green vinyl booths surrounded the shuffleboard table, tops clean and the chairs perfectly situated. Emptiness echoed throughout the tavern in the drip of the faucet and the hum of the ice machine. The smell of beer held in the drains, yeasty and too sour to be flushed away, mixed with stale cigarette smoke and bleach from the previous night's cleanup. The tavern always reminded Jordan of his father, which was one of the reasons he stayed away from it as much as possible.

Jordan sat at the end of the bar, fifteen feet of carved cherry wood topped with black river-bottom slate, fronted with ten worn stools. Sleep had come without effort as soon as he had settled onto the couch in Spider's apartment that pulled out into a bed. It took him a minute to get his bearings when he woke, sore from head to toe and slightly disoriented. But he knew his way to the coffeemaker. Almost an hour earlier, he'd eased out of the apartment in his boxers and a T-shirt, trying his best not to wake Spider. He sat stiffly, drinking coffee, smoking a cigarette, and staring out the window at the Town Hall and police station across the street.

The tavern had a small kitchen of its own, situated between the apartment and the bar. It was crammed with two refrigerators, a freezer, a three-compartment stainless steel sink, a deep fryer, a metal plate grill, and a pantry. The menu was minimal, normal Indiana bar food: deep-fried mushrooms, onion rings, tenderloin sandwiches as big as a plate, and half-pound cheeseburgers. Lunch started at noon and the grill stayed open until nine o'clock in the evening, Monday through Saturday. The tavern was closed on Sunday. Spider avoided the kitchen as much as possible; navigation was difficult at the very least. Angel Lamont, Lem Jacobson's twenty-three-year-old stepdaughter, worked the grill and waited tables. The café was usually twice as busy as the tavern for lunch and dinner, and that suited Spider.

Traffic in Dukaine was usually minimal this time of morning through the middle of the week. The field workers, trying to beat the worst of the heat, had already passed through town an hour and a half before, packed shoulder to shoulder in the back of four pickup trucks and an old school bus painted white and embossed with the SunRipe logo. Two sheriff's department cruisers, followed by a TV news van, had zipped through the stoplight within seconds of each other as Jordan sipped his coffee, and the realization didn't take long to settle in that the traffic on Main Street would be anything but minimal on this day.

He tapped the ash off the end of his cigarette and watched the smoke spiral upward to the ceiling. A sinking feeling settled in Jordan's stomach as he ground out his cigarette. His thoughts focused on the night before, when smoke had touched the stars and the walls of Kitty's house crumbled into a pile of glowing embers and ash. In the blink of an eye, the only familiar place he had to hold onto was the tavern. The one place in his life he'd ever felt sure-footed, at home, or welcome.

He could only hope that Holister had made it through the night. And then he thought of Ginny, and could find no comfort visualizing her perfectly tanned body, their moment together. Everything was all jumbled up in blood, gunfire, and flames.

A loud noise from the apartment startled Jordan, and his body vibrated with an unconscious jump. He spun around on the stool, his hand gripped on the bar for balance. Spider had clanked his wheelchair against the bed frame, metal against metal, and it had sounded like a distant gunshot or a car hitting another car.

Jordan took a deep breath and turned back to his coffee, uncomfortable with his reflexes, relaxing slightly once he realized the noise was just Spider getting dressed.

He had given up trying to help Spider a long time ago. Getting dressed took Jordan a few thoughtless seconds, but took Spider twenty minutes on a good day. In the beginning, it had taken him a lot longer. But their father was not inclined to be soft or patient, even after the accident. Big Joe left Spider to his own devices as he learned to live without the use of his legs. Instead of getting dressed, Spider would lay in bed and scream, cuss, and yell. Big Joe yelled back, and then would close the door and go to work. And, if Jordan was there to help, to pull Spider up if he fell, or clean up the bed if he wet himself, he dared not to lift a hand in fear of Big Joe's angry reprisal that Spider learn to fend for himself.

Spider rolled out of the apartment door, eyes clear, his hair wet and tied into its normal ponytail, wearing a clean white undershirt and jeans. He spun the wheelchair around without any obvious effort, locked the door, and then rolled up on the riser that had been built behind the bar.

Everything had been modified to be within his reach. The cash register was stationed on a shelf under the bar, and a myriad of liquor bottles lined the wall under a large mirror. A television sat on top of the refrigerator next to the sink, and a 12-gauge sawed-off shotgun was mounted under the bar over a three-by-three safe that had been sitting in the same spot since the tavern had been built. The riser put Spider at eye level with anyone who sat at the bar and gave him a view of every inch of the tavern and out the window, a spot he rarely left.

"How'd you sleep?" Spider asked, filling a cup of coffee.

Jordan shrugged his shoulders. "All right."

"Doesn't look like it. Looks like you've been on a bender, man. A bad one."

"You think it's funny?"

Spider rolled over to the bar and sat the coffee cup opposite of Jordan's, not spilling a drop. "No, I'm just saying . . . oh, screw it. You ought to be drinkin' a beer instead of coffee."

"I usually wait until after noon," Jordan smirked.

"Not lately you haven't."

"Like you've got any right to have a problem with that."

"Chill out. Just fuckin' chill out, it's too damn early to argue."

"I feel like I've been hit by a Mack truck. A lotta people been telling me to chill out lately, to calm down. What do you expect?"

"Yeah and the fuckin' grill imprint is still on your face—you look like a dog," Spider said, taking a sip of coffee. "Jesus, this tastes like shit. I'm going to have to teach you how to make coffee if you're going to stay here."

"Who said I was staying here?" Jordan asked, unconsciously touching his black eye.

"Where else you gonna go?"

"I don't know."

"My point exactly."

Jordan tapped his cigarette pack, thought about lighting another one, and then decided not to. He felt tense, all knotted up. "I'm going to need some clothes," he said.

"Help yourself to my closet. I don't think my shoes will fit you, though. Not that I have a great need for extras. Hell, I've had these shoes for four years. Goddamn things will never wear out."

"I've got my boots."

Spider shook his head. "This is really fucked up. You don't have shit, do you? There can't be anything left of the house. One day everything's goin' along fine, you know, little bullshit things, but nothin' major, and then boom, the whole world gets turned upside down."

"Feels familiar, doesn't it?" Jordan said.

"Not really."

Jordan stared at Spider, uncertain if he was being honest. Spider never talked about the accident, and rarely mentioned their mother. "It does to me."

"You really think José knows anything about the fire?" Spider asked, breaking eye contact with Jordan.

"I don't know if any of this is connected to him or the past. It could be something else," Jordan said, glancing out the window.

"We're assuming that somebody set the house on fire just because of what Hogue said. I wouldn't put a whole lot of weight on that. But if it turns out there's meth there, shit's really gonna hit the fuckin' fan."

"I've got enemies," Jordan muttered.

Spider ignored Jordan, lost in a thought, following it like a bloodhound, which he was prone to do after a couple of hits off a joint. "That'd take some doing. Build a lab and then blow it

up on purpose. Not that it'd be hard—those things can go up in
flames if you fart wrong. But whoever did it would've had to
have known where you were and that you wouldn't be back. If
Holister was set up and so were you—I don't know, man,
somebody's got a grudge against the police force in this town,
that's all I can say. Enemies. You got enemies? Who hates you
enough to go to that much trouble? Everybody pretty much
likes you from what I can tell. You're not too much of an asshole, as far as cops go anyway."

"Ed Kirsch for one."

"Why the hell would Ed Kirsch burn down your house?"
Spider asked.

Jordan just stared at Spider, not saying anything.

"You fuckin' slept with her, didn't you?" Spider finally said.

"Yes."

"You're a goddamned dumbass."

"I know."

"Why the hell'd you go and do that?"

"I don't know. I was lonely."

"The stupidest thing I ever fuckin' heard. 'I was lonely.' That's
just bullshit, Jordan. Like Ginny is your only option. Lainie has
an 'Open for Business' sign wrapped around her neck. Hell, it's
flashin' in bright red fuckin' neon."

"Maybe that's the problem."

"When did you see Ginny?"

"The other night. I was on shift and she called. I went over
to see what she wanted."

"You knew what she wanted."

"I know it was a mistake, Spider. But I'm human, damn it. I
haven't been with anybody since Monica and I split up. I
couldn't help myself—I still love her, Spider. I always will."

"Seems to me it would've been easier to pull over some little
blonde honey for speeding and get a blowjob in the backseat of

the cruiser. Instead, you do to another man what Monica did to you. It wasn't six months ago you were sitting at this very bar, suckin' down beer and whining about being fucked over."

Jordan exhaled, felt his shoulder draw tight. Pain tingled in his fingers. "Monica and I had other problems, you know that."

Spider squinted, then ran his hand over the top of his head. "Doesn't fuckin' matter. You swore you'd never go near Ginny again, Jordan. That was supposed to be over a long time ago."

"I don't think it'll ever be over between us. At least not until we get our shot."

"She's different now, Jordan. Livin' with Ed's changed her."

"I can save her."

"You're a goddamn fool."

"I feel bad about sleeping with her, I really do, but this is the first time it's happened in the nine years she's been married to Ed."

"You think you deserve an award or something?"

"Funny."

"I'm serious. Ginny's a head-case these days, but Ed's flat-out nuts. That's why you wouldn't come clean about the letter with Hogue, isn't it?"

"One of the reasons," Jordan said.

"If Ed found out you slept with Ginny, he just might've burned down the house. I kicked him out of here a few years ago for pulling a knife on a guy. He's crazy enough, that's for sure. But you know that. You know where he came from—his dad was just like him. Beat the shit out of all nine of those kids just for the fuckin' fun of it. I really wouldn't blame Ed for kickin' your ass now that I know this bullshit. Hell, I might hold you down for him, if I could."

"Ed couldn't have burned the house down—he was at the hospital with Ginny. He said he wanted to talk to me when this thing with Holister was all over with. I think he knows. Dylan saw me leave."

Spider shook his head. "Man, you're such a dumbass. Some days you make me glad I can't feel anything from the waist down."

"Thanks, I appreciate your confidence." Jordan hesitated. "But I still think Ed might be into meth. I'm not saying he's not involved in setting the house on fire, but somehow it just doesn't fit."

"How'd you figure?"

"There was a needle and an aluminum foil rock in the medicine cabinet. When I asked Ginny about it, she said Ed was diabetic."

"Diabetic, yeah, right. And I'm gonna walk day after tomorrow. Most people smoke meth, not shoot it, Jordan—the needle could be for anything. Ed's on the road a lot, though, so like I said last night, he might be stickin' his veins to make the long runs."

"That's what I thought. So I let it go. But the more I think about it, the more I think there might be something there. Ginny was complaining about never having any money, and Ed always being gone, but he's never where he's supposed to be. She thinks he's fucking around, and she's right, he is. But he might be transporting, too. You know anything about that?"

"Why the fuck would I know whether Ed was running meth? Because I get high? That's bullshit, Jordan. You believe that brainwash shit that pot leads to harder drugs? That's like saying beer leads to hard liquor. You there yet? You need a shot o Johnny Walker to jump-start your fuckin' day?"

"No."

"Exactly my point. I get high. I don't put ammonia and drain cleaner into my body. You ever seen those fuckers tweaking They tear shit apart just to be doing something. Air conditioners, toasters, TVs, you name it. They stay awake fo days—don't eat, don't shower, probably don't even shit. I'm not having anythin' to do with that crap. It's wicked, wicked stuff. One time out and your head's fried. I just toast a few brain cells every so often, and enjoy the fuckin' scenery."

Jordan stiffened. "Sorry I brought it up. I just thought you might've crossed paths with some people in the know."

"I run the other way." Spider's face was hard with anger. He barely blinked. "Besides, Ed is too small time to be making runs. The Mexicans run the big labs, and you know as well as I do Ed Kirsch doesn't care too much for Mexicans."

"Unless he needs to score a bag."

"Like I said, he's small time. Always has been. We all break our codes every once in a while—especially when it comes to scoring a bag."

"Or answering a call from an old girlfriend," Jordan said.

"Nice try—but fucking someone else's wife is not the same thing."

After a second or two of long silence, Jordan said, "None of this makes sense. Holister was set up and then shot. The house burned down, maybe because a meth lab exploded—I was set up. There's a skeleton at Longer's Pond that is obviously a child. I've got Esperanza Cordova's St. Christopher's medal in my pants pocket. And I'm the number one suspect on the list."

"Don't forget the dumbass part," Spider said.

Jordan looked at him curiously.

"You slept with Ginny."

"That has nothing to do with anything that's happened."

"I wouldn't count on it," Spider said. "But I think you're right about one thing."

"What's that?"

"José Rivero is up to something."

"Turn that up," Jordan said, pointing to the TV.

Spider glared at him and then hit the volume on the remote.

A picture-perfect brunette reporter with wide green eyes was standing in the parking lot at Longer's Pond. She was interviewing Sheriff Hogue.

"Can you tell us what happened here yesterday, Sheriff?" the reporter asked.

Hogue stared into the camera. "Well, we're really not sure at this point. We're waiting on the return of a ballistics test."

"So you have a suspect in the shooting of Marshal Coggins?"

The sheriff cleared his throat. "We have a person of interest. It's a little early to say whether or not he's a suspect."

"Does the shooting have anything to do with the fire that occurred in Dukaine last night? Or was it another meth lab explosion?"

"Again, it's too early to tell, ma'am. But rest assured, the department has every available man on this case. The citizens of Carlyle County are safe."

"So you're saying these aren't random acts, Sheriff Hogue?"

"We don't think so, no."

"There have been reports of a skeleton being found here. How does that play into the investigation, Sheriff?"

"I really can't comment on that. It's part of an ongoing investigation," Hogue said.

Jordan stood up from the bar. "Turn it off," he said. "Just turn it off."

Spider grabbed the remote and clicked the television off. "Man, he *really* does think you shot Holister. How fucked up is that?"

"He just told the whole world I'm a suspect," Jordan said, heading for the door. "I gotta get across the street, see if I even have a job."

"Not like that."

Jordan stopped, realized he hadn't had a shower and only had on his boxers and T-shirt. He turned and headed for the apartment, frustrated. "I need the key. Do you have any aspirin?"

Spider dug into his pocket, and tossed Jordan a set of keys. "Hold on," he said, reaching under the bar. "You'll need this, too." He slid a snubnose .38 down to the end of the bar.

Jordan caught the keys, waited, and then stared at the gun as it came to a rest in front of him. He nodded, picked up the .38, and checked to see if it was loaded. It was. "Thanks."

"Not a problem," Spider said. "There's a bottle of aspirin under the sink."

"I might need to borrow the van, too," Jordan said. "I want to go to the house after I go across the street."

Spider shook his head. "No way, man. Nobody drives my van but me."

"You gonna leave during the day?"

"Angel can handle things. Besides, I got the feeling you might need a little help."

"I can take care of myself."

"Have you looked in the mirror lately?"

"I thought you weren't going to get involved?"

"No—I said I didn't like it when you pull me into your crap. I didn't say I was going to sit back and watch it happen and do nothing. I get fuckin' tired of sitting around. Besides, it was my house, too." When Kitty died five years ago, she willed equal ownership to both of them—Spider chose to continue to live in the tavern. Moving would've complicated his life even more.

"Yes, it was."

Jordan took a deep breath. He knew there was no use arguing with Spider, and he was silently glad his brother was coming along. "If we're going to leave, I want to lock up the note and the medal in the safe."

"Great, so Hogue can bust *me* for possessing evidence. I really don't like that idea."

"I told you, once the ballistics come back I'll give them to

Hogue. Not until."

"All right. I guess I better stash my stash, just in case Hogue comes snooping around," Spider said, pulling a joint out of his shirt pocket.

"That's probably a real good idea."

CHAPTER 13

July 11, 1986, 7:15 P.M.

José Rivero stood at the back door with blood on his hands. The first thing Jordan noticed was a little Mexican girl sitting in the passenger seat of José's pickup truck, in the alley between the fence and the grain elevator, her head hung low, tears in her eyes. José had obviously knocked over the bowl of milk for the black snake when he'd bounded onto Kitty's porch. The milk spread across the wood planks like a river breaking through a dam, draining slowly between the cracks. Jordan looked away from the truck to the milk, and then to José's leathery hands. A tiny drop of blood dripped off the end of José's finger and splashed softly into the milk. The splash was no louder than the buzz of a bee zipping past his ear, but Jordan heard it, saw snow instead of milk, his mother's head slumped onto the window, Spider's legs twisted and crushed, and a familiar fear in José's eyes.

"Please, I must speak to the *abuela*," José said, agitated. "The grandmother, I must speak to the grandmother," he repeated when Jordan responded with only a blank stare.

Kitty eased up behind Jordan, her apron untied, flour on her fingers. The smell of hot grease filled the air from the iron skillet on the stove. Two pork chops sat on the kitchen counter along with three peeled potatoes and a bowl of freshly snapped peas.

"What is it, José?" Kitty asked, pulling Jordan to her side.

"Nina Martinez, her baby is stuck inside her and won't come out," José said. "She is very weak."

"You should take her to the hospital," Kitty said, and then hesitated. "You're bleeding."

"No, no, it is from Nina. She bleeds badly. Please, *señora,* she is asking for you. The hospital is too far away. They will only make her wait. They do not care if she dies."

"I can't come running to the camps all the time, José. I have Jordan to care for now."

"I beg of you, *señora.* Nina is my *sobrina,* my niece. My brother will never forgive me if I let her die. Surely you understand?"

Kitty drew in a deep breath, exhaled, and stared into José's pleading brown eyes. "All right, José. Get your shoes on, Jordan," she said, pulling her apron off. "Let me get my things and we'll be right out."

The sun was slowly dropping in the evening sky, tall gray thunderhead clouds lined the western horizon, and the streetlights hadn't come on yet. Blue sky still hung overhead, but it was being pushed away, swallowed up by the certainty of a coming storm.

Jordan did as he was told, running quickly to the bedroom that was now his to grab his tennis shoes. He could hear Kitty rummaging through the closet in the bathroom. He'd seen her launch into action before, knew her routine of preparation like it was written down.

Jordan felt numb, afraid as he sat on the edge of the bed to put on his tennis shoes. He had never been to the Mexicans' camp before, and the sight of blood on José's hands made his stomach queasy. More than anything else, he wished Spider was with him, was able to go with them. He wouldn't be so afraid then. Spider would be teasing him, smacking him in the back of the head when Kitty wasn't looking, making him laugh when he wasn't supposed to.

Kitty appeared at the door, her arms full of towels, and a heavily worn blue canvas bag thrown over her shoulder. "Maybe you shouldn't go," Kitty said. "Holister and Celeste are gone, and I don't know if Ginny's home or not to watch you. I really don't want to leave you here by yourself."

"I want to go," Jordan lied. He didn't want to stay by himself, either.

"Are you sure?"

"Somebody's hurt, right? And you can help them?"

"I hope so," Kitty said, her soft eyes focused on Jordan, a sad frown on her face. "Come on, then, let's go."

He followed Kitty into the living room, a small twenty-by-twenty room with a red brick fireplace centered on the outside wall, the mantle lined with trinkets and family pictures. Heavy wool rugs covered the hardwood floors, and furniture that had been there ever since Jordan could remember surrounded the fireplace. A green brocade sofa his mother called a Davenport, two light yellow high-back winged chairs, the arms covered with lace doilies, and a coffee table with a glass top that never had seen a fleck of dust on it. It looked the same as it always had. Nothing ever moved or changed in Kitty's house.

"There's not anything to be afraid of at the camps," Kitty said, making her way into the kitchen. She sat the canvas bag onto the simple wood kitchen table, and started searching through the pantry where she kept her herbs. It only took her a second to find what she was looking for; the jars were in alphabetical order. Kitty quickly packed the jars in the bag and slung it over her shoulder.

"I know," he answered. "Will I have to see any blood?"

"No, heavens no, you can sit in the truck and wait if you like."

Jordan sighed and followed her out of the house. "Okay."

The thunderheads on the horizon had reached the house, covered it with a thick gray blanket, and the breeze was now a constant wind coming out of the southwest.

Jordan climbed into the truck's bed and sat in the opposite corner of the girl, who had moved from the passenger seat. She looked to be nine or ten, and just stared at him, her eyes big and wide like buttons on a black leather coat. She was barefoot and wore a thin blue flowered dress with mustard stains on her chest. Her feet were dirty and her knees were caked with dust from the fields. He could see tear streaks down her cheeks, dry riverbeds etched in a red dirt desert.

"*Hola,*" Jordan said softly. It was one of the few Spanish words he'd learned since coming to live with Kitty.

The little girl looked away, toward the darkness on the horizon, and coughed.

Kitty eased into the passenger seat and slammed the door closed. The back window was open. José yelled out for the girl and Jordan to hold on, first in Spanish, then in English, and let his foot off the brake.

Jordan watched the dust dissipate behind them as José gunned the truck down the alley and out onto Lincoln Street. The wind blew in his face, and he could hear nothing but the truck's engine rumbling as they passed through town. He saw Sam Peterson delivering newspapers from his bike and eased deeper into the bed of the truck so Sam wouldn't see him. The last thing he needed right now was Sam giving him a hard time about hanging out with the Mexicans. They'd fought the week before because Sam called Kitty a spic lover.

They headed west toward the SunRipe plant on Main Street, crossed the railroad tracks, passed by the American legion, and turned left onto an unmarked gravel road. Tomatoes by the truckload had already started to arrive from as far away as

Arkansas. A small crew of migrants came in the spring to hoe the fields, and they were trickling into town now for the coming harvest. The early arrivals worked in the fields pulling weeds the herbicides wouldn't kill, and in the plant coring and sorting the out-of-state tomatoes. Jordan could smell the sour, acidic odor from the plant. It wasn't as bad as rotten eggs, but it was close. He pulled his shirt over his nose as they drove by the plant.

The little girl laughed, and started coughing again.

"Do you speak English?" Jordan yelled.

The little girl shook her head.

"Are you all right?"

The girl stared at him and cupped her hand over her mouth.

Jordan didn't know whether to believe her or not. Most Mexicans said no when they were asked if they spoke English.

The sun had disappeared behind the clouds, darkness was coming earlier than normal due to the impending storm. Rain was in the air, the smell sweet and fresh, overwhelming the odor from the plant. The first clap of thunder rumbled in the west, barely loud enough to hear over the roar of the truck's engine.

Kitty looked out the back window and yelled above the noise of the wind and truck the best she could. "You all right?"

Jordan nodded. The little girl smiled at Kitty and coughed again.

"I've got some medicine for that cough—I'll give it to you once we stop," Kitty said.

José said something Jordan did not understand, and Kitty agreed, sadly shaking her head.

The road straightened for about a half mile past the plant. The girl stared at the sky, and Jordan followed her gaze. The clouds were rippling in layers; thin whispers of white wandering aimlessly under the thick gray thunderheads, swirling, dancing like scarves thrown from an invisible army of ballerinas. Every once in a while he felt a raindrop. He could taste nothing but the dust rising from the road, and the vibration from the gravel road under the truck sounded like popcorn popping.

Jordan saw a house off to the side of the road, vanishing in the dust as José sped up trying to outrun the storm. It took him a minute to realize the house was where Tito Cordova had lived. It was abandoned, the front yard covered with tall weeds and all of the windows broken out. He tried not to think about Tito anymore.

José slowed the truck and Tito's house disappeared completely. They turned right onto another gravel road, and then turned immediately right again onto a dirt lane that ran between two tomato fields. A line of shacks fronted the road, and old beat-up cars and pickup trucks were parked haphazardly, anywhere they could fit, among them. Some of the shacks, which didn't look any bigger than Kitty's living room and were in need of a coat of paint, had the lights on, but most of them were dark, still vacant. He peered over his shoulder, through the windshield, and saw a crowd of people, seven or eight Mexicans, standing on the front porch of the last shack on the lane. They were waving at José. Not because they were glad to see him, but because they were panicked.

Sprinkles turned into an earnest rain with large drops blowing sideways in the wind.

"My momma is going to die," the little girl said.

"What?" Jordan asked, pulling his shirt over his head to keep as dry as he could.

"*El diablo es flojo.* The devil is loose. And he's coming to take us all away." Her English was broken, but a lot clearer than Jordan expected. He couldn't tell if her tears had returned or if her face was wet from the rain, and he didn't care because she had lied to him about not speaking English, had made him feel stupid.

The truck came to a stop and José and Kitty jumped out.

José reached into the bed and picked up the little girl. She broke into a coughing fit. "Come on now, my little Rosa, your momma will be all right. The *abuela* will not let her die," he said.

Kitty hurried to the tailgate and pulled it open. "I want you to wait in the truck, Jordan."

He took Kitty's hand and jumped down onto the road. It was already turning to mud. Kitty ushered him into the cab and said, "No matter what, Jordan, I want you to stay right here. Don't move unless I call for you. Do you understand?" She looked after José and the girl, a concerned look in her eyes that frightened Jordan.

He knew that tone in her voice, and he wasn't about to argue. He wished he'd stayed at home the way it was. "Yes, ma'am."

The crowd on the porch parted as Kitty and José made their way inside the shack. The little girl vanished into the arms of an older Mexican woman wearing a red shawl. Rain bounced off the roof of the truck and flowed down the windshield. It was like he was sitting behind a waterfall. The people on the porch were distorted; he could barely tell one from the other and they all looked connected, swaying back and forth.

His T-shirt and baseball hat were soaked to his skin, and he was cold. The inside of the truck smelled like cigarette smoke and beer, like his father's tavern. As odd as it was, the smells gave Jordan the first bit of comfort he'd had since they'd left the house, and he quickly fell asleep.

A loud voice, followed by a long extended scream, woke him up. Jordan sat straight up and looked at the shack. It was lit from the inside and he could see shadows moving beyond the thin curtains. The crowd had left; only the little girl was sitting on the front step, holding a candle. He looked at the clock in the dashboard, drew his face close so he could read it, and saw that it was almost midnight.

The door opened and Kitty's silhouette filled the doorway. She stepped out, stopped and crouched down by the girl, hugged her, and pulled a bottle of homemade cough syrup— honey and whiskey—out of her bag. Rosa was crying again. Kitty stood slowly, her bag slung over her shoulder, and made her way to the truck.

José Rivero followed, carrying a small bundle of blankets. Even in the dark Jordan could see the redness in José's eyes, and his shoulders were slumped as if he had just been beaten in a basketball game after trying to win really hard. Kitty opened the door and motioned for Jordan to slide over. He did, not taking his eyes off José as he put the bundle of blankets in the bed behind the cab.

"I'm sorry it took so long, honey," Kitty said as she eased into the seat. She smelled like sweat, like she'd been working hard in the garden. She smelled like something else, too. The smell was metallic, he could taste the sharpness of blood on his tongue.

"Did you help her?" Jordan asked, pulling away from Kitty.

"We did the best we could."

José climbed into the truck and put the key in the ignition. He hesitated, touched the crucifix, and then made a cross against his chest. His shirt was covered with blood.

"Shouldn't you go to the priest, José? To Father Michael?"

"Please, *señora,* you do not understand."

"There is nothing to understand, José, there is only the right thing to do, and the wrong thing to do."

"Padre Michael can do nothing, would do nothing even if he knew what has happened. Nina was unmarried. The baby is . . . was a, oh, how do you say, um, a *bastardo.* It had no father, the church will not baptize a child of this sort. It is condemned to eternal damnation. I am sorry to speak this way in front of you, Jordan," José said.

The engine revved to life as José turned the key. He flipped on the headlights, catching Rosa in the beams. She stood still as a statue as they pulled away, the candle stiff in her hands. Jordan wondered if she was trying to keep the devil away with the flame.

"You must take the baby to the funeral home then, José," Kitty said.

"It is not the way things work for us, *señora*, not here, you know that is true. There is no money to pay the mortician. It is different for us."

"What will you do?"

"It is best not to worry about it, *señora*. You have done enough for us, and I am very grateful that you saved my Nina's life. But please leave this to me, trust me to do what I must."

It was silent all of the way back to town. José pulled up in front of the house on Harrison Street and stopped. Kitty grabbed the door handle. "This is not right, José," she said.

"You must forget this night has happened. No one will ask any questions, so you will not have to lie. They would not care as it is. Just a dead Mexican baby. As invisible as the rest of us who toil the fields. It may be better off."

"That's a terrible thing to say, José."

"It is the truth," José said. He reached over and pulled the door closed. "*Gracias.*"

Kitty stepped up to the curb and headed to the house. Jordan followed, but he stopped midway to the front door. He watched José's taillights as he pulled away, watched the red lights all of the way to Main Street where the truck turned right, east toward Longer's Pond, and then disappeared from sight.

July 11, 1986 10:15 P.M., *Patzcuaro, Mexico*

They called him *El Fantasma,* the ghost, because of his light skin, blue eyes, and his silent ways. One minute the boy would be standing next to the hundred-foot ceiba tree in the middle of the courtyard, and the next minute he would be gone. It was a game he played with the other children. He knew he was different, and he was accustomed to that, but he had found a new power since he'd arrived at *El Refugio*. Power in fear, power in making the other children uncertain of him. And he found he liked that. It evened the playing field when he was at a loss for words, when he didn't understand what someone was saying.

Slowly, the nuns were teaching him the language, and to his surprise, it was coming easy. The lessons made the days pass a little more easily, along with Mass and schooling and visits to the doctors—his life had fallen into a routine that was far different than what it had been before he arrived in Mexico.

But at night, when the owls hooted and screamed like an injured woman, he became scared. The nuns assured him that his mother was dead, that they were most certainly his legal guardians—but his dreams told him otherwise. His dreams told him she still walked the earth, but she was trapped in paradise, and she longed for him as much as he longed for her.

The owls were calling him home, and there was nothing he could do to escape what he heard in the wind as night fell and the lights in the orphanage were put out.

"Tito, Tito, where are you? Please come home. Please come home. Tito, Tito . . ."

CHAPTER 14

August 22, 2004, 7:29 A.M.

Angel Lamont was sitting in Spider's lap when Jordan walked out from the apartment. She looked over her shoulder when she heard him enter the tavern, smiled, and then gave Spider a deep, passionate kiss.

"Damn, Jordan, you look like shit," Angel said, standing up.

"Seems to be the general consensus," he said.

Angel chuckled, and took Spider's hand in hers. "You want some breakfast, baby?" Angel was about five foot five, with short blonde spiky hair cut around the ears like a man, and penetrating blue eyes set in a face that looked older, harder than it should have. She didn't wear makeup, and had a line of gem-studded earrings in her right ear and a single gold hoop in her left ear. When the light caught the earrings just right, her ear looked like a rainbow or a neon sign. Her body was tight, her arms muscular from lifting weights. A thin black leather bracelet adorned her right wrist, and a tattoo of a simple red heart with a sword through it peeked out of the black tank top she wore without a bra, just above her right breast.

Spider never had trouble attracting girls, especially after the accident. He never gave up the conquest. He loved women and they loved him. Jordan was never sure how he did it, how Spider drew so many women into his life, but the best he could figure was that Spider never played the victim, never felt sorry for himself once he took over the tavern. What happened beyond that was none of Jordan's business; he'd never asked and he didn't want to know.

"Sure, I'm starved," Spider said to Angel.

"Got the morning munchies is more like it," Jordan added.

Angel let go of Spider's hand, grabbed the joint out of the ashtray, lit it, and took a deep hit. She exhaled and smiled. "You going to arrest him, officer?" she asked.

"I'm off duty, last I heard." He sat down at the bar, took a quick look out the window across the street at the police station, tapped his fingers nervously on the bar, and reached for the pack of cigarettes he'd left there before showering.

"How do you like your eggs, Jordan?"

"I'm not eating. I've got too much to do."

"Your choice," Angel said, offering the joint to Spider.

He shook his head no. She ground out the roach and disappeared into the kitchen. They both watched her walk away.

"A little young for you, isn't she?"

"You should eat some breakfast and mind your own goddamned business," Spider said. "She's had a tough time of it. There's a lot worse places she could have ended up than sittin' in my lap."

Angel had succumbed to the lure of meth, tried it once and forever after had a taste for it that could not be quenched. She'd stole money from her mother, got caught shoplifting clothes in Morland to sell for drug money, and spent six months in jail. Spider had rescued her—Jordan knew the story, knew full well why Spider had her working in the tavern. He just didn't totally trust Angel, and truth be told, he was a little jealous of Spider. Jealous that Spider could save Angel, while he would not allow himself the same kind of heart to pull Ginny out of her horrible, fucked-up life.

Jordan put up his left hand and scrunched his shoulders. A

motion that meant: *All right, I get it. You're right. I overstepped my boundaries.* Regardless of how separate their lives had been, there was still an unspoken language that existed between them. Subtle glances of victory and defeat, and silent acts of redemption that only they understood. They had not lost their ties of blood, or the bindings of the past, as they had grown into adulthood. They had just chosen to walk in different worlds, even though they only lived two blocks from each other.

"I need to get over to the house and see what's left," Jordan said.

"I'd put that off as long as I could if I were you."

"Well you're not me, you didn't . . ."

". . . Grow up there? Yeah, here we go. The same old pissin' contest."

The air suddenly grew stale. Jordan regretted what he'd said as soon as he saw Spider's face tighten. "I'm sorry," he said, grabbing the bar to steady himself as he stood up. Every muscle was stiff and sore, but he refused to take painkillers. He walked to the refrigerator behind the bar, pulled out a beer, and downed it.

"No big deal, man, I'm used to it." Spider rolled to the end of the bar so he was a few feet from Jordan, face to face on the platform. "It's the truth. I'd be devastated if the tavern burnt down. I really would. But I can't imagine Kitty's house not bein' there and you not living in it. Just knowin' it existed gave me some comfort. A normal place that felt like home, even though I wasn't there a lot. I could still feel Mom there."

"Me, too," Jordan said, wiping his mouth.

"I need to go with you for my own reasons."

Jordan nodded, glad the air had cleared so quickly. Surprised Spider had mentioned their mother. There were moments when Spider was open, lucid. Maybe it was the morning joint. Or maybe seeing the house on fire had turned something on that had been turned off. Jordan wasn't sure he could put his finger on it, but something had changed between them. He was still numb, still reeling from the events of the last couple of days. Somehow he'd woke up in Spider's midst, and it was starting to feel like he had returned home after a long, tiring trip. "I need to run across the street. If you could have Angel fix me a BLT, I'll eat it when I get back."

"Will do."

"How are you going to get in to see Buddy?" Spider asked.

Jordan started to walk away and then stopped. "Haven't figured that out yet. But I think we should go look for José. He might be our only way in, don't you think?"

"If he'll talk to you."

"He will. If he'll let himself be found. Maybe I was seeing things last night—but José looked afraid. I've seen that look in his eyes once before."

"Unless he's the one that set fire to the house."

"You don't know him like I do. He hasn't forgotten everything Kitty did for him, for the migrants and his family."

Spider stared at him. "You don't know Mexicans like I do, either."

"That's an old argument, too, Spider. Things have changed. José might've been there to help us, not hurt us."

"If you think so."

"No, I hope so. He's not as bad of a man as you think he is."

"All right. It's a place to start. I agree with that. But I haven't seen Buddy Mozel in years, man."

"Nobody has."

Jordan had found a pair of jeans and a button-up white and green striped short-sleeved shirt in Spider's closet that fit him after he'd taken a shower. He grabbed the pack of cigarettes off the bar and put them in his shirt pocket. The .38 snubnose was stuffed in a holster in the small of his back. He wore the shirt untucked, and Spider's pants were just a little big for him, so the gun was reasonably concealed. The clothes made him feel physically out of sorts; he wanted his own jeans, his own gun. He wanted to put his uniform back on—it fit him like a glove, and he wore it eighty percent of the time. He did stick his badge in his wallet, though. A touchstone. A reminder to himself that he was still a cop, that everything wasn't lost, that a part of his own world still existed.

He glanced out the window again. Ginny's car, a ten-year-old gray Ford Taurus, was at the stoplight. He froze. Watched her turn and park immediately in front of the police station entrance. She hurried out of the car around to the front passenger door, and ushered Dylan quickly inside.

"What's up?" Spider asked.

"Ginny. She just took Dylan into the station. Louella's been watching him while she stays at the hospital."

"Man, I wouldn't want that old fuckin' bat watching my kid."

"I don't think she's got much choice. Celeste is at the hospital, too. I imagine that's where she's heading."

"That's gotta be a good sign for Holister. You should call and check on him," Spider said.

"It won't do any good; they won't tell me shit."

Jordan didn't move, barely breathed while he waited. Ginny always made him stop when he saw her. Even before the night in her bed. Knowing he couldn't have her only made him want her more. No matter the damage it did to anyone, or the damage that had already been done. Nobody knew him like Ginny, nobody had loved him like Ginny. Not Monica, not anyone. And Jordan doubted anyone ever would. Or that he could love anyone like he loved Ginny. One more reason why turning off Lainie's open sign didn't appeal to him. He couldn't make the same mistake again. He either needed to get Ginny out of his blood or rescue her from Ed. Neither seemed possible. Or the right thing to do.

Ginny ran back out the door of the police station, her hair neatly fixed, dressed in a similar jogging suit she'd had on when he saw her in the waiting room of the hospital, only this one was red. She jumped in the car, turned around in the parking lot, and drove off. He shook his head as she passed by the tavern, heading out on Main Street toward the SunRipe plant.

"What's the matter?" Spider said.

The smell of frying bacon permeated the tavern, covered all of the other smells. Angel had turned on the radio, a country station out of Indianapolis was playing a Dixie Chicks ballad, and she was singing along.

"Nothing," Jordan said. But he didn't even convince himself. Morland, the hospital, was east. Ginny had headed in the opposite direction, in a hurry. "It's probably nothing."

He walked out the door and stopped at the curb. The heat and humidity had not changed from the day before, it was oppressive and unbearable. The sky was clear of clouds and there was no wind, no hint of rain, and a thin haze wavered in the distance. A carbon copy day, typical for August, typical for the drought that had settled over Dukaine and refused to leave.

A small flock of pigeons roosted on the rusted dome of The Farmer's Bank and Trust building. It was not unusual to see a Cooper's hawk swoop in out of nowhere and grab a pigeon for lunch. Hawks were not an unusual sight around Dukaine. He mostly saw red-tails sitting on telephone poles or high in the trees overlooking the fields, waiting for an unknowing mouse to make a run for it. The Cooper's hawks fed on other birds, and the pigeons were all huddled together in a clump of cooing gray and iridescent greens and blues, always aware that they were targets, always on the alert, always looking to the sky for shadows.

Jordan thought of the shooter. Appearing out of nowhere,

relentlessly driving his prey into the corner, and then disappearing with a flurry of silent wing flaps, as if he had never existed at all. He understood how it felt to be a pigeon, and he didn't like it.

All three police cruisers were parked next to the police station. Holister's, Johnny Ray's, and his. He wondered for a second who had driven his cruiser back from Longer's Pond, and realized just as quickly that it didn't matter. In his own mind, the cruiser belonged to him. He'd driven it home after every shift for the last nine years, parked it in the driveway, washed it, waxed it, and took care of it as if his name were on the title.

But the cruiser didn't belong to him. It belonged to the town of Dukaine. His gun though, his 9mm, that *was* his, and he'd lost that, too. And if nothing else came back to him today, he was intent on getting the Glock back. The .38 stuffed in his back was a pain in the ass, uncomfortable as hell. He had no confidence in it, and he felt like a half-baked criminal trying to hide a gun to use for a convenience store holdup.

He took a deep breath and walked inside the police station. Knowing Holister wasn't there, not knowing what to expect, made it seem like the first time he was entering the building. The ancient sour smell seemed even stronger, more disgusting than it had ever smelled before.

Louella was sitting at the dispatch desk, dressed in her normal uniform. The door to Holister's office was closed. Voices chattered on the radio, distorted and fuzzy. She looked at him as he entered the room, and a funny, almost surprised look fell across her face. As quick as it appeared, the look disappeared back into its hard shell.

"I didn't expect to see you so early this morning," Louella said, laying down a pencil. "Are you all right?"

"I'm fine. A little sore." Actually, it hurt just to breathe, but he wasn't telling her that. Louella had never asked Jordan how he was doing in the entire time he had known her. Her tone, though, was not of genuine concern, but expected concern, so it was easy to disregard. "Any word on how Holister is doing?"

"He's holding his own. Ginny said it was a rough night for him. They didn't really expect him to make it to the morning, so there's hope."

"Good," Jordan said, exhaling. "Where's Dylan?"

"He's in your office."

"Did Ginny go back to the hospital?"

Louella looked at Jordan and shrugged her shoulders. "I guess. She didn't say."

"Who's in Holister's office?"

"Johnny Ray." He'd stopped at the front of her desk. Louella rolled back in her chair, staring at him with pursed lips.

"What's he doing in there?"

Louella drew in a deep breath. "The Town Board had an emergency meeting last night. Johnny Ray's the acting marshal now."

Jordan shook his head in disbelief. Power by attrition. The idea of it pretty much suited Johnny Ray's character. Something always told Jordan that Johnny Ray was a vulture, and the impression he had was not entirely because Johnny Ray tried to make extra spending money impersonating a dead man. Whenever there was food around, Johnny Ray took as much as he wanted, without concern for anyone else. And he always talked about getting his mother's house when she died, even though she was one of the healthiest seventy-year-olds Jordan had ever met.

He hadn't even thought about who would replace Holister. Holister was irreplaceable. But it made sense that the Town Board would appoint Johnny Ray acting marshal. He could see Johnny Ray standing up, the last fat kid in line, wanting desperately to be on the Wyatt Feed baseball team. *Pick me! Pick me!* And the Town Board had no choice, because he was the only cop left to pick. At least for the moment. "He wants to see you," Louella added.

"Good for him. I'm not on duty," Jordan said. He stared at the closed door to Holister's office, and then turned away from Louella and walked into his own office.

Dylan Kirsch was sitting on the floor playing with three small die-cast metal cars. The little boy looked up as Jordan stopped at the doorway, and then returned to his imaginary world, banging one car into another, over and over again, doing his best to add sound effects.

"How you doing, Dylan?" Jordan asked softly.

"My cars crashed."

"I can see that."

"I'm not supposed to go anywhere."

"Well," Jordan said, squatting down, ignoring the pain as he did. "That's probably a good idea. It's no fun here, though, is it?"

"It smells funny."

Jordan smiled. "It does." He hesitated. "Can I ask you a question, Dylan?"

Dylan shrugged his shoulders, twirled a little police car in his right hand, and made the sound of a siren.

"Did you tell your daddy you saw me the other night?"

Dylan shook his head. "No."

"Are you sure?"

The little boy shook his head again. "Yes," he said as his voice cracked.

Jordan drew in a deep breath. "All right, then." He stood up. "I gotta go."

"Are you going to see my grandpa? He's hurt."

"Not right now. He'll be all right, though. Your grandpa's

pretty strong." Jordan felt a pang of guilt ricochet in his stomach. He'd been lied to as his mother lay dying in the car. *"She's going to be fine,"* Holister had said to him as they put him in the ambulance next to Spider. He saw the irony in his statement as soon as he said it, but that didn't make the lie any easier.

"Do you promise?" Dylan asked.

"No, I can't promise you that. I wish I could. But I'll tell him you said hello when I see him. Is that all right?"

Dylan nodded, forced a smile, and then returned to playing with his cars.

Jordan turned to leave the office and came face to face with Johnny Ray.

CHAPTER 15

August 22, 2004, 8:09 A.M.

A half-eaten peanut butter and banana sandwich sat on the desk. Two more uneaten sandwiches wrapped in wax paper sat on a stack of papers next to a Diet Coke. Johnny Ray had already tacked up a picture of Elvis in his karate uniform on the bulletin board. Not much else had changed in Holister's office. Jordan wondered how long it would be before the black velvet portrait of The King in full Vegas regalia that was in Johnny Ray's office would be moved and hung behind Holister's desk. Holister would just go fucking ballistic if he walked in and found Johnny Ray at home in his office.

Johnny Ray ambled behind the desk and sat down heavily. "Have a seat, Mac," he said.

"I'll stand."

A half-smile crossed Johnny Ray's face. His trademark smirk. The promotion had obviously motivated the normally lethargic Johnny Ray. His uniform was neatly pressed, his silver badge polished, and his Elvis hair and pork chop sideburns were freshly trimmed and dyed coal black for the new gig.

"Sheriff Hogue will be glad you came in," Johnny Ray said.

"Why's that?"

"He, uh, wants me to detain you."

"Detain me?" Jordan hesitated. "Am I under arrest? Do I need a lawyer, Johnny Ray?"

Johnny Ray reached for the Diet Coke and took a swig. "I don't think that's necessary. The sheriff just wants to talk to you, Mac."

"You mean interrogate me." If Johnny Ray called him Mac one more time he was going to reach across the desk and slap him upside the head.

"Whatever you want to call it."

"You're enjoying this, aren't you?"

"Not really."

"Where's Hogue?" Jordan asked. He steadied himself by leaning forward on the chair that faced the desk. Anger rose steadily up the back of his neck. His muscles tensed, and the aspirin he'd taken earlier was already wearing off.

"I don't know where he's at."

"Well, have Louella find out."

"Calm down, Jordan."

"Look, you idiot, I didn't do anything. I didn't shoot Holister, and I sure as hell didn't have a meth lab in my house. Would I be standing here if I did? Or are you just as much of a fucking lunatic as Hogue is?"

"No need for name calling, Mac." Johnny Ray leaned back in his chair. To his credit, Johnny Ray seemed unruffled, at ease. That in itself was disconcerting to Jordan. Johnny Ray was usually pretty quick to fly off the handle. He'd drop into his Elvis persona and puff out his chest in two seconds if he felt threatened. But at the moment, he was more like a cat who'd eaten the family parrot, feathers sticking out of his mouth, denying he'd done anything wrong. "You really need to sit down," Johnny Ray said, his voice low, an octave deeper, the trill restrained.

Jordan ignored the command again.

"All right, have it your way. I need your badge."

The words hung in the air. Not that Jordan hadn't expected

to hear them; he was just shocked that he *was* actually hearing them. He looked away from Johnny Ray's stare and had an almost uncontrollable urge to pick up the peanut butter and banana sandwich and shove it into Johnny Ray's fat face. "You're not serious."

"Serious as a heart attack. You're suspended until further notice."

"Fuck."

Johnny Ray crossed his arms. "There's nothing I can do about it, Mac. It was the Town Board's decision. And I don't think they'll change their minds. At least until this mess is all cleaned up."

"I'm not giving you my badge."

"I didn't figure you would, but you're still suspended."

"There's a shooter out there, Johnny Ray. A smart, conniving shooter who hid in the weeds and shot Holister. I was there. I got shot, goddamn it. Explain that. Did I fucking shoot myself? Whoever it is is up to something. I don't think they're done yet. I think they burned down my house. You need me, damn it!"

"You don't look like you're in much shape to help out," Johnny Ray said, taking another sip of Diet Coke. "Why do you think, uh, this person, this shooter, isn't done yet? What do you think they're up to? You know something we don't?"

"Damn it, I don't know anything. If you're any kind of cop at all, think about it. Making me a suspect doesn't add up."

"The ballistics test will clear you then. And you have nothing to worry about, right? So you should just go along with the program. Cooperate. Talk to Hogue. It can't do no harm if you haven't done anything wrong."

"Did they find a lab in the house? Is that what this is about?"

"I don't know. Hogue wouldn't say. All he told me was the fire was obviously intentionally set."

"Big surprise. It was arson, at the very least. So, I purposefully set fire to my house? How in the fuck could I have done that when I was in the hospital in Morland?"

"Hogue's checking on that."

"Do you really think I'm capable of shooting Holister and setting fire to my grandmother's house, Johnny Ray? Jesus, even you know me better than that."

"I don't know *what* you're capable of, Jordan."

Jordan started to walk out the door but he stopped. "What about the bones? What about the skeleton, Johnny Ray? Don't you think it's a little odd that Holister called me out to the pond after finding the bones, and the shooter waited until we were both there to start firing? Why didn't they just shoot Holister when he showed up? If the bones really belong to Tito Cordova, like Holister thought, then maybe you ought to reopen *that* case instead of going along with Hogue, trying to pin this shit on me. What about the goddamn bones, Johnny Ray?"

Jordan looked over Johnny Ray's shoulder; the padlock was still on the gun cabinet. He really wanted to ask about the Cordova file, but he wasn't sure if Johnny Ray knew where Holister kept it locked up—and he damn sure wasn't going to be the one to tell him.

"That's an ongoing investigation, I can't comment," Johnny Ray said. The comfortable look on his face had changed. There was a look of confusion, mixed with a touch of anger, in his eyes, as if Jordan had told him something he didn't know.

Johnny Ray sat up in the chair, sweat forming on his lip, and started tapping his fingers on the desk. The air-conditioning had been running constantly, but Holister's office was still warm. The air was moving, but there was no hint of coolness to it, only the humidity had been drawn out of the air. A ceiling fan whirled overhead, the on and off chains clinking together. Louella's radio buzzed with unintelligible voices in the background.

"You didn't know Holister thought it was Tito, did you?"

"I said I can't comment."

"Did you?" Jordan insisted.

"No," Johnny Ray answered, lowering his eyes. "Jesus, after all these years."

"Exactly. Now tell me any of this makes sense?"

Johnny Ray exhaled. He stared at Jordan warily.

"Why don't you help me, Johnny Ray? Help Holister. Hogue's just going to use you, treat you like you're nothing."

"He put me in charge of watching you. And I'm supposed to show the INS agents around when they get here tomorrow."

Jordan saw a familiar look cross Johnny Ray's face: He'd just said more than he was supposed to. "Hogue doesn't have the power to put you in charge of anything. See what I mean, he's already at it. What's INS got to do with this, Johnny Ray?"

"I don't know."

"Bullshit. Tell me, goddamn it—Hogue's playing you, can't you see that?"

"The sheriff is leading the investigation. And I'm part of it."

"Then how come he didn't tell you about Tito Cordova? Why's the INS coming? It's too early for them to show up."

Johnny Ray exhaled and stared at Jordan. "They found a meth lab out at the pond. A small one. You know, a home-cooker. But Hogue mentioned he'd been working with some federal people tracking a distribution line from Texas to Chicago. Things picked up when the Mexicans came back this year. The DEA is working with INS to see if we have anybody connected here."

"So, he's got his eyes on a bigger prize. Damn it, I'm such a fool," Jordan said. "Hogue wants the shooting to go away so he can make a national name for himself by shutting down a major drug ring. He'd be a shoe-in for mayor, or something even more powerful." The thought solidified his hunch that Hogue was up to something by trying to pin the shooting on him. It gave him even more reason to focus on Tito and the shooting.

"I don't know nothing about that," Johnny Ray said. "He just asked for all of the missing people files we had. There are only three, but we can't find Tito's—Hogue's pissed about that. I didn't think anything about it until now, Holister's never been real organized. You know where it's at?"

"No," Jordan said. *Lying's becoming too easy,* he thought.

Johnny Ray shook his head. "Tito Cordova. Man, I haven't heard that name in years."

Holister didn't include Johnny Ray in the annual review of the case, and Jordan always figured it was because of the marshal's lack of confidence in him. He had to rethink that, now—question everything that had anything to do with Tito and Esperanza.

The memory of Johnny Ray participating in the search for Tito had not risen in Jordan's mind until that moment. There were so many people, so much going on then, that it was impossible to remember everything, but he was trying harder, trying to pull the memories into focus so he could find a clue, match it with the years of his own existence in Dukaine. It was impossible when he tried, but flashes were coming to him, little boxes opened when he encountered someone new, when he encountered someone who reacted to Tito's name being said out loud. Everyone revisited the past, their past, their version of what happened, what they did or didn't do. *The trick,* Jordan thought, *is to get people to tell me as much as possible.*

Tito was at the heart of everything that was going on, and perhaps the answer to what was happening now lay in the memory of someone who could remember something he couldn't, or tell him something, anything, big or small, that he didn't know had happened.

If he was going to get his life back, or any semblance of it,

Jordan knew he was going to have to find out what happened to Tito and Esperanza Cordova. Finding José was at the top of his list. But he had other things to do first. It would be easier to get people to talk to him if he wasn't a suspect in Holister's shooting. At least now he had an idea what Hogue was up to.

For a brief second, he thought about telling Johnny Ray about the note and medallion, but immediately knew it would be a bad idea. No matter how much he wanted things back to normal, it wasn't worth taking Johnny Ray into his confidence. He'd made that mistake before.

"You remember the search?" Jordan asked.

"Sure I do."

Jordan had a flash of Johnny Ray when he was a kid, before he idolized Elvis. He was a lonely fat kid. He had no brothers or sisters and lived on Wilson Street, across the street from the Catholic church. Johnny Ray's family belonged to the church, and Johnny Ray had been an altar boy. Jordan had seen him in his altar boy outfit once, a long white puffy tunic that kind of looked like a cape. He still lived in the same house with his mother. His father had worked as an accountant for the Sun-Ripe plant; he died ten years ago, wasting away with bone cancer in the front room.

And then he thought of Father Michael, a tall, white-haired man with a funny accent. Father Michael was from Boston and oversaw the small church with an iron hand. Jordan remembered being scared of the priest. Scared of the man in black. He had coffee and cigarette-stained teeth, and spoke in a sneering, pompous way that made you feel like you were slimy, sinners beyond redemption, not good enough to be in his presence. Migrants came and went from the church at all hours of the day and night. Father Michael always looked tired, and kept pretty much to himself. Kitty avoided the priest. The only thing she ever said about him was that they didn't believe in the same God.

Jordan and Johnny Ray were not friends, even then. Johnny Ray went to the private Catholic school in Morland. They played on the same baseball team, swam at Longer's Pond at the same time, but beyond that, they had nothing in common.

"Father Michael made all of us help," Johnny Ray said. "He never liked this town much. Especially after that."

Jordan remembered that there were trays of food on tables inside the volunteer fire department. Fried chicken. Cakes. Green beans that had been canned from the summer before. Coffee and hot chocolate to take the edge off the November wind. Father Michael stood next to Pastor Gleen, dishing up food for the searchers. Every time Jordan saw Johnny Ray, he was in the food line, never in the search line, never in the pickup trucks that transported searchers to and from the muddy fields.

"What happened to Father Michael?" Jordan asked.

"He went home after the diocese closed the church. Retired. He died a couple of years later. At least that's what I heard. I quit going to church around then."

After you found Elvis, Jordan thought. "That's the problem," he said. "A lot of people that would remember anything about Tito are dead. They went to church there, didn't they? Tito and his mother?"

"Yes," Johnny Ray said. He squirmed in the chair. "I really shouldn't be talking about this, Jordan. Not if them bones are Tito."

"Did you ever hear about Tito's father, who he was?"

Johnny Ray shook his head no. "His mother never took communion, and I never seen her at confession. I don't think she was allowed to. Maybe that was the reason, Tito not having a real father. But you know the rumors. Nobody ever said anything out loud, though. That kind of talk was forbidden in my house. One word against Buddy Mozel was like taking the Lord's name in vain. He'd fire anybody who speculated he was Tito's father—you know that."

"Did Tito take communion?"

"Why is that important?"

"I don't know—I'm just trying to figure things out."

"I don't remember."

"Did you ever talk to Tito? You saw him every Sunday. Were you friends?"

Johnny Ray stood up. His forehead was wet with sweat. "I told you, Jordan, I don't remember. I'm not talking about this anymore. I can't. Just give me your badge and go out and wait for Sheriff Hogue. I got a headache. I'm not talking anymore."

"I'm not giving you my badge, Johnny Ray. I got shot. My house got burned down. And I'm going to find the mother-fucker who shot Holister. You can help me—but if you won't do that, the least you can do is help Holister. You owe him that much."

"I am helping."

"Fine, help Hogue. But I guarantee you this: The ballistics test will clear me. Other evidence will clear me. Even if Hogue takes me in, which he can't at this point, I'll walk out of jail and be right back here, where I belong. And while you're sitting on your ass eating peanut butter and banana sandwiches, playing Mr. Big Shit, the shooter is still out there. How are you going to feel if he strikes again? Shoots somebody else? Or if Holister dies? Tell me none of that matters, Johnny Ray, and I'll leave you alone."

"Get of here, then. Just get out of my office." The Elvis trill returned with a vengeance.

Jordan ignored the claim of possession to Holister's office, other than it reignited his anger, threw a little more gas on the embers that were already about to flame up. "Where's Hogue?

We need to get some things straight. And, I'd like to talk to those INS agents myself."

"I told you, I don't know. Hogue's supposed to be here sometime this afternoon."

"I'll find him and get this straightened out. All I got to do is turn on the TV to figure out where he's at. My guess is he's out at the pond, anyway," Jordan said.

"They won't let you near it."

"We'll see about that. Get on the radio and tell him I'm heading his way."

Jordan couldn't remember the last time he was so angry. His mother's funeral? When he caught Monica? When Ginny broke it off with him and eloped with Ed Kirsch?

Those were all times when he was on the verge of losing control, but now—now he felt like beating the shit out of Johnny Ray, ramming his head into the nearest toilet. He wanted a piece of Hogue, too. Jordan knew if he got started, he wouldn't stop. He was frustrated. He wanted answers and he wanted to hurt something. And he wanted it bad. So, he turned away from Johnny Ray before it was too late, stalked out of the office, past Louella and into the blinding sunlight.

The heat had intensified, but Jordan didn't notice. He stopped, started to head toward the tavern, but went the other way. He knew he needed to calm down. He didn't want to talk to Spider. He didn't want to talk to anybody.

In the distance, the heat shimmered off the sidewalk, distorting his view of the street, the houses and the trees. They looked like a mirage, no matter how close you got to it, everything seemed even farther away, just out of reach. But Jordan walked forward anyway, taking the same path home he'd walked for years. Knowing with each step he took that Kitty's house wouldn't be there. His home was gone. The past was a big pile of ashes. The promise of an oasis in the desert was nothing but sand.

CHAPTER 16

August 22, 2004, 8:57 A.M.

Jordan stood at the corner of Lincoln and Harrison. He could see yellow police tape surrounding the house from a block away. Or what was left of the house. The roof had collapsed. Even from a distance there was nothing to see except three or four blackened poles that had supported the beams, standing straight in the air, monuments to the hardwood the house was built with. A white van was parked in front of the house with ARSON INVESTIGATION painted across the side in bold red letters. Two other cars, a county police cruiser and a black unmarked sedan, were parked in the driveway. The hum of air-conditioners and cicadas joined together, a loud resonating chorus rising and falling like a heartbeat, and drowned out the silence, the empty street, the screams inside Jordan's head.

He was frozen, couldn't move. It was like standing at the back of the funeral home, knowing he had to walk up to his mother's casket, but not wanting to, not wanting to believe he was there, that she was really dead. God, he didn't want to see death one more time. He didn't want to see the house, what was left of it, what was gone. Kitty's books, the piano, all of the family pictures.

The wound on his shoulder had begun to burn, throb with pain. He touched it, put pressure on it, but that only made the pain worse. Sunlight stabbed through the leaves of the tall oaks and elms that lined the street. There was no breeze, just the thick, heavy air that made the pavement sweat. His knees grew weak, and Jordan sat down on the curb.

He had been too young to consider his own mortality when the accident happened. All he understood then was that he had lost something very dear, that his life and Spider's life had changed forever. There was no way he could imagine his own death, not at twelve. But now, reality crept up on him. If the bullet had hit him a few inches to the left, it would have gone straight through his heart. No second chances, no time to change anything, no time for regrets. The curtain closed, and the world as he knew it, gone, swallowed up in darkness, game over.

The thought churned his stomach. He shivered, spit bile into the street, cupped his face, and felt a tear stream out of his right eye. Reflecting on his life was not a strong suit. If there was pain he numbed it with beer, with busyness. He probably should have gone back to the tavern, got Spider, and came to the house like he planned. He would've been strong then, put on a false face to hide his pain from Spider. But Johnny Ray had tapped his rage and brought it so close to the surface that it would've taken a lot more than a few beers to numb what he was feeling. Tears filled his hands and evaporated on the street. The cicadas laughed at him.

Everything was a jumble in his mind. Fleeting images of Tito Cordova walking alone on the road, head hung down, books under his arm. Esperanza at Miller's Grocery, standing in line, solemn, stiff as two migrants walked into the store, standing her ground against Maddie Miller behind the cash register. Buddy Mozel's black Lincoln torn and twisted, the front end smashed beyond recognition—just like Buddy's face. Ginny's body writhing under his, biting his shoulder, her fingernails raking across his back. Kitty waiting for him on the porch after school. Spider lying in piss on his bed. His mother playing the piano, Beethoven's *"Sonata Pathetique,"* on Sunday mornings. Easy summer days walking to Longer's Pond, swimming, laughing, wishing he were a grownup so he could do what he wanted, when he wanted. And Johnny Ray singing "Kentucky Rain" at the Super Six Motel, the last bass lines quivering in his memory.

The barren landscape of his marriage followed, a death unto itself. Monica on their wedding day, her eyes hopeful, her brown hair silky, perfect on her shoulders, a striking contrast to her white lace wedding gown. Silence and anger in the midst of their many arguments. The time two years into the marriage when they sat in front of a marriage counselor, his eyes glued to the floor, searching for an answer to the prickly woman's question: "Why are you so afraid of intimacy, Jordan? What are you scared of losing? Can't you see that Monica really loves you?" She tried with all of her might to unlock the bank of his tear ducts, but that vault was sealed shut.

The counselor's words echoed in his memory. He didn't have an answer then, and he didn't have one now. It was more than Ginny. Monica faded away. He could barely remember what her voice sounded like. Nine years of his life vacant, stuck in a pattern, his marriage like his job. A job that required little of him other than showing up, where one day meshed with the next, driving up and down the streets of Dukaine hoping to catch a glimpse of Ginny. Mostly his job was mundane; a complaint about a barking dog, migrants sleeping on private land, writing speeding tickets, Earl Crebbs beating the shit out of his wife again. And that was OK with him. He had very little aspiration for anything else. He was just passing the time, day after day. Eventually, he had thought, taking Holister's place as marshal would be in his future. Becoming an old man in Dukaine, working his way slowly to Haven Hill, into the plot reserved for him next to his mother.

He kept his hands cupped, the darkness shaded the bright sunlight. He had little awareness of himself, of a grown man sitting on the curb crying.

Monica knew about Ginny. But she didn't know everything. Nobody knew everything. Not even Holister. And that hurt worst. That hurt the worst, now.

Jordan had kept his memories of Holister at bay, afraid to look at them. There were so many. Beyond the car wreck, especially once he went to live with Kitty. Simple things like Holister mowing the yard in his work pants and an undershirt on a summer evening. The many Christmases, knowing the holidays were the darkest for Jordan, when Holister would force him to help string lights on the house. Taking him sledding when it snowed. Stepping into Big Joe's shoes, but somehow staying out of the middle, somehow not trying to be his father, but always willing to be his friend. A mentor in the police station, and an advice giver when things were going south with Monica. Holister had always been there. Always. Even when things with Ginny got bad. Even when Holister caught them together on the cot in the basement when Jordan was sixteen, and they had got into a fight that had threatened everything.

Holister's words at the pond came to mind. "Tell Celeste I'll make things right," he had said. "Tell Ginny it was my fault."

Jordan didn't know what Holister meant then, and he was even more uncertain now. What did Holister have to make right? What was his fault? What had Holister done to his wife and daughter that his last words, or his potential last words, were steeped in a painful apology?

Like every other question that came to mind, he didn't have an answer. The questions were dots that needed connecting, and beyond hoping to find the truth, Jordan hoped to find the one thing that had eluded him: a clue leading to the identity of the shooter. He really needed to get ahold of the Cordova file, refresh his memory—see if he could find more details about Esperanza. The details Holister had kept hidden, even from him. And, the hard part: finding out if Buddy Mozel was truly Tito Cordova's father. Somehow it made sense, and for some reason, Jordan felt in his gut that that was where the motive existed to the shooting. He had to see that file to make sure. And he had to get Hogue off his ass.

He took a deep breath, opened his eyes, and uncupped his hands. Spider was right, now was not the time to shift through the ashes. He needed to get ahold of himself. In an odd way, he was beginning to feel refreshed. Fuck Johnny Ray. Fuck the Town Board. He could prove his innocence with the note and medallion. The ballistics test would exonerate him. There was no way the timing of the fire could be traced to him. He was in Morland, in the hospital, and on his way home. Hogue was grabbing at air, making something out of nothing to make himself look good, to ease the fears of everyone, assure them that there wasn't a madman running loose in Dukaine shooting policemen and setting houses on fire. Hogue was wrong, and the sheriff had known it from the beginning.

The arson van pulled away. Jordan reached for a cigarette and lit it. Sweat rolled off his forehead. He grabbed a handkerchief out of his back pocket and wiped his face, and took a deep hit off the cigarette. He exhaled, focused on relaxing.

A helicopter thumped in the distance, growing closer. The laughter of the cicadas was drowned out, and a brief wind whipped the leaves as the helicopter passed overhead, flying south, toward Indianapolis, at high speed. The chopper was painted bright red, a white stripe down the side with the number 8 plastered on the tail. A television news helicopter rushing back to the station with a story. An update at noon? Or was their work done? There was no way to know, but the chopper looked like a dragonfly fleeing a kingbird. Whatever the news,

Jordan sensed it was urgent, not good. Perhaps the perky little bitch that interviewed Hogue finally got her scoop.

The county cruiser and unmarked sedan backed out of the driveway and followed the van. He watched them drive slowly down Harrison, in the opposite direction from him, and turn left on Tyler Street, probably taking the back way out of town, the shortcut to Morland.

A siren warbled in the distance, far away, to the south. He couldn't tell if it was coming or going. Jordan decided to go back to the tavern and get Spider. He took another puff of the cigarette and ground it out with his boot. Going to the house seemed to be a stupid exercise that would only bring more pain. It was no longer an option. He could see from here that there was nothing left. The time would come to shift through the ashes, but it wasn't now. Answers from the arson investigation was all he needed.

It was time to find Hogue. José would have to wait.

He stood up a little too fast, his vision blurry, a little dizzy. A car stopped on Lincoln Street at the stop sign behind him, the engine rumbling. The car was loud, like it had a hole in the muffler, and the driver revved the engine to get his attention.

His throat was parched. A grasshopper lit on his shoulder. Jordan brushed the insect off and caught a glimpse of the car out of the corner of his eye. It was an old El Camino, mid-70s, dark brown with the wheel-wells rusted out, the rear-end jacked-up with air shocks. Ed Kirsch was sitting behind the steering wheel. "I've been looking for you, McManus."

"Looks like you found me," Jordan said. "How's Holister?"

Ed put the car in park and left the engine idling. Wisps of blue smoke trickled upward out of the tailpipes, dual-exhaust with chrome extenders.

"I don't know, and at the moment I don't fucking care," Ed said. He opened the door and pulled his lanky frame out of the

El Camino. A ten-inch metal pipe dangled from his right hand.

Jordan tensed when he saw the pipe, realized Ed's intent. For a fleeting moment, he thought about running. He looked beyond Ed, considered bolting to Corney Lefay's house and beating on the door, but he doubted he could make it, that he could outrun Ed. The thought vanished as quickly as it came. Running never ended anything. Running only prolonged the eventual outcome. He knew this was coming. "I take it you got a problem with me," he said.

"Yeah, you're my problem, McManus. You always have been," Ed answered, walking toward him. His eyes were glazed, a wildness in them Jordan had seen before when busting a meth house.

"You better just stop right there." The tone of Jordan's voice dropped an octave into cop mode. Everything, his body, his thoughts, turned to forming an exit strategy, apprehending the suspect without getting hurt.

"Looks like you're on your own, now. No badge, no radio, no backup. It's just you and me, McManus."

Jordan backed up onto the curb. "Why don't you drop the pipe and fight like a real man?"

"Why don't you shut up? You been fucking my wife. What do you know about being a real man?" Ed said, his teeth clenched, his breathing heavy. Five feet from Jordan, he took a swing at him with the pipe and lunged at him at the same time.

Jordan jumped out of the way. But he felt the breeze off the pipe, could smell Ed's sweat. "You're making a big mistake, Ed."

"You made the mistake by messing with Ginny."

"Good thing I didn't mess with your little waitress friend at the truck stop then, isn't it?" He got his footing, planted his feet.

Ed stopped.

"Who's been fucking who, Ed? You think Ginny doesn't know

what's going on when you're supposed to be out on the road?" Jordan said.

Ed Kirsch's face turned red. Jordan could see the anger rising from his throat up to his beady brown eyes. He knew he only had a second or two to put things on even footing, so he reached behind him as he took another step backward, and pulled the .38 from the holster.

"Now, motherfucker," Jordan said, aiming the gun at Ed's forehead. "Lose the pipe. Lose the fucking pipe."

Ed laughed. "You ain't gonna shoot me, McManus."

Jordan pulled back the hammer with his thumb. Click. "I told you you were making a mistake." Sweat rolled over his eyes, the salt stung. A mosquito bit the back of his neck. He was numb. Any pain he had before Ed showed up was forgotten, lost in the moment of trying to survive.

The only thing Jordan could hear was his heartbeat thumping a million beats a minute.

"Leave her alone, McManus. Just leave her alone."

It was a concession and Jordan knew it. Ed's shoulder slumped an inch, his breathing lessened. Rock, paper, and scissors: a .38 beat a metal pipe every time.

"Not a problem, Ed, I'll leave her alone as long as you pay her some attention and quit fucking around on her."

"You don't get it, do you, McManus?"

"I'm a little hard-headed."

Jordan blinked, wiped his eye with his free hand.

Ed threw the pipe at him. Jordan dodged it, but the tip of the pipe caught him on the shoulder. Pain shot through his arm, and he staggered backward with a gasp. Ed rushed him, tackled him. As they fell to the ground, the gun fired.

The bullet hit the sidewalk, missing Ed. The retort echoed in Jordan's ear. Ed grabbed his wrist, trying to wrestle the gun from his grip. They rolled on the ground, Ed on top of him. Ed punched him in the stomach, knocking the air out of him, but Jordan held onto the gun.

Never let go of your weapon. Never. Or you're a dead man.

Jordan kneed Ed in the crotch, elbowing him in the face at the same time. Blood exploded from Ed's nose. He could hear the cartilage snapping, a thousand little bones stabbing the inside of Ed's face at the same time.

Ed screamed and rolled off Jordan.

Jordan bounded up to his feet and staggered back, pointing the .38 at Ed's chest, holding his shoulder at the same time, panting heavily. "You move another inch, fucker, and you're a dead man!"

Ed groaned, his hands covering his face, blood gushing between his fingers, like his jugular had been cut, the nuts cut off a pig. Rage filled Ed's eyes. "No, you're the dead man."

Jordan backed up, bumped into a tree. He pulled the hammer back again, lining another round up with the barrel. The line had already been crossed. He had no choice but to shoot Ed Kirsch. A breath escaped his lungs as he put his finger on the trigger.

"Put the gun down, Jordan!" a voice behind him yelled.

Everything went silent. The cicadas had stopped their taunting song. No sirens or helicopters made any noise in the distance. Only the reverberation of the voice bounced inside his head. It made everything inside of him stop, made everything inside of him go cold.

"I said, put the goddamn gun down, Jordan!" Big Joe McManus yelled. "Put it down now!"

CHAPTER 17

September 21, 1991, 2:15 P.M.

Jordan sat in the backseat of Charlie Overdorf's car, the door open, smoking a cigarette, occasionally taking a swig of beer from the bottle he hid between his legs. "Come on, man, let's go," he yelled to Spider. Time was ticking. Weekends were short when you were still in high school.

"Not until I miss," Spider said. He was in his wheelchair at the free throw line, eyeing the rim, the square of the backboard, dribbling the ball without concentration, without looking. He wore a red plaid flannel shirt, unbuttoned, over a white T-shirt. Kitty had bought him the shirt for his twenty-first birthday, which was the day before.

"We could be here all day," Jordan answered.

"So? What's the big fuckin' hurry?" In a swift, flawless motion, Spider aimed the basketball, released it into the air, and watched it glide perfectly through the rim, swishing the net. He raised both arms up in the air, clenched his fists, and yelled, "Yes. Nothin' but net, fuckers. How many is that?"

"Forty-two," Charlie Overdorf said as he grabbed the ball from behind the goal and tossed it back to Spider.

"A new world record!" Spider said, catching the ball, spinning the wheelchair in a circle, the front wheels off the ground.

A cool autumn breeze whipped up a pile of scarlet oak leaves and scattered them across the basketball court at the elementary school. The afternoon sun beamed overhead. Hard skeins of light poked through cumulous clouds in the distance, spotlighting distant tomato fields. The quietness of a normal Saturday was evident beyond the continual bounce of a basketball as Spider lined up for another shot.

"Charlie said he'd let me drive," Jordan said, climbing out of the beat-up Electra 225. He'd got his driver's license a year before, just after he turned sixteen, and always wanted to drive. He loved it. It didn't matter if all he did was drive up and down the streets of Dukaine in Kitty's Oldsmobile, there was no way he could ever be bored driving. The freedom he felt behind the wheel was akin to riding his bike the first time, when he could go anywhere in town he wanted to go. Only now the distances were farther, the means quicker, his taste for speed unquenchable, restrained only by his lack of wheels, his lack of a car of his own, that he wanted desperately. According to Kitty, Jordan was not going to get a car until he graduated from high school.

Spider stopped dribbling the ball. "Are you fuckin' nuts, Charlie? I'm not ridin' with him."

Charlie scrunched his shoulders as a goofy look crossed his face. Charlie's eyes were set a little far apart on his face and any time he tried to smile, or show an expression, his eyes looked like they were staring sideways. Other than that, he was a normal, tall, brown-haired kid with a good complexion. But he blamed his eyes for his continual lack of a girlfriend.

"What're you afraid of, Spider? I'm a good driver," Jordan said. He tossed the cigarette, chugged the remainder of the beer, and walked to the center of the court.

"How many beers you had?" Spider asked.

"Two," Jordan said.

"Liar," Charlie said. "He had three."

"Like I said, I'm not ridin' with him. I ain't got any legs, I sure as hell don't want to lose my arms, too. What time is it?"

"Almost two-thirty," Charlie said.

"Shit. We better go. I'm supposed to be at the tavern by four," Spider said. "My record will have to stand until another day."

"I'm going home then," Jordan said.

"You better not let Kitty smell beer on your breath or my ass is grass," Spider said.

"She hasn't got a clue about what I do."

"Yeah, right." Spider wheeled himself to the passenger side of the car and opened the door. He hoisted himself up with the strength of a gymnast doing an iron cross and flopped into the seat. Jordan folded up the wheelchair and hoisted it into the trunk. He staggered backward before he sat it down, drawing laughs from inside the car.

"You're in great shape to put one over on Kitty—I think you better just stay with us for a little while," Spider said.

"Shut the fuck up," Jordan said, slamming the trunk.

"You're not man enough to make me."

"Would you two knock it off?" Charlie said.

"Chill out, we're just fuckin' around," Spider said.

"One of you is."

Anger hardened Jordan's face, and stiffened his walk. He got in the car, slammed the door, and hit the button to lower the electric window. Some days he wished he and Spider could go at it, throw some fists, and get their fucking fight over with. But that was never going to happen.

"Time to roll," Charlie said, digging in the ashtray for a roach.

"I'm tellin' ya," Spider said, pulling a tiny joint out of his pocket. "Last one. We need to go see if we can score another bag before I go to work. Bad thing is, there's only one place to go right now."

Charlie shot Spider a sideways glance. "Gotta do what you gotta do."

"I hate buying off that motherfucker," Spider hesitated, stared out the window for a second. "Let's go."

"Excellent," Charlie said. He slapped in a cassette tape, Honeyboy Edwards, *Devil's Train,* into the player mounted underneath the dash. A slow four-note riff thumped the speakers, and Honeyboy Edwards's bluesy voice sprang forth, promising a good time as the riff rounded off in a bend and flurry of quarter notes. The smell of pot immediately filled the car.

"Yeah, man, now that's what I'm talking about," Spider said. "Where'd you get that tape? I can't wait to start playing the kind of music I like, once the old man turns over the tavern to me."

"When's he leaving?" Jordan asked.

"He's packing. Soon, I guess."

"Not soon enough," Jordan muttered under his breath.

"My cousin in Chicago sent me the tape," Charlie answered. "I can hook you up with him. He knows a lot of the old dudes who still play in the clubs."

"Cool."

Charlie eased the car out of the parking lot and headed west on Lincoln Street. He held the joint between the seats, offering it to Jordan. "You want any of this? Bogart here'll smoke it all if you don't take it now."

Jordan shook his head. He preferred beer. Pot made him sleepy, and it was something he knew he just didn't like. His mind wandered aimlessly, he obsessed over hopelessly small things, grew sad quickly. With a couple of beers he felt lighter, relaxed; the recipe worked for him, it tasted good, and sometimes it seemed as if he could never drink enough to quench his thirst. Spider was always good for a couple of beers, but he was also leery of getting caught providing beer to Jordan—Spider's only rule was that he had to be around when Jordan was drinking.

"I'll have another beer," Jordan said.

"You're done, pal." Spider turned around from the front seat and gave Jordan his "I'm the big brother . . . and you'll do what I say," stare.

Jordan gave him the finger. Spider slapped the universal fuck-you sign away. Jordan reached back and smacked Spider upside the head. He hit him a little harder than he'd intended, and pulled back immediately, then fell back into the seat out of Spider's reach.

Charlie exhaled loudly. "Would you two knock it off? Jesus! You're worse than two four-year-olds."

"I ought to beat the shit out of you," Spider said.

"How you going to do that?" Jordan laughed.

"Pull the car over, Charlie," Spider demanded. "I've had enough of his shit. It's time the little punk learned a lesson."

"How you going to catch me?" Jordan persisted, grabbing hold of the door handle, ready to flee.

"You can't outrun Charlie. He'll hold you down, and I'll do the punching. Think about that, fucker," Spider said.

"Shit," Charlie said suddenly, in a tone that drew Spider's attention away from Jordan.

"What?" Spider asked.

As Charlie turned left on Kennedy and headed toward Main Street, he slowed the Electra to a crawl. "It's Holister."

Jordan rose up in the seat, peered between the front seats, and saw the white police cruiser sitting at the corner of Kennedy and Main.

Charlie turned down the music, Honeyboy's voice fading to static, and hit the button that rolled down all of the windows. "Be cool," he said, pushing the Buick back up to normal speed. Cool air washed the pot aroma out the window.

Charlie stopped at the stop sign, pulled right up next to the police car, and waved at Holister. Holister nodded. Charlie hit the turn signal and slowly turned right onto Main Street, heading west toward the plant.

"Oh, man," Charlie said. "He's following us. What should I do, Spider?"

"Just keep driving," Spider said, watching the rearview mirror closely.

Jordan's heart was beating rapidly. It was difficult to resist the urge to look behind him, to see Holister following them. A million scenarios jumped through Jordan's mind. Getting caught drinking was one thing, deep shit for sure, but getting caught with pot in the car was another. Holister had little tolerance for drugs. And at the moment, he had little tolerance for Jordan—a week earlier Holister had caught Ginny and him in the basement making love. Holister damn near kicked Jordan's ass, grabbed him by the scruff of the neck and dragged him up the stairs. Jordan's big mistake was taking a swing at Holister—he caught the marshal right under the chin and sent him tumbling back down the stairs. Holister broke his wrist in the fall and had a cast on his arm—and the marshal still hadn't decided if he was going to press charges, but he did write up a report.

Jordan figured the report was to scare him—which it did. But not enough to stay away from Ginny. Nothing could cause that. He'd loved her for so long, and they were finally together as more than friends—he'd do anything to be near her. He just wished Ginny felt the same way he did. She was embarrassed to be seen in public with him because he was so much younger than she was. Every time he was around Ginny, he thought he was going to burst.

"Thank God," Charlie said, exhaling loudly. "Good thing he didn't see Romeo in the backseat or he would've stopped us for sure. I got to give it to you, though, Jordan, for taking down Holister."

Jordan looked through the back window and saw Holister turn into the Sunoco station. "Shut the fuck up, Charlie."

"That was close," Spider said, laughing.

"Ginny Coggins," Charlie said, shaking his head. "You think you were the first, Jordan? Think again. Ginny is easy street, man. I wouldn't touch her if she offered it to me on a silver platter."

"Bullshit," Spider said.

"Shut up, Charlie, you're making me mad," Jordan said.

"What are you going to do, kick *my* ass? I seen you fight with Sam Peterson." Charlie laughed and turned the music back up as they passed by the SunRipe plant, passed by the city limits sign. He punched the accelerator and air whooshed inside the car, bringing a chill inside the Electra as they headed out into the country.

Jordan dug into his pocket, lit a cigarette, and rolled up his window to just a crack. He told himself Spider and Charlie were just jealous . . . but he knew Charlie was partly telling the truth. Ginny had been with other guys—she'd told him as much, but wouldn't say who. Jordan, though, had lost himself to Ginny. She was his first, his only one, as far as he was concerned. He'd run away with her tomorrow if she would—then they'd both be free of the suffocating, boring small town they lived in. They could see the world together if Ginny would love him as much as he loved her.

The music moaned with Honeyboy's throaty black voice, and Jordan felt the intensity of the lyrics, slowly remembering a day, a long time ago, when he visited the camps, and had been warned by a little Mexican girl that the devil was coming to take them all away. He shivered at the memory.

The fields rolled by in a haze. The three beers, mixed with the pot smoke, had left Jordan numb. He didn't gain any clarity until Charlie passed Lem Jacobson's house and turned down another familiar road and rounded a curve.

Charlie slowed down as they passed by Tito Cordova's

abandoned house, and threw an empty beer bottle in the front yard.

Jordan sat up in the backseat.

"What's the matter?" Spider asked.

"Nothing," Jordan said. "That house gives me the creeps."

"That house gives everybody the creeps," Spider said.

Charlie drove for another mile, turned farther into the country, away from town, and finally pulled the Electra to a stop in front of the Kirschs' house.

The house didn't look like it had been painted in years. White flecks of paint dotted the clapboard siding and half of the windows had water-stained plywood nailed to them. The screen door was ajar, and the front door was open. Loud heavy metal music rose and fell rapidly, twice the speed of Honeyboy Edwards. A black mutt lay on the porch, its ears up, a low growl growing in its throat. The dog had splotches of bare skin on its legs, and a few fresh wounds like it had been in a fight recently. Probably with a coyote.

Charlie turned off the engine and jumped out. Spider clicked the tape off and swiveled around. "You stay here. Ed gets nervous with too many people around."

"No problem," Jordan said.

Charlie opened the trunk and wheeled the chair to the passenger door. He grabbed Spider's wrist and popped him into the chair in one fluid motion.

Jordan watched Charlie pull Spider backward onto the porch effortlessly, as if they had been performing circus tricks together since they were kids. He realized that Charlie and Spider had their own language, too. He'd never noticed it before.

Charlie spoke to the dog, said its name, which Jordan couldn't decipher over the music, and knocked on the door. A shadow appeared behind the screen, nodded, and Charlie pushed Spider inside.

Jordan tossed the cigarette out onto the barren yard. Four vehicles were parked haphazardly in front of the house. A one-car garage stood next to the house, tilted, as if it were ready to fall over. Two rusted fifty-five-gallon drums sat in front of the garage filled with unburned trash. Old tires were stacked on the far side of the garage. After about ten minutes, Charlie wheeled Spider back outside. Ed Kirsch followed, along with Ginny, tagging close behind.

Jordan slumped down in the seat, but eyed Ginny closely. When she leaned up and kissed Ed, he started beating the back of the driver's seat as hard he could with his fists.

Spider and Charlie laughed all the way back to the car.

September 21, 1991, 11:15 P.M., *Patzcuaro, Mexico*

The large dormitory room had been dark for over an hour. Tito slowly moved his hand under his bed and pulled out a small bundle of clothes wrapped in a sheet he had stolen from the laundry a week before. The boy in the next bed stirred.

"What are you doing, Tito?" Cirilo Cruz whispered. Cirilo had only been at *El Refugio* for a year, but he and Tito had become fast friends even though Cirilo was three years younger. Tito remembered how scared he was when he arrived in the creaky old building, and could not ignore the boy's pain in the bed next to him. Cirilo's parents had crossed the border and never returned—they had suffocated in the back of a semi-truck that had broken down in the desert. When Cirilo's grandmother died, he was sent to live with the nuns. Cirilo cried for the first month, and then slowly began to accept Tito's offer of friendship.

Tito pointed his finger to his lip. *"Me estoy yendo,"* he said. I'm leaving.

"But where will you go?" Cirilo asked in Spanish. "You are

only a boy. You're only fourteen, not near old enough to be a man on your own."

"I cannot wait any longer," Tito said, a forlorn look crossing his face. "The nuns would have me be a priest or a peasant, and I am neither. I do not belong here. I am going home."

"To America? To this place you call Dukaine?"

Tito nodded. *"Sí."*

"But you can't go by yourself. It is too dangerous. I will come with you," Cirilo said.

"You are too young. I am going alone." Tito dropped the tone of his voice and stared at Cirilo. Even with only a small amount of moonlight filtering through the windows, Tito could see tears welling up in his friend's eyes. "Someday, maybe, I will be able to come back and get you—take you back to America with me."

"To paradise? You would come back for me?"

"This is paradise," Tito said. "Look at the birds in the sky, the mountains behind the town—and the nuns love us all very much. I have never been afraid here, not once I got used to it. But it will never be my home. My memories are too strong. My original language fades. I can barely see my mother's face in my dreams anymore. If I wait any longer, all of my memories will be gone. I must see her face again, breath the same air I once did."

"I will be afraid without you," Cirilo said. He stood up and hugged Tito.

Tito withdrew quickly. "You will wake the others. Tell the nuns nothing of this. I want to get as far away as I can tonight before they come looking for me. Will you do that, Cirilo, my *amigo?* There are men on the other side that hurt me, that brought me to this place. I cannot explain the feelings in my stomach to you, but I must understand what happened. I cannot forgive, as the nuns instruct me to—I cannot quiet the monster who speaks to me at night and begs me to pick up a sword and slay all that have brought harm to me and the one I love."

"But your mother is dead."

"I have never believed that." Tito leaned over and kissed his friend on top of the head. "We will meet again, Cirilo, I promise. *Adiós.*"

Before Cirilo could object anymore, Tito edged away from the bed, tossed the makeshift linen sack over his shoulder, and let the shadows of the large room swallow him up. He turned back as he ducked out the door to catch one last glimpse of his friend, standing fearful in the dark. It was all he could do not to cry himself.

The sounds of night welcomed Tito, as if they agreed with his plan. The crickets' chirps heightened into a productive chorus, as owls and other night birds hooted and buzzed in the black sky. With their song so loud his footsteps would not be heard. He knew if he was lucky, he could travel ten miles along the road north . . . and perhaps by first light, find a farmer's shed to sleep away the day. He did not worry about money or food. He had learned many of the Mexican customs since coming to *El Refugio,* and many of the foods he needed would be growing in the fields—there for the taking at night. Being a thief did not worry him, either. He did not think it a sin to make his way home. And the nuns had taught him that God would provide. The meek would inherit the earth. If they were right, then all would be well. He trusted them . . . as much as he could trust anyone.

But he did worry about the journey, about the long miles to San Luis Potosi. From there he would have to get to Monterrey, and then to Nuevo Lareado . . . where he would have to cross the border. The stories of Nuevo Lareado were enough to frighten anyone—stories of slavery, and murderers, and highwaymen that robbed from the old and desperate. He would have to face those fears when the time came—he knew he was young and weak. For now, though, he knew he must get as far away from *El Refugio* as possible. The nuns did not take lightly to runaways. That was his worry. He knew what would happen if he was caught.

As Tito walked out of the gate an owl flew from the ceiba tree, and its shadow passed over him as a light turned on in the Mother Superior's room. If there was ever a time that he wished his nickname, *El Fantasma,* was true—it was now. He ran north as fast as he could, hugging the shadows, avoiding any noise, any human, not turning to look behind him until dawn started to break in the east.

CHAPTER 18

August 22, 2004, 9:59 A.M.

Big Joe pulled the rental car to the curb, parking it in front of the tavern. Jordan stared at him, the interior of the car silent. He hadn't seen his father in thirteen years.

"You gonna tell me what that was about, or do I have to guess?" Big Joe said.

When he was young, Big Joe McManus could fill a room when he walked in. Now, his thick black hair had turned white, as solid as snow on top of a mountain peak, and thinning like vapors—like retreating clouds. His skin was dark and leathery from the Florida sun, and his body was leaner, but Big Joe would never be skinny. He wore a light blue polo shirt, khaki pants, and sunglasses shielded his eyes. Jordan barely recognized him, but there had been no mistaking his voice.

"What're you doing here?" Jordan asked.

"It seemed the right time to come back."

"Who called you?"

"What do you mean, who called me?"

"Spider said you called him. Somebody had to call you and tell you what was going on. That Holister got shot. That I got shot."

"Louella called. She thought I should know you were hurt."

Jordan stared out the window. His shoulder ached. Blood seeped out from underneath the bandage, staining Spider's shirt. "And that's why you're really here?"

Big Joe clenched the steering wheel with both hands. "I didn't come back for an inquisition. What the hell are you implying?"

Jordan grabbed the door handle, preparing to exit the car. The air conditioner was on full force. The pain was now intense, and he was not certain that Ed Kirsch was finished with him.

Big Joe had given Ed a chance to make a run for the El Camino once Jordan dropped the .38. Ed had squealed his tires and drove off in a cloud of blue smoke.

"I'm not implying anything. Just asking a question. What do you think happened to Tito Cordova? Did what happened between you and Buddy Mozel have something to with all of this?" Jordan asked.

"Excuse me?"

"You heard me."

"What's that got to do with anything? Buddy and I had a score to settle. We settled it out of court. I paid off the bar and made sure your brother had a job for the rest of his life, if that's what you mean," Big Joe said.

"And Buddy's hardly been seen since the accident."

"What happened to him or how he handled it isn't my problem," Big Joe said. "He deserved what he got. Like I said, what's Tito Cordova got to do with anything?"

"Maybe nothing. Maybe everything."

Big Joe let go of the steering wheel, his face flush, the deep wrinkle lines at the corners of his eyes almost vanishing as he narrowed his glare. "I don't know what's been going on around here. But that's old news. The past. That kid disappearing doesn't have a damn thing to do with the present." He paused, looked into the tavern window. "Why is it every time we're in each other's presence it turns into an argument? I haven't been home in years and the first thing you do is accuse me of something I had nothing to do with. When are you going to grow up?"

Jordan watched Big Joe's temples throb, heard the tension rise in his voice, and saw a familiar angry look erupt in his father's eyes. In a flash, Jordan was a twelve-year-old boy crumbled up next to his mother's casket. He wasn't afraid of Big Joe then, and he sure as hell wasn't afraid of him now. "I'm not accusing you of anything. Just asking a question. All hell breaks loose, and you decide to show up unannounced. Just seems a little strange to me. I don't get it."

"Spider knew I was coming. He didn't tell you?"

"Obviously not." Jordan opened the door. The heat reached inside the car immediately, and his own anger was growing, rising against the numbness he'd felt since he heard his father's voice.

Just when he was feeling comfortable, starting to totally trust Spider, he found out nothing has changed. A hidden line of communication with their father still existed, a bond that would always be there. And Jordan would always be left on the outside. "You didn't answer my question," he said.

"You didn't answer mine, either. Why in the hell were you about to put a bullet in Ed Kirsch's head? You been messing around with Ginny again?"

"Looks like you got it all figured out. Now answer my question," Jordan said, hoisting himself up out of the car. He leaned his head back inside and waited for an answer. "What happened to Tito Cordova? Did Holister have something to do with it? Did you?"

He wasn't sure if Spider had told Big Joe about the note and medallion, and he wasn't going to bring it up if he hadn't.

Big Joe put the car in gear and shook his head. "You always were a smartass. Took after your grandmother, always sticking your nose where it didn't belong. I bet you're just like her. You got a soft spot for wetbacks, too, Jordan?" His tone was cold. Cold as a winter day standing in a cemetery.

Jordan barely had time to stand back as Big Joe sped away, the door slipping from his grasp, banging closed.

"Son of a bitch. You're a son of a bitch!" he yelled. Ginny's words echoed in his memory, calling him the same thing. "I'm nothing like you, goddamn it. Nothing!"

The car headed straight down Main Street, and Jordan realized as he watched it that it was the same black sedan he'd seen backing out of the driveway. Big Joe had either been looking for him, or he was up to something. His gut told him that the latter was true.

"Damn it," he said as he kicked the curb and walked into the tavern.

Spider was sitting at the bar in his usual spot. "What happened to you now?"

Jordan walked straight to the bar. "Why didn't you tell me he was coming? Why the hell didn't you tell me?" he asked, pointing through the window at the vacant stoplight.

Spider leaned back in the wheelchair. "Because I knew how you'd react. What was I gonna do, tell Big Joe not to come? Sure, like that's going to happen."

"You coulda told me."

"Look, man, you can be pissed at me all you want. You had enough shit going on. Tellin' you Big Joe was coming home was like . . . well, throwing gas on the fire."

"Not funny."

"Not trying to be," Spider said. "Now what the hell happened?"

Jordan leaned against the bar and took a heavy breath. The air-conditioning was on full blast, the air cool and dry. Angel was banging around in the kitchen, the radio turned up loud.

"Johnny Ray wanted my badge. The Town Board suspended

me," Jordan said, taking a cigarette out of his pocket.

"Your shoulder's bleeding."

"I'm all right." He lit the cigarette, ignoring the pain, the blood. "Give me a beer."

Spider raised an eyebrow, wheeled himself to the cooler, pulled out a bottle of Budweiser, popped the top off, and slid it in front of Jordan.

He took a swallow, then another. "I was mad. So mad I couldn't see straight. Fucking Johnny Ray's an idiot. He looked like a smiling cat."

"That dude just weirds me out. Always has," Spider said.

"I walked to the house. But I couldn't do it. I couldn't go see it. So I sat down on the curb at Lincoln. Ed Kirsch showed up and came after me with a pipe," Jordan said, finishing off the beer.

"See, I told you he was a hothead. I *knew* he was going to come after you."

Jordan told Spider the rest of the story. The fight. Putting his finger on the trigger, wanting more than anything to shoot Ed between the eyes. But Big Joe showed up.

Spider stared at him, didn't say anything for a minute. "You and Ed aren't done yet."

"I know. I'm beginning to think he might be more involved in this mess than I thought."

"Why?"

"I don't know—Ed was manic, probably stoned. Maybe he's just on a tear because I slept with Ginny, but right now it feels like more. If a meth line's running through Dukaine, Ed's probably in the middle of it. Maybe Hogue is getting close to home?"

Spider shook his head no. "Ed's not going to be in the same room with the Mexicans. And I guarantee you that's where that crap is coming from. He's small time, always has been, you know that. This meth thing is bigger than you think. You fucked his wife in *his* bed—that's enough to send anybody off the deep end. It did you."

"You're right," Jordan said, ignoring the reference to Monica. "Johnny Ray said the INS and the DEA were coming here. Hogue's been working with them, tracing the distribution. If he makes the case and brings down the supply, he's a shoe-in for mayor."

"Or any other office he might want."

"He is a greedy bastard," Jordan said. "Who knows what his plans are—but I think the shooting, the discovery of the bones is a distraction. He needs to solve it quickly so he can get on to bigger and better things."

"And you're the scapegoat?"

"I was in the wrong place at the wrong time."

"Maybe," Spider said. "Look, I didn't want to get too involved, but I'm going to make a call—see if I can find out if Hogue and Ed Kirsch have anything to do with each other these days. Maybe you're right. Maybe Ed's in deeper than I think."

Jordan drew a sigh of relief. "Who are you going to call?"

"I'd rather not say," Spider said.

Jordan knew Spider wasn't going to name his pot supplier, and he wasn't going to push it. At least, not at the moment. "Thanks."

"No problem. And, I'd say I'm sorry for not telling you Big Joe was coming home, but I'm not. Regardless of what you believe, he does give a shit about you. You're his son."

"This doesn't have anything to do with that," Jordan said, stubbing out the cigarette.

"I don't know, man, maybe it does. The old man isn't getting any younger. Maybe it's time to lay down the swords."

"Really? Is that what you think? That this is a chance for a happy fucking family reunion?"

"I don't know what to think," Spider said. "What you gonna do now?"

They stared at each other, silence thick between them, a brick wall built by Big Joe that was too tall to climb, and fortified with razor wire to keep them away from each other. Jordan was still angry, still leery of Spider. "What else aren't you telling me?" he asked.

"Whaddya mean?"

"I don't need protecting, Spider. We've hardly talked about any of this. I think you're holding back . . . you know more about this town than I do, see a side of it I don't."

Angel walked out of the kitchen carrying a plate heaped with French fries and a BLT buried underneath. She sat the plate down in front of Jordan. "I thought I heard you two arguing. What the hell happened to you?" she asked Jordan without missing a beat.

"I keep hearing this echo," he said.

"Every time I see you, you're bleeding," Angel said.

"He's a magnet for nut cases," Spider said.

"That's why I enjoy hanging out with you," Jordan shot back.

Spider smiled and slid him another beer.

"You need new bandages," Angel said. "I think I have some in the back. You want me to get them?"

"Sure," Jordan answered.

"Who did this to you?" Angel asked as she walked away.

"Ed Kirsch."

"Figures," she said, disappearing into the kitchen.

Neither Jordan nor Spider said anything for a minute. Jordan hadn't realized how hungry he was. The aroma of the food made his stomach growl. Nobody made BLTs like Angel.

Spider watched Jordan eat half the sandwich before he said anything. "I have no clue what's going on, Jordan. I've seen everything sitting here. The worst possible things human beings can do; cheat, lie, steal, and betray each other. But I've never seen anybody lure somebody out in the open and start taking shots at them. I've never seen anybody mad enough that they'd burn down somebody's house. Beat the shit out of each other, yes. But not crazy, not the madness that this thing has turned into."

Jordan wiped mayonnaise from the corner of his mouth and took another swig of beer. "What about Tito?"

"Why are you so insistent that this goes back to that?"

"The medallion and note for one. The bones for two. And maybe how Holister was acting, some things he said. It all started with the bones. Nobody is willing to talk about that, not even you."

"Nobody wants to remember," Spider said.

"Why?"

"Me, personally? I had legs. I had a whole different life ahead of me then. I was going to go to college and get the hell out of this town. I would've given anything to be a high school coach. But things didn't work out that way, did they? Two months after that kid disappeared I end up in a wheelchair and I've been sitting here ever since. What makes you think I want to reflect on that?"

"I'm sorry," Jordan said.

"Fucking don't be. My life's okay. I get through the day just fine. Now. But everybody's got their baggage, and most people don't like to pull it out of their back pocket in broad daylight and take a close look at it. Why in the hell do you think people drink? To have a good time?"

"There's more at stake here," Jordan said, finishing his sandwich, dragging a couple fries through ketchup. "Tito vanished. And it seems like nobody noticed, nobody cared. And now, twenty years later, everybody's walking around with amnesia. It's as if he never existed."

"Tito and Esperanza were fuckin' Mexicans, Jordan. Haven't you been paying attention? They come and go. Nobody cares. Nobody wants them here. But they're here, and there's nothin' anybody can do about it except live with it. It's the way it is. The way it's always been. We weren't even allowed to talk to the Mexican kids, for Christ's sake. Who knows what happened to Tito, or why? It wasn't any of our business. I'm sure José knows. And Buddy Mozel, too. Try and get into that fortress with your questions."

"It's my business now," Jordan said.

"So what are you going to do?"

The plate was empty. Jordan was tempted to have another beer, but he needed to keep his head as clear as possible. "I'm going to find Hogue. I want my gun back. And then I'm going to find José Rivero and get some goddamn answers about Tito and Esperanza."

"And you just think he'll tell you everything you want to know?"

"Yes." Jordan lit a cigarette and looked across the street at the police station. He wanted to talk to Ginny, too. But he wasn't telling Spider that. "I need to get to the hospital. See how Holister's doing. And if I still don't have any answers, I'm going to get Tito Cordova's file out of Holister's office. Johnny Ray can't find it, but I know where it's at."

"How you gonna get it? You know Louella won't let you snoop around while she's there."

"I'll wait until she's gone for lunch."

"Oh, great. Now you want me to help you break into the police station?"

Jordan nodded.

"In broad daylight? This heat has made you fuckin' loony. You smoking meth, too?"

"I'll only go after the file as a last resort."

"You're going to get us both thrown in jail before this is all over," Spider said.

"Maybe they'll put us in the same cell."

"I hope not—I'll end up going crazy for sure."

Jordan laughed.

Spider hoisted the shotgun up onto the counter.

"What's that for?" Jordan asked.

"Just in case you attract any more bullets, I want to be ready. It's not like my kickboxing skills are gonna do me any good."

Angel walked out of the kitchen carrying a handful of bandages, and sat them on the stool next to Jordan. "Take your shirt off."

Jordan hesitated then did as he was told.

"Give me a wet towel," Angel ordered Spider and then turned her attention back to Jordan. "If you let anything happen to Spider, you won't have to worry about Ed Kirsch or anybody else coming after you. I'll kill you myself," she said, sponging the dried blood off his shoulder.

CHAPTER 19

August 22, 2004, 10:46 A.M.

A dead pig was lying square in the middle of the road. It wasn't just any pig; it was one of Lem Jacobson's prize Hampshires.

Lem kept a small herd of pigs on a farm he owned on Huckle Road, five miles from his big house, far enough out in the country so the rancid smell would only annoy the closest neighbors. Those consisted of a few trailers on one-acre lots, and old man Longer's house a mile away. The Hampshire was all black with the exception of a wide white band around its broad shoulders. The pig had died in the center of the road, forcing anyone driving by to go off the pavement to get around it. Flies swarmed around a cup-size pool of blood that had gathered under its neck.

"What are you doing?" Jordan asked Spider.

"I'm going to the pond."

"I think we should stop."

Spider looked at him oddly, shook his head, and then brought the van to a stop along the side of the road. "Why?" he asked, shifting into park.

"I don't know," Jordan said. "It's a little weird, don't you think?"

"I think everything is weird right now." Spider reached for a roach in the ashtray.

"You think that's a good idea?" Jordan asked. "The pond is

swarming with cops. We really don't need to give Hogue one more reason to haul us in."

"You're probably right," Spider said, popping the unlit roach into his mouth and swallowing it. He chased the roach with a swig of water. "That's all I had with me anyway."

"Good."

The van was idling, the air-conditioner blowing warm tepid air. Exhaust fumes immediately saturated the interior. Jordan pushed the door open and eased out. He was sore, even after taking some more aspirin and cleaning up. The new bandages were tight on his shoulder. He'd snagged a clean white T-shirt from Spider's closet, and the .38 was snug in the holster against his back. It was too hot to hide the gun.

Anxiety heightened his pain. Confronting Hogue felt like he was walking into a hornet's nest. Everything felt constricted, even his lungs. It was time to lay his cards down with the sheriff. But the pig made him uncomfortable. Pigs didn't just die in the middle of the road, and it didn't look like it had been hit by a car, either.

Soybean fields sat on both sides of Huckle Road, stiff and unwavering in the breeze. Longer's Pond was two miles southwest. Spider had taken the back way out of Dukaine, assured by Jordan that the main entry would be sealed off tighter than a drum. He wanted to avoid the chaos as much as possible, stay as far away from the TV cameras and reporters, in case Hogue made an issue out of their arrival. The last thing he wanted was his face plastered across the TV, being hauled away in handcuffs.

The fields were dry. Acres of soybeans were turning bright yellow at the base, the leaves withered and brittle from the drought. Lem's farm was half a mile up the road. A small white house sat just off the road, and was usually vacant, except during migrant season, and then it was full of Mexicans. Jordan had answered more than one call at the house to break up a fight, been there with INS agents as they checked green cards. Most of the migrants would be working today, out in the fields salvaging as many tomatoes as possible. A big red barn, in need of a coat of paint, rounded out the lot, surrounded by pens that were normally muddy and full of pigs. The mud was gone. The pigs were still there, snorting and squealing, their smell hanging in the air in an invisible cloud of methane gas.

Jordan swallowed to get his breath. Even on the coldest day, you could smell the farm from a mile away. The heat only made it worse.

A line of trees followed the river on the north side of the fields, and another line of trees divided the field to Jordan's left, creating a windbreak for a huge tract of tomatoes. Dukaine seemed like it was a million miles away.

He stood at the front of the van, staring at the pig, looking for skid marks, looking for any explanation he could find about the pig's demise. He reached around and pulled the holster a little closer to his side, closer to his reach.

Cicadas droned in the trees. He wanted to yell at the insects, tell them to shut up so he could hear clearly, but he knew it wouldn't do any good. He'd just be a crazy man standing in the middle of the road, looking at a dead pig, screaming into the air, into the nothingness.

There were no visible paths through the soybean field that butted up to the farm. Jordan saw nothing that lead him to believe that the pig had escaped from one of the pens. If anything, the pig had edged its way along the road . . . but then what? The pig just fell over and died in the middle of the road? Could pigs die of heat stroke?

The answer came quickly as Jordan neared the pig. He pulled his shirt up to cover his nose to ward off the smell and the flies.

The two-hundred-pound Hampshire had been shot in the head. A perfect circle the size of a pencil eraser, probably from a .22, sat between the pig's cloudy eyes. Blood had trailed through the coarse black hair and pooled underneath the throat. The smell of blood, of death, of the methane gas mixed with the hot, humid air, penetrated the shirt over his nose and made Jordan gag.

He started to back up once he realized the pig had been shot. There was nothing to protect him. He was completely exposed, standing in the middle of the road. Suddenly, it was very much like standing at the pond with Holister, only the chills up his spine and the hair standing up on the back of his neck warned him of what might come next. He expected to hear the echo of a gunshot at any second.

The pig had been put there on purpose. Probably dumped from a truck.

Just like the skeleton had been placed at the pond? Put there to lure Holister to it so he could be shot? *Is the pig bait?* he wondered.

He stopped backing up halfway to the van. His eyes darted in every direction, looking for movement, looking for anything out of place. There was something else about the pig, something he'd noticed, but didn't really see until now. He looked over his shoulder. Spider had a curious look on his face, obviously wondering what the hell was going on.

Jordan drew the .38 and did a one-hundred-and-eighty-degree sweep. There was nothing to be seen for miles. No cars. Nobody out in the yard at the farmhouse. The only sounds he heard were pigs and insects. Mosquitoes buzzing his ear. Flies anxious for a pork buffet. Muffled squeals. He hurried back to the pig, every sense on high alert, his fear of getting shot again drawing sweat out of his pores like a fountain. Something was written on the back of the pig's neck, across the broad white band, in blood:

2 Dead Pigs

The writing looked familiar, like the writing on the letter. Chicken scratch. He took another deep breath and stepped back. There was no way to really tell if the writing was from the same hand. Maybe he wanted to see it that way. Maybe it just made sense that the person who wrote the letter wrote this message on the pig. And maybe—that same person was sitting in the woods, hiding, zeroing in on him with a high-powered rifle . . .

Jordan ran back to the van as quickly as he could, the .38 tight in his grip, ready to fire. He was looking for anything that moved so he could dive to the ground if he had to. Spider pushed the door open and he jumped in. "Get the fuck out of here, now!" Jordan yelled.

"What the hell's going on?"

Jordan reached over to the hand-controls on the steering wheel and threw the van into gear. "Let's go. Let's go!" he shouted.

The van lurched forward. Spider grabbed the steering wheel and pressed the accelerator lever harder, a look of absolute fear crossing his face. The tires caught, kicking gravel in the air. Spider swerved to miss the pig, jarring Jordan to the left and then back to the right, the .38 waving wildly in his hand.

"Put that thing away, you're making me nervous," Spider said.

Jordan steadied the gun and watched the pig disappear in the rearview mirror. They passed the farmhouse, the van pushing sixty miles an hour. The driveway was vacant. Two empty livestock trailers sat in front of the barn. A mangy long-haired dog appeared out of nowhere and gave chase, giving up quickly as they flew past the property line. A cloud of dust drifted across the road in their wake. Lem's farm and the pigs were gone, far enough behind them to breathe a little easier.

"The van might look like shit, but the motor is ripe, man. This baby can fly if she has to." Spider smiled and grabbed the water bottle. "Charlie's a genius when it comes to souping up engines. He'll do anything to get away from those brat kids of his." He pressed the lever even farther, pushing the van up to seventy. "What the fuck are we runnin' from?" he asked calmly, the fear fading the farther they got from the pig.

Jordan put the .38 on the console and grabbed the water bottle from Spider. He was shaking. "The pig was shot in the head. Somebody dumped it there."

"That's not cool," Spider said. "Somebody could have a wreck. But . . . ?"

"Whoever did it left a message. 'Two dead pigs.' " Jordan took a long drink of water.

Spider looked dismayed, his eyes danced back and forth between the road and Jordan. "What the hell's that supposed to mean?" he asked.

"I think it's a message from the shooter."

"For you? Nobody knew we were coming this way."

"For anybody who found it. What's the likelihood a cop's going to come down this road right now? Pretty high, don't you think?"

"OK, then why not put it somewhere easier to find? Instead of taking that chance?"

Jordan pointed through the windshield at a helicopter hovering in the distance, over the pond. "It wouldn't be too easy dumping a pig without raising a little suspicion, would it? Who knows? Who really knows?"

"The shooter," Spider said.

"And the fucker's still out there, just like I thought. Hogue's on me like a fly on shit, but the shooter's free to go about his business. Damn it, this shit pisses me off."

"Two dead pigs?"

"That's what it said," Jordan said.

Spider shook his head. "Pig could mean cop. Nobody says that anymore. But they used to."

Jordan nodded. "But Holister's not dead."

"You don't know that for sure. It's not Holister I'm worried about. The shooter took a shot at you, too. Shot at two cops. Two dead pigs. Fucker's not going to stop until you're both dead," Spider said.

"You might be right. Maybe I really was a target. Maybe the shooter was after me, too. I thought after reading the letter that they just wanted to shoot Holister. For whatever the reason, that's the way it seemed to me," Jordan said, settling back into the seat, letting the thought sink in for the first time.

Spider pulled the accelerator back and the engine wound down, coughing with relief. "OK, maybe you were a target," he said. "But why?"

"I wish I knew," Jordan said. He sat silently for a moment, thinking. "I think me and Ed Kirsch are going to have another talk," he finally said.

"I'll be there with you this time."

Jordan nodded in appreciation.

The road curved and the fields gave way to woods on both sides, edging along the river on one side and floodplain on the other. A police cruiser sat crossways in the road ahead. Red and blue strobes flashing. Johnny Ray was sitting on the hood.

Spider pulled back on the accelerator. "You *do* have a plan, don't you?"

"Yes."

Beyond Johnny Ray's cruiser, more strobes flashed. Two

ambulances. A fire truck. Jordan could only imagine what the scene in the parking lot looked like. He was glad there weren't any news trucks around. But he wasn't real glad to see Johnny Ray.

Spider pulled to a stop just short of the cruiser, gravel crunched under the tires. Johnny Ray bounded off the hood with his hand out. *Halt!*

"Wait here," Jordan said, climbing out of the van. "Don't fuck with Johnny Ray too much. If Hogue takes me in, I'll need you to come and bail me out."

"No problem. You gonna take this?" Spider picked up the .38 and held it out.

"No."

"You're a more trusting man than I am," Spider said as he put the gun back on the console.

"You can't park there," Johnny Ray ordered. "This road's gotta be free of obstructions."

The vibrato at the end of the sentence made Jordan cringe. Johnny Ray was sweating heavily. The cheap black dye he bought at the drug store ran down the back of his neck. Basketball-size circles dotted his armpits.

"He'll move it," Jordan said.

"What are you doing here, Mac?"

"I need to talk to Hogue. I've got some information for him," Jordan said.

"He doesn't want to talk to anybody right now. That's what he said when I relieved the deputy who was here."

"He'll talk to me. Radio him. Tell him I'm here."

"I don't think that's a good idea, Mac. There's some shit going on—"

"I can see that. Radio him."

Johnny Ray shook his head. "He wants to talk to you at the office. I already told you that."

Before Johnny Ray could raise another objection, Jordan reached in quickly and snatched the radio off his belt.

"Hey, give that back," Johnny Ray demanded.

"Hogue, this is McManus. Permission to come down to the site?" Jordan said into the radio.

Static hissed and crackled as Jordan played keep-away with Johnny Ray, tossing the radio from one hand to the other while Johnny Ray grabbed at it like a child who'd lost his favorite toy.

"Damn it, Mac. You're gonna get me in trouble again."

Spider was laughing in the van, muffled like the distant squeal of pigs.

"Come on down, McManus," Hogue's voice boomed over the radio. The radio hissed again. "Johnny Ray, don't let anybody else down here."

Jordan tossed the radio to Johnny Ray.

"Yes, sir. 10-4," Johnny Ray answered. He wiped sweat from his brow and the back of his hand turned black.

Jordan walked around the cruiser toward the ambulances. Sam Peterson sat in the driver's seat of the first ambulance. He waved to Jordan as he veered off the road and onto a newly blazed trail that led down to the pond. Jordan waved back, not surprised to see Sam. Charlie Overdorf was probably in the passenger seat, waiting for who knew what.

The trail had been a game trail, deer traveling from the pond across the road to the woods. Jordan immediately wondered if the shooter had used it for their escape route. Hogue would have thoroughly checked it already, gleaned any footprints if there had been any on the loose dirt before allowing anyone to use the trail.

Stinging nettle swiped at Jordan's arm, making him itch. Most of the low-lying jewelweed was trampled. A mockingbird flushed ten feet ahead of him, flying from one low-hanging limb to another a few feet up. It chattered at Jordan—sat there curiously staring at him. He whistled at the gray bird. It answered back, singing a long song that sounded just like an orchestra of police sirens as he pushed through the weeds, heading back to where everything had started.

CHAPTER 20

August 22, 2004, 11:15 A.M.

The pond was almost completely dry, the bed fully exposed with the exception of a murky pool of emerald green water on the south end, just in front of the concession stand. It looked like a big hole in the ground, twenty-five feet deep, the openings to the limestone caves covered in thick green moss, drying out in the sun, filling the air with a stench Jordan had never smelled before—it was worse than the pigs. A loud hum was coming from a pump that had been set up to drain all of the water into the river. A huge black plastic pipe snaked out of the pond and into the high, brittle bluestem grass of the wetlands and disappeared into the woods. Two open canopies had been erected directly on the pond bed, white plastic tents with no sides, and several unfamiliar people milled about, taking very little notice of Jordan as he walked out of the woods.

He stopped at the end of the trail and took in the sight, fighting off the memory of the shooting, the sight of Holister wheezing, gasping for air. His own throat was dry. The sun was directly overhead, like an interrogation lamp pointed straight into his eyes. He didn't know what to expect, what he'd see, but this scene was the furthest thing from his mind. A forensic investigation that seemed to reach far beyond the shooting and the discovery of the skeleton was obviously under way. The magnitude of it was something Jordan had never seen, had never dreamed possible in his own backyard, in his own town.

One of the canopies was over the skeleton Holister found by the big sycamore, another was near the center of the pond, a few feet from the slide. Three more canopies were erected in the wetlands beyond the NO TRESSPASSING sign, one next to the other, lined up in a perfect row.

Yellow tape was everywhere, rounding the perimeter of the pond. Little pink flags were stuck in the pond near the first tent, marking shell casings from Jordan's gun. More pink flags hung limply in the woods along the spring.

Rotted soil and previously undisturbed leaves released a strong, sour odor that hung in the air, along with huge swarms of no-see-ums and mosquitoes. Jordan batted the invisible gnats away as he swept the area looking for Hogue, looking for some sign that he was in the right place.

Everything had changed so quickly . . . Kitty's house was nothing but ashes, his battered and bruised face was almost unrecognizable in the mirror, and now Longer's Pond was gone, nothing left but stinking earth and skeleton fingers reaching to the sky.

A helicopter flew over the tree line and hovered overhead, the *thump, thump, thump* of the blades dispersing the smell, and creating a heavy breeze that caused the canopies to regimentally snap against their metal poles and the pink flags to rise and flap in the wind. Voices were strained, unintelligible, but there didn't seem to be a sense of panic, an impending sense of doom, or an immediate threat. Three people occupied the canopy over Tito's bones, or the bones Jordan and Holister had assumed were Tito's, all on their knees, digging and brushing material away from the skeleton, focused and intent, methodically going about their business as if they were on a science class field trip.

Jordan thought he heard music somewhere, but it could have been the helicopter or the pump ringing together, creating a consistent beat. A line of deputies walked along the opposite bank of the pond, four brown uniforms staying even, prodding the ground with thin metal poles. Charlie Overdorf stood under another sycamore and watched the deputies; waiting for some sign, it appeared, to move into action. He did not see Jordan, or if he did, he didn't let on that he had. Charlie was talking into a radio, his EMT bag a few feet away.

The largest crowd was gathered among the three tents in the wetlands. A constant stream of deputies, firemen, and normal-looking kids, college students, traversed from the tents up and down the trail that led to the parking lot. It looked as if they were all attending a picnic of some kind, a lazy summer day when there was no hurry to be anywhere or do anything important.

Jordan could not help but search the tree line for unusual movement. He was sure the site was secure, but the dead pig was still fresh in his mind. The message tumbling over and over inside his head like the song he thought he'd heard. It was stuck in his ear and would not go away. *Two dead pigs. Two dead pigs . . . Two . . .*

He took the threat very seriously.

The other canopy in the middle of the pond was empty, save a white sheet anchored securely in the middle, and Jordan began to understand what he was seeing. A thought entered his mind that had never occurred to him until now, until he was standing on the edge of Longer's Pond, expecting one thing and finding another.

There were more bones than what he and Holister had initially found.

More skeletons than just Tito?

"McManus!" Sheriff Hogue hollered as he stepped out from the first canopy in the wetlands. "Over here."

Without thinking, Jordan waved. *Sure,* he thought, as he

headed toward Hogue, *he's real happy to see you since you're both long-lost buddies.* But oddly, Jordan was glad to see the sheriff at that moment, glad to see a familiar face.

Hogue met him halfway, walking directly across the pond, his boots squishing in the rotted leaves. The sheriff swatted away a swarm of gnats that hung over his head and coughed. "I'm glad you came out. We need to talk." Hogue extended his hand for a handshake.

Jordan reluctantly shook Hogue's skillet-sized hand. He'd heard those words before—he hadn't noticed until that moment how much Bill Hogue and Ed Kirsch sounded alike.

The sheriff did not look overwhelmed and was barely sweating. For a big man, he moved with ease through the oppressive heat.

A thousand questions were forming in Jordan's mind—a million cautionary flags shooting into the air, each one warning him not to trust Hogue. He had an idea what the sheriff was up to and the smile on his face telegraphed his intention. Jordan didn't like it. At the moment, he had no choice but to play along.

"I've been stuck here all day, and it looks like I'll be here for a good while longer," Hogue said.

"What's all this?"

"Bones and more bones. It's a fucking graveyard. Five skeletons so far. And I wouldn't be surprised if there aren't more. We started finding them as we swept the area looking for evidence of your shooter. One, then another, and another, and another. . . . The one Holister found is a kid, can't be more than ten or eleven years old. See that lady over there?" Hogue pointed to the first skeleton, Tito, the spot where Holister was shot. "She's a forensic anthropologist from Indianapolis University, Katherine Shead. Says she's never seen anything like it. Goddamned, if she isn't acting like a kid on Christmas morning. She seems to think this has more to do with the Mexicans than it does a serial killer or something like that. Thank God. She's just surprised nobody found anything before now," Hogue said.

"There's never been a drought like this," Jordan said flatly. "The woods get more traffic than the wetlands these days—especially since Buddy Mozel bought the land and closed down the swimming hole."

"I think that's interesting, too," Hogue said, staring at the anthropologist.

Jordan followed Hogue's gaze. Katherine Shead looked to be in her early sixties, her thick, wiry, gray-streaked hair pulled back in a long ponytail, dressed in khaki pants and a short-sleeved linen blouse, a white floppy straw hat at her side. A pair of glasses dangled from her neck, and her movements were swift, akin to someone thirty years younger. Her face was deeply lined with wrinkles, no doubt from spending a lot of time outdoors, practicing her craft, digging in the field. She looked like a walking encyclopedia of knowledge, and she immediately reminded Jordan of Kitty.

"What do you mean five? All kids?" Jordan asked after a long silence, scratching his shoulder.

Hogue shook his head. "That one," pointing to the other tent in the pond, "is a baby. The others up there are all adults."

Jordan let the words sink in. Something sparked in his memory, told him he shouldn't be surprised. He thought of the night José came to the door with blood on his hands, and then it flittered away, overcome by the immediacy of what he was seeing, what he was hearing. He took a deep breath. "The one Holister found? Is it Tito Cordova? Can they tell?"

"Nope," Hogue said and then grew quiet, eyeing Katherine Shead curiously, watching her every move.

Jordan cast his eyes at the sheriff expectantly, waiting. The silence bothered him. Hogue's demeanor bothered him. The truth of what he was hearing was too hard to grasp.

"The lady, the professor, I guess, says that's impossible. The bones belong to a female," Hogue finally said. He pulled a toothpick out of his front pocket and started picking his teeth.

"A girl?"

"Yes. Has something to do with the pelvis. She says there's no mistaking the fact. It was a little girl. So, there's no way those bones can belong to Tito Cordova. Holister's theory doesn't hold up. I think he just wanted it to be that boy. He'd mention it every once in a while to me. We all have cases that haunt us. Tito Cordova was Holister's. We're running checks on missing girls in the last twenty years. Haven't come up with anything yet, though."

"I wanted it to be a boy, too," Jordan said. "I wanted it to be Tito."

"Sorry to disappoint you. I'd still like to take a look at the Cordova file. You know where it's at?"

"No," Jordan said. "Any idea who that skeleton might really be?"

"Your guess is as good as mine."

Jordan wiped sweat from his brow. His heart was beating rapidly. A *girl?* The skeleton didn't belong to Tito. Jesus, who could it be? The bigger question forming in his mind had to do with the note and the medallion. Why was the letter sent to Holister if the bones weren't the remains of Tito Cordova? What did the St. Christopher's medal have to do with all of this?

"You're looking a little pale, McManus. Let's go up and sit in my cruiser and get us some air-conditioning." Hogue led, walking toward the trail to the parking lot.

Jordan hesitated. He wanted to talk to Katherine Shead. He wanted to know how she could tell for certain that the bones belonged to a girl. He still wanted to believe the skeleton he had touched was Tito Cordova. Finally found. But he followed Hogue. He didn't come to the pond to talk to some anthropology professor. He came to get his gun back. And to tell Hogue about the pig.

"I got five skeletons and a nearly dead local marshal shot in the back, McManus," Hogue said over his shoulder as they passed by the tent with the girl's bones. "And no goddamned answers. The press is a having a heyday with this. I'm trying to find José Rivero. I got some questions for him, too." The sheriff stopped and turned to face Jordan. "You seen him?"

Not since last night, Jordan thought. "No, I haven't," he said, looking to the ground.

"Well," Hogue hesitated, "I do have at least one answer for you."

"What's that?" Jordan asked, turning his attention to the inside of the closest tent. The skeleton was free of dirt and mud, lying in a hole as if someone had gently placed it there on purpose. A tall college student said something about transport to another student who was brushing dust off the skull.

"Preliminary ballistics came back on your gun," Hogue said.

The bones looked brittle, butterscotch yellow in places and black in other places. Jordan had tried to put Tito's face on the skeleton, build a body of flesh and blood in his imagination, but he could barely remember what Tito had looked like when he tried. Now, there was no face, no skin to put on the bones. It was a simple skeleton, the only remains of a person who could not tell their own story. *A girl? It's a girl. . . . Who are you? What happened to you?*

The memory of José at the door came back stronger . . . the baby had died, and José had argued with Kitty about the burial. Was one of the skeletons the baby? If so, he'd been right all along—he needed to talk to José. And something told him he better find José before Hogue did, or there wouldn't be any talking to him.

But what about the girl? Rosa. She had a deep cough, looked sickly in the truck, predicting the devil's arrival. Had she died, too? Did José bury her at the pond along with the baby?

"I'm sorry, what'd you say?" Jordan asked. Pain rippled through his body, and he wished Kitty was still alive so he could ask her some questions about the Mexicans, about José.

"Come on, let's go to the car." Hogue turned and bounded up the trail.

Dazed, Jordan followed, keeping the skeleton in sight as long as possible. The parking lot was full of Carlyle County cruisers, all lined up, polished but covered in a thin coat of dust. Roll call. Two more fire trucks sat idling, blocking the lane. A third of the way down, yellow tape had been strung between two trees. Two deputies stood sentry against the crowd that had gathered beyond. In the distance, Jordan saw television vans with their satellite antennas reaching high into the air. The helicopter buzzed away, the thump of the rotors growing dim like a fading heartbeat.

"Fucking vultures," Hogue said as he climbed inside his cruiser. He hit the ignition and turned the air-conditioning on full blast.

Jordan's throat was raw. "You need to send a deputy down Huckle Road," he said, sitting gently on the hot leather seat.

"Why's that?"

"There's a dead pig in the middle of the road."

Hogue reached around to the backseat and pulled two cans of Coke out of a small cooler. He handed a can to Jordan, looking at him as if he had just said something in a foreign language.

"A what?"

"A dead pig." Jordan popped open the Coke and took a long drink. "It was shot in the head. Had a message written on it. 'Two dead pigs.' In blood."

"Jesus Christ, what next?"

"I don't know." Jordan took another drink, the cold liquid biting his throat as he swallowed. "I didn't have anything to do with this, Hogue. I didn't shoot Holister, and I didn't burn down my own house. I want to know what's going on as much as you do. I want to do my job."

Hogue tapped his fingers on the steering wheel. Cool air was beginning to circulate in the cruiser. He picked up the mike and ordered two deputies to investigate Huckle Road, and secure the pig as a crime scene.

Static and an affirmative answer blared over the radio. Hogue turned down the volume.

"Timewise you're in good shape for the fire. A nurse saw you leave the hospital five minutes before we got the call," the sheriff said, mounting the mike in the bracket on the dash. "It was definitely arson. Can't pin down the meth lab aspect yet. But the investigators found starter fluid cans. Might never be able to tell; there's nothing left."

"I know." Jordan breathed a quick sigh and took another drink of Coke. He wanted to tell Hogue "I told you so," but he just nodded.

"I still think the fire is connected with all of this mess," Hogue continued. "But I'm a little confused why somebody would do that. You got any enemies, McManus?"

"Everybody's got enemies. I've been a cop for seven years. I'm sure I've got my fair share."

"You didn't answer my question."

Jordan stared out the window at a thick stand of devil's plague. His answer was stuck in the base of his throat. "Ed Kirsch," he finally said. "But I think you already know that."

Hogue's face did not change, his stare was expressionless, waiting for Jordan to continue.

"Ginny and I have a history. Ed found out we, uh, spent

some time together recently. He came after me with a pipe a little while ago, down from the house. I don't know if he burned it down. But I wouldn't put it past him."

The sheriff nodded. "I'll talk to him. That boy's been a pain in my ass since the day he was born. He's just like his father—no good. I don't know why my sister put up with it all these years. Nine kids and no man to fend for her. Lord knows I've done my share, but I couldn't be a father to all them kids. She thinks the Lord will provide—her and that damned church . . ." Hogue stopped, apparently realizing he was talking about personal business to Jordan. He looked embarrassed, but only for a second. "What happened after Ed found you?" Hogue continued, his tone quickly all business.

"We got into a fight. My father broke it up."

"Big Joe's back in town?"

"Came back today, as far as I know."

"Interesting. You want to press charges against Ed?"

"No." Hogue's response concerning his father did not escape Jordan's attention. Why would the sheriff think Big Joe's return to Dukaine was interesting?

"Well, that gives us something else to look into," Hogue said. "Maybe Ed shot the pig. He doesn't like you—never has. He's the jealous type. And that wife of his, well, I don't mean to speak ill of Holister's daughter, but she's a wild one, too. Not very smart of you to go skinny-dipping in another man's pool—especially knowing the circumstances like you do."

"I've already been beating myself up for days. I know it was a big mistake," Jordan said. "But why would Ed shoot the pig?"

"You don't believe he'd do that?"

"I don't know what to believe. Could Ed Kirsch have set my house on fire? Yes. Was he the shooter? I don't know. I don't know whether or not he's got a grudge against Holister. I can't make the connection. I know he and Holister didn't get along.

But Ginny and Holister didn't get along very well, either. Not after she married Ed."

"All right. Like I said, we'll talk to him. I don't think he's the shooter either. Ed's a dumbass, but I don't think he's a killer."

For the moment, Jordan decided not to implicate Ed as a meth user. He wasn't sure. But Hogue would figure it out for himself—or maybe he wouldn't. Maybe he already knew. The drug bust Hogue was planning with the INS and DEA was not his problem at the moment. "You don't think my father has anything to with this, do you?"

"A lot of old news is becoming new again. We'll talk to him, too, now that I know he's in town."

"What about the ballistics report?" Jordan asked, letting the words about his father settle in his mind. The interior of the cruiser was cold now, the extreme change in the temperature made him shiver as he asked the question. Hogue was still being coy.

Hogue looked at Jordan, made eye contact and held it. "It wasn't your gun that shot Holister. Plain and simple."

It took everything Jordan had not to let his rage boil out. "I told you I wasn't involved from the beginning, Sheriff. This whole damn time you had me pegged as a 'person of interest' and you could have been out looking for the real shooter. The Town Board fucking suspended me—and asked for my badge. I'm a cop with a mark on my record, thanks to you," Jordan said, his voice escalating with each word.

"You're not off the hook yet, McManus," Hogue said.

"What do you mean I'm not off the hook?"

"The gun wasn't your gun. But the bullets that came out of Holister's back belonged to you. The serial numbers match the box of ammunition on your sign-out sheet from the day before. We found the casings near the spring. Right where you said the shooter was. Everything matches. You're still a person of interest, McManus. More so now than you were before. You're directly connected to the shooting. At the very least, you're a possible accomplice. I'd get a search warrant for your house, but that obviously won't do us any good, will it?"

"No, it won't do any goddamned good—someone burned it down, remember? Jesus Christ, Hogue, you're tellin' me I'm still a person of interest? You can't be serious?"

"I am. And I'm getting a search warrant for your brother's tavern. He's going to need to come up with an alibi for the time Holister was shot and for the fire."

"He's in a wheelchair. How in the hell could he have been the shooter?"

"Did he ever have access to your weapon?"

Jordan hesitated. "Yes."

"Then he's a suspect," Sheriff Hogue said.

CHAPTER 21

August 22, 2004, 2:09 P.M.

It was the hottest part of the day and the hospital parking lot was full. The six-floor building cast a long shadow over the entrance, and Jordan had to force himself to walk toward the door. Pigeons fluttered on the eaves, coming to light on top of a two-story limestone white cross to huddle in the shade. Four marble saints stood watch, defiant with swords in one hand and a bible in the other, stationed in an alcove below the cross. The red brick building had not lost its luster of the past, the windows gleamed as if they had all just been cleaned, and the lawn facing the parking lot was manicured and neat, even though it was brown and nearly dead. Sprinklers sprayed water all across the grass in front of the building, a futile ballet of mist rising and falling from the steady clicks of spinning metal heads that pretended to be rain clouds. Two large cement urns full of freshly watered red geraniums sat on both sides of the door.

Jordan hit the handicap button and the automatic doors slowly swung open.

"I still think you oughta go see a lawyer," Spider said, his hands resting on both wheels of his chair.

They'd been arguing since leaving the pond. Jordan was insistent that they go to the hospital, while Spider was adamant that they get help. Hogue was doing everything he could to connect Jordan to the shooting, and Spider felt it was time Jordan faced the reality that they were both suspects. Both of them were dumbfounded by the sheriff's statement that the bullets that were extracted from Holister's body could be traced back to Jordan. For a while, they both had sat in the van silently after Jordan told Spider everything that happened, trying to make sense of it all.

"I'll call a lawyer when they arrest me," Jordan insisted. "Hogue's got some work to do to charge me as an accomplice. Meanwhile, I'm going to do everything I can to make sure that doesn't happen."

He was a little more comfortable with the .38 out of the holster—he'd left the gun in the van next to the shotgun under a blanket.

"You sure about this?"

"What choice do I have, Spider? I can't just sit back and wait for them to come and get me. I still have the note and the St. Christopher's medal, and I still have questions Hogue can't answer. Especially now, since those bones aren't Tito Cordova. We really need to find José."

The doors swung completely open and jerked to a stop.

"I'd be looking for Johnny Ray if I were you. He tore out of there right after you walked down to the pond. Who else had access to your ammunition?"

"I told you, he was off the night before. Holister was on shift. Johnny Ray probably left because he got a call. He *is* the only cop Dukaine has at the moment."

"That's comforting."

Jordan hesitated, stepped aside as an elderly couple made their way out of the hospital. The pair walked slowly by, lost in their own world, faces expressionless, eyes glazed. "But you're right," he said as the couple stepped off the curb, out of earshot. "I need to figure out who could have snatched some of my bullets and who else has a Glock."

"Then why are we here?"

"To see how Holister's doing. He might be able to help, if he can talk."

"How come I get the feeling you're not telling me everything?" Spider asked.

Jordan stared at the sky, watched a pigeon flutter in for a landing on the eave. Spider knew him better than he thought. Jordan *wasn't* telling him everything. He could hardly bring himself to admit what he was thinking, but the sad fact was there was only one place he was at before all of this happened, when his gun wasn't on his hip, when the ammunition was not locked up and accounted for. And that was when he was in Ginny's bed.

He was at the hospital to see Ginny as much as he was Holister. There was no way he was going to tell Spider that, and start another argument. "Trust me," Jordan said, trying to deflect Spider's remark. "I've worked with Johnny Ray for a long time. He isn't capable of anything like this. His only crime is being an idiot."

"And a bad singer."

"That doesn't make him a psychopath."

"Fine. Have it your way. But you still need a lawyer, and obviously I do too," Spider said, rolling ahead of Jordan with a vigorous push on his wheels.

A long glass corridor stretched out in front of Jordan. The sun beat through the windows, the heat's intensity overcoming the blast of air-conditioning that did little to welcome him. He watched Spider speed through a second set of entry doors and followed slowly, running his brother's concerns about Johnny Ray through his mind. No matter how he looked at it, Johnny Ray as the shooter just didn't make sense. But maybe Spider was right, maybe he ought to have another talk with Elvis if his hunch about Ginny was wrong. There were starting to be too many people to talk to—at the moment Johnny Ray would have to wait. Right now José Rivero was number one on his list after they left the hospital.

A tall young Mexican man dressed in blue jeans and a T-shirt with a gray smock over it was washing windows on the doors. He stood back as Jordan walked by.

The sight of migrants working outside the fields was becoming more and more common in Carlyle County. The Mexicans were beginning to stay year-round, fill low-level service jobs. Jordan had given very little thought to the change, had barely noticed it was happening because the way of life in Dukaine was so entrenched in his thinking, in his view of the world. But washing windows surely had to be better than picking tomatoes, less labor intensive, safer, steadier income. He could hardly blame anyone for not wanting the kind of work he saw in the fields, but he wondered immediately if the man knew José, and then realized how stupid the thought was. The world José walked in, held power in, was twenty miles away. Asking the Mexican if he knew another Mexican was like assuming all black people knew each other or all white people knew each other. It was a flash of his own prejudice, his own lack of understanding, and he didn't like how it felt.

Jordan nodded to the Mexican as he passed through the second set of doors.

The man lowered his eyes to the floor, refusing to nod back, to acknowledge the gesture.

The lobby was brightly lit, row after row of fluorescent lights beaming down on a field of padded gray chairs. A fish tank sat in the center of the seating area, and in the corner a table for children was filled with Dr. Seuss books, blocks, wood puzzles, and other small toys. Keeping the children occupied was not working. Three small children were running around the chairs, playing tag, screaming and laughing, while their overwhelmed mother sat in a chair and stared at the ceiling. A baby was crying. The television in the opposite corner of the play area was tuned into a daytime talk show, the participants lashing out loudly at each other. A parade of people walked through the lobby, coming and going to the gift shop that sat at the right of the entrance, stopping at the service desk, or leaving the hospital. All with stone faces, eyes half-closed, their expressions restrained and their voices low. The bronze Christ stood with open arms against the wall and watched the world go by.

Spider was at the service desk talking to a young blonde woman in a white uniform. She giggled and picked up a black telephone receiver as Jordan eased up behind him.

"She's checking ICU," Spider said, looking up, over his shoulder.

Jordan tensed as he saw the smile fade from the girl's face. She gently hung up the phone and said, "There's somebody you can talk to in the waiting room."

The blonde, who couldn't have been more than twenty-one years old, pointed down a long hall that extended south of the desk.

"It's through the second set of doors on the right-hand side. You'll see it."

"Is everything OK?" Jordan asked.

"I'm sorry," the girl said softly. "You need to talk to the people in the waiting room."

Jordan heard Spider exhale, his face had turned ashen. Gray with dread. He nodded and started to roll away.

"Hey," the nurse called out. "Here's my number." She hesitated, flashed a smile, her teeth perfect, her blue eyes holding onto their initial sparkle. "Just in case you need somebody to talk to." She scribbled on a torn piece of paper quickly and offered it with a steady hand.

Spider stopped, rolled back, and grabbed the paper.

"Thanks . . ." He stuffed the paper in his pocket and returned the smile.

Jordan watched the transaction and shook his head—he was still surprised by Spider's ability to get a phone number. His gut told him to expect the worst from the girl's reaction on the phone, even though he didn't want to believe it.

Spider rolled off again, his hands flicking the wheels forward, the sound echoing off the sterile white walls and the glossy, waxed white floor. Jordan followed, his footsteps matching and reverberating with Spider's pace. He slowed as he passed a large refrigerated vending machine with an all glass front, offering flowers for all occasions. Blue carnations for the baby boy. Pink roses for the baby girl. Purple irises mixed and daisies centered delicately around a get well card. He could smell the flowers, a hint of sunshine that fought to overcome the constant antiseptic odor filling the hospital.

An image of Kitty's garden entered Jordan's mind—in his memory he saw her stooped over, her floppy straw hat on her head to shield the sun, digging up irises along the house, splitting the rhizomes for a new bed. "One thing always leads to another, Jordan. You just got to hope things will grow, have faith that they will bloom after the long winter. Sometimes, that's all you have when things seem to be the worst, when things are hopeless. The bloom is the reward," she had said. "It'll come if you tend to it right."

Damn it, he wanted to ask Kitty some questions . . . not hear her fables about flowers. *"Did you know what happened to Tito Cordova? Or Rosa? Why did you keep secrets from me?"* Kitty could not answer his questions from the grave—and if they existed in his memory, he couldn't find them.

Faith, it seemed to Jordan at the moment, was an overrated concept. It had nothing to do with reality. Not his reality. Not now. Walking with lead feet toward the ICU.

The second set of doors flung open with a tap on a button on the wall.

Jordan and Spider entered the waiting area, a smaller version of the main lobby, fish tank and all, and came face to face with Big Joe. He was the only person in the room.

It took Jordan a second to recognize his father, even after the ride back to the tavern from the house. It was hard to see him as an old man, shrunken and white-haired, a little bent over, yet still strong, with eyes that belied surprise. It was the eyes that finally registered with him, the sunglasses gone.

"I didn't expect to see you boys here," Big Joe said, standing back against the wall, making room for Spider to navigate past a row of chairs.

Silence settled between the three of them for a moment, tension bouncing off each one, growing stronger by the second. The feeling was as normal as a summer storm.

"You're a little late," Big Joe said, easing into a chair, facing Spider.

Jordan remained standing, unconsciously holding onto the handle grips of the wheelchair.

"I didn't know we had an appointment," Spider said.

Big Joe shook his head. "Holister died about a half an hour ago, smartass."

"Fuck," Spider said, barely audible, a loud whisper that echoed in the small room.

Jordan's chest constricted. He'd expected to hear those words once he saw the girl's face turn solemn on the phone. But actually hearing them was different than he imagined. A million images flashed through his mind, all of them starting and ending at Longer's Pond.

"Where's Celeste?" Jordan asked.

"She had some calls to make. Albert Patton. Some family. And she's trying to find Ginny," Big Joe said.

"Man, this sucks," Spider said.

"What do you mean, she's trying to find Ginny?" Jordan asked, unwrapping his fingers from the wheelchair. He sat down in a chair, leaving an empty space between himself and Big Joe.

"She was supposed to be here a long time ago," Big Joe said.

"I saw her drop Dylan off at the station this morning," Jordan said.

Spider sat silently in the wheelchair, his face as expressionless as the people in the lobby, obviously lost somewhere in his own thoughts.

"That's what Louella said. Nobody's seen her since."

"I don't like this," Jordan said. "Not after my run-in with Ed."

"Celeste is pretty upset that Ginny isn't here, but there was so much going on it was hard for her to do much about it. She wasn't going to leave Holister's side to go looking for her. She's been chasing after that kid all her life."

Spider stiffened, stretched his arms like he just woke up, an action that was as normal for him as it was for someone else's chest to flex in rhythm with their heart. "What happened? Why did Holister die?"

Big Joe looked at Spider oddly, as if he was unsure where the question came from, why the question came at all. "His heart gave out. The surgery and wounds were too much for him."

"So now it's murder," Spider said, staring directly into Jordan's eyes.

"I suppose it is," Big Joe said.

"One dead pig," Spider said, holding onto Jordan's gaze. "One to go."

"What the hell's that supposed to mean?" Big Joe asked.

"It's a long story," Jordan answered quickly.

"But part of the fuckin' story, nonetheless," Spider said.

Jordan shot him a look. *Would you shut the fuck up?* But it didn't do any good.

"Somebody left a dead pig in the road on the way to Longer's Pond. They left a message: 'Two dead pigs.' Written in blood. Jordan doesn't think it has anything to do with him, but I think it has everything to do with him," Spider said, finally looking away from Jordan.

"Sheriff Hogue knows about it," Jordan interjected, flashing the look again.

"He needs to know what the hell is going on around here, Jordan. Holister is dead, for Christ's sake. Kitty's house is toast, and you're walking around dodging a sniper while you try to outwit that hardass we call a sheriff," Spider said.

"I know that." Jordan felt tears welling in his eyes. He was angry. Sad. Concerned about Ginny. Uncomfortable in his father's presence. Just the sight of Big Joe made his fingers unconsciously curl into fists.

Big Joe studied them both, remained silent. The aquarium bubbled, a plastic diver in a red suit floated to the top of the water and then floated back down.

"I think there's a lot of things we need to talk about, but this isn't the time or the place," Big Joe said. "I'm going to make sure Celeste gets home . . ."

". . . We'll look for Ginny," Jordan said.

Big Joe nodded. "I'll be at the tavern later. We can talk this all out then. In the meantime, stay the hell out of trouble." He stared directly at Jordan.

Spider stuffed his right hand into his pocket and pulled out the St. Christopher's medal. "Hang on to this," he said, handing the dime-sized gold piece to Big Joe.

"What are you doing?" Jordan said incredulously. "I told you to put that in the safe."

"And I told you I didn't wanna be an accomplice to your bullshit when Hogue came sniffing around. Good thing I got it with me now that he's gettin' a search warrant for the tavern. My guess is he's gonna show up anytime, and I'm not goin' to jail for withholding evidence. You can if you want, but I'm not."

Jordan tried to grab the medal out of Joe's hand, but the old man closed it in a fist. If he'd been a dog, he would've growled. The look on his face was enough to force Jordan to stand back and stuff his hands in his pockets.

"Where'd you get this?" Big Joe asked, examining both sides

Spider looked up at Jordan. "You gonna tell him?"

"Holister had it at the pond. He got a letter the day before the shooting," Jordan said uneasily. "There was a note with it. Poorly written, like someone was trying to disguise their handwriting. It said to meet at the pond."

"Holister was set up?" Big Joe said.

"Yup, and Mr. Potatohead here wants to keep that information to himself."

"It's leverage, Spider. I want my gun back. I want my job back. How many times do I have to tell you that?"

"A million times. But it's still stupid. I don't like Hogue any more than you do, but . . ."

Big Joe stood up. "Both of you shut up." He shook his head and tumbled the St. Christopher's medal in his hand, caressing both sides gently. "Esperanza," he said, his tone softening, his eyes lifting to the ceiling.

Spider reached in his other pocket, pulled out the letter, and handed it to Big Joe.

"So, the past really has come back to haunt us. This is why you asked me about Tito Cordova in the car, isn't it?" Big Joe asked Jordan, taking the letter from Spider.

He nodded.

"This would surely get Holister's attention—get him to the pond," Big Joe said.

"And you home from Florida," Spider said.

CHAPTER 22

January 5, 1995, 6:19 P.M.

Kitty stood at the window, watching it snow. A fire crackled in the fireplace, lazy yellow and blue flames dancing along the bottom of the logs, and the sweet smell of hardwood filled the room. She had on a thick white hand-knitted sweater that matched the color of her hair, and a pair of gray wool slacks. A pot of chili sat simmering on the stove—Indiana chili, mild in taste, a thick sauce full of big chunks of tomatoes, green peppers, onions, hamburger, and macaroni. Dusk settled in early in the winter, and it was totally dark outside, even though it was barely evening. Jordan stopped as he crossed the living room. The sight of Kitty's spindly frame made him uneasy.

His grandmother was nearly eighty years old. Her health was failing quickly—so much so that she had turned herself back over to the world of modern medicine. The windowsill above the kitchen sink was lined with medicine bottles, all in alphabetical order, each for a malady that he did not understand because Kitty would never tell him the extent of her troubles, of her illness, or what the doctor had diagnosed.

He knew, however, that her death would come sooner rather than later. She had lost a lot of weight since the autumn winds turned cold, and now she was little more than a withered tree with all of her leaves decaying on the ground at her feet. She'd always looked old, but now she looked haggard, more tired than he could ever remember. He tried not to think about the certainty of what lay ahead. Jordan could barely imagine a world without his grandmother.

She had seen him through the roughest years of his life, given him a home, and worked hard at being a parent when she was long past the time in her life to do so. He loved her for it, even though he had not been very appreciative of it at the time. But things had changed. His life was just starting, he knew what direction he was heading, and for once, he was happy.

Everything had fallen into place once he and Holister had mended their fences, and Jordan had decided to become a cop. Everything but his relationship with Ginny. And that was going to come to an end, or a beginning, soon. He had finally decided that it was time for an ultimatum: Ginny would have to pick Ed Kirsch or him—and they'd both have to live with the choice she made. If only he could convince himself to stick to his guns, to *really* force Ginny to make a choice . . .

"I talked to the lawyer today," Kitty said, turning from the window. Her face was gaunt, her skin ashen, but her eyes were still sharp, still deep blue, the color of a summer sky.

Jordan stiffened. He knew the conversation that was coming, and he didn't want to have it. "Do we have to talk about this now? I have a date."

Kitty nodded and eased her way over to the sofa that was centered in front of the fireplace. She sat down and pulled a purple afghan over her lap. "Sit with me a minute." It was an order, not a request.

Jordan obeyed. These days, he found comfort in rules and orders. Not that he had given up his own mind, but he was starting to feel a peacefulness that appealed to his own sense of right and wrong in being told what to do, how to interrupt the laws of the world. He had two weeks to go before he started a three-month course at the police academy in Indianapolis, and he couldn't wait. Not only would the time away from Dukaine be an adventure, it would be the start of his new life. He was excited and scared at the same time.

"I need you and George to go with me before you leave so I can sign the house over to both of you," Kitty said. She hated Spider's nickname and refused to utter it aloud, or join the rest of the town who had happily donned her grandson with a moniker wrought with ironic pain.

"Can't that wait?"

"No, I don't think it can. I want to make sure I have everything in order before you leave." Kitty drew a deep breath. Jordan could hear her chest rattle. "I know you might be disappointed that I've left the house to you and George, but it is the only fair thing to do. What your father did was wrong, but this house is as much George's as it is yours."

Jordan's stomach growled. The smell of the chili made him aware of his hunger, but he'd lost his appetite. He had not heard a word from his father since he had left town four years ago. Essentially, Jordan had been disowned. The tavern belonged to Spider, one hundred percent, and even though the thought had never occurred to him that Kitty would leave him total ownership of the house, the act did bring the wound on his soul to the surface. It was almost as if Kitty was asking him to relive the death and abandonment of his childhood all over again. He had to fight with everything he had not to fly into a rage—even though he didn't understand why he felt so angry.

"I know that," Jordan snapped.

Kitty feigned a smile. "I wanted you to know now. Spider is all the family you have, and some day you'll need him. I don't want this to put a wedge between the two of you."

"It won't."

"Will you promise me that?"

"Yes," Jordan said, even though he didn't believe he would

ever need Spider. They barely saw each other these days, and barely spoke when they did.

Kitty's eyes flickered. She knew he hadn't told her the entire truth—her facial expressions always spoke louder than her words. But she didn't pursue the conversation. "All right, then, as long as it's settled."

"I don't care about the house—I mean, I'll take care of it for you, you know that. Spider hardly leaves the tavern."

"I know you will," Kitty said, easing the afghan off her lap. "Sometimes I think the best thing that ever happened for both of us is when your father left. And it was the worst thing, too. I never liked your father, didn't trust him any farther than I could throw him, but I never thought things would turn out like they did. He was an alley cat—I just wish I could have warned your mother off of him. Lord knows I tried. She knew he had a roaming eye, knew he would be a hard man to pin down. But then I wouldn't have you and George if she hadn't followed her heart, would I?"

Jordan answered her with silence. He'd heard all of this before. Kitty repeated herself constantly, especially in the last few years, never straying from the stories he'd heard since he'd come to live with her.

"If I thought it would do any good," Kitty continued, "I'd tell you more about him. I know you have questions, I know it hurts. But you can't change the past, can you? Your life is ahead of you, not behind you."

Jordan shook his head and rose to his feet. "I need to go."

Kitty reached out and grabbed his hand, stared into his eyes. "I'm really proud of you, Jordan. I'm really happy you're finding your way. Being a policeman is an honorable thing. There aren't many choices in this town—I feared for a long time you would end up working at the SunRipe plant or working in Morland like your grandfather. He was a very unhappy man. Neither is the place for you."

"I could never work for Buddy Mozel, or in any kind of factory for that matter," Jordan said.

"No, I don't suppose you could. Holister is a good man." She hesitated, drew in a deep breath. "But he has his secrets too. We all do. Some days, I think this town is cursed. We've all treated the Mexicans poorly. Try not to carry on that legacy, will you?"

"I don't have anything against the Mexicans," Jordan said as he pulled away. "I'll be back later, we can talk about this tomorrow."

"There's always tomorrow, isn't there?" Kitty smiled, but it was a hard smile, a knowing smile, an acerbic grin that made Jordan shiver.

"Jordan," she called out as he grabbed the doorknob to leave, "You should stay away from Ginny. She's no good for you. Just like your father was no good for your mother. Don't make the same mistake she did—it cost her her life."

A tremble ran up Jordan's spine. The continuation of the conversation about his mother and father brought immediate visions of blood, of anger, of faces and voices he could barely see and hear in his memory. A picture of his mother, all decked out in her senior prom dress, sat on the mantle—a beautiful girl he did not know, who had grown into a woman and was lost in a senseless car accident. A ghost who had been gone almost half of his life. Pictures after she married Big Joe were put away, bound in heavy string, locked in a trunk in the attic. Rarely, if ever, did Kitty speak so openly about his mother, so directly, and she had intentionally touched a nerve—he could see the pain of it in her eyes.

"Why do you hate Ginny so much?" he asked.

"I don't hate her. I've known Ginny since she was born. She was the most beautiful baby I've ever seen. Her hair was golden. It was so pure it turned white in the summer. People would just stare at her, treat her as if she were royalty. If her last name had been Mozel instead of Coggins she would have owned this town even more than she did. A person gets used to that kind of attention, comes to expect it. Trust me, Jordan, you will not be enough for her. Nor will you be able to give her enough. For whatever the reason, Holister has pulled away from Ginny now that she's grown, and his attention is the one man she can't capture. Don't think you can fill the hole that exists within her, because you can't."

"Why?" Jordan asked softly. He had never heard this story before. "What happened between Ginny and Holister? They can't stand to be in the same room with each other."

"I don't know. It's probably just a natural thing between fathers and daughters. And I suppose Celeste and Holister are like every other married couple. They've had their ups and downs. My guess is they had Ginny to hold them together. Bad thing is, it worked out just the opposite. Holister spends more time in his police car than he does at home. I suppose that's a blessing to us, and a curse to Celeste. But I wouldn't know, she hasn't taken me into her confidence for years."

Jordan knew there was a strain between Kitty and Celeste, but he never pried, was never really interested in finding out why. He was only interested in spending time with Ginny. Sometimes when he was younger, just being in the same room with her had been enough. "Did Holister ever step out on Celeste?" he asked.

Kitty eyed Jordan seriously. "You always were one for questions, weren't you?" She chuckled with approval in her eyes, but grew serious quickly. "Do you mean was Holister like your father? No, I don't think so. But I don't really know. How could I? Like I said, he's a good man. He was a friend of your father's a long time ago, when they were young. Buddy Mozel, too. The three of them were real close. But they went their separate ways, like most young people do. Don't gauge Holister by your father's deeds, Jordan, that's a dangerous way to live." She stood. "I've said too much already. I'm going to bed. But, Jordan, please be careful."

"I love her, Kitty."

"I'm sure you think you do. Just be careful, and stay away from her. Find someone else to love—someone who will love you back."

He opened the door as Kitty padded down the hall to her bedroom, her words still ringing in his ears. Her stern order to stay away from Ginny was one he knew he would disobey. Kitty didn't know Ginny like he did, didn't know how much he loved her. He was bound and determined to win Ginny over, no matter what Kitty thought, or how much Ginny claimed she loved Ed Kirsch.

A cold rush of air stung his face and snowflakes quickly covered his head before he could put on his black ski cap. In the distance he heard a snowplow scraping Main Street, could see the glow of pulsing yellow lights cutting through the darkness. As he stepped onto the sidewalk, Jordan stumbled and almost fell. He hadn't paid any attention to the drift piling up in front of the stoop. His mind was elsewhere . . . wondering how love could be so great if it hurt so much, if the whole world was against you.

January 5, 1995, 11:13 P.M., *Monterrey, Mexico*

Tito stood silently behind the curtain. Light slid underneath the thin sheer, illuminating his feet. He could barely breathe, and could not move, could not take his eyes from Aidia Marquez's silhouette as she bent over on the toilet and brushed her hair. His thoughts were dark, unimaginable, as he envisioned Aidia's lustrous brown skin and tried with all of his might to fight off the curiosity of her nakedness.

Aidia had been kind to him, and he knew the lust he felt was wrong. The nuns would condemn him, instruct him to say the rosary a hundred times, go to confession to be absolved. But there was no God in Aidia's house, no way to rid oneself of sin. She would only laugh at him, shoo him out the door to fetch her tequila or groceries for the week, make him sweep the porch and sing a silly song, or clean her paintbrushes, all the while listening to *ópera* music. Her punishments confused him . . .

"Sueñe sus sueños," Aidia commanded in Spanish. Dream your dreams. "I am going to turn out the light now, Tito. Tomorrow we go to Barrio Antiguo, and show my new paintings to that miser Chavez. I am finally ready, after working so hard all these long months. Money is thin, and his *galería* is very popular right now. We may have to turn you back into a *mendigo* to beg from the pious pigs coming and going from the *Museo de Arte Contemporaneo* if Chavez takes nothing from me. Get your sleep. It will be a long day."

Tito's face flushed. Aidia might as well have caught him masturbating. She was one of the most beautiful women he had ever seen. Even in middle age, Aidia was in fine shape. Her frame was small but curvaceous, her black hair streaked with strands of white, and the lines under her eyes only added to the depth of her beauty, especially when she smiled, showing off her perfect white teeth. The clothes she wore were always light and airy, the colors of the jungle and sky, and more often than not, the thin linens exposed the fact that she wore no bra, that she hated physical and emotional restrictions of any kind. Her breasts were perfect.

Aidia's family was wealthy. Her father was the owner of a large manufacturing plant in Monterrey, but she was an artist. She had long ago left the comfort of money behind, pursuing her own dreams instead, getting by meagerly on the sale of her paintings, and doing odd jobs if she had to. The *casa* was full of canvases depicting scenes of the poor side of Mexico; peasants in the field, *nómadas,* migrants, crossing the big river, their bundles of clothes, the whole of their life, floating away in the distance. And of the street boys, the *mendigos,* panhandling the *turistas* on the corners of Makro Plaza, where he had met her.

Three weeks after he had arrived from San Luis Potosi, he spied Aidia under a tree watching him, painting him and the other boys he had befriended. Orphans, or those without parents, since Tito did not consider himself an orphan, it seemed, made friends more easily than most people. A lost and lonely look was all one needed to join a gang—even if the danger of it outweighed begging on the street alone. After Aidia had finished the painting, she had sought him out, offered him a roof over his head and food in his belly every day, if he would do her chores, run her errands, clean her paintbrushes. . . . She was intrigued by his blue eyes, by his light skin, his perfect English, of which she knew little. She said he was, "Copper among the rubble of deaf stone."

God had sent him an angel, and he had been with her ever since—trying with all his might not to love her. But five minutes after he met her . . . it was too late.

Rain pinged off the metal roof. A cool breeze circled through the small cement-block house, mixing the smells of Aidia's home into a bouquet of comfort: Turpentine. *Achicoria,* chicory, for the morning coffee laid out on the sink, and the sweet fragrance of honey and almond bath soap. The light clicked off, and Tito undressed and lay down on his cot. He pulled the blanket up over his shoulders and closed his eyes, but images of Aidia mixed with the remembrance of his days as a *mendigo,* of his journey to Monterrey from *El Refugio.*

He grasped the St. Christopher's medal that forever dangled around his neck and wondered how so much time had passed.

He wondered if he could ever free himself from the pull of Aidia's kindness, of her heart and passion that seemed to throb out of every pore of her body. He needed her love as much as he needed to breath . . . but he knew deep in his heart that one day he would have to leave her. And his heart, his growing desire to be with a woman now that he was nearly a man, told him that his leaving would have to come soon, or he would stay in Aidia's *casa* for as long as she were alive. He would never make it to Nuevo Laredo, never cross the border, never step foot in the place he once called home.

Tito was indebted to Aidia for saving him, for pulling him from the streets before he fell victim to the flesh sellers and glue-sniffers, and the thought of leaving her pained him. But he was losing himself, losing his dreams, his memories, and sometimes, he felt just as trapped in her presence as he had with the nuns.

Slowly, he settled in to a comfortable position. The rain lulled him to sleep.

The soft sound of Aidia's steady breathing, a few feet away, was nothing but a simple lullaby that reminded him of distant tomato fields and the smell of *menudo* simmering on the stove.

CHAPTER 23

August 22, 2004, 4:39 P.M.

After knocking on Ginny's trailer door three times, Jordan kicked it in. He stepped back, gripped the .38 a little tighter, and swept inside.

The front room was a mess; the television shattered, a chair turned on its side, papers strewn across the floor. He made his way through the kitchen, inching along the wall, listening for any sounds of someone else inside. There was no air-conditioning, no fans running, no windows open. The trailer was sweltering under the tin roof. The kitchen smelled like sour milk, the faucet was dripping steadily, and the refrigerator door was standing wide open.

He stopped before heading down the hall, anchored his hand on the sweaty paneling, and remembered leaving, Ginny's sobs, the fear in Dylan's eyes. Goddamn it, he should have taken them with him, should have done what Ginny wanted—ran away and became something else, someone else. A fishing guide in Minnesota, or a ranger in Yellowstone. Either one sounded pretty good, but he knew he couldn't leave, not then, and certainly not now. He finally had to ask himself a tough question: Did Ginny know what was coming? Is that why she wanted so desperately to run away? If she took his bullets, then the answer to that question was yes.

Maybe she was trying to protect him as well as herself.

Maybe? Maybe she still loved him. Maybe not.

While Jordan was inside, Spider waited in the van with the shotgun in his lap. There was no way Spider could provide backup for Jordan other than to crawl up the rickety steps, dragging his legs behind him. That was too dangerous, too slow, since they didn't know what Jordan could be walking into. Ginny's car was gone, and Ed's El Camino was nowhere to be seen. It looked like the trailer was empty, like no one was home. Spider was less than thrilled about Jordan's plan, but he'd gone along with it, keeping the van idling, ready to get help or get the hell out of there on a second's notice. It was all he could do. Just sit there and wait, one more time. Only Spider had a cell phone—Jordan had never felt the need for one since a radio was always strapped to his hip. But he wished he had one now so he could call Spider if he needed him.

Jordan edged down the hall, hesitating, listening, before he entered the doorway to Dylan's room.

The small ten-by-ten bedroom was empty, the bed unmade, bright red and blue Spiderman sheets in a tangle. Toys were scattered across the floor; a Tonka semi-truck, an army tank, action heroes missing a leg, an arm, a head, laying in a pile in the middle of the floor. The closet door stood open. Jordan quickly cleared it, assuring himself that the boy was still with Louella. He'd seen Dylan that morning, being led into the station by his mother. All things considered, that could've changed, and the police station was the next place he'd go if he didn't find Ginny home.

Sweat dripped off Jordan's forehead. The thin hallway was like a sauna. Early evening light dappled through the curtains of a single window no bigger than a cement block, casting seashell-shaped shadows on the dark walnut-paneled walls.

He could hear the van running outside. A cat meowing next door. The constant *drip, drip, drip* of the faucet matched the beat of his heart.

The bathroom door was open and Jordan ducked low, ready to roll into Ginny's bedroom if he had to. He eased up next to the door casing, peered inside, and saw nothing but his own reflection in the mirror as he jerked the .38 in front of him. His black eye had ripened, and was starting to fade from its original deep purple. His face glistened with moisture in the soft light. He hardly recognized himself, standing in front of the mirror, pointing a gun at himself.

Nothing seemed like it had changed in the bathroom since he was there a few nights ago, after making love with Ginny. Nothing except his face, the wounds on his body, Big Joe's return to Dukaine, the discovered graveyard at Longer's Pond, and Holister dead and gone. The guilt Jordan felt from not being able to save Holister was heavier than anything he'd ever felt in his life. A lot had happened during his life that had been out of his control—except the shooting. He was trained for that. If only he'd done one thing different Holister would still be alive, would be there to answer his questions . . . if only. If only . . . He knew he had to push the thought away or he'd go crazy, beating himself up with one more thing.

Everything had changed once he'd left Ginny's bed. And now he was back under her roof, fearing she was dead, or at the very least, had come to some great harm—or worse, was somehow involved in this mess. Had Ed led her down one more dead-end path?

With that thought in mind, Jordan went to the medicine cabinet and opened the door. The needle was gone. The aluminum foil rock was gone. Only the ordinary, everyday items were there. Something did catch his eye, though, as he went to leave the bathroom.

Ten empty packages of cold and sinus medicine were littered across the bottom of the bathtub. A coiled piece of black tubing lay in the corner. Several empty pickle jars sat on the edge of the tub. The only thing missing was a hot plate, antifreeze, muriatic acid, and the rest of the necessary chemicals. He had been right, his hunch verified; Ed was home-cooking meth.

He took a deep breath, saddened by the discovery, and pushed his way out of the bathroom. Ginny was more involved than he had hoped, she had to have known what Ed was up to . . . and he had to seriously consider the fact that she did take his bullets—he just couldn't figure out why she would do something so drastic. But he would.

An odd smell permeated the bedroom, and he edged up to the door to check the final room in the trailer, unsure of what he'd find. His shoulder knocked a picture to the floor. An 8 × 10 Wal-Mart portrait of Ginny, Ed, and Dylan smiled up at him from the floor. Almost unconsciously, he cocked the .38, pulled the hammer back, and entered the bedroom, expecting the worst—only to find it empty as well.

The bedroom was a shambles. Drawers pulled out, emptied on the floor and on the bed, mixed with the piles of dirty laundry. The fan was off, and the window was closed, the sheer curtains torn from the rods, hanging sideways on one nail. Perfume bottles lay shattered, and the smell was immediate and overwhelming; a mixture of jasmine, sandalwood, and musk that attached itself to his pores, causing him to shudder. Each fragrance triggered a memory of Ginny at various stages in her life, his life, their life.

Not finding her at the trailer eased his mind. But only for a moment. It was obvious somebody had tossed the place. The question remained whether it happened when Ginny was there or not. Did Ed and her get into a fight? Or did somebody take her away against her will? Only pieces of the meth lab were present—did Ed take them somewhere else, along with Ginny? There was no telling what had happened, especially if Ed was stoned. And that was likely, considering what had happened earlier when Ed came looking for him. The rage Ed was in would be notched up times ten if he was high.

"I should have shot the son of a bitch in the head when I had the chance," Jordan said out loud, "and put him out of his misery."

His gut told him Ginny hadn't been abducted, not unless it had happened after she dropped off Dylan. Fighting with Ed made more sense. But when did that happen? This morning before Ed came looking for him with the pipe? Or later? Or was she using too? On a binge with Ed? She'd headed in the wrong direction when she left the station and should have been going to the hospital. Where did she go?

There were signs that Ginny was using, now that he thought about it, but he hadn't wanted to see them. He had wanted nothing more than to be nineteen again, nothing more than to have one more chance at winning her over. Spider was right. He was a fucking dumbass . . . He would have done less harm by climbing into bed with his ex-wife, or Lainie, or the redheaded waitress at the Flying Tiger.

Jordan saw no blood, no sign that there had been any physical harm done to Ginny. All he knew at that moment was that he had to find her. Make sure she was all right and go from there. Take her to Celeste once he found her. To another reality that was even less pleasant than the one he stood in right now.

How could he still want to save her if she had betrayed him, used him, put him in harm's way?

He pushed that question away, too, then thought of Holister—of the reality that his friend, his boss, Ginny's father, was really dead.

"They were laughing like it's all a goddamned joke," Holister said.

Jordan backed out of the bedroom with Holister's voice ringing in his memory. The first undistinguishable shot had twisted the old man's puffy face into a surprised burst of pain. And then the laughter. It seemed familiar. Distant but familiar. He stopped, tried to place the laughter, and then reentered the bedroom, his eyes searching the top of the dresser. He was sure he was missing something here, a clue staring him straight in the face, waiting to be found.

Two of the bottom drawers remained intact, and he opened them quickly, rummaging through the drawers of T-shirts and socks . . . looking for a bullet, something that would prove or disprove his theory that Ginny had taken the bullets from his Glock. He really wanted to find something to prove himself wrong, that Ginny hadn't betrayed him.

He found nothing to convince him either way, so he eased his way outside. He had a recurrent feeling, the same one he'd had the other night: He was in another man's house looking for something that did not exist.

Spider revved the engine of the van as Jordan stepped out the door of the trailer, sending a big blue puff of smoke into the air.

Jordan shook his head, telling Spider he hadn't found Ginny. He removed the bullet from the .38's chamber, stuffed the gun back into the holster, and walked slowly to the van, eyes on the ground, looking for anything that might provide a clue to Ginny's whereabouts, or what had happened inside.

Nothing. Unless he was going to analyze every brand of cigarette butt littering the gravel where Ginny parked her car. There wasn't time for that, there were too many butts to choose from.

"Let's go to the station," Jordan said as he climbed into the van.

"Are you fuckin' crazy?" Spider asked, setting a bottle of water into a cupholder on the dashboard console. "Strike that. I know the answer. Why? What'd you find?"

"The place is a wreck. Somebody either tossed it looking for something, or Ginny and Ed got into a fight. Hard to say which," Jordan said, taking a drink from his bottle of water. "There's remnants of a lab. Somebody was cooking—maybe Ed, maybe Ginny."

"I'm not surprised."

"Me, either. I should have seen it . . ."

"You were blinded by . . ."

"Stop it," Jordan said, hitting the dash. "I know it! Goddamn it, I know what I should have seen, what I should have done, and what I shouldn't have done!"

"Sorry, man."

"Don't be. Just lay off. There's enough shit going on. I don't need to be taken to the cleaners every time her name comes up."

"You're right."

Jordan stared at Spider for a second. *Let the anger go,* he told himself. *Let it go.* "Damn, I could use a beer," he said.

"You didn't answer my question. Why do you want to go to the station?"

Jordan looked at Spider curiously. "I want to check on Dylan. Make sure he's all right."

Spider nodded. "That's cool. But what if Hogue or Johnny Ray want to keep you there?"

"I doubt Hogue'll be there. He's got his hands full at the pond. I can handle Johnny Ray." Jordan looked at his watch. "Louella will be leaving, or is already gone, it's after five. Unless they got her working overtime because of everything that's going on. If she took Dylan home with her, then we'll have to go there."

"What if they detain you? What then? I'm supposed to bail your ass out of jail?" Spider asked.

"Then you'll have to find Ginny and Ed."

"And you think it's worth the risk, checking on the kid?"

"Yes."

"I don't."

"All right. Here's the deal," Jordan said, frustrated, still not sure he wanted to tell Spider the whole truth, even though he had no choice. "I left my Glock on the nightstand when I was at Ginny's. I was on duty when I slept with her."

Spider laughed uncomfortably but said nothing, probably in response to the look he was getting from Jordan not to say a goddamned word.

"She—could've taken the bullets," Jordan continued. "Put it all together. If Ginny really did take the bullets and gave them to the shooter, then she's involved. She knows what's going on. Knew what was going to happen. The call was a set-up—just like the letter to Holister. We had sex for one purpose—so she could get the bullets. The rest of it was bullshit."

"That's got to make you feel even better, huh?"

"Oh, yeah, great. Just great. Can't be much more stupid than that, can I?" Jordan said, mocking himself but letting the tone go quickly. "Maybe Ed's the shooter. Maybe I'm right. Maybe he's transporting, dealing again, and he pulled her into it. Dylan was there, too, that night. I've seen too many kids in houses that have had labs in them. I just want to make sure he's safe."

"But why would Ed shoot Holister? He's Ginny's father."

"I haven't figured that out yet. Maybe this has something to do with the INS and DEA coming—Hogue's big bust. Not only was Holister Ginny's father—but he was a cop, too."

"You, too."

"Yeah, two dead pigs. I know. There's been a lot of activity at the pond, cookers using the woods to hide in. Me and Johnny Ray have both had calls out there in the last couple of months. If somebody was getting too close to making a bust, then maybe it was time to take action. If Holister got shot with bullets from my gun, and I was the only one there . . ."

". . . Then you're more than a suspect—you're directly linked to the shooting. Case closed. Which is exactly what's happened."

"Thanks to Hogue."

"Ed Kirsch's motherfucking uncle. You think the sheriff's involved in this?"

"I don't know. He runs a clean department, has high aspirations. It doesn't fit, even though Hogue's been acting strange from the beginning. Maybe I just don't want to believe a cop is involved in something like this . . . a cop shooting another cop."

"He was quick to believe it when it was you."

"It still doesn't fit."

"All right—some things are starting to make sense," Spider said. "But that doesn't explain the St. Christopher's medal with Esperanza Cordova's name etched on the back. Or the house burning down. Or the bones at the pond. Just thinking about *that* weirds me out."

"Me, too. There's a lot I can't explain. I might have an idea about the bones, though."

"What? You know how they got there?"

Jordan exhaled. "I think I might. If we can find José, I'll know for sure, and then I'm . . ."

". . . Right back where you started from. Knocking on Buddy Mozel's door."

"He bought the land. Closed it off. That has to be why. He knows what's there. I'm sure of it."

"So, maybe you're off base about Ed."

"What would Buddy's motive be for shooting Holister, for shooting me? Why would he send the letter, the medal—which at this point looks like it has absolutely nothing to do with anything."

"Like I said, it got Big Joe to fuckin' come home," Spider said.

"That it did. Are you sure he was in Florida when he called?"

"I don't know. How can I be sure of that? I didn't hear the ocean in the background or anything like that—but I wasn't listening for it, either. What're you saying?"

"Maybe Big Joe's the shooter."

Spider didn't say anything. He stared at Jordan as if he wanted to say something, but couldn't. His eyes glazed and he looked away quickly, out the window toward the SunRipe plant.

"It's something to think about," Jordan said, grabbing a cigarette out of a pack on the dash. He knew he'd crossed a line, implicating their father . . . he was just thinking out loud, trying to make sense of everything. "Let's go. I want to make sure Dylan is all right—make sure he's nowhere near Ginny and Ed until we know what the hell is going on."

"I swear to God, you're gonna get us fucking killed."

"You want to go back and sit by the phone?"

"Nope. I don't wanna be there when Hogue shows up with his search warrant."

"I didn't think so."

The trip to the police station took five minutes. Main Street was nearly vacant. There was very little traffic. A pickup truck full of Mexicans passed by as they stopped in front of the station. It headed out of town, toward the camps. The late afternoon sky was blistered white and it was a little early for the workers to come out of the fields, but Jordan didn't think too much of it. The drought had changed a lot of things—they could have been going back for a break, more water, anything at this point. He had no idea what the shift schedule was at the moment.

Johnny Ray's cruiser was nowhere to be seen and all of the vehicles at the fire station were gone as well. Jordan sighed a breath of relief, glad there were no cruisers in the parking lot. Only Louella's Buick sat in its normal spot. Spider eased the van next to it.

"I'll be right back," Jordan said as he grabbed the door handle.

"Hey, wait," Spider said as Jordan opened the door. "I need to tell you something."

"Right now?"

"I shoulda told you sooner. A lot sooner."

Jordan looked at Spider curiously, uncertain of the cracking tone in his voice. There were tears in his eyes. "What?"

"I know what happened to Tito Cordova," Spider said, staring straight at Jordan.

"What do you mean you know what happened?"

Spider took a deep breath. "I was there. I saw everything, goddamn it."

CHAPTER 24

August 22, 2004, 5:41 P.M.

Dukaine was eerily silent for early evening. Jordan tried not to notice, but all of his senses were on hyper-alert. The window of the van was rolled down, the air-conditioner blowing lukewarm air. He could hear pigeons cooing, smell and taste the rank odor of tomatoes being processed into ketchup, and feel each drop of sweat rolling down the back of his neck. He would have been cooler, more comfortable in his police uniform. Oddly, he felt like he was acting like a cop—but he didn't feel like one. He felt desperate. Hunted. On the run . . . winded and in pain, like he'd just been hit upside the head with a two-by-four.

He could not remember the last time he'd seen Spider cry. Tears streamed down his brother's face, and Jordan could do nothing but stare.

"All right," he said as he sunk back into the passenger seat. "You need to tell me what the fuck is going on. All of it, right now."

"I wanted to. Yesterday. Ten years ago. But I couldn't. I was scared. Jesus, I been scared every day of my life since it happened," Spider said, wiping the tears from his eyes. "Damn it, I wish I had a fuckin' joint."

"That's the last thing you need right now." Jordan looked over his shoulder as a semi rumbled through the stoplight on

Main Street. It wasn't a SunRipe truck. "What're you scared of?"

"What isn't there to be scared of? Going to jail. Losing the tavern. Fuck, I don't know. I figured I'd get shot long before you ever did. But nothing happened."

Jordan exhaled deeply. He grabbed a cigarette and lit it. All of his concerns about Dylan and Ginny still existed, but they'd have to wait. "You need to tell me everything."

Spider nodded. "You're gonna be mad."

"I don't give a rat's ass. Tell me what the fuck happened."

Sweat beaded on Spider's forehead. He tapped his fingers on the steering wheel. "I thought this was over. Day after day I sat in the tavern staring out the window, watching, listening, waiting to hear something. The memory was like white noise— always in the background. Life went on, if you want to call it that. . . . You thought everybody forgot about Tito, but I didn't."

Jordan stared at his brother impatiently. "Holister didn't."

"A lot of people didn't—haven't." Spider took a swig of water, his eyes still moist, glazed, and red-eyed. "Nobody knew who Tito's father was, right?" he said. "Everybody always thought Buddy Mozel was his father. It made sense, since Esperanza worked for him. They may have even loved each other in an odd, secret way—I don't know, that would explain a lot of things. Buddy went off the deep end after Tito disappeared, after Esperanza—"

"—I know all this," Jordan said.

"Kitty found out who Tito's father was. That's what started it." He stopped tapping his fingers, turned his body so he was facing Jordan. "And it wasn't Buddy Mozel."

"If you're about to tell me that Big Joe was Tito's father . . ."

"It'd probably be easier if that were true," Spider said. "And it very well may be, for all I know. I didn't say I knew everything. I just said I was there."

"So, Kitty found out who Tito's father was, but you don't know?"

Spider nodded. "She never told anybody as far as I know. Took it to her grave."

"How'd she find out?" Jordan asked. He took a long drag off his cigarette and exhaled. *Why didn't Kitty tell anybody? Especially after Tito disappeared?*

"How'd Kitty find out anything?" Spider said. "She was thick with the Mexicans—you know that. She went to see Esperanza and Tito every month. I don't know when it started, probably from day one since she helped deliver him. Buddy was giving Kitty money to make sure Tito had everything he needed, stayed healthy."

"That doesn't add up," Jordan said. "Why didn't Buddy just include the money in her check? Why feed the fire that he might be Tito's father, especially if you say he wasn't?"

"Kitty said he wasn't. And Esperanza feared more than anything that Buddy would find out who Tito's father was, that Kitty would tell Buddy."

"She told you that?"

"Yes."

Jordan took one last drag off the cigarette and flipped it out the window. "When?"

"After the accident. We talked about a lot of things back then when nobody else was around. You lived with her, but you weren't her only fuckin' grandson."

Jordan ignored the comment, ignored the old divide between them. "She never said a word to me about any of this."

"You were too young."

"You were only sixteen—"

"—When Tito disappeared, not when Kitty told me. Why does it matter?" Spider asked.

"It doesn't." But it did matter to Jordan. He couldn't believe

Kitty had kept this information from him. He wasn't sure why he thought he had a right to know—but if she'd told Spider, she should have told him too. "I still don't understand. Why would Buddy Mozel give Esperanza money secretly through Kitty when he could have paid her in a million different ways? She was right there in his house. Why would he do it anyway, if he wasn't Tito's father? And how in the hell did Buddy convince Kitty to do this for him? She despised his treatment of the Mexicans."

"You're going to have to ask him."

"At least now I know what questions to ask." The world outside the van had completely vanished from Jordan's view. He had a nagging headache, pain throbbed through his shoulder. The nightmare he'd woke up in after leaving Ginny's bed continued rolling forward. Everything he thought was true for so long was getting turned upside down on its head. Spider had secrets he'd kept hidden for half his life—and even though that wasn't a big surprise, Jordan was numbed by the knowledge that Spider had known all along what had happened to Tito Cordova. Even more unsettling was how involved Kitty was in all of this. God, he wished she were still alive. "What's all this got to do with what you did?" he asked.

"I didn't do anything, goddamn it. I was there. I saw it!" Spider yelled and then recoiled against the door.

"You didn't tell anybody. That's doing something."

"I'm tellin' you now."

Jordan shook his head. *OK, but it's a little late, don't you think?* He didn't say it out loud, but he wanted to.

Spider turned again in the driver's seat, stared out the window at the volunteer fire department. A light breeze kicked up some dust in the parking lot, swirled it in a funnel, and vanished just as quickly as it had appeared. He turned the key off and the van's engine chugged and choked with an extended rattle before it went silent. "I was sixteen," he said. "What the hell did I know? I sure didn't think life would turn out like this." He smacked his legs, twisted his lips into a frown. Tears brimmed his eyes.

Ginny had told Jordan the same thing. It was as if living in a small town was an incurable disease, an illness slow to show its symptoms. And when it did, it was too late to treat it. You just died a slow miserable death, one day at a time. Staying in Dukaine had infected them all—even him. Sitting there, staring at Spider, looking into his eyes, Jordan felt empty, lonelier than he'd felt in a long, long time. Nobody's life had turned out like they thought it would.

The wound in his shoulder throbbed harder, and the loneliness turned to anger, but Jordan restrained it. *I got shot because of you,* he wanted to scream. *Holister is dead because of you.* But he said nothing. He just continued to stare and waited for the truth to seep out of Spider's mouth.

"Tell me what happened," Jordan said.

"All right. Better now than later, I suppose." Spider sniffled, wiped his eyes and nose.

Jordan remained frozen. Waiting. It unsettled him to see Spider like this.

"It was a normal day," Spider began. "I was lookin' for a bag of pot. Charlie was doing something else after school—working on a car, something, I don't remember now. We were in the tenth grade, and Charlie was always working on that damn Electra his grandfather gave him. Anyhow, I was walking home, and Ed Kirsch passed by. I waved him down."

Jordan bit his lip, pressed down hard enough so he wouldn't say what he was thinking. *You motherfucker. How could you not tell me?*

Spider took a deep breath. "Ed's a year older than me, was in the grade ahead of me, and I never liked getting pot from him—

you know that. The Mexicans were gone, so pot was a little hard to come by. But Ed always had something when I was desperate, even if it was just homegrown, or a dime bag that was always a little short, which in those days didn't matter too much. Hell, a damn dime bag would last a week or two. . . . Sure isn't that way now."

"You should have warned me about Ed," Jordan finally said, glaring at Spider.

"I told you to stay away from him, from Ginny."

"You don't get it."

"Yes, I do. More than you think. Do you wanna hear this or not?"

"Go on."

"Ed said he'd have to go to the house to get me a bag, but he had something to do first. Did I want to ride along? Sure I did. Didn't fuckin' want to go home. Mom and Big Joe were at war. He should have left Dukaine then instead of waiting until he did."

Jordan nodded.

"So, I got in the car and Ed and I smoked a doobie, kind of a try before you buy, you know? No, you wouldn't. Never mind. Anyway, we drove out in the country, the opposite way of Ed's house. I didn't know where he was going. Fuck, I didn't care. Ed started ranting about the Mexicans. It was November and they were gone. I thought it was a little odd, but people around here carry that hate year-round, so I didn't pay much attention. Ed was just blowin' off, like usual. We slowed down about a half-mile from the Cordova place, and Ed stopped. He turned to me and said, 'You tell anybody about this and I'll have to kill you.' He was serious, and it scared the holy fuckin' shit out of me. I should have got out of the car right then, should have never gotten into it to begin with, but by then it was too late. I was so stoned I could barely move. I had cottonmouth, couldn't say a word.

"I don't know why he took me with him. I suppose he thought he and I were just alike. Everybody in town knew how Big Joe felt about the Mexicans—Ed's father was in the tavern all the time. And he was right—I didn't like the Mexicans any more than the next guy. But I never had anything against that kid. I barely knew he existed. What the hell did I care back then who his father was, or that he was a half-breed? Buddy Mozel was barely on my radar. He was just the jerk with the black Lincoln who owned the plant and half the town. All I cared about was getting stoned and getting laid, which hadn't happened yet, by the way."

"Not much has changed," Jordan said.

"Yeah it has. Everything has changed. I still wish I could get laid—and getting stoned isn't what it used to be. Anyway, I think Ed took some satisfaction that I was with him because of Kitty—he mentioned her. Asked me how I felt about her tending to the migrants. I said I didn't fucking care what she did. Parents, grandparents, it didn't matter, I didn't like anybody that had any kind of authority. Kitty was great for a meal, but what she did beyond that didn't matter to me, I had to deal with her every once in a while, but I didn't have to like what she did anymore than I had to like Big Joe and what he did. Everything was all fucked up back then. Our world was fallin' apart, not that it was ever great to begin with, and the only time I wasn't mad was when I was stoned."

Spider took a deep breath, ran a hand through his hair, and tightened his ponytail. He stared off into space, searching for details. "Ed pulled up in the driveway. The kid was standin' on the porch. When Ed got out of the car, Tito started runnin'. It was like watchin' a rabid dog chasing down a rabbit. By then I was really freaked out—I just sat there and watched, I couldn't breathe. Ed caught him, started punchin' him and dragged him back to the car, opened the trunk, and tossed him in, hard. The kid kept screamin', beatin' on the lid to get out. Ed got in the car—looked at me and started laughin'. Tito had scratched his face and a thin line of blood ran down his cheek. But Ed couldn't take the noise. He got out again, opened the trunk, and beat the kid until he was quiet. I could see through the rearview mirror and the crack of the trunk lid. He really hurt that kid. I don't know if he killed him then or not. But he could have—he really went at it. He could have done it right then and there."

Tears streamed down Spider's face again, and he began to cough.

Jordan tensed up. Without the engine running, the interior was getting hotter by the minute. Every once in a while, a breeze would flitter through the open windows. He could taste the dust from the parking lot. His skin itched with sweat, but he sat motionless, totally restraining himself from saying anything, from moving. He had to hear this, had to separate the fact that Spider was his brother, that a crime had been committed and he was hearing the details—but it was getting harder and harder not to play cop with Spider.

"We went to Ed's house, got a bag of pot, which was a huge, generous dime bag, and then he drove me to the spot where he picked me up and dropped me off."

"What happened to Tito?"

"He was in the trunk the whole time. I never heard a peep out of him, no movement, nothing. I figured he was dead. When those bones were found at the pond, I figured it was him, just like you did. I was relieved. It was finally over with," Spider said. His face glistened with sweat and tears, but his eyes seemed clear now. His breathing returned to normal. He looked truly relieved, lightened. "When Ed came after you, I figured all I needed to do was sit back and watch—make sure you knew to be wary of him. The cops would do their job, figure out sooner or later that Ed dumped the kid at the pond."

"But it's not Tito's bones. And you don't know what Ed did with him after you left the car?" Jordan said.

"No, I don't."

"I still don't understand why you never told me, told Holister."

"I told you, I was scared. Even more so after the accident. How would I defend myself against Ed?"

"Why'd Ed take Tito? I don't understand—it doesn't seem to me he was doing it for kicks. He was heading there, right?"

"Yes," Spider said, turning away. "I didn't ask why. All I know is what had happened that day, and what happened in the next week or two. And then the accident happened, and that changed everything for a long, long time. Nobody talked about Tito to me—and I sure the hell wasn't going to bring it up."

"What happened after that day?"

"Everything went back to normal. Ed never said anything else about it. When the search was going on, he was nowhere to be found. But who would expect any of the Kirschs to help out? Nobody. But over the years, he would let me know that it wasn't a good idea to say anything. We had that bond. I was tied to Ed and Ed was tied to me. The fact that you're my brother—a cop—never seemed to matter. Ed knew we lived in different worlds. He seemed to take satisfaction that he had something over on me. He'd won. Don't you get it? He kept you at bay with Ginny, and me with information. He could do anything he damn well wanted. And obviously, he did."

Jordan grabbed the door handle and pushed the door open. "You could have gotten me killed."

"You want an apology?" Spider asked. "You got the truth. Take that for what it is. I didn't have to fuckin' tell you."

"I got one more question for you."

"What's that?" Spider asked.

"Do you still buy off Ed?"

"I'm not answerin' that question. I don't think I have to."

Jordan pushed his way out of the van. He wanted to be as far away from Spider as possible. His concern for Ginny and Dylan was utmost now that Spider had told him that Ed was involved in this deeper than just cooking and dealing meth. He trembled from head to toe.

He stalked across the parking lot. He could hear pigeons cooing, and the smell and taste of tomatoes was ranker than ever—the air smelled of roadkill; death and rot baking in the sun. Grabbing the door to enter the station, he looked up and down the empty street before ducking inside. The musty smell immediately greeted him, along with another smell that he did not immediately recognize.

Until he stepped fully into the room and saw Louella Canberry reclined in her chair as far back as it could go, staring at the ceiling with a bullet hole set squarely between her eyes.

CHAPTER 25

March 9, 1995, 11:22 A.M.

The sixteen-week course at the police academy in Indianapolis had flown by for Jordan. Day after day, his time had been regimented between classes and all the necessary physical training it was going take to become a deputy for the Dukaine Police Department. The book work had been the most difficult for him, learning search and seizure laws, basic laws of arrest, handling of evidence and report writing; while the physical side was surprisingly more interesting, more fun. Until now, Spider had always been the athlete in the family.

Weaponless defense, the firearms range, the driving course, daily exercise and obstacle course, and uniform inspections provided Jordan with a confidence he'd never felt before. He finished sixth in his class out of thirty, and finally, graduation day had arrived.

An auditorium the size of a football field housed the ceremony. At least a hundred and fifty people sat in wood pullout bleachers on one side, while on the other side a small stage had been erected with cadets facing it, sitting in cold metal chairs.

Jordan looked over his shoulder and scanned the audience. Spider sat in his wheelchair, freshly shaven with the exception of a thick black goatee, and dressed in jeans and a heavy black sweater. The glint of Spider's gold earring caught Jordan's eye, and they made eye contact, each of them forcing a smile. Spider looked a little uncomfortable sitting in a room full of soon-to-be cops and their families.

Holister, who was in full dress uniform, sat behind Spider, and Celeste sat next to him, as always, prim and proper, a pink pillbox hat atop her perfectly coifed white hair. Like most everyone else, she had on her coat, a thick dark blue wool affair that had surely come straight out of the window of one of the better woman's shops on the courthouse square in Morland.

The wind outside howled and Jordan could feel a cold draft on his feet. There was a threat of a late winter ice storm hanging over the day, and a growing nervousness was obvious among the crowd, an underlying sense of urgency to get home before the storm hit. The threat of bad weather was evident to everyone except the captain of the cadets who was taking as long as he felt necessary handing out certificates to each graduate.

Jordan's toes were almost numb, but he barely noticed. There was no sign of Ginny in the crowd. Not that he had expected her, but still, he'd secretly hoped she would show up, even though he doubted her new husband, Ed Kirsch, would allow it.

He had only seen Ginny once since she'd got married, since she'd ran away one snowy night a few months ago and took the vows of matrimony in Kentucky, in the presence of two strangers and a justice of the peace. They did not speak then—just stared at each other and turned away. As far as Jordan was concerned it would be a long time, if ever, before he would speak to Ginny again—he wasn't sure if he could restrain himself, his anger, even though he knew he would have to now. He'd been heartbroken at the news of the marriage, but not nearly as much as Holister and Celeste had been.

Ginny's absence hurt—he would've loved to have seen her bright smiling face standing out from the crowd, her eyes focused only on him, smiling, rescuing him from the drudgery of another ceremony—but it was Kitty who he really missed, who he really grieved for.

Three days before his training started at the academy, Kitty had died quietly at home in her sleep. Just like Ginny's choice to run off with Ed, Kitty's death had not been a surprise. Jordan had seen it coming for months, even though he denied the possibility, the certainty of it. But Kitty had known she was dying, and she'd tidied up as many loose ends as possible, as if she were preparing for one last journey. Everything was in order, funeral arrangements, transfer of ownership of the house, all divided equally between Jordan and Spider, and that had made her death much easier to navigate. At least physically. Jordan could barely sit still at the funeral—he'd wanted to run from under the tent, flee the cycle of death that always ended up at the same place.

He had seriously considered putting off going to the academy. But Holister had convinced him to go forward instead of sitting in the empty house, jobless, hopeless, doing nothing but feeling sorry for himself. And like usual, Holister had been right. The training distracted Jordan—engaged him, and after a few days, focused his thoughts on the future. There would be time enough once he had graduated, once he was back in Dukaine, to settle his grief. Kitty wouldn't have wanted it any other way. He had ventured to Indianapolis as much for her as he had for himself.

In both instances, at Kitty's funeral, and now, at the graduation, there had not been one word from or one mention of Big Joe. It was as if he, too, was already buried in the Haven Hill cemetery.

Jordan's certificate of completion was securely in his hands. The captain, Peter Eastman, a cross between a priest and a drill instructor with a gray handlebar mustache, was finally wrapping the ceremony up. Taps played for all of the policemen who died while on duty by a single trumpet player. A melancholy reminder that eased into his heart, and brought the realization closer to the surface that every time he put his uniform on he was putting his life at risk. The trumpet player stepped back, and almost magically, the room was filled with a high school band performing a rousing Sousa march. The glory of duty, of brotherhood, of daily victory over darkness, was evident in each powerful note, each strike of the drum. The music announced the risk was worth taking. While one life might be lost, hundreds more might be saved. A smile grew halfway across Jordan's face as he lost himself, his thoughts and fears, in the rhythm of the music.

Once the echo quit reverberating from the rafters, the cadets were ordered to stand, to take the oath that would see them through their careers.

Almost finished, Jordan thought. He was excited about going home, about working with Holister. But he dreaded seeing Ginny, dreaded the quietness of the house on Harrison Street, dreaded separating himself even further from Spider, especially now that he was all alone.

"Repeat after me," Captain Eastman's voice boomed over the PA system. "As a law enforcement officer in the state of Indiana, my fundamental duty is to serve mankind. To safeguard lives and property. To protect the innocent against deception, the weak against oppression or intimidation, and the peaceful against violence or disorder; and to respect the Constitutional rights of all men to liberty, equality, and justice. I will keep my private life unsullied as an example to all; maintain courageous calm in the face of danger; develop self-restraint; and be constantly mindful of the welfare of others. Honest in thought and deed in both my personal and official life. I will be exemplary in obeying the laws of the land and the regulations of my department."

Jordan could hear coughs, throats clearing, along with Captain Eastman's steady tenor ringing in his head. Could he do all of these things? The commands were not far from Kitty's imposed morality—the same one that had gotten him here, gotten him to consider law enforcement as a career choice. Not that he had many choices in Dukaine—other than leaving or working at the SunRipe plant, of which he wasn't willing to do either. Dukaine was his home, he was comfortable there, couldn't imagine living anywhere else in the world. He spoke the words with enthusiasm, and a nagging feeling of doubt.

"Whatever I see or hear of a confidential nature or that is confided to me in my official capacity will be kept forever secret," Captain Eastman continued. "Unless revelation is necessary in the performance of my duty. I will never act officiously or permit my personal feelings, prejudices, animosities, or friendships to influence my decisions."

Jordan looked over his shoulder again. Spider looked away.

"With no compromise for crime and with relentless prosecution of criminals, I will enforce the law courteously and appropriately without fear or favor, malice or ill will, never employing unnecessary force or violence, and never accepting gratuities or favors. I recognize the badge of my office as a symbol of public faith, and I accept it as public trust to be held as long as I am true to the ethics of the police department I serve. I will constantly strive to achieve these objectives and ideals, dedicating myself before God to the brotherhood of law enforcement."

Jordan nodded. *I can do this,* he thought. *This is who I want to be. Thank God I have Holister to show me the way.*

A few more final words from Captain Eastman followed—the tossing of hats, applause by the audience, rain tinkling on the windows as it froze on the glass panes. The band struck up another song, a celebratory tune that he didn't know the name of but could feel in his bones. He had a new family now . . .

bound by the daily risk of doing the right thing, standing for something that was more than he could grasp—but he could reach for it. And he would . . . with all his might. Being a cop was more than a job—it was a life. And, finally, he had a life of his own . . .

The huge room erupted with noise and movement. Cadets were glad-handing each other, a slap on the back, a promise to keep in touch. Holister and Celeste pushed their way to him.

"Congratulations, Jordan," Holister said, clasping his hand and giving him a hearty handshake. "I'm proud of you. The Town Board's approved you now that you've completed your training. You can start Monday morning, first thing."

"Don't rush him," Celeste said. "Let him celebrate." She reached up and kissed Jordan on the cheek. "Kitty and your mother would be so proud," she whispered, pulling back, wiping tears from her eyes.

"I'm just happy for the boy," Holister said, beaming.

"You two'll have a lot of time together. He should enjoy this."

"Yes, we will," Holister answered with a wink.

Spider rolled up and stuck his right hand out to Jordan. "Congratulations."

"Thanks."

They stared at each other for a moment. A vacuum of tension pushed all the noise away. Jordan wanted to ask Spider if he had told Big Joe about the ceremony, but he didn't, couldn't bring himself to. It was a miracle that Spider was there to witness the event as it was.

Before he could say anything else, someone grabbed Jordan's shoulder and spun him around, pulling him back into the moment, away from the family divide.

"Hey, we made it, man," Lonnie Marovich said with a huge smile.

"Yeah, we did."

Holister and Celeste stood proudly next to Jordan.

"These your parents?"

Before Jordan could say anything, Holister stepped forward and shook Lonnie's hand. "Marshal Holister Coggins. Jordan's gonna work with me."

"Glad to meet you Marshal Coggins. He's going to be a good cop. Just watch him when he drives—he damn near got me killed."

They all laughed. Jordan nodded at Holister, a silent thank you they both understood. He was always uncomfortable when the subject of his parents came up. "The front end on that car was out of whack," he said.

During the driving course, they had practiced a controlled slide on wet roads. Jordan lost control and stopped the cruiser inches from the crowd of cadets waiting to drive next.

"Whatever you say, Jordan." Lonnie laughed again. The bond between them had been quick. Lonnie's strength had been the books, while his weakness was the physical side of things. They'd helped each other through the daily grind of the academy, and Jordan was happy for the friendship, but he felt bad that he had never told Lonnie about his family—he avoided that topic as much as possible, and Lonnie didn't push it. Lonnie's enthusiasm for police work was contagious, made his life in Dukaine seem distant, less painful.

"Hey, I want you to meet someone," Lonnie said. He put a little pressure on Jordan's shoulder and pushed him forward through the crowd, and stopped in front of a good-looking brunette who looked similar to Lonnie. "This is my sister, Monica, the one I've been telling you about."

Monica Marovich shook Jordan's hand softly. She had a beautiful smile and deep brown eyes—the kind you could get lost in if you let yourself. "Lonnie, you're such a jerk. Don't believe a word he says, Jordan."

"I don't."

"Hey," Lonnie said. "We're having a little party at my house. You should stop by if you can. I know the weather's supposed to be bad, but I'd really like it if you did."

"I don't know . . ." Jordan turned away from Lonnie and Monica. Spider was rolling toward the exit. Holister and Celeste had promised to take him out to dinner, but beyond that he had nothing to go home to but an empty house. Spider disappeared in the crowd. "Sure. That would be great," Jordan said.

Lonnie grinned and stepped back. Monica leaned up and kissed Jordan on the cheek. "Congratulations, Jordan McManus. Lonnie's told me a lot about you, too."

"Well, I think you better believe every word of it, then."

They all laughed again. Lonnie and Monica disappeared into the crowd, and Jordan watched them walk away, watched her walk away. She really was beautiful. He felt the same thing he had when he was taking the oath: excitement and doubt.

March 9, 1995, 5:25 P.M.*, Monterrey, Mexico*

Chavez was standing at the door, trying to flag in customers. The *galería* was just inside a *callejón,* an alley, two blocks from the *Museo de Arte Contemporaneo.* It was a busy, bustling time in Monterrey. *Turistas* were thick, escaping the winters up north, delighting in Mexico's cheap goods and the warmth of the ever-bright sun. Most people walked right by Chavez without giving him any notice.

Tito could barely remember winter. Snow. The feel of biting cold on his skin. He tried not to remember on most days, because when he did, he saw the man that grabbed him, beat him, saw the other one sitting in the car, a spider drawn on his arm. And then blackness, the smell of gasoline . . . until finally when he awoke to a soft Mexican voice that promised he was safe. Memories came in flashes. He could never remember whether it was a male voice or a female voice, and he'd finally decided that it was the voice of a nun. Blackness bordered in white, surrounding a caring face. At least he had awoke—had escaped death, but to this day he no idea how or why.

Aidia hurried him along, past the *muchachos,* the street boys begging for food money, past the tamale stands that made his stomach growl. The air was filled with celebration and sadness, the smell of wonderful food and hunger was everywhere—it was, as Tito learned, the way of life in Mexico, especially in Monterrey. "Chavez will not be in his shop forever, Tito," Aidia said, scolding him.

The festival-like atmosphere entranced Tito. The last few months had been filled with a sense of desperation as they waited for Aidia's paintings to sell, for the burden of poverty to be lifted from them. He was getting tired of eating *brooth del pollo* for dinner, but he could not bring himself to leave—to run away in the middle of the night one more time. Aidia needed him.

Chavez was a portly man with a severe face pocked with tiny scars and shiny, moist skin. He was always dressed in a white suit that seemed much too tight for his body. Tito did not like Chavez, did not trust him, but Aidia refused to ask for money from her family, and Chavez owned the only *galería* in town that would sell her paintings.

"*Senorita* Marquez, how nice to see you," Chavez said, stepping aside to allow Aidia and Tito inside the *galería.* "I fear I do not have much good news for you. A pittance, really."

Aidia stopped in the middle of the small room and scanned the walls, the floor, for her paintings. Tito stood next to her—waiting for a sign to show on her face, a sign that said whether or not she believed Chavez. They had been to the *galería* many times since Aidia had taken Tito in, and each time was a mix of haggling and deciphering Chavez's lies. A frown was frozen on Aidia's lips, as if she was trying to think of something to say, to think of a different tack to take with Chavez.

The *galería* was a jumble of colors and familiar smells—it was very much like Aidia's *estudio*. The walls were packed with paintings of every kind. Sculptures and vases littered the floor with more paintings leaning against anything that would keep them erect. There were a lot of Frida Kahlo imitations—an artist that Aidia held in high regard, but she could not stomach those who tried to feast off the artist's dead bones—and more landscapes and peasant pictures than Tito could count. He had followed Aidia's eyes and saw, too, that none of her pictures were displayed anywhere in the room.

Chavez waddled behind a long counter made of mahogany, and disappeared underneath it for a moment, searching for something, it seemed.

Aidia was cussing under her breath. Tito had never seen her so angry and he feared what would come out of her mouth next. There were times when she would fly into a rage at the drop of a pin—if Tito chewed wrong, stood wrong, asked a question at the wrong time. Afterward, she would apologize and act as if the outburst never happened. But Tito had learned to see the anger coming, to know when to step back into the shadows and when to avoid it.

Now was one of those times. Tito eased away from Aidia and stood next to a bronze statue of a *conquistador*.

Chavez reappeared with some coins in his hand. Aidia's face flushed red.

"How am I supposed to make any *dinero*, Chavez? You do not have any of my paintings on the walls."

"I only have so much space."

"That is what you always say," Aidia said.

"You should learn to paint like Kahlo."

"*Usted es un cerdo gordo.*"

Tito moved behind the statue when Aidia called Chavez a fat pig.

"Take your *dinero* and leave my shop, *Senorita* Marquez." Chavez extended his hand with the coins in it. "And take your paintings with you. I do not have to put up with such treatment."

Aidia's shoulders tensed. She bit her lip, tears glistened in her eyes, and she took a long, deep breath. "*Estoy apesadumbrado.*" I'm sorry, she said. "I truly am, Chavez. It is just that money is thin and I cannot bear to give up my painting. It is my life. I know of no other way to live."

Chavez's beady eyes did not change. He looked bored—as if he had heard Aidia's story a million times. "Perhaps," he said, rubbing his chin with his index finger, "we could make another arrangement," wrapping a fist around the coins.

It wasn't until Chavez licked his lips that Tito understood what the offer meant.

Aidia swirled around to Tito, her eyes glaring. She picked up a small vase about the size of a football and threw it directly at Chavez's head. The plaster shattered into tiny pieces as it struck the wall, barely missing the man.

"*¡Fuera de! ¡Salga!*" Chavez screamed. Out! Get out!

He threw the coins at Aidia. They scattered across the floor and Tito ran to pick them up.

Aidia found a larger vase and heaved it. Chavez ducked. Shards of the vase flew everywhere. Ceramic pieces the color of a rainbow fell at Tito's feet. He looked up and saw Chavez move from behind the counter with a walking cane in his hand, arched up ready to strike Aidia.

Aidia's eyes were wild, searching for something else to throw. She did not see Chavez until it was too late. He swung the cane down and smacked Aidia's hand with great force. The sound of breaking bones echoed in the room, followed by a horrible shriek of pain.

Chavez reared back again, readying the cane to strike Aidia again, all the time yelling, ordering them to leave. *"¡Salga! ¡Salga! ¡Salga!"*

Tito was panicked, afraid of what would happen next. He picked up a shard of the vase at his feet, and without thinking, only seeing Aidia's dangling wrist and agony on her face, he lunged at Chavez, putting himself between them, and drove the sharp end of the vase directly into the fat man's throat.

Chapter 26

The dispatch radio was silent and Jordan listened closely before moving another inch inside the police station. The ceiling fan whirled, spreading the smell of death and blood throughout the room. In the distance he could hear the air-conditioner droning. Warm, sticky air swirled around him. His skin felt clammy, and for a moment, he panicked at the sight of Louella.

The fluorescent lights were still on, buzzing overhead, the light harsh and void of shadows. There were no other sounds indicating anyone else was in the main room, only Louella, who sat rigidly, silently in her chair, staring upward, her gaze fixed. Blood ran down the left side of her face from the bullet wound in her forehead. It had already congealed. One of the knitting picks from her hair had fallen to the floor. Long, wild gray strands dangled motionlessly over the back of the chair. A fly landed on her right eye.

As soon as Jordan regained control, pushed his panic away, he realized he'd touched the door handle. He stuffed his hands in his pockets. His fingerprints would be everywhere—but after being scrutinized so closely by Sheriff Hogue, after being a suspect in multiple crimes over the last two days, keeping himself free of suspicion seemed very important to him. For about two seconds.

Sweat ran down his back as he pulled the .38 from the holster and checked the chamber, making sure a bullet was ready to fire.

There was no question that Louella was dead. But he could not bring himself to move toward her.

He took a deep breath, pushed away the conversation he'd just had with Spider—for the moment—and felt a shock of terror rise from the bottom of his feet to the top of his head as a single question formed in his mind: *Where's Dylan?*

The shock of the question, the instant image arising from his memory, put him in the backseat of the family station wagon. He could taste the blood, feel the glass stuck in his face, the intense pain in his legs, a cold wind pushing in the open door as he saw Spider laying in the middle of the road, broken and feared dead. He wasn't sure he could bear to find the little boy dead, too . . . but he knew he had to look, to try and find him.

Jordan bolted to the door of his office, ignoring Louella. Dylan's toy cars were strewn across the floor. Nothing was out of place—no one was there.

His thoughts were a jumble. He checked the janitor's closet. Nothing. The door that exited to the front half of the building, the Town Hall, was locked. From there he checked the door that led upstairs to the storage room. It was locked, too. He scanned the room again, and his gaze fell back on Louella. Slowly, cautiously, he made his way to the dispatch desk, searching the floor, looking for shadows, hoping to see movement under the desk.

He glanced quickly under the desk, hoping the little boy had sought refuge there. But he found nothing. From there he forced himself to touch Louella. Images of Grandpa George and his mother lying in a casket briefly flashed in his mind's eye.

Louella's skin was cool but not cold. He touched her neck, her carotid artery, with his left hand, still keeping the .38 ready in his right hand, and could find no pulse. She hadn't been dead long. There was no sign of any residue on her head—and he figured she was shot from a distance, figured the shooter walked in the front door and fired without warning. He felt incredibly sad, recoiled from the cold touch. Even though he'd never liked Louella, she had been a stable presence in his everyday life. He could depend on her to be behind the desk, to be snippy, bossy, and judgmental. And now she was gone, too.

The console was shut off. Her purse was at her feet—she was obviously getting ready to go home when the shooter came in. He couldn't be sure, but that's how it looked to him. There was nothing left for him to do—he couldn't save Louella, it was too late for that. It may be too late to save anybody, Ginny, Dylan, himself . . . but he had to do something.

The beating of his heart overwhelmed all of the other noises in the room as he made his way to Holister's office. He peered around the doorjamb, hoping, praying, that Dylan was there. His hopes were futile. The office was empty, too.

But the door to the gun cabinet was standing wide open. The padlock was laying in the middle of the floor. Four Remington Model 700 rifles stood securely in a line, untouched. Several cases of ammunition were butted against the back wall of the gray metal cabinet; magazines for the rifles, bullets for the Glocks they all carried. A sign-out sheet hung on the open door. Everything looked in order.

Jordan inched into the office, ignored the picture of Elvis in his karate uniform on the bulletin board, and kneeled down to take a closer look inside the cabinet. Dread filled him as he searched for the one thing he couldn't see from outside the office.

As he suspected, Holister's briefcase was missing.

He stood straight up and began to put everything together he was seeing, piece together the crime scene he was standing in the middle of. He slid the .38 back in the holster.

Someone had come into the office and shot Louella. There was no sign of a struggle, so Louella must have known the shooter—or they surprised her. The shooter obviously knew what he was after—the Cordova file. But did the shooter know Dylan was there? Did he find the boy before or after Louella was shot? Did he find him at all—or did the little boy escape, run away, and let somebody know what was happening? There was no way for Jordan to tell exactly what had happened, not in the span of time he had to consider it.

If Dylan did get away, did alert someone to the shooting, then Jordan knew full well that he needed to get his ass out of there—get as far away from the police station as possible. But he was like a dragonfly caught in a bird's beak. He couldn't bring himself to pull away, find the strength to break away and escape without losing a wing. He obviously had been minutes behind the shooter, seconds away from finding out who the shooter was, a heartbeat away from facing a demon.

There were answers in front of him, all around him, and even though he knew he was putting himself in more jeopardy, he had to take the risk to ask more questions, to hopefully find some answers, so he could figure out where to go next.

He leaned down and examined the padlock on the floor without touching it. It was open, and uncut. The shooter had the key. Or knew where the key was.

Jordan grabbed a piece of paper off the top of the desk and slid open the bottom drawer. He felt for the key—knew where it was hidden—and found nothing. The key was gone. He slid the desk drawer door closed and looked around the room again. Did the shooter drop something? Leave something behind? Nothing jumped out at him—everything looked pretty much the same as it had the last time he was in the office.

So, after the shooter grabbed the briefcase, what then? Jordan asked himself. *Where was Dylan while all this was going on? What did the shooter do to him?* He shuddered at the thought, shuddered at the possibilities of another child in Dukaine being abducted. Being killed.

After his discussion with Spider, there was no way he could *not* suspect Ed Kirsch. But why would Ed shoot Louella?

To get the briefcase, Jordan answered himself. That made sense. But how did Ed know where the file was—that it even existed? Or where the key was? And, what was in the file that was important enough to kill Louella for? Did Holister know Ed was involved in the abduction? If so, he had never mentioned anything to Jordan about it. That was one piece of the case Holister *wouldn't* have kept from Jordan. He knew that in his bones.

It has to be Ed, he thought to himself. Ed took Tito Cordova. And Ginny was nowhere to be found—did she know about the file? Did she tell Ed where it was? It was possible. If Ed had convinced her to take the bullets from his Glock, then telling Ed about the briefcase didn't seem like much of a stretch—if Holister had ever told her about the file, if she had ever seen it.

God, he wanted to talk to Holister . . . but that was impossible. Just like talking to Kitty was impossible. He began to get angry again—furious that people made a mess of things and left them for other people to clean up, to pay for.

No, stop, Jordan told himself. *Keep your head about you . . .* Why would Ed Kirsch want the Cordova file? Louella wouldn't have given it to him—so he shot her, and then took Dylan. If Ed was planning on making a run for it he would want to take the boy, too.

Jordan took a deep breath. There was no question he had to find Ed Kirsch. But could he trust Spider to help him? Did Spider tell him everything? Was what he had told him in the van the entire truth?

But what if the shooter wasn't Ed? The question kept coming back into his mind. Each time it did, Jordan pushed it away, thoroughly convinced, at the moment, that Ed was responsible for killing Louella. Nothing else added up. Even if Spider hadn't told him everything.

He reached into the cabinet and grabbed one of the Remingtons. The rifle weighed nine pounds and had a twenty-six-inch barrel. On a normal day, picking up the rifle didn't even draw a flinch, but a twinge of pain shot through his shoulder as he slung the rifle over his arm. He ignored the pain the best he could. A rush of adrenaline was coming from somewhere deep inside him. He was afraid for Dylan, for Ginny, and angry as hell at Spider.

A spare radio sat next to the boxes of ammunition. Having a radio would keep him apprised of what was going on—give him the option to call Hogue or Johnny Ray if he needed them. He grabbed the radio, attached it to his belt, and started to walk out of the office. He stopped at the entry door and checked the battery. It was dead.

Jordan shifted the weight of the rifle, skirted the desk, and eased around Louella as carefully as possible.

A fresh battery sat in the charger next to the microphone. He thought about closing her eyes, honoring her death. But he knew better. Instead, he snatched up the battery, exchanged it with the dead one, and flipped on the radio. Static hissed and echoed throughout the room.

"Copy. 1187 out," a male voice said.

"Huckle Road entrance is secure. 1218 clear," another male voice said.

The radio hissed and crackled again.

"10-1. Could you repeat 1218?" a female dispatcher.

"Huckle Road entrance is secure."

"10-4."

Hogue was still keeping the pond secure. That was good to know. The work on the graves—digging up all of the skeletons out of the muck, would take some time. Gawkers would be everywhere now. Driving up and down the road, hoping they could catch a glimpse of a bone, a body. Some would park as close as possible to the pond, congregate in small groups like they were at a summer picnic, waiting to hear the latest rumor, the latest tidbit of news over the radio, or from a friend of a friend whose brother-in-law was a sheriff's deputy. Jordan could just about name the people who would be standing there. Maybe they watched so they would feel better about their own lives— safer, happy that tragedy had passed them by one more time. Whatever the reason, it pissed Jordan off that people stood along the sidelines, watching death and destruction as if it were a Friday night football game.

Until that moment, he had no idea what was going on with the investigation—other than what Hogue had told him: He was still under suspicion, still considered a "person of interest" in the shooting.

Holister had died since he'd talked to the sheriff at the pond. Ginny had gone missing—at least unofficially—and her trailer had been trashed. Was Ed looking for the file, the briefcase, there? It was something to think about.

Beyond the unanswered questions about Ginny, Louella was officially dead—and Dylan was nowhere to be found.

And to top it all off, Jordan thought as he moved from the dispatch desk, Spider had confessed to him that he'd been there when Tito Cordova had been abducted. Which not only had pointed the light of suspicion directly on Ed Kirsch, but he had to rethink his own footsteps over the last couple of days. Revisit everything Spider had said and done. Did Hogue have a good reason for suspecting Spider, for issuing a search warrant for the tavern? Had it been served yet?

He had no idea, no answers to the questions that kept scream-ing in his mind about his brother, about what was going on. But having the radio in his possession would help level the playing field—at least when it came to Sheriff Hogue.

"1187," the female dispatcher said. "Unit 01 is requesting you meet him in Dukaine at the corner of Jefferson and Main. Code 2."

"01 is en route. ETA is five minutes."

"Copy 01. Did you get that 1187?"

"10-4."

"01 clear."

The radio hissed and crackled again. Jordan froze. Unit 01 was Hogue. Code 2 was no lights or siren. Fuck . . . Hogue was heading his way. He needed to get the hell out of there . . . he should have left as soon as he walked in and found Louella dead.

He couldn't very well walk out the front door with the Remington on his shoulder and an armload of ammunition. The only other way out was the door that led upstairs and then down the rickety metal fire escape on the back of the building. But the door was locked. He'd already checked it.

"I'm heading that way now," unit 1187 said.

The radio went silent. Jordan thought about switching channels, checking to see where Johnny Ray was—he didn't know what the shift schedule was or what Johnny Ray's duties were since becoming the acting marshal—but he decided not to. For all he knew, Johnny Ray had hung up his gunbelt for the day, and donned his Elvis garb for a gig at the Super Six motel.

A sign on the stairway door said to keep it locked at all times. Jordan jiggled the doorknob and pulled on it again to make sure it was fully locked. It was.

The lock was old, tarnished brass, and took a skeleton key to open. He had picked the lock before—last month, just before Holister's birthday party, to hide his gift in the landing. After a quick tour around the room, he picked up Louella's needle from her hair off the floor.

His hands shook as he jimmied the lock and pulled on the door. Sweat ran down his nose. The radio remained quiet. After a few minutes of struggling, the door finally popped open.

The staircase was narrow and dark, and the musty smell was even worse inside than it was outside. Jordan flipped on the light, closed the door behind him, and made his way up the creaky stairs. Another door stood before him at the top of the stairs. He pushed it open slowly.

Soft gray light filtered into the room from the window over the fire escape. A five-by-five-foot plastic Santa Claus was propped up against the far wall, staring at him with a wide smile. Boxes of garland, files, and old law books littered the floor. A mousetrap sat underneath an old office chair, a mouse's remains half decayed, the flesh rotted off its head, exposing a perfect skeleton.

Jordan tried to ignore the familiar aroma as much as he could, adjusted the rifle over his shoulder, and looked away from the mouse, to the floor, to see if there were any fresh footprints in the dust.

No one had been upstairs in a long time.

He relaxed for a second and moved to the window. The view from the second floor did not allow for much. He could see over the roof of the volunteer fire department, see a few houses beyond, but the tall maple and oak trees that lined Jefferson Street obscured everything else.

Dusk was settling in, daylight was fading into a cloudless night sky. But it was still hot, and the second floor was stifling and humid. He could barely breathe.

The wood window was swollen and Jordan had to put some effort into pushing it open. His shoulder screamed with pain, and he felt something tear, felt the first drop of blood ooze out of the gunshot wound.

The radio crackled again.

"01 is 10-97. What's your 20, 1187?"

"I just passed the city limits sign."

He leaned outside and eased the boxes of ammunition onto the metal grate and then stepped outside, trying his best to stay in the shadow of the building. Hogue was close, on the other side of the building or across the street.

Jordan hoped he could make it to the van without being seen, but his hopes were dashed when he stood up and looked down into the parking lot. The van was nowhere to be seen.

Spider was gone.

CHAPTER 27

August 22, 2004, 7:01 P.M.

The only car in the parking lot below was Louella Canberry's Buick. Jordan stood with his back against the wall, trying to blend in, unsure of what to do next. The maddening chorus of cicadas and other insects buzzed high in the trees—would they ever shut the fuck up? Cars stopped and idled at the intersection on the other side of the building. The ever-present rumble and groan of the SunRipe plant pulsed distantly beneath all of the other noises, pumping stinking excesses from tomato sauce and ketchup into the sewers. A smell that was hardly noticeable to anyone who had lived in Dukaine for any length of time, but for some reason it was more noticeable tonight, and it made him nauseous.

The heat of the day would not relent until the wee hours of the morning, and then it would be a brief respite, if that. There was nowhere to run, nowhere to escape the drought, the presence of the plant, and the anger Jordan felt as he searched the empty parking lot for Spider's van.

He couldn't go back downstairs, or inside the second floor for that matter. Hogue would discover Louella's body soon enough, and the entire building would be searched, would become another crime scene wrapped in yellow tape.

He couldn't go across the street to the tavern, either.

And he couldn't go home.

The radio was turned down low, crackling with voices, and Jordan knew he had to move. Finally, he decided to head to Holister's house—to see if Celeste had made it back from the hospital, if there was any word on Ginny, and borrow Holister's pickup truck. If she wasn't home, he knew where the keys were. He would just have to break into the house to get them.

He made his way down the fire escape as quietly as he could with the Remington over his shoulder and two boxes of bullets tucked under his good arm. Blood was beginning to soak through his shirt from the wound, but it was not gushing, just a steady dribble. The pain was minimal, quelled by his growing rage and distrust of Spider.

Jordan's mind was chattering like the police radio—only he was not on a search and find mission, or serving a warrant at the tavern, which Hogue was now in the process of—he was silently screaming at Spider. *Goddamn you, Spider . . . Goddamn you. Where are you? How could you do this to me?*

Once on the ground, Jordan hunched and scurried his way across the parking lot, staying in the shadows as much as possible, using Louella's Buick for cover, and then on to the nearest telephone pole where he stopped and took stock of what was going on across the street. He could see the tail end of Hogue's brown and tan cruiser parked in front of the tavern. The other unit was nowhere in sight, but he figured it was parked at the back door.

He wondered if Angel knew what was coming her way—if Spider had gone to the tavern and got caught up in the search.

Still, it was no excuse for leaving him. Spider had a cell phone—he could have called Angel.

Jordan regretted not having a cell phone, they could have stayed in contact if he did. But as it was, Spider didn't know what he had found once he left the van and entered the police station. From Spider's point of view, when Jordan went inside, everything was as it was supposed to be. Louella was watching Dylan and the Cordova file had not been stolen. How could Spider know Louella had been murdered and Dylan was missing?

He drew in a deep breath. Now he was rationalizing Spider's actions. It was better than looking at the other side of things—assuming Spider was involved as much in the present as he had been in the past. All Jordan knew was Spider had left him when he needed him most. One more time.

The garage doors to the fire department were open. All of the vehicles were gone, still out at the pond. A collection of pickup trucks and cars with blue strobe lights sat behind the building. Jordan hunched down again and navigated through the maze of vehicles and made his way down the alley that led to Lincoln Street.

A dog barked as he passed Sam Peterson's parents' old house—a mixed-breed Doberman was tied to a tree and danced at the end of its chain, baring its teeth. The alarm signaled other dogs in the neighborhood to start barking, and before long, all of the sounds of early evening were drowned out.

Jordan hurried along the fence lines, past the one-car garages that faced the alley, ignoring the dogs, trying to stay as hidden as possible, still hunched down. He felt like a little kid playing army.

Someone would see him. Call the police. Louella wouldn't answer. They'd call the county dispatcher then. Hogue would put two and two together, and know Jordan had been inside the police station, make him a suspect again. He squelched the radio at the thought, turned up the volume slightly, and hoped he would make it to Holister's house before someone made the call.

The alley ended at Lincoln Street. Holister's house was a block away and there was no easy way to get there, no alley to cut through, no other path to take but the sidewalk, which would leave him totally exposed. He thought about cutting through yards, but most of them were fenced in, home to more barking dogs. He stopped and hid on the dark side of an oak tree to get his bearings. For the moment, he was safe, a good distance from the tavern, from Hogue, from Louella staring at the ceiling.

A car was coming. Jordan pulled tighter into the shadows, brought the rifle to his chest, and leaned face first into the bark. The street was lined with fifty- and sixty-foot oak and elm trees. Even on the brightest summer days the full foliage cast long shadows across Lincoln Street. All of the yards had patches of dirt in them where grass would not grow. Ivy clung at the bases of each tree—which even now was a vibrant green. The overhead shade had its benefits, huge limbs towering over almost every house, creating a natural form of air-conditioning, protecting black shingled roofs against the beating sun. But the air was still, there was no breeze, and Jordan felt more like he was in a jungle than a block from home.

As the car passed, Jordan peered around the tree. It was not a car, but a truck. A red truck. It was José Rivero.

Jordan took a deep breath and stepped out of the shadows into the street and waved his arms. He knew he was taking a risk, but he trusted José . . . as much as he could trust anyone right now. The truck slowed and the brake lights came on. Jordan hoped he wasn't making a mistake.

"I've been looking for you, *señor,*" José said through the window as the truck came to a stop in reverse. "Get in."

Jordan hesitated until Hogue's voice came over the radio calling for another unit. He tossed the boxes of bullets on the floor, slid the Remington off his shoulder, and climbed into the truck. The .38 poked his back and he reached around and pulled it out, keeping the gun in his lap while he propped the rifle up between his legs.

"You are bleeding," José said.

"I'm all right," Jordan answered as he pulled the door closed and José put the truck in gear.

"You do not look so all right, *Señor* Jordan."

Jordan said nothing. He gulped in some cool air-conditioning and wiped the sweat from his face. He closed his eyes for a second. When he opened them, the first thing that caught his attention was the plastic Jesus glued to the dashboard. "I've got a lot of questions for you, José," he said, thinking about the St. Christopher's medal and letter.

"I am sure you do. There will be time enough for those once you are not bleeding. Once you are safe." José looked at Jordan sideways, and then returned his sad eyes to the road.

They turned at Lincoln and Kennedy and headed out of town away from the SunRipe plant, toward the camps.

"Where're we going?"

José turned up the air-conditioning so it would blow even colder air. "There are many places no one knows about but us. I think it is best to get you as far away from here as I can. I owe the *abuela* that much."

Jordan scrutinized José's face at the mention of Kitty. "Louella Canberry is dead."

José nodded. "It continues. I am not surprised."

"What the hell's going on, José?"

"I am not sure. But it will not end. Not now. Not until the truth is known by everyone. I must leave soon. You know that."

"Because of the bones? The graves at the pond?"

"Partly. *Señor* Buddy will face many questions because of my actions, because of the secrets we share. If he lives to see another day. I fear my protection of him is coming to an end."

Jordan settled back into the seat. José's weathered face was drawn long with sadness. His brown eyes were glazed and distant, barely fixed on the road ahead. "Why were you looking for me?"

"To warn you."

"About what?"

José shook his head no. "There are many things you do not know. I wanted to tell you before now. I tried to find you, but when I did it was not safe."

"At the house? When it was on fire?"

"*Sí.*"

"Spider was with me," Jordan said, realizing what José meant when he said it wasn't safe.

José nodded.

"He already told me. I didn't know it then, but I know now. He was with Ed Kirsch when he took Tito Cordova."

The Mexican exhaled. "I suspected as much. But that is not why I fear your brother. Though now knowing this, I am glad I trusted my *instinto*, my instinct."

As the houses thinned and the fields began to take over the landscape ahead of them, daylight dimmed even further, covering the entire world in a blanket of thick gray shadows. It was not yet dark, but not light either. The sky remained cloudless. Wispy clouds of vapor hung over the fields, holding steady as if they were attached to the ground by invisible strings. Kitty called this time of day the gloaming—a moment between night and day that was as magical as it was dangerous.

Jordan coughed. Pain rippled through his torso. He cringed, grabbed his shoulder, and put pressure on the wound.

"*Resto, por favor, señor.* Rest, please. . . . There will be time enough for this once you are better."

"There's no goddamn time, José. You don't understand. Dylan is missing. Ginny's son. Holister's grandson. He was at the police station. Louella was watching him. He was gone. Vanished just like Tito Cordova . . ."

"Do not say that," José commanded harshly.

"It's true."

"Maybe. But please, do not say that name."

"You have to believe me. Louella was shot in the head. No skirmish, no mess. It was as if someone walked in, aimed and fired, and then went about their business."

"I do believe you," José said. "There is nothing that surprises me now. I am too old not to expect the worst."

They turned onto a gravel road and then turned quickly again down a well-worn path that was just wide enough for the truck to pass through. Tall trees skirted both sides of the road. Darkness filled the inside of the cab. The dashboard lights cast long shadows on José's face. Jesus glowed in the dark, a little green man now, with His arms stretched out to both sides like he was taking a sobriety test.

"Unit 01, please be advised of a 10-66 in the alley behind Lincoln Street. Subject is white male, six feet tall, wearing blue jeans and a white shirt," the dispatcher on the police radio said.

"10-4. I'm finishing up here right now. We'll check it."

"01, also be advised that the subject was carrying a rifle. The caller said they tried to call Dukaine dispatch but received no answer." Static hissed through the small radio speaker.

"Can you repeat?"

"10-4, 01. The caller tried to call Dukaine dispatch, but received no answer. The dispatcher's car is still in the lot. Could you check that out?"

"10-4. Did the caller identify themselves?"

"It was the dispatcher's brother. He's concerned because she should have been home by now."

Jordan turned down the radio. He knew what was coming. He looked at José and sighed. "All hell is about to break loose," he said.

"It already has, *Señor* Jordan. It already has."

José slowed the truck as they rounded a bend. The headlights swept through the darkness, catching tall dry brush and the rough trunks of hickory and walnut trees, until the bright lights finally came to rest on a small travel trailer partially hidden by a tall bank of weeds.

Jordan saw the shadow of a man walk slowly past the window as José brought the truck to a stop. He clutched the .38 and stared at José curiously.

"You will be safe here for now," José said. "I have been moving often. Soon, I will leave for Mexico for good. But I cannot leave until I have done what is expected of me."

"Who's inside?"

José did not answer. Even in the shadows of the cab, Jordan could see José take a deep breath, look away from him sadly.

"There are some things you need to know," José said. "Tito Cordova did not die. It is not his bones you found at the pond."

"I already know that," Jordan said, his fingers wrapped tightly around the grip of the .38. He was watching the window of the little trailer. "Who is it?"

"There are many of my *amigos* there. But that was Rosa's grave. Do you remember her?"

Jordan nodded yes. He wanted to ask what happened, why she was at the bottom of Longer's Pond, but he restrained himself and waited.

"I know you do not understand this, our world in the fields. We are not to be seen in life or death. But I convinced *Señor* Buddy many years ago that we needed a place to bury our dead, a place where we could go and mourn even over unmarked graves. For a long time he knew nothing of this. But after Tito disappeared, that changed. He changed. I had placed Rosa's worn-out little body in the pond by then—and her sister, the baby that had been born dead in the *abuela*'s hands."

Jordan nodded, remembering the night Kitty and José argued

fiercely about giving the baby a proper burial.

"I feared this day would come," José said. "As the drought took hold there were many *malavisos,* bad omens. The night before Holister was shot, I saw *seis buhos,* six owls, lined up all together on the branch of a dead oak tree, and the shadows of four more flying through the air. The next day, a hungry coyote jumped out of the woods and into the road in front of me in broad daylight. I barely missed hitting him and came stop a few feet from it. I yelled at the coyote to move, but the ragged beast planted its paws firmly and showed its teeth." José's face paled as he stared into the darkness.

The radio was buzzing with activity. They had found Louella's body. Jordan reached down and turned it off. He knew the procedures, knew everything Hogue would do next, including putting an APB out on him.

"I feared the spirits were walking the earth, so I went to the pond. But I was too late. It was surrounded by the *policia.*"

"Tell me about Tito," Jordan said.

José drew a deep breath. "I would rather wait until we are inside. It is not my story to tell."

"Who's in there?"

The Mexican did not answer again. "The past never sleeps. It is a river that runs south and then returns as rain. Sometimes as a great storm uprooting trees, other times soft and gentle, just when it is needed. A storm comes soon—see how the leaves dance and the clouds gather?" José pointed through the windshield. "Great trees will fall."

Rosa's voice swam up from deep inside Jordan's memory. "*El diablo es flojo.* The devil is loose." He looked up through the trees and could barely see the sky. A few stars twinkled, but he could see heavy clouds gathering in from the reflection of the moon. A wind had kicked up and the leaves looked like they were turned inside out, shining silver in the darkness.

José opened the door and stood up out of the truck. "Come, I need to tend to your wound. You will not need your *armas*. Your guns will do you no good for now."

Jordan followed, taking each step cautiously as he stuffed the .38 in the holster. He wasn't going anywhere without a gun.

José knocked on the door once, opened it, and stepped aside for Jordan to enter.

Jordan hesitated, eased up onto the weak metal step, pulled himself slowly inside, aware of every sound, every movement.

Buddy Mozel sat in the corner, waiting for him.

CHAPTER 28

Tito Cordova stood outside of CERESO I, the Central Facility for Social Rehabilitation, and sucked in his first breath of freedom in nine years.

The inmates called the prison *el agujero grande,* the big hole, but Tito had mixed feelings about leaving. Time had stood still as he had grown into a man, had become part of a *familia* inside the whitewashed walls. Now, he was alone again—no one waited for him outside the gates. Aidia had stopped visiting him a few months after he'd been convicted of murdering Chavez, and beyond her, there was no one he could call family. Thankfully, he had a place to go, a mission to carry out, and that made leaving *el agujero grande* easier than he thought it would be.

His dream of returning to paradise would come true soon.

He was left a pauper in a prison system that relied on bribes and payoffs to survive. It was lucky for him that he could speak both Spanish and English, and Tito quickly came under the protection of *El Príncipe,* Jorge Estavantes, The Prince of cellblock C, as a translator between the Americans, who were mostly there on drug charges, and the Mexicans.

Inmates with no money spent their days in small cells with as many as twelve other men and only two bunks—they earned money shining shoes, doing laundry, or scrubbing the floors of the *células del visitacion,* visitation cells for conjugal trysts that cost an inmate ten dollars a night. The Americans could receive money from the outside, and buy comfort and security at a relatively cheap price. It was because of this system, allowing wives and girlfriends to spend the night, that male-to-male rape was uncommon. Tito's main worry during his nine-year stint was the warring drug cartels that continued their territory battles on the inside.

He had lived comfortably once *El Príncipe* marked him with a tattoo on the nape of his neck. Before then, though, life had been hard. His heart grieved for Aidia, and he had to fight for his life, for his own space, more than once in the packed cell he was first assigned to. But once the crude devil's face over a set of crossbones was etched into his skin with blue ink, he had his own cell, his own toilet and shower that he paid for with money he would owe to *El Príncipe*. From then on, rape or harm was out of the question. Being in debt was far more agreeable to Tito than spending his time in prison constantly looking over his shoulder.

The big hole was very much like the orphanage, and just like when he was boy, Tito looked to the day when he could cross the big river. Except now, instead of running away in the middle of the night, he had to pay off *El Príncipe* before he could truly be free.

Tito looked to the sun overhead and picked up his small linen bag of belongings. His instructions were simple: Go to the corner of Juarez and Belden, take a seat in the small café, order *cabrito*, and wait.

He jingled a few pesos in his pocket and caught the first bus downtown. Flat-bed trucks, loaded with soldiers, passed by every few minutes as Tito stared out the dirty window, guns sticking up in the air, bored looks on the soldiers' faces. There was a war on with the cartels, but it was a war the government could not win. The cartels outnumbered the soldiers four to one in Nuevo Laredo, and everyone knew who was really in charge of the city. But people bustled through the streets as if it were a normal day.

It had been so long since Tito had seen so many people. He was overwhelmed, a little frightened now that he was on his own. He stared through the smog and exhaust from all of the cars and searched the distant horizon for blue skies, trying to fight off the loneliness he was beginning to feel.

The café was no bigger than two cells put together, and only three people sat inside. Garlic and vinegar filled the air. A man with a giant belly led him to a table in the corner away from the other patrons. The table was covered with a plastic red and white checkered tablecloth, dotted with cigarette burns. Flypaper dangled overhead, and a painting of a mountain hung on the wall. The painting was yellow and faded, a copy of a copy that had probably been there as long as the restaurant had been in business. The man smiled at Tito as he ordered *cabrito*, barbecued kid goat, and a draft of Negra Modelo.

"*No se apresure,*" Tito said. Don't hurry.

The cook smiled again, nodded, and disappeared through a swinging door next to the cash register. Folk music played on the radio, accordions at a fast pace with a group of male harmonies matching each note. Outside, cars and bicycles zoomed to and from the Historic District, and Tito let his mind wander to his days in Monterrey, with Aidia, as he turned his attention back to the painting overhead.

He had thought about searching for Aidia, see if she was still alive. But it was an easy choice not to. Aidia had abandoned him, and besides, she was nothing to him now. Her home was not his home. His home only existed in his dreams. No, he would go north, not south. He would go forward, not backward. It was the only thing he knew to do—the only thing he had ever wanted to do. Aidia was an old woman—probably ordering around another boy in his place. But he never regretted fighting for her, even though he had not meant to kill Chavez.

It was hard for Tito to believe so much time had passed since he had left *El Refugio*. He hoped Cirilo had had a better life than he had.

The food came, and it looked like a feast compared to prison food. Tito sat still and stared at the tender meat covered in thick spicy tomato sauce and fresh vegetables until he could no longer restrain himself. He devoured the meal in a matter of minutes. The beer tickled his throat, the taste very different from the homemade beer and wine that the inmates made from fruit and bread. He wanted another beer but could not bring himself to spend the money. He was going to need every peso and dollar bill he had in his pocket.

Tito finished his meal and did as he was told; he sat and waited. He watched people come and go. Two beautiful women came into the café and ate their meal a few tables from him. He could smell their perfume. Their long black hair glistened as if it had just been washed with rain water. He could almost taste their skin, and he had to keep reminding himself not to stare. It had been a very long time since he had been so close to a woman, and he realized how much he missed their company. And how much he wanted to touch them, hold them privately in the darkness and truly become a man.

The women left without noticing him, and he continued to wait. Daylight faded into night, but the pulse of the street outside the café did not lessen. He sat transfixed, watching the world go by, wondering how long he should wait, and what it was that he was waiting for. He thought of running, not paying his debt, but Nuevo Laredo was *El Príncipe*'s land as much as the prison was. Tito did not know the streets, and he was much too old to beg or sell his body, which he would not do. Moments of anger pulsed in his heart as he took stock of his life.

How could he not be angry? Not be enraged? He did not ask to be in Mexico—and yet, it was all he knew now. Was it a stupid little boy's dream to push north to a place he did not know?

The answer came quickly to him: *Yes—even if it is for revenge.* He had to find out what had happened to his mother. He had to find out what happened to him. There were those in the faraway land of Dukaine that were in debt to *him,* and he was bound and determined to collect on that debt. Just like *El Príncipe* was collecting from him. Prison had taught him to be smart with his anger. He could kill a man if he had to.

Finally, the cook began to place the chairs on the table. Tito locked eyes with the man questioningly. The cook laughed.

"Grab the mop, little *pollo,* we will leave soon," the cook said with a huge smile on his face. "*El Príncipe* did not tell you I was his uncle?"

Tito shook his head as he stood.

"Jorge always was a distrustful little fuck. It has served him well, I suppose, lost inside the walls of *el agujero grande.* His mother will not even go see him these days. Did you know that?"

Again, Tito shook his head no, grasped the mop, and began to slop the floor with murky water that stung his nose with bleach. He did not take his eyes off the cook.

"There is no place in heaven for *asesinos.* Murderers are assigned to hell, even though my dear sister prays for her son every day, asks the dear Lord for his mercy, she does not believe it will do her any good. Her son is a very bad man, but you know that, don't you?"

"He was kind to me," Tito said.

The cook laughed again. "Only because you're an *asesino* who speaks English. He is not done with you yet, *amigo.* I would withhold judgment about his kindness if I were you."

Tito wanted to ask the man his name, but he knew better

than to seek information that was not readily given. The less he knew, the better off he was. His gut told him not to trust the fat man, but he was not in a situation to do anything else.

"My nephew promised you passage across the border?"

"*Sí*," Tito said, nodding.

"And you will be free of his debt?"

Tito nodded again.

"Your life will be at risk. Now is the time to run if you are not willing to die. I will turn my back, if you like. But do not stop. *El Príncipe* will find you and take no mercy on you. Either way, you risk dying. Which way is it, *pollo?* We leave now."

Tito stopped mopping. "I am ready to go."

The cook took off his apron and walked to the swinging doors. "Once you're on the other side it will not be any better for you there than it is here. I hope you know that."

Tito said nothing. He followed the man outside and climbed into the passenger seat of a plain white van. The city lights flashed by quickly and soon they were on the highway, Interstate 35, fighting for a position among the hundreds of semi-trucks that headed north. The fat man remained silent for the entire drive until they exited the highway a few miles from the border.

"The *migra* will be plentiful on this night, *pollo*. The moon is full."

Tito took a deep breath, thought about all of the stories of the Border Patrol he had heard, and pushed them aside. He did not answer. He did not want the cook to know he was scared, excited, and sad. How could he not think of his mother's story about being duped by the coyote? He could only wonder if something worse awaited him.

They drove two hours to the west, getting farther and farther out into the open country. Darkness wrapped around them like a charred blanket. The night air was hot—but sweet. Finally, the van slowed and the cook turned onto an unmarked gravel path that led up to a ramshackle house.

"There are others," the cook said, shutting off the engine.

Tito followed the man into the house. There were at least twenty people packed into the small front room. It smelled of urine and sweat.

"*Espera aquí*," the cook said. Wait here.

Tito stood next to a man dressed in peasant's clothes, a few years younger than himself. The man looked to the floor and grasped his wife's hand, who was standing next to him. They were mumbling, praying.

For the next hour each person in the room was led to another room and disappeared behind closed doors. Tito heard murmurs and whispers of those that came back out. When it was his turn he knew what to expect, and he understood the cook's warning about his life being at stake.

The smell in the room was even fouler than the room packed with people. It was a chemical smell, a thousand times worse than the bleach in the café. Cardboard boxes filled the room with the exception of a table that sat in the middle. A bare light bulb dimly lit the room. The cook and another man stood waiting next to the table.

"Ah, it is your turn," the cook said. He motioned for Tito to sit at the table. "Swallow all of these until you can swallow no more." The table was loaded with buckets full of white sausages. Two bottles of cooking oil sat next to the buckets. "But be careful, do not puncture the packet, *pollo*. It is mostly pure ephedrine that we get from China. It is used to make meth. Poor man's cocaine. One packet is enough to send your heart into a racing frenzy." The cook laughed and shook. "You will look like you're being electrocuted. But don't worry. It will not last long. And then you will be dead—free of all your debts on this earth."

Tito picked up a packet carefully and stared at it. This was his ticket to paradise.

"Dip it in oil so it will slide down faster," the other man commanded.

Tito looked up, saw the man's beady eyes and a scar that ran down the side of his throat, and decided he had no choice. He had come this far. It only took him ten minutes to digest as many as the packets as he could.

An hour later all of the people in the house were packed in the back of the cook's van. Women coughed. Men stared into the darkness. The van was packed so tight with migrants Tito could barely move. Oddly, no one spoke, or when they did, it was very little, hushed—each with their belly full of deadly drugs. Fear was the only taste, the only smell inside the van.

After a long bumpy ride the van stopped. The cook shepherded them all out and made them stand in a single line. He pulled Tito to the side.

"You are to make sure everyone gets across. There is another van on the other side. They will take you to a house where you will wait. From there, you and some of your group will be taken to Chicago—but it will still be dangerous. The truck you will be in will be loaded with meth underneath as well as inside your body. The *migra* and American *policia* will not take any mercy on you. They are at war with us, too. Ask no questions. Do as you are told. But do not even think you can outrun my nephew in America. He is everywhere. If you betray him, he will hunt you down and have you killed—even as he sits in his lowly prison and awaits his journey to hell.

"Once you arrive in Chicago and dispense the meth, you are free to go wherever you want. Your debt to *El Príncipe* will be repaid. You should be able to find plenty of work this time of year."

"I am going home. To Indiana," Tito said.

"Then you will not be far. There are many tomato fields in the north near Chicago."

Tito watched as the others waded into the river, knapsacks over their shoulders, heads down, all listening for the *migra*'s trucks. He walked to the riverbank and looked over his shoulder. The cook was sitting behind the wheel of the van smoking a cigar. He hung his head out the window and hollered, *"¡Buena suerte!"* Good luck!

Tito put his foot into the river, followed the line of people as the water reached his waist. He looked up. The sky was clear. The stars glistened. The man in the moon smiled. In the distance, a coyote howled and a truck engine started. Headlights flashed across the river, and then grew dark. Tito stopped. He could not go back. Not now.

A van drove to the bank and sat idling. Tito quickly realized it was the van sent to pick them up. He pushed forward, running in the water as fast he could, splashing the river water everywhere until he was thoroughly soaked from head to toe.

He stepped out of the river and looked back at Mexico. The cook's van was gone. The city, Nuevo Laredo, lit the night sky in the distance like dusk after a long, gray day. Darkness covered all of Texas, but in the east, dawn was starting to break and the Big Dipper was falling behind the hills. He'd never been so happy in his life.

Tito genuflected for the first time in years, dug out the St. Christopher's medal around his neck, kissed it, and then caught up with the rest of the *mojados.*

CHAPTER 29

August 22, 2004, 9:05 P.M.

Buddy Mozel's face was twisted and scarred by years of plastic surgery. His skin was shiny, pulled tight on his forehead. One eye and cheekbone was higher than the other. Age had not been kind to him. What hair he had left was pure white, thin wisps exposing scars on his skull, and his eyebrows were nonexistent. His once regal Roman nose was crooked and tiny spider web veins had risen near the surface of his skin, a purple roadmap that reached under both eyes and vanished in the glare of the single overhead light. An ornately carved cane bearing a lion's head on the handle supported his skinny frame. But, for Jordan, there was no mistaking Buddy Mozel's presence or his stature. Buddy's shoulders were squared, though thinner, and he was dressed in fine casual clothes, navy blue slacks and a blue and white striped oxford shirt.

"It's been a long time, Jordan," Buddy Mozel said, extending his hand.

Jordan had to duck inside the small travel trailer. He tilted his head, shook Buddy's hand, and tried to restrain the look of shock that must have been on his face. "Yes, it has."

The trailer was a typical weekend camper, and Jordan suspected it was José's year-round home, but he didn't know that for sure. It was probably less than twenty feet long with a low rounded ceiling covered with blonde wood. The front room, if it could be called that, consisted of two bench seats with a small table that folded down between them. The seats, covered with fading orange flowery upholstery, could be converted into a bed. A small sink, along with a dorm-sized refrigerator and a hot plate, rounded out the tiny kitchen. Beyond the kitchen, the camper held a tiny bathroom and a bedroom big enough for a twin-size mattress. There were a few personal effects in the trailer. A collection of votive candles with religious figures sat on the counter next to the hot plate along with another plastic Jesus, sitting in a chair with lambs at His feet.

Buddy sat down on one of the bench seats and motioned for Jordan to sit. José closed the door and remained standing, looking outside.

The windows were open and a small metal fan circulated warm muggy air. Tree frogs and crickets sang outside. Somewhere in the distance a great horned owl hooted forcefully, celebrating darkness, starting the night's hunt.

Jordan sat down and adjusted the .38 so he could be comfortable. "Mind if I smoke?" he asked.

"Go right ahead," Buddy said.

"You should let me look at your wound, *Señor* Jordan," José said, stepping away from the window next to the door.

"I'm fine." The bleeding had subsided, but the pain remained. The right side of his shirt was covered in dried blood.

"Are you sure?"

Jordan lit a cigarette and put his hand out to stop José. "Seriously, I'm all right."

José nodded and returned to his post next to the door.

Jordan turned his attention back to Buddy Mozel, still a little unsettled by his appearance. Buddy had been a handsome man. Not only because he had money for nice clothes and fancy cars, but his genes had all cooperated and joined together to form that special kind of physical magnetism that attracted both men and women—albeit on different levels. The accident had butchered what nature created, and it was obvious there was not a man on earth who could restore nature's original creation. To see Buddy as a shadow of his former self saddened Jordan, regardless of his feelings toward the SunRipe owner—though he had always been much more forgiving of the man than Spider had been.

Buddy sighed and looked down at the table. "I never meant for it to come to this," he said softly, almost a whisper.

"Holister's dead," Jordan said.

Buddy shook his head. "I know."

"So is Louella Canberry."

Buddy looked up. His eyes were red. Jordan couldn't tell if Buddy was about to cry or if it was a normal condition. "When did that happen?" Buddy asked.

"A little while ago. I walked into the station. She was sitting at her desk with a bullet in her forehead. Hogue's there now." Jordan took a drag off the cigarette and stubbed it out in an ashtray on the table.

The old man looked Jordan directly in the eye. "I didn't have anything to do with this. You realize that, don't you?"

Jordan didn't acknowledge Buddy's denial, but he didn't break eye contact. "Dylan Kirsch is missing. Along with his mother, Ginny."

José stood motionless. He looked like a statue guarding the door.

"I can offer you little information about what's going on now. That is not why I wanted to see you. I'm afraid I won't be much help," Buddy said.

"I'm not so sure about that. Sheriff Hogue is convinced I shot Holister, or at the very least, that I had something to do with it. My house, Kitty's house, burned down, and he suspects me for that, too. He just got done searching the tavern. And if I were a betting man, he's pegged me for Louella Canberry's murder, too. He put an APB on me. You can call him off. I didn't have anything to do with any of this, either."

"I have little influence over Bill Hogue these days."

Jordan didn't believe it.

"Hogue is a persistent man, Jordan," Buddy continued. "And sly as a fox. Don't believe everything you see with him. Of course, it would be easier if you would just turn yourself in."

"I'll ask for Hogue's help when the time is right."

Buddy nodded. One eyelid seemed to be frozen, never opening or closing. "I don't know who killed Holister."

"Why do you think he was killed?"

Buddy took a deep breath. "He stopped by the house the morning he was shot. He showed me a letter and a St. Christopher's medal that belonged to Esperanza. I knew nothing about it then—or that the bones had been exposed. But as soon as I saw that medal I feared it was just beginning. Holister never gave up on that case. I think he had some new information, he implied as much, but did not share it with me. My relationship with Holister has had many faces."

Jordan thought back and remembered noticing the gates to the mansion being open. But Holister did not tell him that he had been to Buddy Mozel's or talked to him. He had to wonder why. "So the medal really did belong to Esperanza?"

"Yes."

"You're certain?"

"Positive."

Jordan had never doubted the St. Christopher's medal belonged to Esperanza, but he had been curious where it came from, especially once he learned the bones at the pond did not belong to Tito Cordova.

"Did you know about the bodies buried at the pond?"

"Of course," Buddy said, glancing at José. "But not always."

A sad look crossed his face, which was hard to read. "I am an old man, Jordan. I have made many mistakes. You have to understand the times, the nature of my business. Things were different in the old days."

Jordan wasn't convinced that "things" had changed all that much. The Mexicans were still commodities, cheap labor to bring in the crop and process the tomatoes. Living conditions were still virtually the same as they were twenty years ago—only now, Buddy exerted more control over them. No, he didn't understand the nature of Buddy's business. He had never wanted to.

"Holister thought the bones belonged to Tito Cordova. Did he tell you that?"

"No. Like I said, he hadn't found them yet. He only had the letter. I would have told him that that was impossible, though, if I'd had the chance. There is no way Tito Cordova was buried at the pond."

"Why is that, Buddy?"

"Because José took him to Mexico."

Jordan stared across the table. Buddy's face showed no emotion.

"The day Tito disappeared, Esperanza went to Holister," Buddy said. "Your grandmother, Kitty, had discovered who Tito's father was, and Esperanza was afraid she was going to lose her son. Kitty had warned her to leave Dukaine, but she wouldn't. Her life was here. With me."

"I'm a little confused," Jordan said. "Are you Tito's father?"

Buddy Mozel shook his head. "I wish I was." He drew in another deep breath of muggy air. "You need to understand a few things. I have no children. It is impossible. I have always been sterile. I am the last of the Mozels. My relationship with Esperanza goes back a long way. Her mother worked for my mother. She was very much like the sister I never had, as much as that was possible. Later in life, I made sure she was taken care of, but could not do that directly because we had become closer than brother and sister. Like the rest of us, Esperanza made her share of mistakes. The rumors were nearly true. I loved Esperanza, but we could never be together. Not like normal people."

"Tito was her mistake." Jordan looked up at José, who had not moved.

"Yes. Kitty took care of a lot of things for me. I know you may find that hard to believe, but I was bound by tradition, by culture, and by my own ignorance and pride. Your grandmother was a forceful woman, and would do whatever it took to see that the migrants received good care. She felt I could always do more. And maybe she was right. But like I said, my business is a difficult one."

"Is Tito Cordova still alive?" Jordan asked.

"I do not know. The day he disappeared, José went searching for him and found him at Longer's Pond, discarded like a pile of trash. He was barely alive. I felt it best that we get Tito away from here as quickly as possible. We told no one that he was found. It seemed more important to keep him safe. Another of my many mistakes. It was very difficult to watch Esperanza in such pain, and I had planned on telling her where Tito was once José returned. But it was too late by then."

A tear slid out of the corner of Buddy's right eye, the most functional of the two.

Jordan's mind was racing, filling in the blanks of Buddy's story with the story Spider had told him.

"For years after, I sent money to the orphanage that we put Tito in. The stories died away, and the boy was forgotten, not mentioned. But when Tito was a teenager he ran away from the orphanage, and we have no idea what happened to him from there. So, yes, he may be alive. Esperanza told me she gave him her St. Christopher's medal to protect him—but it had failed. When Holister brought it to me, I feared Tito had returned. A grown man seeking revenge." Buddy's shoulders sagged, and he lowered his head. "I wouldn't blame him."

Silence engulfed the small camper. Finally, Jordan told Buddy and José what Spider had told him about the day Tito disappeared.

"We suspected it was one of the Kirschs," Buddy said. "I'd fired Ed's father a few months before, but we could never prove anything. Holister suspected as much, too, for a long time. Not long after Tito was taken Lee Kirsch ran off with another woman, so his involvement was always an unanswered question."

"So you don't know if Lee Kirsch had Ed take Tito?"

"No. But like I said, I think Holister found some new information. I think he finally discovered who Tito's father truly was. There was no way he could ask Esperanza. But he always felt that was the missing link. If he could find out who the father was, then he'd know who took Tito. Or at least, knowing what you know now, who had Ed Kirsch abduct him."

Jordan sat back in the seat and tried to remember the last time that he and Holister discussed the Cordova case. It had been nearly a year ago, last November. Holister hadn't hinted to him that he was on to something new. Maybe something had come along recently—but still, Jordan couldn't remember anything. All he remembered about the conversation was that Holister seemed focused on the days after the search ended. Specifically, the day Esperanza Cordova walked into the police station, put a gun to her head, and pulled the trigger.

"Do you know who Tito's father was?"

Buddy nodded yes. "It may be difficult for you to know."

Jordan exhaled deeply. "It was Big Joe, wasn't it?"

Buddy nodded again. "Yes," he whispered.

Jordan let the information swirl around his head for a second. He was suddenly very cold. A thousand more questions jumped into his mind, but he held back and waited for Buddy to finish.

"Big Joe made sure he had an alibi for the entire time the abduction took place. He was with your mother. He was very vocal about it to everyone. There is no one in this town that doesn't know how he feels about Mexicans or the plant. He even helped in the search. And, there was no link between Lee Kirsch and your father that we knew of. Until now, knowing that Spider was with Ed," Buddy said.

"But Kitty knew. You knew. How come you didn't tell Holister?"

"After Esperanza killed herself, it didn't seem to matter. What good would it have done to bring Tito back here? He was safe. Cared for. Your parents were in the midst of getting a divorce. Your mother had found out, of course. She was very angry at Kitty for not telling her sooner. But I think that wound was beginning to heal before the . . ."

". . . Accident," Jordan said.

"Yes. That night forced the memory of Tito even further into the past. I was trying to rescue your mother from your father. I feared for her safety. The loss of Esperanza was difficult for me. I felt I had pulled the trigger. If I had told her the truth, she would still be alive. Your mother and I had always been friends, and we sought solace in each other's company. Our lives were in the midst of tragedy, so we had something in common."

"You and my mother were having an affair?"

"Hardly. I was in no shape to love anyone. Neither was she. But your mother had a big heart. Something she got from her mother. Her life with your father was not what she had expected it to be. She was trapped with two young boys and little skill to survive other than to come to work for me, which she would not do. She would have survived though—she was a strong woman. She just could not break away from Joe McManus as easily as she thought she could. She was afraid of him. Even I could not promise her safety from him. I was a fool to go to the tavern that night. But I only know that now, twenty years later. I didn't want to be alone, and she had asked me to come."

Jordan thought of Ginny—trapped too, like his mother, in a marriage that did not turn out like she thought it would. A marriage based on fear. The cold chills had gone away and he felt confined, trapped inside the tiny trailer. He needed to get out of there and find Ginny and Dylan. If it wasn't already too late.

"In a matter of a few months," Buddy continued. "I was responsible for killing the two women in my life I truly loved, Jordan. I am sorry." His shoulders collapsed. He put his head on the table and began to sob.

Jordan was stiff with rage and confusion. He still had a lot of questions. But there were some answers forming in his mind. He looked to José who was still standing by the door rigidly. He noticed a cell phone attached to his belt.

"Can I borrow your phone, José?"

José nodded and handed it to him.

Jordan punched in the number to Spider's cell phone. Spider answered immediately.

"Where in the fuck are you?" Jordan asked.

"Looking for you," Spider said.

"Bullshit. Where'd you go? You left me stranded, mother-fucker."

"I went to get Charlie. I figured you needed another set of legs. I was tired of sitting around not being able to help."

Jordan bit his lip. He didn't know whether to believe Spider or not.

"Look, man," Spider said. "There are cops everywhere. Hogue was at the tavern serving the search warrant and he got called across the street. Somebody killed Louella Canberry."

"I know. I found her."

"Charlie and me hauled ass out of there. Anyway, we just followed Ed Kirsch. He's at the SunRipe plant."

"Where are you at?" Jordan asked.

"In the parking lot at the liquor store, across from the plant," Spider said.

"All right. Stay there. I'll be there in a few minutes."

"I'm not a killer, Jordan," Spider said.

"Just stay there."

Jordan flipped off the phone and handed it back to José. "We need to go," he said.

Buddy Mozel did not move from the table. He had quit crying. His face was ashen and gray. The plastic Jesus stared down compassionately at the withered old man as he prayed to die.

CHAPTER 30

August 22, 2004, 11:17 P.M.

The wind was blowing leaves and small limbs across the road. In the west, the sky lit up with the first strikes of lightning. Flashes of hot yellow light gave Jordan a brief glimpse of a tall roiling cloud bank intent on gobbling up the stars and the moon. A cold front was sweeping toward them, finally pushing stagnant heat and the drought east, into the realm of memory that was sure to last a lifetime.

But the promise of rain did not matter now. A midnight storm was brewing and the darkness and rage that was evident in the sky only matched what Jordan felt in his heart.

Redemption was the last thing he had on his mind.

It took José ten minutes to drive to Peg's Keg & Spirits—a longer than normal drive since he had to skirt Dukaine and avoid the multitude of police cruisers that clogged the corner of Jefferson and Main.

A news helicopter hovered over the center of town and a bright searchlight was aimed down at the police station, sweeping across the streets in search of a criminal or story. Whichever one came first. After a loud clap of thunder and a heavy gust of wind, the chopper turned and flew over their heads south toward Indianapolis.

Spider's van was parked on the outskirts of the lot, facing toward the gate of the SunRipe plant. The liquor store was still open for business, but only one other vehicle sat in front of the cement block building. The ten-year-old Chevy that belonged to the clerk working the late shift.

José pulled up next to the van and turned off his headlights.

Jordan turned down the police radio. When he rolled down the window to talk to Spider it was difficult for him to see past his anger, not see Big Joe's face instead of his brother's.

Spider followed suit and rolled down his window. Charlie Overdorf was in the passenger's seat—he leaned forward and gave Jordan a nod.

José sat back silently, leaving his hands on the steering wheel. The Mexican had been exceptionally quiet on the ride to the liquor store. Pensive. Almost as if he were unsure, or scared, of what his words would evoke from Jordan.

"Is he still in there?" Jordan asked after returning Charlie's nod.

"He drove to the back, where they park the semis," Spider said. "What the hell's going on?"

Jordan glared at Spider and looked away—through the windshield at the plant. The wind had replaced the rotting smell of tomatoes with the cleansing aroma of rain. Bright lights from the plant lit the interior of both the cab of the truck and the van like it was daylight. He wanted nothing more than to hunt down Ed Kirsch and kill him. But he remained frozen, unable to act on his darkest desire.

The SunRipe plant looked like it was up and running, operating as if everything in the world was proceeding normally, but the parking lot was empty. José had meekly told Jordan that the third shift had been cancelled.

"Was Ed by himself?" Jordan asked Spider.

"As far as I could tell. He was in the El Camino."

"I'm going in after him. My guess is he's got Ginny and Dylan in there—or at the very least he knows where they're at,"

Jordan said.

"I'm not going to fuckin' argue with you," Spider said.

Good, Jordan thought. *I don't have the patience for it right now.*
Nor did he have time to grill Spider about Big Joe or tell him
what he'd learned from Buddy Mozel. He wasn't sure it was
important at the moment. He still wasn't sure whose side Spider
was on.

"We don't have much time. Hogue is looking for me. I took a
rifle from the gun cabinet in the station. Somebody reported
seeing me run down the alley on the way to Holister's house.
Downtown is lit up like a war zone. I think you guys ought to
stay here and keep a look out. José's got a cell phone—you can
call him if something comes up," Jordan said.

"You're taking him with you? I think you should take Charlie. You can trust him."

"Can I trust you to be here if I need you? José's already
agreed to help," Jordan snapped.

Spider threw his hands up in the air. "All right, all right. I
should have waited for you. I'm sorry. I saw a police car pull up
in front of the tavern and I panicked."

Charlie sat silently, watching.

Jordan didn't accept the apology. He didn't move or change
his stoic expression.

"You think Ed's the shooter? That he killed Holister and
Louella?" Spider said.

"I don't know," Jordan answered. But in reality, he doubted
Ed really was the shooter, though he was convinced Ed was
involved somehow—Ed was at the hospital with Ginny, so there
was no way he could have set the house on fire, and as far as
Jordan was concerned the two events were linked.

His list of suspects had shrunk from every resident in Dukaine to two: Big Joe and Tito Cordova.

There was no sign that Tito had returned to town other than

the existence of the St. Christopher's medal. Buddy Mozel's confession led Jordan to believe that Tito was still alive. And revenge seemed like a logical motive—but there were a lot of holes in his theory, a lot of unanswered questions. It would be easy to place Tito at every crime scene that had occurred since the shooting began. Easy to think a stranger had returned to town with nothing but vengeance in his heart. Too easy. Especially after talking to Buddy Mozel.

When Jordan thought of his father, the holes filled in quickly. But they were still there, even though the logistics seemed a little harder to peg down.

Deep in his heart, Jordan hoped he was wrong about his father. He hoped beyond all hope that Big Joe McManus was not capable of murder, even though he was certain Big Joe was behind Tito's abduction—which solidly linked Big Joe and Ed Kirsch. And at the moment, he had to reconsider his thought process. Maybe he was wrong about Ed being the shooter.

If Ed had found the bones at the pond during a meth deal and thought the skeleton was Tito Cordova—then he could have alerted Big Joe that they were in trouble, they were about to be found out. What did Big Joe say at the hospital? *The past has come back to haunt us.*

But, as far he knew, Ed didn't know the bones weren't Tito's. Buddy had told him that José found Tito at the pond near death—not dead. Ed didn't know what he knew. All Ed Kirsch knew was that Tito Cordova's body was dumped at the pond and a skeleton had been exposed by a drought twenty years later. Ed had assumed what Holister had assumed; the bones were the remains of the little boy he'd killed.

But that would still not explain the St. Christopher's medal. Or why Big Joe had Tito taken in the first place.

"Have you heard from Big Joe?" Jordan asked.

"Not since we left him at the hospital," Spider said. "He's

probably still with Celeste."

"I hope you're right."

The storm edged closer. The first sprinkles of rain began to dot the windshield. Thunder rumbled close enough to send a vibrating wave through the truck.

The police radio was alive with chatter. Jordan listened for a minute. "Change of plans," he said. "They're looking for your van, Spider. You can't stay here."

"Damn it!" Spider said, slapping the dashboard.

"I have a solution," José said.

"I'm listening," Jordan replied.

"The controls to the parking lot lights are on the south side of the building. Next to the docks. I can shut off the lights and we can hide the van and the truck behind the plant. No one will see us. Not Ed Kirsch or the *policia.*"

"Is the box locked?"

"I have the key," José said. "Once the lights are off, take the truck and follow Spider. I will meet you there." He opened the door and stepped outside. "I am sorry, *Señor* Jordan, I fear this has been difficult for you. The past cannot be changed any more than the course of a river can be changed. We all should have dried our feet long ago."

Jordan didn't know what to say. He leaned forward and offered José the .38. "You might need this."

"Do not worry. I am prepared," José said, forcing a smile as he ran toward the plant.

The Mexican was still spry for his age and it only took a second for José to cross the road and disappear into the shadows.

Jordan turned his attention back to Spider, clutching the .38. "If you betray me, I'll shoot you if I have to."

"We got your back, Jordan," Spider said. "I promise. I want to catch Ed Kirsch as much as you do. Maybe more."

"You know I never liked that motherfucker," Charlie added.

Distant voices on the radio distracted Jordan again. The parking lot lights went off. "We need to go," he said. "Hogue's heading this way. The liquor store clerk just called us in. Everybody's really jumpy right now."

"Why not wait for 'em?" Charlie asked.

"It's a long story," Spider said.

The van rumbled to life. Jordan slid over to the driver's seat of the truck and followed Spider across the street.

All of the lights on the outside of the four-story building flickered off. Lightning danced in the sky, closer. Thunder exploded above them almost immediately. Jordan could barely see through the windshield as the wipers pushed away the heavy rain. He wasn't sure if José had turned off the lights or if lightning had struck a transformer.

The wind buffeted the truck as Jordan drove through a maze of semi-trailers and came to a stop behind the van. When he opened the door he heard a chorus of sirens competing with the thunder and wind. The temperature had dropped an easy ten degrees in the last five minutes.

José was standing on the dock. A tall garage door was open behind him, and it exposed the interior of the plant—lit only by dim emergency lights. Jordan grabbed the Remington, all of the magazines he'd taken, and the police radio. By the time he reached the dock, his jeans and bloody T-shirt were soaked to the skin.

"I shut off all the lights except the emergency lights," José said.

Ed Kirsch's El Camino was parked next to a semi-tractor attached to a trailer. He was nowhere to be seen.

Charlie jumped out of the van, holding his shirt over his head with one hand and a sawed-off shotgun in the other. He ran to the sliding door behind the driver's side of the van and popped it open. He didn't wait for the automatic lift to fold out. He put the shotgun down and disappeared inside, exiting a second later with Spider thrown over his shoulder.

The rain was blowing vertically and Jordan and José stepped to the right of the large garage door, out of the rain.

Jordan listened for movement and scanned the inside of the plant for anything that would alert him to Ed Kirsch's presence. He had checked the exterior locks on the plant nightly, but had not been inside more than a handful of times. The sheer size of the building was overwhelming. Seventy-five foot ceilings extended as far as the eye could see, and every inch of the football field–sized floor seemed to be filled with machinery that looked like a roller coaster inside a giant's kitchen. Several silver vats, each the size of a small car, lined the far wall. A water flume traversed up and over his head, an inclined conveyor belt with small paddles on it that was used to wash the tomatoes once they entered plant. The flume eventually angled down onto another conveyor belt where the tomatoes were manually sorted. Beyond the sorting stations, a series of large blades hung in wait to begin the chopping phase. Stacks and stacks of fifty-five-gallon drums were piled everywhere. Tomato paste waiting for transport. There were a million different places for Ed to hide. If that was his plan.

The plant smelled worse on the inside than it did on the outside. Yellow emergency lights gleamed softly overhead. There was much more than just the shipping and receiving section of the plant, and Jordan was glad José was with him.

Charlie sat Spider on the floor next to Jordan.

"I'm not sittin' this one out," Spider said.

Charlie disappeared outside again.

"What now?" Jordan asked José, ignoring Spider.

"There are many places to hide. If he knows we are here," José said.

"I don't think he's here to hide," Jordan said.

José nodded. "No, me either, *señor.*"

Charlie ran up the ramp of the dock, pushing Spider's wheelchair. The shotgun was in the seat, wet from the rain. Charlie picked up the gun, wiped it down quickly, and hoisted Spider off the floor and into the wheelchair.

Thunder boomed. The wind whistled, and pushed more rain inside the door. Small pebbles of hail danced on the roof of the van. Lightning flashed every couple of seconds, and the sirens had quieted.

Jordan turned up the volume of the police radio. Hogue was at the liquor store.

"You guys stay here. Keep an eye on Ed's car in case he slips by us and tries to get away," Jordan said.

"What if Hogue shows up?" Spider asked.

"Tell him José and I are inside. We might need the help."

"What if he still thinks you're the shooter?"

"I can prove I'm not. I'm going to have to take him at his word that he was just doing his job. Hogue might be a lot of things—and I've got a lot of reasons to believe that he might be involved in this. But there's one reason to believe he's not."

"What's that?" Spider said.

"He's always been a good cop. He cleaned up the sheriff's department and kept it that way. I can't see him risking everything he's worked for to cover for Ed."

"If you say so."

"Just stay here," Jordan said. "Call us on the cell phone if you need help, or if you see anything."

"I need the number."

José gave his cell phone number to Spider, and quickly followed after Jordan, who was making his way up a ladder on the wall.

Jordan stopped halfway up the ladder. "Call Big Joe, Spider. Find out where he's at. You've got his number, don't you?"

Spider nodded. "I always call him on his cell phone these days."

Pain screamed through his body as Jordan pulled himself upward to a catwalk that extended outward through the plant, branching off in several different directions. He was exhausted. The Remington on his shoulder was heavy, and he wasn't sure he was going to make it to the top. But he had to. Ginny and Dylan's life depended on it. On him.

José followed Jordan up the ladder. Jordan stood back and allowed José to take the lead. He chambered a round in the .38, put it back in the holster, and loaded a magazine in the rifle.

They moved slowly, quietly, searching for any sign of movement. The storm echoed through the metal building and the rattling hail on the roof made it difficult to detect any sound out of the ordinary. There was nothing but shadows and machinery below them. It did not take long for Spider and Charlie to disappear from their sight.

The air cooled as they passed over a row of freeze dryers. José stopped. A second later they heard Charlie yell from far behind them. A gunshot. Followed by another. And then the distinct retort of a shotgun echoed throughout the plant. They ran as fast they could back to the ladder.

Spider was sitting in his wheelchair holding his right leg. Charlie was out on the dock, the shotgun at his shoulder, aiming out into the darkness.

The fiercest part of the storm was past them—the thunder rolled east, shaking the ground as it went. Lightning still lit the sky every few seconds.

"That son of a bitch Ed Kirsch came out of nowhere and shot me in the leg," Spider said. His hand was covered in blood as he put pressure on the wound. "Good thing I can't feel a fucking thing."

Even in the dim light Jordan could see that Spider's face was pale, pasty. "We need to get him an ambulance." It didn't matter that Spider couldn't feel anything, his body would still go into shock, still react to blood loss.

A semi rumbled to life, the engine as loud as the thunder. Jordan brought the rifle up to aim and ran to Charlie on the dock.

"He's getting away," Charlie said.

"Your shotgun won't do any good. You're out of range," Jordan yelled. He zeroed in on the tires of the semi and then inched his sights up to the cab. The semi lurched forward. He locked onto his target—he was going to try and shoot Ed through the passenger window. His finger was on the trigger, ready. He tried to regulate his breathing. There was only going to be time for one shot before the semi was gone.

Lightning flashed in the black sky and Jordan saw Dylan Kirsch sitting in the passenger seat as he pulled the trigger.

CHAPTER 31

August 23, 2004, 12:29 A.M.

Jordan lowered the barrel of the rifle and staggered back against the wall. The trailer's taillights swerved, but the semi continued rolling forward, picking up momentum as it sped toward the back gate. The wind had died down and the rain had slowed—it now fell in buckets instead of sheets. Distant thunder met the echo of the shot from the Remington in a rousing crescendo. He had no idea if he'd hit Dylan, no idea whether or not he had just killed the little boy he was trying to save. But he was sure of what he had seen. It was not a ghost in the cab of the semi.

Spider groaned. Charlie was on the phone calling an ambulance. The semi passed through the gate and the engine whined as Ed accelerated, pushed on the gas to get out of range as fast as he could.

It only took a few seconds for Jordan and José to make it to the truck. Jordan's body was numb—he was not thinking, or at least trying not to. He pushed an image of Dylan, covered in blood and dying, as far out of his mind as possible.

José put the truck in gear, muttering softly, and Jordan quickly determined the Mexican was praying as they tore after Ed and gave chase.

If God could help them now, he'd become a believer . . .

The Kenworth was obviously pulling a full load because it was just reaching top speed as José passed through the gates.

315

Dim red taillights shone in the distance—the semi was about a mile and a half ahead of them. Voices on the police radio were constant, shouting orders, static trampling the traffic. Jordan looked behind them and saw the strobes reflecting off the Sun-Ripe plant, and in the distance, he heard the tornado siren go off, wavering three times. It was a call to all of the members of the fire department to come to the station. A few seconds later, an ambulance radioed that it was on the way to the plant.

Jordan glanced over at the speedometer. They were going eighty miles an hour on a wet gravel road.

"Dylan Kirsch was in the front seat. I saw him when I fired the rifle," Jordan said. "I don't know whether I hit him or not. We can't lose the semi."

"We won't," José said, staring straight ahead.

Jordan exhaled. He hadn't realized that he was holding on to the door handle, that his knuckles were white.

"Ed Kirsch is a very bad man, *señor.*"

"I know."

"No. He is a *mula,* a mule. He carries drugs for the *cárteles.*"

"Hogue said he was planning a big bust, that a huge shipment was coming through here. I've thought all along that Ed was transporting."

"The trailer is full of drugs. That is why he went back to the plant," José said. "When he returned from Texas, he parked an empty trailer in the lot and they loaded a new trailer on his tractor for another run. But the trailer was not empty. Many pounds of meth are hidden inside. If he loses the shipment, he will be killed. My guess is that he has transferred the drugs to the new trailer. It is loaded with ketchup for a short run to Chicago. So he fears for his life. But he is a user. He is unpredictable and unreliable. He may not care at this point if he lives or dies."

Rain continued to fall. The windshield wipers steadily cleared the view into the darkness ahead, thumping back and forth like a metronome, a heartbeat. There was no dust on the road, the storm had soaked the gravel and it was slippery. The truck slid as they rounded a curve and gained on the semi. It was a half a mile ahead.

"How do you know this?" Jordan asked.

José drew a deep breath. "I have been in this town for a long time, *señor*, and have had to walk in two worlds. But I am old, like *Señor* Buddy, like your father, and my time here grows short. I, too, have amends to make for my sins. For a long time I turned my back to the drugs that came up with my people. I thought they were harmless and had nothing to do with the harvest. How could I not know of its existence?"

Jordan did not take his eyes off the semi.

"But this meth. It is *muy malo*, very bad. Almost overnight it has poisoned us all. I have worked silently with the *policía* for some time. The *cárteles* are powerful and smart. I suspect they know I am working with the authorities."

"For Hogue?"

"And the DEA."

"Undercover?"

"*Sí*." José looked away from the road to Jordan. "Even Holister did not know. Ed Kirsch is related to him."

"And to Hogue."

"The sheriff is a good man," José said, turning his attention back to the road. "The law burns in his heart. He will send his *sobrino* to jail if he has to rid the county of this scourge."

Jordan tried to get his bearings. The semi was heading out into the country and they'd come a long way fast. He gripped the Remington tightly. Shooting out the tires was never a consideration, knowing Dylan was inside, but he had not considered what to do next, other than follow Ed. Oddly, it did not appear that Ed was trying to outrun them now . . . he had to know he was being followed, pursued. He was leading them somewhere—away from the plant, from the police.

"What about the bones?"

"It is bad timing, divine intervention, or a plan to put an end to me. I am not sure which. Many of my people are aware of the *sepulcros,* the graves at the pond. It is no secret among us. The markings are quite clear to those who know what to look for. There are some who are tied to the *cárteles* working in the fields. It would be a way to silence me, to be rid of me. Killing me would be simple. Punishing me for my sins would be far more painful. They would like nothing more than to see me bound in an American prison."

"You're between a rock and a hard place."

"*Sí.* I have betrayed people on both sides of the law. I have already confessed. Now I must make my atonement."

"To who—Hogue?"

"No," José said. "To God."

The semi turned north. "What does Tito Cordova have to with all of this?"

"I don't know. And that is why I am still here. Otherwise, I would have left as soon as the *sepulcros* were discovered so *Señor* Buddy could have blamed that on me. He is very weak, and I fear he is not up to the trouble he faces." José slowed the truck to make the turn. They were twenty yards behind the semi.

"Something's wrong," Jordan said.

The semi geared down to a crawl and José was inches from his bumper. It wasn't until he saw the brake lights come on that Jordan realized where they were.

The truck's headlights flashed on a small white house sitting alone on a rise. Drops of rain were intermittent. The storm had been fast moving. A thin line of thunderclouds on the dark horizon was all that was evident of the front that had brought much needed relief to the air and to the ground. Lightning flashes faded and the wind had quieted back down. With everything that had happened, Jordan could only wonder why Ed Kirsch had led to them the abandoned house—to Tito and Esperanza Cordova's house.

José brought the truck to a stop, and they watched the semi lurch up the driveway and park about ten yards from the house. José's headlights were pointed directly at the cab.

José flipped on the brights, illuminating everything in view with intense white light.

The Cordova house stood to the left of the semi in the shadows. No lights shone in the windows. Withered weeds dotted the yard, glistening with moisture from the rain. A broken screen door was on the ground along with a scattering of empty beer bottles and old tires.

José stared silently at the house, and almost magically pulled a Glock out from under the seat. The sight of the gun made Jordan's heart skip a beat.

He had to consider that he'd made a huge mistake by trusting the Mexican. It was very possible that he had been tricked, that he had been sitting next to the shooter all along.

Slowly, Jordan let go of the Remington, propped it against the door, and eased the .38 into his grip. His mind ran back through the series of events that led them to where they were now. Could José be the shooter? Yes, he thought—as his mind clicked through the shooting at the pond, the house fire, finding Louella dead in her chair. Did José have access to his bullets? That was where he had to stop thinking and consider he was overreacting. But he was still uncertain of the man who was sitting next to him.

The expression on José's face did not change. His gaze was fixed on the semi like a hunting dog on a bird, his leathery brown skin tight—the hardness of years spent in the sun and fields etched in every wrinkle. His eyes were hard to read in the darkness of the cab.

Ed pushed open the door of the red Kenworth tractor, and in a flash Dylan climbed out the driver's door. The little boy's blonde hair glowed in the bright headlights like the sun on a summer day. He looked OK, no blood, no apparent injuries. Jordan breathed a sigh of relief.

Before he could say anything to José, Jordan saw Ed wave his hand. And then saw that there was a gun in his hand. Ed slid out of the cab, pulled Dylan to him, and put a 9mm to the boy's head. Blood covered Ed's right shoulder. The shot at the SunRipe plant had missed Dylan and hit Ed.

Jordan looked over to José, to the Glock in his hand. There was no time to mistrust the Mexican. He decided José had had plenty of time, plenty of opportunities to kill him before now. It was a risk—trusting his gut, but it was one he felt he had no choice but to make.

He took a deep breath, opened his door, and pointed the .38 through the open window, using the door as a shield. José did the same.

Ed headed for the house but stopped halfway between it and the semi, leaving himself fully exposed. Jordan hesitated, fearful that the shot would hurt Dylan.

The rain had ceased and the air had cooled. Sweat dripped off Jordan's forehead.

"Let him go, Ed." The voice came out of the darkness. A tall looming figure stepped out of the front door of the house.

Jordan almost dropped his gun when he realized it was Big Joe.

"The boy doesn't have anything to do with this." Big Joe walked into the cone of light from José's headlights. He was pointing a gun at Ed.

"Fuck you!" Ed shouted as he pulled Dylan closer, jammed the barrel of the gun, a Glock, harder against the boy's head.

Tears streamed down Dylan's face.

Jordan could hear the little boy whimpering.

"You're not going to get away, Ed," Jordan yelled. "Give it up!"

Ed pressed his finger tighter on the trigger. His eyes were wild, darting between Jordan and Big Joe.

Jordan pulled the .38 out of the window and slowly made his way up the drive, the gun leveled at Ed's head. José fell in behind him.

Sirens resounded in the distance, drawing closer. Ed backed up slowly against the Kenworth's giant front tire.

"I should have never trusted you in the first place," Big Joe said, taking a slow step toward Ed. "You fucked everything up once, and now you're doing it again."

"I thought he was dead!" Ed yelled. Pain twisted on his face as blood ran down his arm.

"I didn't tell you to kill him," Big Joe said, coming to a stop ten feet from Ed. "Let the boy go."

Ed shook his head no.

Big Joe reached into his pocket with his free hand and pulled out the St. Christopher's medal. He held it up in the air. The gold glinted in the light. Fear danced in Ed's eyes. "He's not dead, is he?"

"No." It was a whisper. Dylan struggled, but Ed gripped him harder.

The sight of the medal stopped Jordan in his tracks.

"How'd you get this, Ed?" Big Joe demanded.

The sirens grew closer and Jordan heard José come to a stop just behind him.

"It's over, Ed. Let Dylan go," Jordan said.

"I'm not going down on my own for all of this."

"Where's he at?" Big Joe screamed. "Where's Tito Cordova?"

Ed cocked his head to the trailer. "In there. I didn't know it was him until he recognized me. Fucker tried to kill me on the way back from a pickup in Texas. I should have just killed him then, but I knew about the bones at the pond. I figured if Holister thought they belonged to him, then I'd have some time."

Jordan glanced over at José. The Mexican was already backing away toward the rear of the trailer. He could see strobes flashing down the road. The sky was lit up like a Fourth of July finale.

"Time for what?" Big Joe asked.

"To get the load I'm hauling out of town. To leave . . . period. Fucking Ginny told Holister I took Tito. She thought she could get rid of me, but I had it all worked out. Kill Holister and that would be that—a big enough distraction to cover me, and it'd get me off the hook for taking Tito," Ed said, nodding at Jordan.

"So you sent the letter to Holister?" Big Joe asked, gripping his gun tighter.

"I had Ginny do it. Once I had Tito locked up, once I had that goddamn St. Christopher's medal so I could bait Holister with it, I knew I was home free. I knew how much he wanted to find out what happened when the kid first disappeared. But I didn't count on Ginny fucking Jordan. I didn't think she'd go that far. When Jordan showed up at the pond, it changed everything."

"How'd you get the bullets?" Jordan demanded, inching closer, trying to figure out how to shoot Ed without hurting Dylan. He had no idea what Big Joe's plans were. But as long as Ed was talking, he wasn't going to worry about his father. Big Joe seemed as interested in getting the truth out of Ed as he was.

"I made her call you. She took them."

"Why?" Jordan said. He had a clear shot at Ed's head—but it was risky, still.

"I told you—she told Holister. I had no choice. Paybacks are hell, man. I knew I was going to have to get rid of Tito again. No big fucking deal there, except he was carrying drugs for Mexicans, so I had to be a little careful with him until the delivery was made. But if I set you up for Holister's murder, I'd kill two birds with one fucking stone. I'd be rid of you and Holister. I didn't tell her to fuck you. . . . Once that happened I was out of my head, man. I didn't give a rat's ass about the deal. . . . It's personal between me and you. Always has been. If Ginny wouldn't have done what I wanted her to—then I showed her what would happen, what I'm showing you now." He slid the barrel of the Glock from the side of Dylan's head and pointed it under the little boy's chin. "My finger's on the trigger pretty hard motherfucker. You can shoot me—but you'll kill him, too. I'll take him down in the fall." Ed's face was pale. Blood dripped from his fingers to the ground.

Keep him talking, Jordan said to himself. *Keep him talking until Hogue shows up.* He glanced over at Big Joe. His father was trembling—his eyes were red with anger. Anger and something else he had never seen in his father's eyes before. Fear.

Big Joe remained standing in the same spot—the gun still aimed at Ed.

"But you didn't know about the file Holister kept on Tito Cordova, did you?"

"Once Ginny told me about it, after I shot Holister, I knew I had to get rid of it." Ed cast his eyes toward the back of the trailer. José had opened the door and was climbing inside. "I always wanted to kill Mrs. Canberry anyway. I've hated that bitch since second grade. She treated me and my brothers and sisters like we was dirt."

"Where's Ginny?" Jordan yelled.

"Inside," Big Joe said. "She's fine. He told her to wait here so they could get away. He kept Dylan with him for insurance. I found her after you left the hospital—I figured Ed was involved in this once I broke up the fight between you two. But I knew he was involved for sure when Spider gave me the medal. I should have let you shoot him then and there. But it's not your place to take care of my mistakes. Not anymore."

Flashes of blue and red light covered the ground, reflecting off the side of the white trailer. The sirens whooped and hollered and several vehicles ground to a halt.

Ed looked to the road, to the back of the trailer.

Out of the corner of his eye, Jordan saw two men emerge around the side of the trailer, saw Ed Kirsch take the Glock from under Dylan's chin, and heard the echo of a gunshot.

Ed Kirsch's head snapped back and slammed against the tire. Blood erupted just under his right eye, raining down on Dylan. The little boy screamed and jumped forward as Ed slowly crumpled to the ground. The Glock fell to the ground with a soft *thud*.

Jordan refocused his vision on Big Joe. A thin wisp of smoke wafted upward from the barrel of the .38 his father was holding. The gun was Holister's—he hadn't paid any attention to it until that very moment, until he could see it clearly in the spotlights and strobes from the parade of police cruisers that had circled the Cordova house.

Jordan ran to Dylan and scooped him up.

"Drop the gun, Big Joe!" Hogue's voice boomed over a bullhorn. The road was lined with county cruisers, Johnny Ray's cruiser, a white INS van, and a couple of black sedans that Jordan figured belonged to the DEA.

Big Joe looked into the light, ignored the command, and walked over to José and Tito Cordova. He extended his hand, the St. Christopher's medal securely in his grasp, to Tito. "Here," he said. "I think this belongs to you."

CHAPTER 32

August 23, 2004, 1:13 A.M.

Jordan watched as Johnny Ray led Big Joe to the back of a cruiser. He had barely been able to catch his breath before the whole area was swarmed by county deputies, state police, and DEA and INS agents. Once Big Joe was in custody, the rhythm of the investigation began in earnest. Yellow tape surrounded the Cordova house, the semi, and José's truck. There was nothing he could do but stand inside the perimeter and wait for Sheriff Hogue.

Ginny sat inside an ambulance as Sam Peterson treated Dylan for some minor cuts caused by breaking glass. The little boy wouldn't have any scars. At least on the outside. Jordan watched Dylan being tended to with a great sense of relief.

Ginny was unharmed, but in a very distressed state. Her clothes hung limply on her body, and she looked like she hadn't slept for days. They hadn't had a chance to talk, only exchange glances, smiles only the two of them could see.

Jordan feared her recovery from this incident, from her life with Ed, was going to take more than time to heal. From what he knew and what he saw, a trip to drug rehab would be in order. He could barely begin to think of the future, but there was no question that he would help her and Dylan through the tough times. If that was what she truly wanted.

The fact she'd gone to Holister and told him about Ed

convinced Jordan that she really wanted out of the marriage, that she had really done something to change things. But Ed had her trapped, had used Dylan and drugs to control her. No wonder she was afraid.

Stacks and stacks of ketchup cases sat on the ground next to the trailer. A small compartment in the back of the trailer had housed at least five hundred pounds of meth.

Ed's body had not been moved. A police photographer was taking pictures, while more deputies stood around and watched.

Finally, Sheriff Hogue made his way to Jordan.

Hogue extended his hand to Jordan. "Good work, McManus. This one almost got away from us."

Jordan shook the sheriff's hand and then withdrew it. "What's the status on my brother?"

"Looks like he's going to be all right. He's going to be treated and released. I thought he was involved in this mess. But I guess he's not."

"No," Jordan said. "Not this."

"You know why I thought that, don't you?"

"I've got a good idea."

"You need to have a talk with him about the way he lives his life."

Jordan stared at Hogue and ignored the suggestion. "I guess one of the things I'm still curious about is the house fire. Any word on that?"

He wondered about the pig, too. But it didn't matter. It made sense that Ed shot it, and left the message—just like he'd sent the letter.

Hogue shook his head yes. "Ginny just cleared it up. Ed got to the hospital just as you were leaving. He had just enough time to set the fire, and get there. It's a twenty-minute drive, so it fits. The arson guys found some materials he left behind, so now that I have a good idea it was him, we'll see if we can link some prints back to him. He sure went to a lot of trouble to get even with you."

"Looks that way."

"You going to be up to talking with us? Or do you want to wait until the morning?"

"I'd just as soon get it over with."

"All right. We can do that." Hogue shifted his weight. Red and blue flashers swept across his face as a look of contrition entered his eyes. "I guess I owe you an apology."

Jordan looked away, stared past the sheriff as the coroner wheeled a gurney toward Ed's body. He wanted to ask Hogue if he wanted a little ketchup to sprinkle on the crow he just ate, but he restrained himself.

"I'll return your gun to you first thing in the morning," Hogue said.

"That's a start."

"Just doing my job, McManus. Look at it from where I was standing. You would have done the same thing."

"Maybe. Maybe not. But I understand. It doesn't make it any easier to take, though."

"Well, I think you did a good job here. I got no problem with recommending you to the Town Board to take over Holister's job. Lord knows I don't want to deal with that fuck-up Johnny Ray Johnson any more than I have to."

"It's a little early for me to think about that. I've got some things to sort out first."

"You're not going to quit the department, are you?"

"I don't know. I'm not sure I was meant to be a cop. I've broken some serious vows in the last couple of days, turned my head on more things than I should have. Maybe if I wouldn't have, none of this would be happening."

"The drugs would still be here, McManus," Hogue said. "Trust me on that. This haul is just a pebble in the ocean. We still don't know who Ed's contact in Chicago was—or where this crap came from. We got a good idea. But there's not much the DEA can do across the border in Mexico.

"This is a war. Meth is my biggest concern, and I'm going to need every good man I can find to help with the fight. So I'm asking you man to man, cop to cop, not to let our misunderstanding get in the way of the job you do."

"I'll think about it."

The coroner and a deputy loaded Ed's body onto the gurney. Jordan's mind flashed back to the pond, to Charlie and Sam loading Holister's limp body onto a similar gurney. It seemed like another lifetime—so much had happened since then that he'd barely considered what lay ahead for him in the not-so-distant future. Holister's funeral. Rebuilding the house. Making sure Spider was all right—and not on the hook legally for anything he did when he was sixteen. Then there was Big Joe. Sitting in the back of the cruiser in handcuffs.

"If you're worried about Big Joe, I think he'll walk on self-defense," Hogue said, almost as if he could read Jordan's mind.

Jordan frowned. "You might change your mind once we have our talk. He was behind Tito Cordova's abduction. I don't know all of the details. Ed Kirsch took Tito from his house, beat him, and left him for dead at the pond. José Rivero found Tito and took him to Mexico to an orphanage so he would be safe for a little while. That changed when Esperanza committed suicide—José left him there. Tito eventually ran away from the orphanage, and José lost track of him. Tito obviously recognized Ed on this drug run, and Ed tried to use the past to get Holister off his trail. Ginny told her dad about the abduction, and probably the drugs too, but I don't know that for sure."

"You mean to tell me Tito Cordova is still alive? What does Buddy Mozel know about all of this?" The sheriff stared at Jordan, waiting for more information.

"Yes, he is . . ."

"Son of a bitch."

". . . And I can't speak for Buddy Mozel."

"So, Big Joe was behind all of this after all?"

"He started it, I guess," Jordan said.

"And finished it."

"Yeah, well a lot of people got hurt along the way just because he wasn't honest, because he didn't want anyone to know he'd had a relationship with Esperanza Cordova and fathered a child while he was still married to my mother. I'm not sure finishing it accounts for much."

"He's going to be in some trouble then—if he doesn't clam up about the abduction. Might be a little hard to pin that on him after so long. Especially with Ed Kirsch out of the picture."

"You really need to talk to José Rivero and Tito Cordova," Jordan said as he scanned the crime scene. They were not by the trailer, or on the stoop in front of the house among the group of deputies standing there. He turned around and scanned the road, looked along the line of police cars, and saw nothing.

"José Rivero and Tito Cordova are here?" Hogue asked.

"They were," Jordan said as a slight smile came over his face.

José and Tito were nowhere to be seen. It was as if they had vanished—like bronze-skinned ghosts at the first sign of frost . . .

August 27, 2004, 11:15 A.M., Patzcuaro, Mexico

Tito stood at the gates of *El Refugio* and watched a group of children playing. Their laughter reached up into the pure blue sky as they ran in circles around the ceiba tree. He laughed as a tall priest came outside the old building and yelled at the children to stop before someone got hurt.

The mountains that surrounded Patzcuaro stood tall, looking

down on the white buildings with red roofs. Birds sang. The smell of tamales filled the air.

He took a deep breath of fresh air and walked toward the priest. *"Padre,"* he yelled.

The priest looked up and stared at Tito, shielding his eyes from the sun.

"I hope you can help me," Tito said in Spanish.

"I will try," the priest answered, shooing away a little boy who had ran up to his side and pulled on his sleeve.

"I am looking for someone, an old friend who lived here a long time ago. His name is Cirilo Rodriguez."

The priest had warm brown eyes and perfectly cut black hair that matched his cassock. A flicker of recognition flashed across the man's face. He looked to be a few years younger than Tito. "What is your name, *amigo?"* A smile accompanied the question.

"Tito. Tito Cordova. I, too, spent time here as a child."

The priest threw his head back, laughed, and then embraced Tito with a tight hug. "You have found him, my *amigo.* I am Cirilo."

"No!"

"Sí!"

Tito laughed and returned the hug. Once he stood back and examined the priest's face, he could see the man his friend had grown into.

"I didn't believe you would ever come back. I thought you were surely dead. I kept a candle lit for you," Cirilo said. "And now, here you are. Come let us get something to drink, to eat. Are you hungry?"

The children had stood and watched as the priest spoke to the stranger. They parted when they passed, arms around each other's shoulders.

"You became a priest," Tito said.

"*Sí*. The nuns showed great patience with me. Especially after you left. I could never leave here, and this is the only way they would let me stay. Tell me, did you ever make it to paradise? To the place of your dreams and find your mother?"

"Ah, I am afraid she is dead. My heart would not believe it."

"So, you had to find out for yourself. And paradise?"

"This is paradise, Cirilo. Just as I told you it was."

The priest nodded and then smiled. They walked inside the front door of *El Refugio* and stopped. Nothing had seemed to change since he had left. But yet, everything did. Everything looked brighter, smaller, and warm, even though they were old.

"Are you planning on staying long?" Cirilo asked.

Tito hesitated, took in a deep breath of rich mahogany wood and the smell of *almuerzo,* lunch, cooking far off in the kitchen. "I have no place else to go, *Padre*. I was hoping to find out what happened to you. I hadn't thought about where to go from here."

Cirilo put his hand softly on Tito's back. "*Hogar agradable,* Tito," he said. "*Hogar agradable.*"

Welcome home, Tito. Welcome home.

ABOUT THE AUTHOR

Larry D. Sweazy (www.larrydsweazy.com) won the WWA Spur award for Best Short Fiction in 2005, and was nominated for a Derringer award in 2007. He has published over 50 nonfiction articles and short stories, which have appeared in *Ellery Queen's Mystery Magazine; The Adventure of the Missing Detective: And 25 of the Year's Finest Crime and Mystery Stories!; Boys' Life; Hard-boiled; Amazon Shorts;* and other publications and anthologies. Larry is also the author of the Josiah Wolfe, Texas Ranger series (Berkley). He is a member of MWA (Mystery Writers of America), WWA (Western Writers of America), and WF (Western Fictioneers). He lives in the Midwest with his wife, Rose; two dogs, Rhodesian ridgebacks, Brodi and Sunny; and a black cat, Nigel.